THE SAINT

RESURRECTION

THE SAINTHOOD – BOYS OF LOWELL HIGH BOOK 1

USA TODAY BESTSELLING AUTHOR
SIOBHAN DAVIS

Everything changed the night my dad died.

The night I met Saint, Galen, Caz, and Theo.

Those manipulative a-holes set out to ruin me after our hot night together, but they didn't realize you can't destroy something that's already broken. And it only works if the victim cares.

Which I don't.

Because I've been in hell for years, and nothing penetrates the steel walls I've erected.

Until The Sainthood decides I belong to them and cracks appear in my veneer. Their cruel games, harsh words, and rough touch awakens something inside me, and now, I'm in trouble.

They draw me deeper into their dangerous world, until I'm in the middle of all the violence and gang warfare, tangled up in all the secrets and lies, and there's no turning back.

Because they own me.

And nothing has ever felt so right.

I'm exactly where I should be.

But with enemies on all sides, survival becomes a deadly game with no guarantees.

And, sometimes, saints become sinners.

PRAISE FOR RESURRECTION

"Heart-stopping, intense, and hotter than hell! Five VENGEANCE IS HOT stars!"
K Webster. USA Today bestselling author

"Siobhan! Goodness. What have you done to me? Resurrection is freaking amazing!"
WSJ Bestselling Author Ilsa Madden-Mills

"I devoured Resurrection in one sitting. It was sinfully sexy, dark, and taboo."
Ava Harrison. USA Today bestselling author

"Resurrection was the ultimate page-turner. Deliciously dark, I never wanted it to end."
Parker S. Huntington. USA Today bestselling author

"The only thing better than a Siobhan Davis book is a Siobhan Davis REVERSE HAREM book!!!"
S.E. Hall. New York Times bestselling author

"You want this book in your life. No, you NEED it! AMAZING!!"
Bestselling Author Shantel Tessier.

"A brilliant, mind-blowing, fast-paced, intense, edge-of-your-seat read."
Bestselling Author S.B. Alexander

"HOLY HOTNESS! I've never been a big fan of RH....until this book!"
The Masque Reader

GANG STRUCTURE & CONTROL

The Sainthood (Prestwick & Lowell)
President: Neo/Sinner Lennox
Junior chapter leader: Saint Lennox
Junior chapter second in command: Galen Lennox
Junior chapter members: Caz Evans, Theo Smith, Bryant Eccleston

The Arrows (Prestwick)
Leader/President: Archer Quinn
Sergeant at arms: Diego Santana
Junior chapter leader: Darrow Knight
Junior chapter second in command: Bryant Eccleston (Sainthood spy)

The Bulls (Fenton)
New Leader/President: Marwan

Ex-Lowell High School gang
Leader: Finn Houston
Second in command: Brooklyn Robbins
Finn's girlfriend: Parker Brooks
Parker's bestie: Beth McCoy

LOCATIONS
Prestwick: birthplace of The Sainthood and The Arrows.
Lowell: where Harlow lives and where the new chapter of The Sainthood has been established
Fenton: birthplace of The Bulls

SCHOOLS
Prestwick High – The Arrows reigns supreme
Prestwick Academy – The Sainthood reigns supreme

Lowell Academy – A private school Harlow used to attend
Lowell High – The Sainthood reigns supreme

KEY CHARACTERS
Harlow Westbrook – 18, MC.
Giana Westbrook – Harlow's mom.
Trey Westbrook – Harlow's dad (deceased.)
Saint Lennox – 18, MC
Galen Lennox – 17, MC. Saint's cousin.
Caz Evans – 18, MC.
Theo Smith – 18, MC.
Alisha Lennox – Galen's mom.
Diesel – Harlow's friend/trainer & VERO employee
Sariah Roark – Harlow's best friend.
Emmett – Harlow's friend.
Sean – Sariah's boyfriend.
Lincoln – work associate of Trey Westbrook.
Howie Young – DEA Agent
Randall Solice – Head of VERO
Taylor Tamlin – Parker's half-sister
Ashley Shaw – Harlow's friend
Jase, Chad – Ashley's boyfriends

Copyright © Siobhan Davis 2020. Siobhan Davis asserts the moral right to be identified as the author of this work. All rights reserved under International and Pan-American Copyright Conventions.

This is a work of fiction. Names, characters, places, incidents and dialogues are products of the author's imagination or are used fictitiously. Any resemblance to actual people, living or dead, or events is entirely coincidental.

This book is sold subject to the condition that it shall not, by way of trade or otherwise be lent, resold, hired out, or otherwise circulated without the prior written consent of the author. No part of this publication may be reproduced, transmitted, decompiled, or stored in or introduced into any information storage and retrieval system, in any form or by any means, whether electronic or mechanical, including photocopying, without the express written permission of the author.

Printed by Amazon
Paperback edition © December 2020

ISBN-13: 979-8603938325

Editor: Kelly Hartigan (XterraWeb) editing.xterraweb.com
Cover design by Robin Harper https://wickedbydesigncovers.wixsite.com
Photographer: Michelle Lancaster
Cover Model: Josh Elton
Formatting by CP Smith

NOTE FROM THE AUTHOR

This is a dark reverse harem romance, and it is not suitable for young teens due to mature content, graphic sexual scenes, and cursing. The recommended reading age is eighteen-plus.

RESURRECTION

THE SAINTHOOD – BOYS OF LOWELL HIGH BOOK 1

THE SAINTHOOD

PROLOGUE

Spring Break before Senior Year

SHARP PAIN PENETRATES my chest cavity, aiming straight for my heart, like a thousand tiny pinpricks digging into smooth flesh.

He's gone.
Left this world without any warning.
And I'll never see him again.

It hurts, and the pain wants to embed deep. To burrow straight through to my soul. To inflict the worst damage imaginable. The pain pushes and pokes at soft tissue, but it's no good. It won't advance any further. Because I learned to lock that shit up when I was thirteen years old.

I grab the bottle of vodka from the empty passenger seat of my Lexus SUV, uncapping the lid and bringing the glass to my lips. I chug it like it's water, feeling lost as the alcohol glides down my parched throat.

This car was the last gift he bought me, a couple months ago,

SUV with bullet-resistant glass, an explosion-mitigating floor, and a bunch of other protective features I considered way over the top.

But maybe, there was a reason for it.

The car swerves on the road as I take another mouthful of vodka. The approaching car flashes its lights, the driver angrily shaking his fist as he passes by. I shove up my middle finger, hissing under my breath, even if he's right.

The car swerves again as I close the vodka bottle, tossing it back on the seat. I don't care if I die, but it wouldn't be fair to Mom to lose her loving husband and her only daughter on the same day, both from fatal car accidents. I grip the wheel tighter, my eyes stinging with tears that will never fall.

A few minutes later, the car screeches to a halt outside Darrow's dilapidated house. I jump out, leaving the door open, and race up the overgrown driveway. I raise my fist to knock, but the door swings open before my knuckle makes contact with the worn wood.

"He's not here," Rita drawls, bobbing her six-month-old son on one hip while she noisily chews gum. Her gaze rakes over me from head to toe, her lips curling into a sneer at my school uniform. The white knee-length socks, black pleated skirt, white shirt, red and black tie, and red blazer edged in black trim with the school crest confirm my status as a private academy student.

Although, Rita is already aware of that.

It's one of the reasons why she hates my fucking guts.

The other is because I've been screwing her precious brother for the past six months.

"Where is he?"

"I'm not Darrow's keeper." She sniffs, wiping her nose with the back of her sleeve. Her son emits a loud wail, his lower lip trembling as he cries out. Poor kid is probably hungry, and judging by the bulky diaper he's wearing, I'm guessing he needs changing too. He shivers, the cool night air swirling around his naked flesh. "Shut your mouth," Rita snaps, glaring at the innocent child, and the baby cries louder.

Bile floods my mouth, and adrenaline charges through my veins. She's such a lousy mother, and I don't get it. *Why is it that good couples, with the disposition and means to raise kids in a loving environment, struggle to conceive while this junkie gets knocked up without even trying? Where is the justice in that?* My heart aches for that kid. *What kind of future awaits him with a mother like that?* I know Darrow has pulled her up on her shit before, but he's rarely home, and it's not like he can do much.

Grabbing a hundred-dollar bill from my purse, I thrust it at her. "I know you don't like me, and I really don't care. But I know you know where he is. Tell me, and it's yours."

Her scowl deepens, and I know she wants to tell me to screw off. But she needs the money more. She snatches it from my hand like a greedy shrew. "He's partying at Galen Lennox's place."

Shit.

I arch a brow, waiting for her to elaborate, but her lips pinch closed. "And where is that?" I prompt, biting back a frustrated sigh. Bitch knows I'm from Lowell, the next town over. That I don't attend Prestwick High with my boyfriend—her brother. And even though I have a suspicion where that asshole lives, I don't have time to waste driving aimlessly around town if I'm wrong.

She thrusts her palm out, and I grind my teeth. If it wasn't for the baby in her arms, I'd punch her in her heavily made-up face and demand an address. But she *is* holding her son, so I'm forced to play nice. I slap a twenty into her hand, daring her to challenge me with a deadly look. Mood I'm in, I'll come back and pummel her ass to dust just for shits and giggles. We enter into a silent face-off, and I keep my eyes locked on hers, refusing to back down.

She folds first, bouncing the baby up and down as he continues to cry. "Forty-one Thornton Heights."

She moves to shut the door in my face, but I plant my foot

in the doorway, stopping her from closing it. "Don't shove it all up your nose. Buy your son some clothes and formula. I'll be mentioning this to Darrow."

"Fuck off, slut. Mind your own goddamned business." She kicks my foot away, and the door slams shut.

I head back to my car, plug the address in, and set off for Galen Lennox's place.

I know who he is.

Everyone does.

Because The Sainthood is revered around these parts.

The organization is one of the oldest criminal enterprises in the US, with chapters in most states, but the gang started in Prestwick, and it's the largest branch with the most power.

It's split into two levels—junior and senior. The junior chapter controls the schools and teen drug supply and generally lays down the law among their peers until the members successfully pass initiation and "jump in." Then they become members of the senior or main organization, and successors take over their crown at the junior level. Typically, the transition occurs once the members graduate high school.

All the local gangs are structured similarly, and regular crew wars are the norm. The Sainthood are known rivals of The Arrows, the crowd Darrow runs with, and I'm guessing Dar's presence at this party is a way of pissing The Sainthood off. While Darrow has Prestwick High locked up tight, The Sainthood rules the hallways at Prestwick Academy, and they *own* the streets. The Arrows are small fry, and Dar despises The Sainthood because they have what he wants—control, respect, loyalty, and fear.

I could do without this tonight, but I need the distraction of sex and alcohol more, so I drive toward the nicer part of Prestwick where Galen Lennox lives.

Bile fills my mouth as I pull up in front of the familiar house. Cars, trucks, and bikes are parked haphazardly across the wide front lawn as I drive up the sweeping driveway. I pull into an empty space in front of the monstrous gray brick two-story building and kill the engine. Swiping the bottle of vodka from the passenger seat, I hop out and head toward the open front door.

Chills creep over my spine as I step foot into the gloomy hallway. A massive chandelier hangs from the ceiling, casting dim light over the marble tile floor below. Mahogany stairs extend upward on either side of the lobby, the steps covered in a drab green carpet that has clearly seen better days. Cobwebs cling to the high ceilings and cornices, and a thin layer of dust obscures the pictures of ancestors covering the walls as I walk toward the sound of the thumping music.

My heels make a clacking sound as I walk through the depressive corridor decorated in dark wood panels and dull green and gold wallpaper. I remember how creeped out I was the first time I was here, but it's worse now with the added obvious neglect. I pass a succession of tall, mahogany-stained doors, all closed with no sounds of life, so I continue toward the music.

Reaching the end of the hallway, I turn left and head straight for party central.

I step into the vast room, glancing at the vaulted ceilings adorned with expensive chandeliers and the myriad of windows draped in heavy ruby-red velvet curtains. A DJ spins tunes from an elevated dais at the end of the room, but other than that, the room is completely bare of furnishings. At one time, this was an ornately decorated ballroom, host to lavish parties that were the talk of the town, but it's clear no one is looking after this place anymore.

A large crowd dances on worn hardwood floors while others sit in clusters on the ground at the edge of the room, talking, laughing, smoking, and drinking. I inhale the scent of weed as I walk through the space, keeping my eyes peeled for Darrow, but I don't spot him or any of his crew.

Exiting the ballroom by the rear door, I head outside. Sounds of laughter filter through the air as I step around the outside of the property toward the back patio. My feet slam to a halt at the sight of the overgrown maze, and I allow my mind to wander back to that night. I was only a kid, which is why I didn't recognize the address even if I remember every other detail of my last visit here.

I uncap the vodka, chugging it down my throat, welcoming the burn and latching on to it rather than letting the memory unfold.

I press on, my feet picking up pace as I round the bend and spot several of Darrow's gang. A group of about twenty is lounging by the old pool, huddled around a makeshift bonfire, sprawled across garden chairs and loungers. The pool is empty now, save for the leaves and debris cloistered on the old blue-tiled floor.

I stop in front of the lounger Bryant Eccelston is lying on. Bryant is Darrow's bestie and number two, and where one is the other is never far. A cute blonde is draped around his broad five-feet-eleven-inch frame. "Where is he?" I ask, drilling him with a look.

"Cute outfit." Bryant smirks, taking a slow perusal of my body, his gaze lingering on my chest out of habit.

"Cut the crap, Bry. Where's Darrow?"

He cocks his head to the side, and the flickering light from the bonfire highlights the deep scar running from his left eye across his temple and into his hairline. "He's back there." He jerks his head backward as his lips kick up ever so slightly. The blonde on his lap giggles, sending me a smug look as she wraps her arms around his neck.

Ignoring the theatrics, I walk in the direction of the pool house, swigging from the vodka bottle, willing it to hurry the fuck up and numb my pain.

The door is open, and I push inside, hearing them before I see them. It's not a surprise. Not after Bryant's carefully staged intervention outside.

I walk across the living area, sidestepping crumpled beer cans, stale pizza boxes, and wrinkled clothing, listening to the pants and groans emanating from the bedroom, cursing that dickhead under my breath.

I open the door with a flourish, leaning against the doorway as I watch a bimbo with brash red hair ride my boyfriend's cock. She's really going for it. Bouncing up and down on him like she's on a bucking bronco. Darrow's pelvis lifts as he grips her hips, sweat gliding across his chest, as he groans in pleasure, thrusting up inside her. She moans, throwing her head back as she succumbs to the sensation.

And I know how good it feels, because Darrow's got a big cock and he knows how to use it.

"Hey, asshole," I say, taking another swig of vodka as I watch them.

"Lo! Shit!" Darrow's eyes pop wide as he finally notices me. "Don't overreact," he pleads, his expression turning frantic. He shoves the redhead off his cock, and she falls to the floor, hitting her temple against the side of the bedside table. He stands, his erect dick saluting me, as he steps over his fuck buddy, ignoring her cries and cusses, making a beeline for me.

"Dar," Tempest whines, climbing to her feet. "Forget about her. Come back to bed." She fondles one of her big tits, while her free hand rubs the bruised skin on her forehead.

"Shut the fuck up," he snaps, glaring at her over his shoulder.

Her lips thin, and a muscle ticks in her jaw. Then, her features smooth out, and a wicked glint shimmers in her eyes.

"Spit it out, bitch," I say, holding up a palm to stall Darrow's forward trajectory.

"He's been fucking me for weeks, any chance he gets," Tempest purrs, grinning smugly as she walks toward us.

I raise the bottle. "Good for you. It's only taken you, what, about two years to worm your way into his bed?" She wraps her arm around Darrow from behind, but he pushes her off. "We've all watched your pathetic seduction attempts, but perseverance obviously pays. You should be proud." I smirk, drinking another few mouthfuls of vodka.

"Oh, I am proud. I'm very proud, because I'm clearly a

much better lay than the high-and-mighty Harlow Westbrook."

"Shut your face, Tempest, or I'll shut it for you," Darrow hisses at his fuck buddy, looking like he's seconds away from losing his shit.

"Not my fault you can't hold on to him," she adds, taunting me further because she's got fluff between her ears.

Darrow loses it, slapping her across the face, and I wince as her head jerks back.

"Real classy," I deadpan, glaring at the asshole. I'm not a fan of Tempest. I actually cannot stand her, but no one deserves to be treated like that. If he had ever dared to lift a finger to me, I would have slapped him back and then tossed his abusive ass to the curb. But Tempest will cling to him like a limpet because she has zero self-respect and even less intelligence.

"She's no one," he says, reaching for me. "A hole to fuck when I'm bored. It means nothing."

The desperate look really doesn't suit Darrow, and I'm wondering how I've put up with him this long. He was a means to an end, and he's outlived his usefulness. Now, I get to walk away like the injured party, and I can keep my secrets close to my chest. It's neater this way. Tempest has done me a favor. Not that she'll ever hear that from my lips.

I snort, and they both pin eyes on me. "You two dumb fucks deserve one another." I push off the door frame. "Enjoy my sloppy seconds." Tempest glares at me, and from the way she's clenching her knuckles, I know she'd love to take a pop at me. "I was done slumming it anyway."

"Lo, wait. C'mon. You know I love you." Darrow makes a grab for me, and I promptly knee him in the nuts. He drops to the ground, cupping his dick, as he roars out in pain. I lift the vodka bottle, ready to pour it over his head, before I think better of it.

I'm not wasting good Grey Goose vodka on that cheating slimeball.

"Enjoy your ho, and lose my number." I hold my head confidently as I walk off.

"Thanks for the heads-up," I say, blowing Bryant a kiss when I walk past Darrow's crew, looking like I haven't a care in the world.

Bryant ditches the blonde and chases after me. "You deserved to know," he says, falling into step beside me.

I glance at him, knowing exactly why he did it. "Like I said, thanks."

"Wait." He grabs my elbow, stalling me. "He was never right for you anyway."

My lips twitch. "And I suppose you are?"

"You know I am." He runs a hand over his shaved black scalp, his hazel eyes confirming everything I've suspected.

"Yeah, that shit's not happening, Bry. Go back to Blondie." I don't wait for his reply, shucking out of his hold and slipping through the back door into the house.

Fuck that asshole Darrow. I really needed to fuck all this shit out of my system tonight. I hug the vodka bottle to my chest. Guess Mr. Grey Goose will just have to do the job instead.

I'm halfway down the hallway toward the entrance lobby when he calls out to me. "Lo! Wait up!"

I glance over my shoulder, spotting Darrow shoving his way through the crowd at the doorway to the ballroom. Ugh. I'm not in the mood to hear his cringeworthy excuses.

I don't have much of a morality code, but cheating is a hard pass for me.

He's burned his bridges, and I was done with him anyway, so there's nothing he can say that will make me change my mind.

I'm done fucking him, and I'm done talking to him.

It's not like there's a shortage of hot guys in Lowell, and I'm finished experimenting in Prestwick.

"Fuck my life," I mutter, racing to the nearest door, yanking it open and darting inside. I lock the door from the inside. Exhaling heavily, I turn around, my breath faltering as I instantly realize my mistake.

Or, perhaps, it's fate meddling, and I've been led here tonight for a reason.

Four pairs of eyes stare at me with varying expressions. The guys are seated around a circular table playing cards. Lighting is real low, the only illumination coming from two lamps, one on either side of the room. Smoke clouds swirl overhead. The smell of tobacco mixes with the heady scent of Mary J.

The guy with the cropped dirty-blond hair swivels around in his chair, stretching his long jean-clad legs out in front of him, his gaze trekking over me with blatant interest. Piercing blue eyes penetrate mine, and I hold his intrusive gaze with one of my own.

His face is a masterpiece of epic proportion. Strong nose. Plump lips. Full, high cheekbones most girls would kill for. His wide ice-blue eyes are framed with a layer of thick black lashes. His chin is coated in a stylish layer of stubble. His left eyebrow is pierced, and tattoos covers his exposed arms and hands right to the tips of his fingers. It's too dark to see them clearly, but it's an impressive display of ink. His black T-shirt stretches across an impressive chest and bulging biceps, and he is drool-worthy in the extreme.

He's hot as fuck, but from the smug tilt of his lips, he knows it too.

A throat clears, dragging my attention away from the guy who can only be Saint Lennox, leader of the junior chapter of The Sainthood. A guy as feared as he is desired.

My eyes lock on Galen Lennox next. Where his cousin Saint's gaze held curiosity as much as a threat, Galen is all cold, hard lines, his expression reeking of tension and disbelief. His jade-green eyes bore holes in the side of my head, and his ripped body is taut, on high alert, ready to strike at a second's notice. Colored tats cover one arm, creeping up the side of his neck. He rubs his plush lips, narrowing his eyes suspiciously, as he dips his head, his brown faux hawk pointed in my direction like he's wielding a weapon.

I don't respond well to threats of any kind, so I push off the door, straighten my spine, and walk toward the table as Darrow pounds his fists on the door outside. "Lo! Open this fucking door right now!"

The guy with dark hair and intense brown eyes cocks a brow in amusement. He drums his fingers off the table, shooting a look at Saint. He's built like a tank. Wide shoulders. Broad chest. Biceps bigger than my head. Muscular legs that snugly fit the dark jeans he's wearing. His expression is the warmest. His gaze bounces from Saint to me to the door behind me. He must be Caz Evans—the muscle. Stories of his brutal strength are legendary around these parts. He's killed men with his bare hands if they are to be believed.

I stop in front of Saint, placing my hands on my hips, challenging him with a look. I feel the daggers Galen sends my way, but my focus is singular and locked on their leader. Saint's notorious cool blue gaze meets mine, and a spark sizzles between us as we stare at one another up close for the very first time.

The Arrows and The Sainthood are sworn enemies, and they don't make a habit of socializing together, but I'm sure he's heard of me. The same way Darrow would know if any of these guys were dating. Saint's heated gaze burns through my skin, and fire blossoms in my chest. An ache spreads lower, my core pulsing as attraction, instant and fierce, slams into me.

"Saint."

Our connection is broken at the sound of *his* husky voice, and my head whips around. My jaw clamps shut as our eyes meet. His expression conveys so much, but it's too damn late. Pained hazel eyes latch onto mine, and the tsunami builds in intensity inside my chest.

I pride myself on my ability to keep my emotions on lockdown, but this day is seriously fucking with my head. Between Dad, Darrow, and now stumbling across The Sainthood, this day couldn't get much worse.

Theo Smith is the fourth member of the gang and he's also

drop-dead gorgeous, but in a different way. His long sandy-blond hair falls to the nape of his neck, tucked behind his ears in a messy, bedhead style that is extremely sexy. He scrubs a hand along his stubbly jawline, holding my gaze, the unspoken plea obvious. For a tech wizard and financial mastermind who is known to be sharp as a tack and cool under pressure, he sure looks rattled now.

He should be.

Because he's a liar and a coward.

And he knows I know.

"Harlow Westbrook!" Darrow is close to breaking point if he's using my full name now. "Open this fucking door, and stop being such a sensitive bitch."

I relax my jaw, loosening my features and planting an amused expression on my face, as I refocus on Saint. He stands, eyeing me with a calculating look that manages to be darkly sinister and drenched in lust at the same time. Shivers course all over my body, and I'm so aroused my panties are soaking.

I'm close to six foot tall in these heels, and Saint still towers over me. I visualize his large frame covering mine in my mind's eye, elevating my desire a notch higher. Heat from his body crashes into me, both soothing my ragged edges and tending the flames building to an inferno inside me. I place my half-empty vodka bottle on the table, planting my hands on my hips again. "Well?"

I put it out there. I'm doing this. Now, the ball is in his court.

The attraction is mutual. He's doing nothing to hide he wants me as much as I clearly want him.

Saint takes a step closer, and his chest brushes against my body, sending a fresh wave of desire cascading through my limbs. "If we do this—"

"I know. This isn't my first rodeo." I know nothing in this life is free. You ask for a favor. You pay the pied piper. Sex is the usual currency. It's the way of the world we inhabit.

A muscle pops in his jaw as he grips my chin tight, tugging my head up. "Don't fucking interrupt me."

"Or what? Let me guess. You'll punish me?" He can't know that rough sex is my favorite, and punishment is rarely a punishment. Not after the things I endured at thirteen. It will take a lot to break me this time.

He stares deep into my eyes, bringing his face in so close we are sharing the same air. "You'd like that."

I don't like that he can read me so easily. Not when I've spent years erecting walls to keep men like him out. But forewarned is forearmed. And it's no surprise Saint Lennox is a master at breaking down walls and uncovering truths. He isn't the brains behind the operation for no reason. My eyes respond affirmatively, and my body hums in anticipation.

"It won't just be me," he adds, carefully watching my face for my reaction. "We're a package deal."

I've heard rumors to that effect, and it only adds to the appeal.

Butterflies invade my chest, and my body throbs with raw need. I wet my dry lips, gulping as a surge of adrenaline sluices through my veins. I know what's on the table. What they will do and the price I must pay. If he thinks this is a dealbreaker, he's so wrong. This is exactly what I need to get through the rest of this hellish day.

"Do it," I say, my voice resonating with confidence, my face showcasing my eagerness.

Saint's eyes darken to the point where they're almost smoldering.

He wants this.

It's a done deal.

"Saint. We should talk about this." Displeasure underscores Galen's tone, and if he fucks this up for me, I'll fuck *him* up.

"The decision is made." Saint turns his head, daring his cousin to argue.

Galen rubs the back of his neck, nodding tersely.

What Saint says is law.

Everyone knows it.

"Lo! I'm not playing games. Open the door, or I'm fucking breaking it open," Darrow roars, his patience reserves all gone as he shoves his body weight at the door, rattling it.

Saint drops my chin, grabs my hand, and pulls me toward the door. He eyeballs me with his hand curled around the handle. "Last chance to back out."

"I'm not backing out." I press into his side, wrapping my arms around his neck and draping myself all over him, enjoying the flurry of shivers racing along my skin the instant I touch him. "I'm all in."

Respect flashes in his eyes, but it's so brief I'm not sure I didn't imagine it.

Slinging his arm around my waist, he holds me close and opens the door, facing my new ex. "Darrow Knight," Saint drawls, sliding his hand to my hip. "To what do we owe this pleasure?" Derision drips from his tone and his expression as he rubs circles on my hip with his long, inked fingers.

Darrow's face darkens like thunder, his gaze jumping between Saint and me. The top button on his jeans is undone, he's bare chested, and his sneakers are unlaced. I'm betting Tempest wasn't too pleased to see him flee so fast in pursuit of me. "Get the fuck out of the room, Lo." Darrow grabs hold of one of my arms, pulling it away from Saint's neck.

"Fuck you, Dar," I say as Saint pries Darrow's meaty fingers off my flesh, reeling me back into his body. "I've never answered to you, and I'm not about to start now."

"You don't want to do this, babe." He folds his arms across his chest, leveling me with a warning look. "You're overreacting."

I laugh. "You appear to be suffering delusions of grandeur. Let me help clear it up for you." I shuck out of Saint's embrace, prodding Darrow in the chest as I force him back. "I. Don't. Care. You were just someone to fuck when I was bored." I love turning his own words back on him.

He slaps my finger away, and Saint steps up behind me,

sliding his arms around my waist, pulling me back into his warm body. "You've overstayed your welcome." Saint's voice could cut glass.

Galen steps up on my other side. "Get your crew, and get the fuck out of my house."

"You touch her... You know what this means." Darrow clenches his fists and puffs out his chest.

"You've crashed and burned, man." Caz blows smoke into Darrow's face. "Now, get lost."

Darrow's face turns an unhealthy shade of red. "Whore." He narrows his eyes to slits. "I was fucking done with you anyway."

"Yeah, that's why you're chasing after her, pounding on our door like some fucking pussy," Saint replies. "You're a mess, man."

"I hope she's worth it," he barks before storming off.

"I'll grab a few minions and escort The Arrows off the premises," Caz says, stubbing out his cigarette on the floor. He tosses a grin in my direction. "Don't start without me." He waggles his brows before walking off after Darrow.

"I need a fucking drink," Galen growls, shoving my shoulder as he pushes past me into the room. Saint steers me back inside, eyeing his cousin with a laser-sharp gaze he should be concerned about.

Obviously, the cousins don't tell each other everything.

Theo closes the door after Caz, attempting eye contact with me, but I ignore him, giving him a taste of his own medicine.

Galen chugs straight from a bottle of bourbon on the table, drinking it like it's soda. Saint drops into a seat across the table from his cousin, pulling me down on his lap. I remove my school jacket, hanging it on the back of the chair.

Saint zeros in on my chest, smacking his lips and smirking. "Nice rack." He palms my breasts through my white shirt, and my nipples instantly pebble. He pulls on my tits, roughly kneading them through my clothing, until my nipples are so hard they're straining against my flimsy lace bra and the thin material of my shirt.

Theo kicks his feet up on the table, lighting a blunt and bringing it to his lips. Galen scowls, his gaze riveted to Saint's hands, and it's almost comical. Snatching my vodka bottle, I knock back a few mouthfuls before swiveling on Saint's lap until I'm straddling him. His hands drop to my waist, and he quirks a brow, waiting for me to make the next move.

I put the bottle on the table and bend down, boldly pressing my mouth to Saint's. His lips instantly part, and I pass some of the vodka from my mouth to his. His eyes pierce mine as we swallow, our mouths still lined up, and I could get lost in those dangerous icy depths if I'm not careful.

He swoops in before I can retract, claiming my lips in a searing-hot kiss that curls my toes. Although, calling it a kiss isn't doing it justice, because it's more like a claiming.

Saint devours my mouth. His tongue swirling around mine. His lips punishing as he takes what he wants with no apology. And I return his ardor, pressing bruising kisses against his lips as my hands sweep over the velvety-soft hair on his head. His hands slide under my uniform skirt, his large palms flattening against the bare cheeks of my ass. He's already hard underneath me, and I grind against him, desperate to feel him inside me. To lose myself before my head starts reminding me my world has upended.

"I thought we were waiting for Caz."

Saint rips his mouth from mine, fixing an arrogant look over my shoulder at his cousin. "This *is* me waiting." He squeezes my ass cheeks, and I bite down on my lower lip to stifle a moan. "I'm getting our girl warmed up."

I place my hands on his shoulder and lean down, licking a path up the side of his neck and along his bristly jawline.

A deep rumble erupts from his chest. "Girl, you've got balls." He removes his hands from my butt, holding my face tight, examining me with clear amusement.

"Her name is Harlow." Theo's voice is clipped, but none of us miss the soft edge.

Saint keeps a hold of my face as he turns his attention to his friend. "Something you want to tell me, dude?"

"Everyone knows who Harlow Westbrook is. She's—"

I yank out of Saint's grip, twisting around so I'm facing Theo, and he stops speaking mid-sentence. "You really don't want to go there." My eyes dare him to test me.

"Interesting." Saint holds my hips, dragging my butt back and forth across his crotch. "But it can wait. I'm horny as fuck." He lifts me off him, temporarily setting my feet on the ground.

In a lightning-fast move, he swipes the contents of the table away with a sweep of his hand. I predict the move at the last second, snatching my vodka before it becomes a casualty. Galen's reactions are equally fast, and he rescues his bourbon before it joins the cards, chips, money, and a few bottles of beer on the floor. Saint lifts me again, placing me on the edge of the table. "Lie back." His eyes blaze with lust, and my panties are fucking drenched, yet he's barely touched me.

Galen curses, and Theo gulps, as I do what I'm told. I lie back and my long, dark hair fans out around me on the table.

"Grab her hands," Saint commands.

Galen fumes for a couple seconds, swigging more bourbon before sending it flying across the room. The bottle smacks into a wall, shattering on impact.

"You done?" Saint levels his cousin with a lethal look.

"Not nearly." Galen's gnarly tone sends shivers racing up my spine. He grabs my hands, yanking them up over my head until it feels like they're being wrenched from my arm sockets.

Saint parts my thighs, gliding his hands up my bare flesh as the door opens and Caz joins our little party. He locks the door with an audible click, stomping toward us in heavy boots. "That handled?" Saint asks, his hands stalling halfway up my thighs.

"We tossed the trash." I can hear the smirk in Caz's tone. "Hey, beautiful," he says, leaning over me and cupping one side of my face.

I stare at him as Saint resumes his upward journey on my thighs. Cool air brushes across my overheated flesh as Saint lifts my skirt. "What's with the uniform?" he asks.

"Didn't have time to change," I murmur, my gaze locked on Caz's as he moves his face down closer to mine.

I got the call when I was in school, and Mom sent a car to collect me. Lincoln, my dad's assistant, drove my SUV home. After a couple hours with the police, the coroner, and the director of the funeral home, I just needed out. Mom retreated to her bedroom with a bottle of wine and some Valium, and I grabbed my vodka and hightailed it out of there. I didn't even realize I was still in my uniform until that bitch Rita Knight made me aware of it.

"You look hot," Saint says, cupping my pussy through my thong. "And I've always wanted to fuck a Lowell Academy princess."

"Guess it's your lucky day," I rasp just before Caz's demanding lips slam down against mine. He destroys my mouth as his fingers make quick work of my shirt. I gasp into his mouth when Saint rips my thong apart, exposing me to the room and plunging two fingers inside me.

"She's so wet for us," he exclaims, adding another digit and pumping his fingers in and out in rough thrusts. I squirm on the table, and Galen holds both my wrists in one hand as he leans over me from above, sliding his free hand down my body, his fingers finding their way into my left bra cup.

He fondles my breast, tweaking my nipple hard, and I cry out into Caz's mouth. Caz lifts his head, licking his lips, his eyes darkening as he ogles my chest.

If any of them notice the scars, they pay them no attention.

In one swift move, he unclasps my bra at the front, freeing my breasts. Saint continues fingering me while Galen kneads my left breast and Caz's delectable mouth suctions around my right nipple.

Between them, they tease and taunt me until I'm a hot, writhing mess.

My eyes land on the chair where Theo is sitting, smoking, and watching with an obvious hard-on tenting his jeans.

"Sit up." Saint pulls his fingers out, and the two guys worshiping my chest pull back. "Take my cock out."

I sit up, peering into Saint's lustful eyes, reaching for the button on his jeans and popping the top one. I slide my hand inside his boxers, and he hisses through gritted teeth when my hand wraps around his long, hard length. I stroke him slowly as he plays with my tits. Behind us, the sounds of clothes being shed send my blood pressure sky rocketing.

I've had a couple of threesomes before. Me with two guys. But I've never been with four all at once. And these guys are hot as fuck and skillful lovers—if the gossip I've heard is reliable.

I yank Saint's jeans and boxers down as he pulls his shirt up over his head. While he kicks his jeans away, Caz strips my shirt and bra off leaving me in only my skirt, which is currently still bunched up around my waist, my pussy on full display.

Theo tosses some condoms on the table, and I whip my head around to him. We stare at one another. A silent communication passes between us. He has his jeans undone, and his hand is stroking his cock, but he's making no move to join us.

Saint yanks my head back around. "Eyes on me, baby."

I scoot to the edge of the table and press my mouth to his chest, looking up at him through hooded eyes as I press hot, wet kisses all over his chiseled abs and chest. He places his hand on top of mine, still wrapped around his rock-solid erection, and he moves my hand up and down, urging me to continue. He lets go, and I pump his cock in strong, confident strokes, loving the dark glaze coating his eyes and the way he thrusts into my hand.

Someone fists a hand around my hair, tugging my head back and to the side. "Open wide," Galen commands.

I take his cock into my mouth, hollowing out my cheeks so I can take him all the way in. He's huge, triggering my gag reflex when he presses against the back of my mouth. He eases out a little, and then I slide my lips up and down his wide shaft, sucking him enthusiastically, enjoying the sounds he's making as I blow him. He fucks my mouth while I pump Saint's cock and Caz fondles my tits from behind.

"Enough." Saint removes my hand from his dick, lifting me up the instant Galen pops out of my mouth. My legs wrap around Saint's toned waist as he walks us to the leather couch.

He drops me down flat on my back, nudging my legs apart and lowering his mouth to my pussy. His fingers dip in and out of me as he alternates with his tongue, ravishing me like a madman. I explode on his tongue, my back arching, hips jerking as I come all over his mouth.

He stands, grinning manically as he rolls a condom on. "You taste like temptation, Harlow Westbrook." He leans over me, slamming his mouth against mine, and I can taste myself on his lips.

He lifts me up and sits down, situating me over his throbbing dick. "Ride me, princess. Show me how much you love my cock inside you."

I lower myself slowly on top of him, feeling him stretch me as I take him inside my body. Alcohol buzzes in my veins, and I'm high on the right sensation as I start fucking him.

"Awesome ink," Caz says, trailing his fingers over the design that stretches from my shoulder blades down to my butt. I flinch for a second, but quickly compose myself.

"The avenging angel, right, Lo?" Theo says.

"Don't call me that." I glare at him over my shoulder as I bounce up and down on Saint's cock.

"Who are you seeking vengeance on?" Galen asks, stroking his cock as he watches my tits jiggle while I ride his cousin and best friend.

"Everyone," I reply without hesitation.

"Fuck," Saint grunts, digging his nails into my hips in a way I know will leave marks. "Your pussy is so tight."

Caz brushes my hair over my shoulder, positioning his cock

at my mouth. I open for him as Galen's mouth latches around one of my nipples. Caz isn't quite as big as Saint and Galen, and I take him all the way in. He thrusts in and out as he rolls my other nipple between his fingers.

Theo just watches.

He's still in his chair, but he's moved closer.

Our eyes meet as he watches me fuck his friends, and I see the pain. I almost feel sorry for him until I remember what he did. And that I'm numb to emotions.

The only time I allow myself to feel anything is when I'm fucking. It's the only pleasure I permit myself, and right now, my pleasure-o-meter is off the charts.

Theo's hand is working overtime behind his jeans, and his face is flushed. I can't resist pushing his buttons when Caz abruptly pulls out of my mouth. "You can take my ass," I offer, eyeballing Theo, my tone seductive, my expression sneering.

"I'm good," Theo says, his voice strained.

"Your loss is my gain," Caz jokes, grabbing a tube of lube from the bookshelf and squirting some in his hand before throwing it to Galen. Caz rolls on a condom and lathers his dick with lube as two wet, cold, slippery fingers push into my ass. I groan, grinding down on Saint's cock as Galen fingers my ass, prepping me. With his free hand, he rolls a condom over his long, thick shaft.

Saint thrusts up inside me with mounting urgency, his hands on my hips hurting as he pounds into me with wild abandon. He orgasms on a roar, his cock pulsing inside me, and I explode when he rubs my clit, spasming around him as his climax dies out.

Then we switch out, and I'm riding Galen as Caz takes me from behind. The sensation is incredible, and despite the hostility wafting off Galen in waves, this is the most fun I've had in ages. I could happily spend all night fucking these guys. Ignoring reality while I delay the inevitable.

As soon as Caz has ripped his condom off and come all over my ass, Galen flips me onto my back, wrenching my legs up over his shoulders as he pounds into me.

His eyes flare with hatred as he thrusts inside me, drilling his pelvis into mine, pushing his big cock inside me as far as it will go, nudging my cervix and causing stars to sprout behind my eyes. Galen has some stamina, fucking me mercilessly for ages, sweat glistening on his chest with the exertion.

Saint strokes his cock while he sucks on my tits. He calls Theo over when he notices he is close, and despite the reluctance in Theo's eyes, he obeys his leader, coming all over my breasts the same time Saint does.

Caz has his jeans back on, and he's drinking my vodka as he watches Galen fuck me like he wishes he was killing me. Galen's hand closes around my throat as Saint toys with my sore nipples, rubbing his and Theo's cum all over my bare breasts. "You have the best tits, princess." He smirks, watching his cousin exorcise his demons. My pussy feels scratched raw as Galen pummels my insides. "And the tightest cunt," he adds, as Galen finally detonates, his entire body tense and straining as he shouts out his release. A few strokes of Saint's fingers against my clit and I'm coming again too.

The second Galen is done, he pulls out, tosses the condom into the trash can, yanks on his jeans, and storms out of the room, slamming the door behind him.

Saint scoops up my clothes, flinging them at me. "Time to go, princess."

I don't protest, but I don't hurry either. Theo hands me some tissues, averting his eyes as I take them from him. I take my sweet time cleaning their spunk off my body and getting dressed. I stand, casting one last glance at the guys before I walk toward the door. I swipe the bottle of vodka from Caz's hands as I pass, and he cranks out a laugh.

"Thanks for the distraction," I say as my hand closes around the door handle.

And the awesome sex.

I think it, but I don't say it because these guys' egos are probably floating somewhere in outer space as it is.

"Distraction from what?" Saint asks, walking toward me in all his naked glory.

Damn, that man is sex on two legs, and my core throbs with need, which is insane after three orgasms and a ton of glorious, sweaty sex.

"Life. Death." I shrug, but they all heard my voice crack.

Theo lowers his head but not before I glimpse the sorrow in his eyes.

He knows my dad just died. Figures he would have heard.

"You realize what you've done here today," Saint says, stepping into his jeans.

"I know."

"We won't protect you," he adds, pulling a smoke from a pack of cigarettes.

"I know that too."

He closes the distance between us, placing his arms over my head, caging me in. "Good, because The Sainthood doesn't do charity work."

"I don't want or need your help. I'm perfectly capable of defending myself."

A lazy smirk ghosts over his mouth. He tugs sharply on my hair, yanking my head back. "I guess we'll see just how vengeful you are, princess." He presses his mouth to my ear. "Let the battles commence."

THE SAINTHOOD

CHAPTER 1

Four months later – start of senior year

"NEVER LOSE SIGHT of your surroundings," Diesel instructs as a guy sneaks up on me from the rear. With one last strong jab, I punch the bloodied woman in front of me in the face, kick her in the ribs, and sweep her legs out from under her. She's out cold before she even hits the grassy floor.

I swing around, instantly ducking down as the man's clenched fist aims for my face.

He's dressed from head to toe in black, like all my opponents are, but this guy is something new. His sheer brutality is different. He genuinely looks like he wants to bash my head in. And he knows his stuff, because I've barely had time to recover before he lands a firm punch in my gut. I stumble back but compose myself before his second punch makes impact.

We go at it like this is a real life-or-death situation. Punching and kicking, swinging and diving, dancing on our feet as we spar, pretty evenly matched. Blood trickles into my eye from the small cut on my brow, and I swipe at it with my sweat-slickened hand.

"Time out," Diesel shouts, holding up bottles of water, and I curse under my breath. I can count on one hand the amount of times Diesel has ended a fight over the years he's been training me. It almost always ends with my opponents out cold or clearly at my mercy. Either I'm losing my touch or he's upped the stakes, choosing better quality targets for me to practice on.

My opponent's smug smile angers me so much I strike the carotid artery in his neck with the side of my hand when he turns away from me, grinning as his legs give out, his eyelids flutter closed, and he crashes to the floor.

Diesel sighs, shaking his head as he approaches, offering me a bottle of water. "I wanted to do some close combat knife fighting today. It's been a while since we focused on knife fighting skills and defenses."

I take the bottle from him and twist the cap. "I know how to use my knife, and I always carry my blade with me."

It took me a couple years to feel comfortable using knives because the sight of one used to trigger my trauma, but Dad arranged for this special form of hypnosis therapy that helped me overcome my fear. Carrying a folding knife is easier to conceal than a firearm, so learning how to defend myself using knives was a no-brainer.

I drain half the bottle in one go while Diesel prods the unconscious guy and girl on the ground. He talks quietly into his earpiece, and I know he's calling in the cleanup team.

They always follow him here in a plain black van. Hiding in the shadows at the edge of the woods surrounding the field where we conduct our training sessions. Only revealing themselves when Diesel summons them to remove my bloodied and battered opponents.

I never fight the same combatants. It's always new men and women. Usually a few years older than me. And I've often wondered who they are and where they come from. But I know not to ask questions. That was another thing Daddy taught me.

I know they are here to help me. That they have kept this secret for years and that Diesel contacted me the day after Dad died to confirm the monthly weekend arrangement was still in place.

It seems, even in death, Dad is still protecting me.

Pain slices through my chest, attempting to infiltrate my heart, but I reinforce my walls and push the pain away. Like I do daily when the toll of Dad's passing hits me anew, threatening to dismantle the armor I've spent years perfecting.

The best way I can honor the man, who meant everything to me, is to live the life he helped create for me. To be the person he shaped me to be. To force my emotions aside and focus on what needs to be done.

"Go shower," Diesel instructs a couple minutes later. "I'll meet you in the cabin."

"Sure thing, Commander." I toss him a sexy grin as I turn around, heading in the direction of the cabin that has been in my dad's family for generations. My hips sway as I walk, and I can feel his eyes glued to my Lycra-clad body every step of the way. I shouldn't tease him like this. Not out in the open where there are vigilant eyes, but sometimes, I just can't help myself.

I walk into the cabin, instantly relaxing in the familiar surroundings. It's been modernized over the years, and it's more like a luxury vacation cabin now.

Originally, our ancestors built it as a hunting cabin, and I imagine it was more rustic and rudimentary back then. Now, it boasts split levels with four en suite bedrooms upstairs and a large open-plan living and kitchen area downstairs. The lower level also houses a game room, bar, small gym, and study.

Dad usually worked while I trained, and on Sundays, I would do homework at his desk while he grilled steaks. Out back, there is a wide decked area with a hot tub, outdoor eating area, and grill that we made good use of anytime we came here.

We're surrounded by thick woodland, and there is no other property for miles. Access is via a high gated entrance, and the entire twenty-acre site is protected by barbed wire and high-tech security cameras. There is only one way on and off this property, and it's always been my go-to safe haven.

Mom doesn't even know about this cabin.

Something else Dad and I were keeping secret from her.

All those weekends he told her he was taking me camping up the mountains, we were actually coming here.

Dad loved my mom so much. Anyone who spent time in their presence could attest to it. They worshiped one another in a way I've never seen with any other couple.

But he kept *a lot* of shit from her.

I've kept a lot of shit from her.

I'm still doing it, but it's necessary.

I've promised myself that if I ever fall in love it will be with someone on an equal footing. Someone I can tell all my secrets to. Someone who will protect me in the same way I protect him. Not someone I have to shelter and lie to in the name of keeping him safe.

I trudge up the stairs and into my bedroom, opening a window to let some cool air circulate, before I head into my bathroom. It takes time and energy to peel my sweaty workout gear off my body, but after exerting considerable effort, I step into the shower, sighing as the cold water hits my flesh.

I let my skin cool down under the cold water, and once my body temp has reduced, I adjust the shower settings to warm. I wash and condition my hair and scrub at my body, and then, I stand under the warm stream of water, allowing it to ease my tired, sore muscles.

I close my eyes and remember the first time Daddy brought me here for training. I was fourteen, and it was a few months after the event which changed my life.

"This nice man is going to help, buttercup," Dad said, *crouching down in front of me and taking my hands as I cowered from the strange man with the disarming smile.* "He's going to show you how to fight so nothing can ever happen to you again."

That piqued my interest. "What kind of fighting?" I asked, directing my question at my dad and not the stranger even *though it was the stranger who answered.*

"We will start with basic fitness and combat training and progress to marksmanship and defensive maneuvering techniques, survival tools, and basic first aid procedures among other aspects. By the time your training is complete, you will be proficient in handling a variety of different weapons and you will be fully competent to protect and defend yourself against any enemy attacks."

"When do I begin?" I asked without hesitation, my thirst for vengeance already in full flow.

As Diesel's strong arms wrap around me from behind, I wonder if Dad would still consider him a nice man if he knew all the carnal ways my commander now knows my body.

I WAKE A couple of hours later with my face pressed into Diesel's chest. I lift my head, startled to find he's still here. We usually have a couple rounds of hot sex, and then he takes off, not lingering for small talk.

We both know what this is.

That it has boundaries and a time limit, and I'm more than okay with that.

I learned how to separate my emotions from the act of sex when I was fifteen and I willingly gave my virginity to the guy I was fake dating at the time.

Back then, I entered into a sexual relationship understanding it wasn't, and never would be, love, and it helped me approach the physical act as just that. A way of experiencing untold pleasure without looking for anything but an orgasm.

It has stood me well.

I've never fallen in love with any of my sexual partners or either of my two previous boyfriends.

Both those relationships served a different purpose anyway.

So, if Diesel is still here, it means he wants to talk.

I prop up on one elbow, placing my hand on the solid wall of muscle that is his chest, peering into his eyes. "Did you sleep at all?" I ask, tracing patterns against his skin.

"No." He runs his hand up and down my back.

"So, you were just watching me like a legit creeper?" I tease, touching the old scar tissue on the left side of his chest.

"Pretty much," he agrees, offering me a rare smile.

Diesel takes his job very seriously, and it still amazes me that we fell into bed in the first place. After the first session I had with him, post Dad's death, I was so consumed with grief I pounced on him, and I think he didn't have it in him to turn me down.

Plus, I'm experienced enough to know how to please a man, and I'm certain he's enjoyed our illicit trysts even if it battles with that sensible, logical part of his brain.

"You're so beautiful, Harlow," he says, placing his hand over my left breast. "And I'm not just talking about the outside. Your inner strength and your indomitable will to survive is the most beautiful thing about you. I wish I was ten years younger so I could be worthy of you."

I lean down and kiss him, surprised to see so much emotion swirling in the depths of his pale-blue eyes. "Even if you were, your strict moral code and unrelenting loyalty to your job wouldn't allow you to permit anything permanent between us. We both know that."

"My boss, and your dad, would not react well to this."

"Your boss doesn't know, and my dad is dead."

"I'm so much older than you, and you were in mourning. It was wrong to respond to your advances when you were vulnerable."

I shake my head. "I'm eighteen now, and I know what I'm doing. You helped me that night. You gave me exactly what I needed, and you shouldn't have any regrets because I don't."

"You were only seventeen that first time," he says, and I see how much he hates himself for taking advantage of me. That's how he sees it in his head, and nothing I say will likely change his mind.

"It was still legal, and you didn't force me into anything. Don't beat yourself up over it." This is becoming too heavy, and I avoid that shit like the plague. I ease out from under his arm, dropping flat on my back. I stare at the stark-white ceiling as I pull the sheet up over my naked chest. "And it's only sex. We can stop this at any time." I turn my head to his, cupping his stubbly cheek, smiling at him with genuine affection. "My heart isn't invested, Diesel. You won't hurt me. I'll miss the sex, but it won't break me."

Not much does anymore.

Although my dad's death came close to it.

He stares deep into my eyes. "Sometimes, I think your dad was so wrong. That we took it too far. That we've taken too much from you."

"You weren't the ones who took from me, and I have no regrets," I lie. I can't admit the truth to anyone, because saying it out loud will only make my suspicion too real. I need to fix it first before I can even begin to come to terms with the consequences of my actions.

That's the end of our conversation, and quite possibly, this is the last time I'll watch Diesel getting dressed in my bedroom.

But I'm okay with that.

This isn't fun if I know he's suffering a moral crisis every time we tango between the sheets.

I signed up for uncomplicated sex and multiple orgasms. If that's no longer all that's on the table, then I want no part of it. It's better we end like this before his doubts ruin something good and true. There is no shortage of willing bodies to share my bed, and I won't go without.

He kisses me passionately at the bottom of the stairs, and as goodbye kisses go, it's pretty damn impressive. I stay in place, watching him walk across the cabin to the door. He stops with his hand on the door handle, talking to me without turning around. "I know we only communicate to confirm our sessions, but you know how to reach me." He glances over his shoulder, his expression fiercely determined. "If you need my help, at any time, you only need to ask and I'm there."

I fold my arms across my chest. "You're a good man, Diesel."

A pained look washes over his face, and I know he doesn't agree, but it's exactly that sentiment which confirms my statement. Any other hot-blooded male wouldn't turn down no-strings-attached sex with a younger woman, but Diesel is a decent guy, and he won't use me for sex.

I watch the security cameras, waiting until I see his car exit the gates of the compound, before I head into the study.

I open the secret panels in the floor, removing the sturdy black box and placing it on top of the desk. I tap in the code on the panel of the box, unlocking the lid and retrieving the stack of files there. Then, I take out my hardback notepad and pick up where I left off last month.

I'm determined to crack the secret code the files are written in. Because I know the truth I seek is somewhere in here, and I won't rest until I've uncovered it.

THE SAINTHOOD

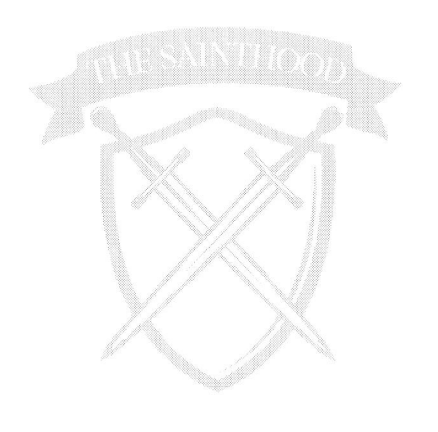

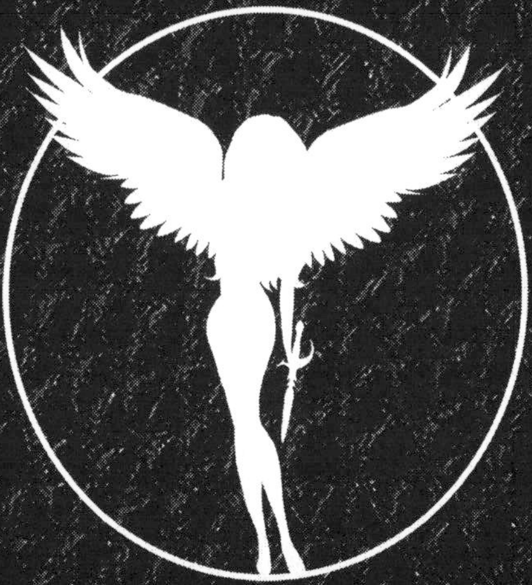

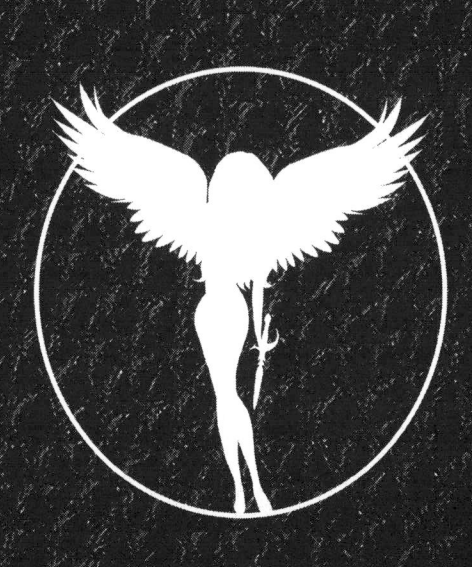

CHAPTER 2

"Your father would never have tolerated this," Mom says. I nurse a cup of steaming black coffee while picking at the shriveled eggs and incinerated strips of bacon she made for breakfast. I want to eat it, because I know she's trying, but I've never been a breakfast lover. I'm never hungry first thing, and Mom knows this. But I shovel another mouthful down, not wanting to offend her.

"I know, but he'd back down if he knew I wasn't unhappy about it," I say, sipping my coffee as I watch Mom studiously. She's pacing the kitchen, looking put together on the outside, but something's nagging at her. And I don't think it's the fact I've been gone all weekend "camping" or that I got expelled from Lowell Academy over a sex tape.

"What's going on with you?" I ask, pushing my half-eaten plate away.

She stops pacing. "What do you mean?" She runs her fingers through her wavy hair in a clear tell.

"You're agitated."

"I'm just concerned for you. Starting senior year at a new

school is a big deal. Especially a public school when all you've been used to is private. It will be a big culture shock, honey."

If she knew I'd been slumming it with Darrow and his Prestwick High crowd for half a year, and that I've seen and heard things that would turn her prematurely gray, she wouldn't be half as worried.

I shrug, tossing my hair over my shoulders. "Not to me it isn't." I stand, taking my plate and scraping it into the trash. "Sariah and Sean attend Lowell High. They have less archaic rules. And no one knows me there."

That last part isn't the full truth, because the video went viral, and now, everyone in my new school thinks they know who I am before they've even met me. But I don't want Mom worrying unnecessarily. She's been a basket case since Dad's fatal car accident, and it's felt like I've lost both parents.

But I've noticed a difference this past month. She's not locking herself in her room crying all the time. She's been going out. Heading into the office and taking an active role in managing her successful advertising agency. Meeting up with friends at night. And she's started to pay attention to her appearance again which is how I know she's beginning to heal.

Giana Westbrook, a.k.a. my mother, is drop dead gorgeous. According to Dad, he had to fight off competition to win her heart back in the day, and he was always fending off would-be admirers.

I can see why.

Even at forty, she is stunning. Tall with long dark hair, piercing green eyes, and a figure most supermodels would kill for, she looks twenty years younger and could easily pass for my sister. She often does, which is something Dad always got a kick out of.

He used to say I was the mirror image of her, and he always showered me with compliments, but I'm a pragmatist. I might share the same height, the same hair, and the same eye color, but that's where the similarities end. I'm curvier with bigger boobs which, when combined with my slim lower body, make me look like I'm about to topple over all the time. And, where Mom has this gorgeous heart-shaped face and delicate porcelain skin, I have Dad's round shape and his facial features with fuller lips, olive-toned complexion, and less defined cheekbones.

I know I'm pretty, but I'm not in Mom's league. Which is fine by me, because I loathe attention.

"You have your dad's confidence and self-belief," she says, gently cupping my cheek. "Nothing ever fazed him either."

"You have self-confidence and belief too," I reassure her, because you don't build a multimillion-dollar business from the ground up without those qualities.

"I didn't possess those traits at your age. I'm not sure I'd have been capable of enduring what you've endured these past few months." She reels me into a hug. "I'm proud of you, honey."

I ease out of her arms, staring at her with my mouth trailing the tile floor. "You're proud of me for making a sex tape?"

"That's not what I meant." She sighs, tucking my hair behind my ears. "I'm not pleased my little girl had a foursome with three guys, but I'm more enraged that those assholes recorded it without your knowledge and then enabled that scumbag to distribute it to everyone at school. I still think we should have sued them."

I gave Mom scant details on purpose. She knows the tape exists. That I had consensual sex but wasn't aware it was being recorded. I didn't tell her the guys were The Sainthood, and I didn't tell her the scumbag who shared it online was my scumbag ex. I know she won't watch it, and she's better off not knowing the truth.

Although, if she knew, she'd understand better.

You don't sue The Sainthood and live to tell the tale.

Dad always said we had to protect Mom, and that hasn't ended just because he's no longer here to fulfil his part of the bargain.

I love my mom, and I'm always going to look out for her.

She's a big part of the reason why I'm not letting it go.

The other is the fact I'm hurtling toward a destiny I don't want and the only way to halt it is to act first.

I need to keep her safe, and unraveling the truth is the only way to ensure it.

Dad is gone, but the mission isn't over. Not even close to it.

"I'm not having my sex life hauled through the courts or being forced to sit in some lawyer's office, facing any of those assholes, while pricks in suits pick my character apart. And it would've only prolonged the whole situation. It's died down now, and we got it removed from the internet," I say, purely to appease her.

I'm not naïve. Once it's out there, it's accessible forever and ever. Just talk to Kim K. Although, at least, she found a way of profiting from it.

I know tons of guys must've downloaded it and are probably regularly jerking off to it, but there isn't anything I can do about that now, so I refuse to lose sleep over it.

What's more upsetting is the number of guys hitting on me now. The suggestive comments from the guys, and the slurs from the girls, roll over my head like water falling over a cliff's edge, but being pawed at, stared at, messaged at all hours of the day and night, and followed around the school halls pisses me off to no end.

So, no, I'm not sorry to be leaving my snobby academy school behind.

Although, I'm under no illusions. I know my rep precedes me at Lowell High, but Sariah and Sean have been working on damage control, and I'm hoping it won't be as bad there.

Even if it is, I've only got to survive another ten months before I can wave sayonara to this shithole town.

"You're probably right." She glances at the clock. "You should go. You don't want to be late your first day."

I grab my Prada backpack from the table and snatch up my jacket.

"You're sure you want to wear that?" Mom asks, and I

know I'm offending her uber-feminine proclivities with my tight ripped jeans, scuffed boots, and off-the-shoulder sweater complete with battered leather jacket.

"Yep," I say, grabbing an apple from the fruit bowl. I tuck it in the front pocket of my bag. "It's great not having to wear that stuffy uniform."

Her tongue darts out, and she wets her lightly glossed lips. "Well, have a good day, and let's talk when you come home."

I SWING BY Sariah's grandma's place fifteen minutes later to pick her up. "Oh, boy," she says, buckling her seat belt. "Rocking up in this car is just asking for trouble."

"They can bite me." I shrug, easing my SUV back out onto the road.

I'm not changing who I am to fit in, and this car was the last gift from my father. I remember how adamant he was that I drive this and not the Gran Turismo Sport that's my favorite of his flashy cars.

She throws back her head, laughing. "Have I told you how cool it is that you go to my school now?"

I grin as I honk my horn at two asshats crossing the road directly in front of me, as if there isn't a car waiting to mow them down. "Maybe once or a thousand times."

Her azure eyes pin mine in place. "Seriously, though. I'm so fucking excited for senior year now, and that's all thanks to you."

"I'm sure a certain six-foot-four football player has something to do with it too," I tease.

"To be honest, I wish Sean didn't go to Lowell High. It'd make things easier."

"Hey." I reach out and squeeze her knee. "If any of those cheerleaders even look funny at you this year, they'll have me to answer to."

Sariah and Sean started dating a year ago, much to

the disgust of the cheerleading squad, and most of Sean's teammates, according to my bestie. A few of the girls threatened her, and when that didn't work, they resorted to pushing her around. But my girl knows how to defend herself.

We've both been attending kickboxing classes downtown for the past two years. I only started attending so I had an explanation for my defensive skills. But it's come to mean so much more to me. The classes keep me fit, and they help to alleviate stress. It's also how I met Sariah, and we became instant best friends.

Still, no amount of skill can help if it's ten on one, and Sariah's taken a few beatings. She's a loner, like me, so she had no one to back her up. At least now, I'll be there. And it's not like I need much incentive to get involved. The pent-up rage inside me has grown even worse since Dad died. Now, I'm constantly battling a wild inferno that blazes out of control inside me, and I grasp any opportunity to uncage the beast with both hands.

"I have a feeling they have a new target this year." We share a look.

"How bad is it?" I ask.

"You're all anyone is talking about. I've heard the usual bullshit from the guys, and the girls' claws are already drawn. Sean has spread the word around, but he's not sure if it's enough."

"If he couldn't keep the bottom-feeders away from his beloved girlfriend, I doubt he's had any more success defending me, but I appreciate he tried." I squeeze her knee again. "Don't worry. I know how to take care of myself. It'll be cool."

"Watch out for Parker Brooks," Sariah warns as I take the turn that will lead us to the school.

"She's the reigning queen bee, right?" I signal and pull off onto the road.

"Yes, and she's also dating Finn Houston. He leads the crew that controls Lowell High."

"I know who Finn is." I had sex with him one time at a party a couple years ago. We were high, drunk, and horny. A lethal combination that almost always ends with marathon sex.

Here's hoping he doesn't remember because I don't want to make an instant enemy of his girlfriend. My agenda is too important, and I don't need additional distractions.

"I'm not after Parker's crown. She'll back off when she realizes that." What I need to do requires me to blend into the shadows. To become almost invisible so I can sneak around undetected. Having a spotlight on my head would cause too many delays.

Sariah pushes her short blonde hair behind her ears. "We both know that's a lie."

"Yeah," I chuckle, as I pull the car through the rusted iron gates at the front of my new school. "But it's fun to fantasize sometimes."

THE METAL DETECTOR beeps as I walk through the scanner, as I expected it would. The female security guard pats me down as other students stream through the doors, gawking at me like I'm a new science experiment.

"You can't bring knives to school," the guard says, frowning as she removes the dull blade from the back pocket of my jeans.

I hold up my palms. "My bad. I'm new."

"That's not an excuse." Her frown deepens, and she eyes me warily. I hold her gaze, refusing to be intimidated. "I'll be keeping this," she adds, dropping it into a brown plastic container along with a bunch of other confiscated weapons. "Move along."

"What was that all about?" Sariah murmurs under her breath as we take off.

"Concealing the knife I have tucked in the inside of my boot," I quietly reply. I wasn't joking when I said I carry my

Strider SMF everywhere with me.

She nods in understanding. "Come on." She tugs on my elbow, steering me around the corner, away from the throngs crowding the hallways. "Let's get the paperwork shit out of the way."

A short while later, we leave the school office. "Everyone's staring." Sariah states the obvious as we clutch our schedules and locker combos. Thankfully, we have lockers across from one another, and we share a few of the same classes too.

"Let them look. No skin off my back." I ignore the inquisitive gazes of my new schoolmates, keeping pace with Sariah as she leads me down the hallway.

I'm shoving books in my locker when Sariah shrieks behind me, and I whip around, knuckles raised, ready to inflict some damage. My shoulders relax when I spot Sean with a giggling Sariah lifted in his arms.

"Hey, Lo." Sean grins at me as he lowers my bestie to her feet.

"Hey, stud." Sean is classically good-looking with dark hair slicked back off his handsome face. With his wide, warm brown eyes, cute dimples, and friendly smile, he's the perfect boy-next-door type.

Which is something I'd run a mile from.

But Sariah is tits over ass crazy about the guy.

And I can see why.

He's massively talented on the field, but he doesn't sport an ego the size of Texas like most of his teammates. He's down to earth, funny, smart, and loyal. He worships his girlfriend, and he's the only reason, besides my parents I believe in the notion of love.

He's the atypical jock, and I would've adored him for that fact alone.

But he's also a decent guy, and there are so few of them around. Just because he doesn't float my boat doesn't mean I can't appreciate him.

"Hey, sexy." A hulk of a guy cages me in, leaning over me

like he deserves to share my airspace.

"Get the fuck out of my face." I shove at his solid chest, but he doesn't budge. "Your breath reeks."

"Back off, Cummings." Sean appears at our side.

"I've got this." I pin Sean with a "back off" look. The last thing I want or need is someone riding to my rescue. Especially on day one.

"Cummings." I smile sweetly at him, utilizing an alternative strategy. "That's an unfortunate name." I trail my finger from his collarbone down lower.

He smirks, and he'd probably be hot if he lost the arrogant entitled look he's currently sporting. "I happen to like my name." He presses his mouth to my ear. "The ladies call me The Cum King."

Gag. "Oh, yeah?" I feign interest, grinning as I run my hand down lower, along the rippling muscles of his six pack, inching toward the band of his jeans.

"Meet me under the bleachers after school, and I'll demonstrate why." He waggles his brows, and the smug expression on his face only adds to the overall unattractiveness of his proposition.

"You know," I say, sliding my hand down over his crotch, palming the semi in his jeans. "I think I'll pass. Because anyone who's proud to be called The Cum King is a Grade-A douche, and I tend to steer clear of arrogant, asshole players." I grab his junk, twisting it in a way I know is painful, digging my nails into the denim.

He howls, pushing away from me, cupping his dick and swearing. "You fucking whore."

I roll my eyes. "So cliché."

Sean chuckles, and I spot a few guys flanking him at the rear; some smirking, some scowling, and some holding their crotches protectively.

"You've just sealed your fate, bitch," Cummings says, straightening up, his face puce.

"I'm quaking in my boots," I deadpan, as a shadow looms

over me from behind.

"Making friends already, princess?" His dark chuckle raises all the tiny hairs on my arms.

I turn around slowly, blood boiling in my veins, hands clenched tight at my sides.

Saint Lennox stares me out of it. His blue eyes radiate challenge, his cocky smirk conveys superiority, and he holds himself confidently, his body a strong, taut, physical weapon, as he silently threatens me with a dark, dangerous look that electrifies my body and fuels the rage coursing through my body.

"What the fuck are you doing here?" I return his stare with a deadly one of my own.

"Didn't you get the memo?" he says, leaning into my face, his warm breath fanning across my already overheated skin. "We just transferred in."

I glance over his shoulder for the first time, locking eyes with Galen, Theo, and Caz. They stand stoically behind their leader with their shoulders back, heads up, and lethal expressions on their faces, danger seeping from their pores, their bodies primed to annihilate anything or anyone who stands in their path.

Galen snaps his gaze to me, glaring in a way that lets me know he still despises me. His hatred is so visceral he can't conceal it.

I flip him the middle finger, returning his venom with my own special brand.

He steps forward, placing his hand on my shoulder and gripping me with iron strength. "Welcome to senior year, angel," he growls, his dark eyes unleashing wave after wave of fury, an unspoken promise that he's never letting this go. "It's going to be your own personal version of hell."

THE SAINTHOOD

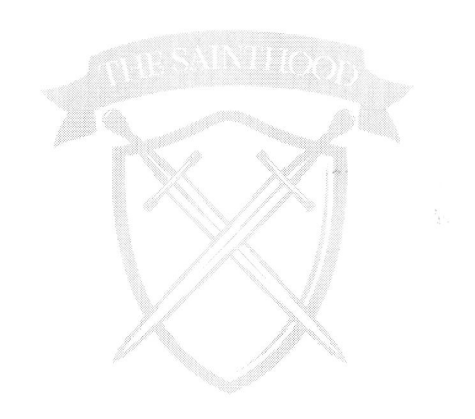

THE SAINTHOOD

CHAPTER 3

"BACK THE FUCK up." A gruff voice commands the crowd that has formed around us, and they instantly part, bowing in deference as if Finn Houston is Travis fucking Scott.

Idiots.

Galen removes his hand from my shoulder as The Sainthood turn en masse to face Lowell High's self-proclaimed king.

Finn spares me a passing look, a flare of recognition sparking in his eyes, and there goes my anonymity. I can only hope he's as keen to keep the news of our past hookup a secret from his girlfriend as I am. A muscle ticks in Finn's jaw as he squares up to Saint.

A flash of vivid color draws my eye, and I lock gazes with Parker Brooks, Finn's purple-haired, blue-eyed queen. She's standing beside her boyfriend, her gaze pinned on me, hatred clearly visible.

Maybe, she already knows I screwed her man. Or she's just a bitch who hates any newcomer. Or she's one of those girls wanting to spill my blood because she's jealous I fucked The

Sainthood.

Whatever the reason, she's already decided I'm her enemy. *Might as well embrace it.*

I cock my head to the side, rubbing my middle finger up and down the side of my nose in an obvious slur. Her nostrils flare, and she looks like she wants to tear me limb from limb.

A low chuckle drags my attention away from queen bitch, and my eyes meet Caz's. "Naughty, princess," he mouths before Galen digs his elbow into his ribs, forcing him to focus.

"Got a problem, Houston?" Saint asks, letting his gaze roll slowly and deliberately over every inch of Parker.

Acid churns in my belly at the seductive look he's giving her, and I want to gouge his eyeballs out so he can't look at her anymore.

The strength of my reaction shocks me, but I refuse to name the emotion. Instead, I turn inside myself, locking all that emotional crap down. Feeling more in control, I plaster a "don't give a shit" expression on my face while I wait to see how this plays out. Out of the corner of my eye, I spot Sean pulling an angry Sariah back from the confrontation. She's struggling in his hold, wriggling and writhing, her face a mask of naked hatred. Sean's eyes lock on mine, and I subtly nod.

Get her out of here.

It's not that Sariah can't hold her own, but she shouldn't have to. She's seen enough violence and bloodshed to last a lifetime.

I only recently discovered she believes The Sainthood was responsible for murdering her entire family. Not that she has any proof. And it could've been one of the other gangs, but she says her gut tells her they were involved, and that's good enough to add another reason to my ever-growing list.

Sariah doesn't talk about what happened, because the trauma is all too real, and I've never pried. All I know is her family was murdered, in front of her, because of some drug deal gone wrong. She survived because she played dead when her brother's lifeless body fell on top of her. She stayed that way for hours, too terrified to move. It was only when the cops showed up, a couple hours later, that she was taken to safety.

She was thirteen when her world upended.

The same age I was when it happened to me.

"Grab your fuck toy," Finn spits, spearing Saint with a vicious look, "and get the fuck out of *my school*."

Saint squares up to Finn. They are matched in height, and it's like watching Goliath face off against The Rock. "Seems you didn't get the memo either." He tilts his head to the side, a familiar sneer gracing his mouth. "This is Sainthood territory now. Your little crew is no more." He firmly shoves Finn's shoulders. "Show some respect, and get the fuck out of my face."

"Fuck you, asshole." Finn shoves Saint, and Galen, Theo, and Caz stiffen, clenching their fists, ready to spill blood. "You don't get to show up here and lay claim to what's mine."

Saint shakes his head, chuckling. "That's exactly what we get to do."

"The Sainthood has no jurisdiction in Lowell," Brooklyn Robbins says, stepping up beside Finn. Brooklyn is to Finn who Bryant is to Darrow. The second in command with the physicality to scare most threats away. He's a couple inches taller than Saint and Finn, and as a fullback on the football team, he's a good bit wider too.

I've done my homework on my new schoolmates. Plus, it's always been in my best interests to understand the gang rivalries in play between Lowell and Prestwick.

One thing I know for sure is Finn, Brooklyn, and their crew stand zero chance against The Sainthood. A lowly school-based gang won't last five seconds against one of the country's deadliest gangs.

People fear The Sainthood for a reason. And now the guys have turned eighteen, they are all undergoing initiation. As soon as they graduate, they'll move up to the senior branch. No doubt, their successors at the junior level are already waiting in the wings, being trained to take over. Most likely, that's who's been left in charge of Prestwick Academy, their previous stomping ground.

"We do now," Galen confirms.

"This doesn't have to be a bloodbath," Caz adds. "Just concede to our rule, and we'll show you respect."

"Over my dead fucking body," Finn barks, cracking his knuckles and baring his teeth.

"That can be easily arranged." Galen drills Finn with a look most men would cower from.

A yawn slips out of my mouth, and several pairs of eyes dart to mine.

"Bored, princess?" Saint asks, fighting a smirk.

"Watching fucktard A face off against fucktard B? You betcha." I slam my locker shut and then slip the strap of my bag over my shoulder as the bell chimes.

"Watch your dirty mouth." Parker nudges past Finn, putting herself all up in my space.

"Free country. I'll say what I want and do what I want."

Her blue eyes flare with wicked intent. "Liar." She prods my chest with one bony finger. "We've all heard you obeying *their* commands." Her gaze jumps between all four guys, and she does little to disguise her interest. If her boyfriend wasn't behind her, unable to witness her unsophisticated flirtation, I doubt she'd be so brave. She makes little quote marks in the air with her fingers as she attempts to emulate a masculine tone. "Take my cock out. Open wide."

Laughter rings out around us from the lingering crowd who is too invested in this stare down to worry about tardy slips.

I flick her finger away, smirking. "I owned and enjoyed every part of that night. *Everything* that happened was on my terms, or it never would've happened at all. I *chose* to obey, and last time I checked, that counted as free will. Not that I expect a dimwit like you to understand. Careful there, Parker." I push her back out of my private space. "Let your GPA slip any lower and even McDonald's won't hire you to scrub their toilets."

Her fist juts out, but I've quick reflexes, and I duck in time, swinging my leg around and taking her down. She falls back on her heels, arms flailing as she squeals like a pig. Gasps and giggles surround us, and it's not surprising some are enjoying this.

Finn narrows his eyes at me as he catches his girlfriend just before she cracks her skull off the ground.

Pity.

"Football field. Tomorrow after school. Your crew against mine," Finn says, raising his eyes to Saint.

Saint cracks his knuckles, grinning like all his birthdays have come at once. "Your funeral."

"Keep your whore on a leash," Finn adds, slinging his arm around a furious Parker as he helps her straighten up. If she wanted to rip me limb from limb before, now, she wants to bury me six feet under, pour gasoline on my broken bones, and piss on me before setting me alight, judging by that look on her face.

"I'm nobody's whore or fuck toy." I step up to Finn. "And if you don't keep *that bitch* on a leash, she'll be sorry."

"You stupid cunt of a—"

Finn clamps his hand over his girlfriend's mouth, muffling her threat. "Watch it, Westbrook." Finn's eyes veer between a warning and an invitation.

I roll my eyes, so over this pathetic shit.

With one final venomous look, slanted in Saint's direction, they walk off.

Sariah finally breaks free of Sean's arms, racing to my side. Her wild, animalistic rage has been rescinded, and she's more in control. "C'mon. You're going to get a tardy." She glowers at The Sainthood as she threads her arm through mine. Sean strides to her other side, casting a protective gaze over the proceedings. I can tell from his face he's unhappy at this latest turn of events, and I don't blame him.

I'm not exactly thrilled myself even if I've been waiting for them to make their next move.

"We're not done here," Saint says, crossing his arms.

"You're right. We're not." I eye each of them one at a time. "I still owe you payback."

"We weren't the ones who shared the video online or distributed it to the entire student body," Theo says, speaking up for the first time.

"He speaks," I drawl in my best sarcastic tone. "And don't pretend to be innocent. You recorded it without my permission. Then you sent it to Darrow to rile him up. And I know you have the skills to configure the file so it's not shareable, but you didn't do that because you wanted him to distribute it."

He doesn't even attempt to protest, which is how I know I'm right.

I think Theo needs a little history lesson. A reminder of exactly who's in charge here.

Little clue—it's not him.

"Just admit it. You messed up. *Again*."

Saint's all-seeing eyes bore a hole in Theo's skull, but he's pretending he can't feel the weight of his stare. Theo's fingers grip his phone tight, and his jaw hardens. I'm betting he regrets everything that went down between us. Because it gives me power over him, and he knows I'll use that to my advantage. I'd love to be a fly on the wall when Saint corners him about this later. Love to hear what bullshit excuse he comes up with to continue concealing the truth.

"You knew the stakes," Saint says, refocusing the conversation. He lounges against the wall of lockers, deliberately looking bored. "And I told you we don't do charity work."

"That doesn't give you a free pass! I knew Darrow would be gunning for me, but you gave him more ammunition."

"Not our fault you were too dumb to ask if there were cameras in the room," Galen sneers.

"How is it"—I extract my arm from Sariah's and push my face into Galen's—"the house is falling apart from neglect, but somehow, there's cash for security cameras?"

"That's none of your business." He grinds his teeth, and his jaw clenches.

I know from talking with Mom that the house was his grandparents' house. His grandma left it to his mom when she died. The snooping I did confirmed Galen's mom is a hardcore coke addict, and that explains a lot.

Except the cameras.

Obviously, the organization paid for them, but I hadn't been expecting them in Galen's house. *Saint's house?* Yes. Because he's the leader. But Galen is only second in command of the junior branch of The Sainthood and I didn't think that level of security would be warranted. Clearly, I underestimated his importance. Or perhaps my head was clouded by emotion that night.

"Lo. Leave it," my bestie says. "Don't try to find an explanation where there is none. They're lying, cheating, murdering bastards who wouldn't know the truth if it jumped up and bit them."

"I know one truth," Galen says, undressing my bestie with his eyes. "I want to nail your tight pussy with my cock."

"Watch your fucking mouth," Sean says. "You don't get to disrespect my girlfriend, and if you come anywhere near her I'll cut your fucking balls off."

The clacking of heels distracts all of us.

"No loitering in the hallways and the bell has already rang," the small, curvy woman with the pinched features says, jabbing her finger in the air in our direction. Her name badge says Vice Principal Pierson. "Get to class now."

"You need to have a word with your superior," Saint says, fixing a dark glare on the woman. "If you ever dare speak to us like that again, I'll raze your house to the ground." He moves closer, and his face is so close to hers his nose is almost bumping hers. "With your husband Travis and your son Cameron in it."

The vice principal pales, clutching a shaky hand to her chest.

I'd like to reassure her that he's spoofing, but I know The Sainthood has no qualms about hurting innocent children.

"Come on." Sean places one hand on each of our lower backs, urging me and Sariah forward. "Let's get the fuck out of here."

THE SAINTHOOD

CHAPTER 4

I*T'S HARD TO* concentrate on my classes after the bomb that's just been dropped in my lap, but I try, because I can't afford to fall behind. There's no way I'll maintain my 4.1 GPA if I allow distractions to derail me. I'm on a countdown to the day I graduate and I can get the fuck out of this town. No one is messing that up for me. Especially not The Sainthood.

I have my heart set on attending Brown, like my father did. The only issue is Mom. I don't like the thought of leaving her here all alone, but I doubt she'll want to move clear across the country. Her business is here, and she's very attached to the house because it's where I grew up and all her memories of Dad are embedded into the bricks and mortar. She knows I've already received an early offer from Brown. That I want to follow in Dad's footsteps, and she's never had an issue with it.

But that was before Dad died.

We haven't discussed it since because Mom has largely checked out of life.

I know it's a conversation we need to have someday soon. But it's all hypothetical anyway until I find a way of squashing fate.

"How is day one so far?" Sean asks as we line up in the cafeteria at lunchtime.

"Nothing I can't handle," I reply, grabbing a bottle of water and a small salad from the refrigerator.

"Batshit Branning made her stand at the top of math class and introduce herself," Sariah says.

"I tried to get away with a vague introduction," I explain as the line moves forward. "But she wasn't happy until I'd given up my life story."

Sariah grins. "The look on her face when you confirmed your favorite sex position was extended cowgirl and how you were the girl from The Sainthood video was fucking priceless."

"She couldn't get me back to my seat fast enough." I grin at the recollection as I hold out my plate. The server slaps two indistinguishable lumps of food on the plate and hands it back to me. I squint at the sludge on my plate, my stomach churning at the unpleasant smells assaulting my nostrils. "I wouldn't serve this to my pet pig," I grumble, abandoning the plate and heading toward the prepackaged sandwiches. I'd rather eat processed meat sandwiched between dry bread than risk the complete unknown.

"You have a pet pig?" a hot guy with cute dimples asks, arching a brow. He's standing with Sean, so I assume he's a friend although Sean hasn't made introductions yet.

"No, but if I did, I wouldn't give it that slop."

He chuckles, and waves of messy chocolate-brown hair fall into his eyes. "Can't disagree. The food here is shit, but it beats starving."

"I think I'd rather starve," I deadpan, inspecting the pathetic sandwich offerings on display.

He chuckles again, moving aside to let Sean and Sariah pass. "I'm guessing the food here is a lot different than the food at Lowell Academy."

I nod as I grab a ham and cheese sandwich that looks like it's the most edible. "That's the only thing I'll miss about the place."

"I'm Emmett, by the way," he says, whipping my tray from my hands.

I glare at him as I grab it back. "Did I ask you to carry it?"

His grin expands, and he's even hotter when he smiles. His warm brown eyes glimmer with interest. "I'm just being a gentleman."

I walk off, following in the direction my bestie and her boyfriend have taken. Emmett keeps pace at my side, and I glance up at him. Judging by his height and his ripped body, I'm guessing he's a football player too. "If you're looking to get into my panties, acting like a gentleman is a surefire recipe for failure."

I'm walking past a long table when a leg darts out on purpose. I jump over Galen's foot at the very last second, narrowly avoiding wearing my lunch. I plaster a bored look on my face as I stare at him. "Real mature, asshole."

I ignore all members of The Sainthood, walking away with Emmett faithfully clinging to my side.

"Let me guess. You're into assholes," he asks, a tinge of disappointment underscoring his words.

"And if I was?" I ask, sliding into a seat at the empty table opposite the jock table. Sariah shoots me a look, but she gets up from her seat beside Sean and moves over to my table.

"Then I'd tell you I've no desire to be an asshole, and I'd go out of my way to prove that nice guys can be bad in all the right ways," he says, waggling his brows as he hovers over the table.

A genuine smile slides over my mouth. "There might be hope for you yet."

"Does that mean I can join you for lunch?" he asks, sharing a look with Sean as he too leaves the jock table, claiming the seat beside his girlfriend, across from me.

"Nope." The chair beside me scrapes noisily along the tile floor as Saint plops down into it. "This seat is taken." He levels a dark look at Emmett. "Permanently."

"Fuck off, Saint." I move to stand, but he grabs my wrist, keeping me in place.

I hate how my skin tingles from the contact.

How his touch coaxes a host of memories from the furthermost place in my mind.

How my brain rejoices at reliving every second of that hot night we shared together.

"I'm not sitting with you or any of your minions," I add as Caz, Galen, and Theo sit down around us. "I'd rather sit at the fucking jock table."

Emmett extends his hand. "You can sit with me."

I place my hand in his, purely to taunt Saint. I attempt to wrench my other hand away from Saint, but he tightens his hold on my wrist, almost crushing my bones as he refuses to let me go.

Caz stands, rounding the table and pulling Emmett's hand out of mine. "Don't be an idiot. Stick with the cheerleaders," he says, shoving him forcefully toward the jock table.

Emmett stumbles back a few feet before recovering. He reclaims the gap, squaring up to Caz. "I don't take orders from thugs."

"Maybe you should," Theo says, not lifting his eyes from his iPad. "Unless you'd prefer your sister get kicked out of the hospital program." He tips his chin up, staring at him with a face devoid of emotion. "She'll probably die without that experimental drug, right?"

I'm not surprised the assholes have done their homework. It's basic survival of the fittest. You don't rock up to a new school without ammunition. And there's no better ammunition than secrets and weak spots. My experience taught me that as well.

Secrets are the most important currency around these parts.

"Sit at the jock table, Emmett," I say through clenched teeth. "It was never going to happen anyway."

In another lifetime, before I was forced down this path, I could see myself with someone like Emmett. A nice guy with a side order of bad. Someone who could push my buttons *and* rein me in.

But this is my reality. And the Emmetts of this world don't belong in it.

He's seething. His fists are balled up and ready to unleash pain. But starting something would not be smart. And he's obviously got smarts because, a couple seconds later, he turns around and wordlessly retreats to the jock table.

"Let go of my wrist," I demand, plastering a neutral expression on my face as I eyeball Saint.

"Are you going to behave?" His thumb makes circular motions against my skin.

"No."

He smirks, and his eyes burn with intensity as he rakes his gaze up and down my body. His inked fingers continue exploring the skin on the underside of my wrist, and I squirm on my seat as a trail of shivers ghosts over my flesh. He notices, his full lips kicking up in amusement, the dark glint in his eyes flaring with liquid heat.

My core throbs, pulsing in fast succession as his intense gaze does funny things to my insides.

Why the hell does the bastard have to be so freaking hot? And why the hell is he the first guy to ever evoke this type of visceral reaction in me?

I don't answer my inner monologue because I already know the answers. I just don't want to admit it or act on it.

"Then, I'm not letting go."

I'm sure the sharp edge of a blade pressed against that growing bulge in his jeans would do the job. And I could easily reach down and remove my knife from the inside of my boot, but showing my hand this early would be a bad move, so I shut my mouth and urge my twitching fingers to retreat.

"Let her go," Sean says, casually peeling an orange as he stares at Saint over the table. "Agree to leave Sariah and Harlow alone, and I'll help you claim the crown at Lowell High."

Saint grins, yanking me in closer to his side. His arm locks around my shoulders, keeping me firmly in place. "We don't need any help claiming the crown. We already own it. Tomorrow's planned little show is just that. *A show*. A demonstration of what will happen to anyone who dares challenge our authority."

"You underestimate Finn's reach if you think a visual threat will bring everyone to heel," Sean coolly replies. "But if you have the jocks and the cheerleaders on your side, any lingering resistance will die out. It'll make for a smoother transition."

Saint runs his free hand over his cropped hairline. "Why would you help?"

"Because I'm a pragmatist. This will happen either way. And I'd rather it happened without anyone getting hurt."

Galen snorts. "What the fuck do you see in this sap?" He directs his question at Sariah. "You need to sample a real man, sweetheart," he adds, cupping his crotch. I don't know if he's flirting with my bestie to piss me off, incite a fight with Sean, or if he genuinely is interested in her, but he's already rubbing me the wrong way, and I hate that he's getting to me.

That they're *all* getting to me.

Galen needs taken down a peg or ten. "I've already had a sample, and trust me, it's nothing to brag about," I drawl, wresting myself out from under Saint's arm. I glare at him as he slams my hand to the table, pinning it underneath his much stronger, much larger, palm. And fuck him. Because he knows how to incapacitate me. If I had the use of that hand, I could free myself. Elbow him in the ribs. Hit his carotid at the perfect point to render him unconscious. Grab his nuts and twist so hard he'd see stars. I could attempt it with my free hand, but I'd have to stretch across my body to reach him, and his reflexes are too sharp. He'd see me coming and stop the move before I'd have time to engage.

"Try telling that to your greedy pussy," Galen replies, slanting me with a poisonous look. "Your pussy was riding my cock so hard I almost impaled your womb." He says this deliberately loud, and chuckles surround me as the crowd gives him the attention he seeks.

"I was squeezing that hard in the hope I'd break your cock," I coolly retort. "Don't convince yourself it was anything but an angry fuck when we both know the truth."

"Enough." Saint hauls me to my feet, wrapping his arm snuggly under my breasts in a way that screams possession. Holding me securely to his body, with my back against his chest, he whispers in my ear, "Make any move, and I'll humiliate you in front of the entire cafeteria."

As if I'd care.

I'm tempted to do it, just to piss him off, but I'm more intrigued to know exactly what The Sainthood's game plan is. Nothing they do is without calculation. And I want to know their angle so I can counteract it.

So, for now, I'll play their little game while I'm in the intel-gathering phase.

"Fuck you," I auto-reply, holding still in his grip.

"That was a one-time thing, sweetheart. The Saints never go back for seconds."

I've heard the rumors. That they never date. They only fuck girls once. And they always fuck girls as if it's a team sport. But I've also heard they ignore their conquests after they've spread their legs. I know why I'm different, but no one else does, and their public expression of interest in me will make others suspicious.

"Good," I say, "because I'd rather slit my throat and die a slow and painful death than fuck any of you again."

"Liar." His warm breath fans over my ear, and my body betrays me, shivering as delicious tremors zip through my limbs.

Most everyone in the cafeteria is watching us, so when he speaks, he has the attention of the entire place. "Listen up." His deep voice projects around the room. "The princess is off-limits. She belongs to us. Touch her and you'll regret it."

I'm still puzzling over it hours later when I arrive home,

parking my SUV in the ten-car garage beside Mom's silver BMW and a strange red truck.

I'm cursing Saint under my breath as I saunter into the two-story beige-brick house, plotting various ways to murder him. I'm resourceful and skilled, and it doesn't take me long to compile a long list. I'm grinning to myself as I imagine ripping his heart from his body and putting it through a blender as I watch him bleed out slowly on the floor, gasping for air as he gradually dies.

I walk through the lobby, past the sweeping hardwood stairs with the mirrored banisters, along the porcelain-tiled hallway. I pass by the closed door of Dad's study, the library, and reading room, and head straight for the open-plan kitchen and dining room, searching for Mom, but she isn't there. Remembering the unfamiliar red truck, I head toward the formal living room next. That's where she usually brings guests. But that room is empty too. Sounds of laughter filter from the main living area, and I head in that direction, unprepared for the sight that awaits me.

I stand stock-still in the doorway, blinking excessively, wishing my eyes were deceiving me when I know they're not.

Mom is lying flat on her back on one of the gray leather couches, smiling up at the man looming over her. They are fully clothed, but their bodies are strategically positioned in a way that confirms familiarity, and I see red. I storm into the room like a wild tornado hellbent on destruction.

"What the fuck is going on?" I roar as I round the couch, stopping in front of them. My dirty boots leave a trail of mud on the gray, pink, and white rug I know she spent a fortune on, but I don't care.

At this proximity, it's even worse. Mom's legs are parted, and the man is thrusting his hips against hers. I don't need to see his erection to know he's sporting one. His hand is kneading her breast through her blouse, and I'm seconds away from personal nuclear detonation.

I cannot fucking believe this.

Her head turns to the side, and she looks at me with a horrified expression, swatting at the man's chest, trying to push him off. But the guy is tall and well-built, and Mom's small hands do nothing.

The man jerks his head up, his icy-blue eyes locking on mine. All the blood drains from my face as I watch a sleazy smile creep over his mouth. My heart stutters in my chest.

"Hello, sweetheart." His gruff voice sends shards of dread coursing all over my body, and hatred blooms in my chest.

A thin line of sweat glides down my spine as my heart starts thumping wildly, careening around my rib cage. Blood rushes to my ears, and pain throbs in my skull.

Inside, I'm a mess. My emotions rage at me, begging to be set free. I've been assaulted on several fronts today, but I won't let this break me. I paint an appropriate mask on my face so he can't see the turmoil turning my insides upside down.

"Who the fuck are you?" I demand, my gaze jumping between him and Mom as I execute my role perfectly.

"I'm your new daddy," he answers, and I lunge at him without hesitation.

THE SAINTHOOD

CHAPTER 5

I HALF-GRAB him off my mom, ignoring her screams as I ram my fist in his face. Rage surges to the surface, and I unleash the beast, thrusting my fist forward again.

He reacts superfast, rolling off the couch onto the floor, grabbing hold of my ankle, and tugging sharply. I go down hard, landing flat on my back with pain darting up my spine. But my reflexes are quick too, and before he can climb over me and subdue me, I lift my leg, jamming my knee into his junk. An animalistic roar rips from his throat as he collapses on his side, clutching his crotch and writhing in agony. I climb to my feet as Mom scurries to his side. "Oh my God. Are you okay?"

"She kneed me in the balls!" he shouts. "Of course, I'm not okay." He squeezes his eyes shut, moaning as I stand over them with my hands on my hips, my eyes fastened on my mom's hand as she sweeps it up and down his arm in a soothing gesture.

Anger pummels my insides, and I glare at her.

"Everyone, just calm down," she says, eyeing me warily. "I'm sorry you had to see that, Harlow. I wasn't expecting you home for another hour."

"Clearly," I deadpan.

"You didn't go to kickboxing class?"

"The instructor got sick. Canceled the class at lunchtime."

"Perhaps, she shouldn't go to kickboxing," the asshole on the floor says, "if that's what they're teaching kids there."

"I'm not a kid. And I didn't learn that technique there. My first self-defense class taught me that handy little trick."

Careful, Lo. My inner voice urges caution. *He can't know that you know who he is.*

Mom's face pales at the mention of my self-defense classes. She knows why I was there, and the guilt continues to eat at her. I hate how she believes it's still her fault. But I can't tell her the truth, because that would hurt her more.

"Are you going to explain who he is, or do I have to figure this out myself?" I ask as the douche straightens up.

Mom helps the monster to his feet, and they sit down on the couch. She pats the empty space beside her. "Come sit beside me."

I remain standing. Eyeing the asshole with thinly concealed hatred that is all genuine. But I can get away with it, because this is a natural reaction for any daughter finding her recently widowed Mom in such a situation with a strange man.

Begrudgingly, I've got to admit he's hot. Even if his dirty-blond hair is unkempt, hanging in loose waves around his face, and his blond goatee could use a trim. He's covered in ink, and he's got muscles stacked upon muscles. His dark jeans hug broad thighs, and his open plaid shirt is stretched across wide biceps. He reeks of cigarette smoke and arrogance, and I cannot believe he succeeded in capturing Mom's attention.

It's as if she deliberately chose someone the complete opposite of my father.

Dad had slicked-back dark hair and zero ink, and while he worked out and kept his body in good condition, he was no muscle-bound freak. At ten years older than Mom, and a certified career obsessive, he was rarely out of custom-made suits. He sure as shit wouldn't have worn threadbare jeans, a creased white T-shirt under a blue-and-black-plaid shirt, and scuffed biker boots.

"Harlow." She sighs, pleading with her eyes, but I'm not conceding.

"I'm fine standing." I glare at him as he circles his arm around her back. "Take your hands off my mother."

An amused grin tips up the corners of his mouth, and the expression is familiar. He removes his arms, holding up his hands, flashing me a row of straight white teeth as he smiles. "We've gotten off on the wrong foot. It's not what you're thinking."

It's exactly what I'm thinking, and it's clear the stakes have just been raised.

My mind churns as I try to figure it all out.

An icy-cold shiver creeps up my spine and I narrow my eyes at him. "So, you're not a gold-digging motherfucker preying on a vulnerable widow so soon after she lost the love of her life?" My tone easily conveys my disbelief, and I deserve a pat on the back for my stellar acting skills.

A muscle clenches in his jaw, and he loses some of his fake warmth.

"Harlow." Mom gasps. "I know you're shocked but that's no excuse for losing your manners."

I snort. "Get real, Mom. The asshole just told me he's my new daddy, and you expect me to mind my manners around him?!"

She cuts him a glare. "Neo shouldn't have opened with that."

I bark out a laugh. "Neo? Are you fucking kidding me? Does he have a swastika tattooed somewhere on his body?"

"No! Of course not. That's the name he was born with." Mom rubs at her temples. "Please just sit down and let me explain."

"I'm not talking with him here." I drill a venomous look at the blond douche.

He stands. "I'll go. I've shit to handle anyway." He pins me with a devious look before he pulls Mom up into his arms and slams his lips down on hers. His arms sweep around her back as he dips her down low, devouring her mouth in a deliberate show of control.

I want to rip his mouth and his hands from her body before decapitating him. I dig my nails into my thighs, visualizing torturing the douche in my head to avoid killing him for real. Doubt Mom would appreciate that even if I'd be doing her a favor. And there's no way I'd risk jail time for the jerk.

This guy is bad news, trouble with a capital T, and somehow, I've got to find a way to make her see that.

"If you're finished assaulting my mom with your disgusting tongue, I'd like to speak with her," I snap, as my emotions get the better of me. I'm sure he did that purely to rile me up, and I'm so disappointed in Mom because she's swooning in his arms like she's never been kissed before.

He breaks the kiss-slash-assault, reeling Mom into his chest, clasping her close so he can eyeball me over her head. "I love your mom, kid. Always have. Always will. I get this is a shock, but it's happening, so you'd better deal with it." His eyes narrow to slits as he sends me a silent warning.

Gone is the pretend warmth.

His mask is down, and the danger is fully evident.

Does he know I know? Or is this usually the way he reacts to daughters of the women he's fucking?

All the tiny hairs lift on the back of my neck, and I swallow a lump of fear as slow realization dawns.

He smirks, pinning me with an arrogant look that says if I get in his way he'll destroy me.

I bury my fear, shove all emotion aside, and confidently lift my shoulders, staring coolly at him with a look that confirms it's "game on." A brief look of admiration flits over his blue eyes before they darken in warning.

"Go." Mom extracts herself from his embrace as the two of us remain locked in our face-off. "Let me talk to my daughter.

All will be okay." She pecks his lips, and I puke a little in my mouth.

"Later, beautiful." He kisses the top of her head while maintaining eye contact with me, and another blast of ice-cold fear slaps me in the face at the calculating quality to his gaze.

I underestimated this man.

He's not just a monster.

He is something else.

Something I'm much more afraid of.

He's the devil incarnate, and he's determined to make my life a living hell.

Bile churns in my gut as my mind whirls at the potential implications.

I watch her watching him leave the room with my heart deflating. *She has feelings for him.* My life is about to become ten million times harder.

The door slams after him, snapping me into focus. I shove my emotions deep inside and concentrate on learning as much as I can.

"I'm so sorry, Harlow." She cautiously walks toward me.

"How could you, Mom?" I shake my head, unable to hide my disgust. "Dad's only gone four months, and you're already fucking someone else?"

She flinches at my words and my tone, but I won't apologize for speaking my mind.

"I've known Neo since I was eleven years old," she explains. "He was my childhood sweetheart and the man I was engaged to when I met your father."

My stomach drops to my toes as I realize this is even worse than I feared. "What? Why have I never heard of him before?"

My mind is whirling ninety miles an hour as I struggle to process this latest puzzle piece.

Dad told me he'd had to win my mother's heart, but he never told me she was engaged to another guy, and Mom has never spoken of any other man but my father. I knew she was only twenty when they met, after Dad moved back here to take up a position with a leading law firm, and that he was thirty and steadily progressing his legal career.

Mom's from Prestwick, and they didn't have much money growing up. At the time my parents met, she was attending business classes at the local community college and she had plans to set up her own business. My dad swept her off her feet, and they were married within the year, and I arrived the following year. Dad helped make Mom's dreams come true, and I have never ever doubted what they shared was the real deal.

Until now.

Because now, I'm wondering if Dad was only a meal ticket for Mom.

If that dangerous asshole that just left this house is really the love of her life.

If this is all part of his game plan.

Or it's possible my mind is warped from my fucked-up life experiences and I'm fitting the wrong pieces in the wrong holes.

"Were you fucking him when Dad was alive?" I bluntly ask, while I watch her struggle to form an answer to my previous question.

"What!" Her eyes pan wide. "Of course not! I have always remained faithful to your father." Tears prick her eyes. "I loved him so much." Her voice cracks, but I'm immune to it.

For the first time in my life, I don't trust my mother, and I doubt I ever will again.

"Sure, you did. That's why he's barely cold in the grave and you're hooking up with your old childhood sweetheart behind my back. How long has it been going on, Mom? Did you warm his bed before my father was even put in the ground? Did you forget Trey Westbrook the instant his heart stopped beating? Was Neo"—I spit out his name, lacing it with hatred—"always your end game, huh?"

She lifts her hand to slap me, stopping herself at the last second. "I know you're hurt, but you don't get to speak to me like that. I am still your mother, and you are still living under my roof. You will sit the fuck down, and let me explain."

I shake with rage, and my natural instinct is to storm out of the room, pack a bag, and get the hell out of here. *But what if my initial instinct is wrong? What if Mom's in danger?* If she's being manipulated, then I can't leave. I need to start gathering more intel, so I need to know everything she knows about Neo.

I draw deep breaths as I drop onto the couch, urging my body to calm down and my mind to get with the program.

Mom's shoulders visibly relax as she sits beside me. "I never told you about Neo because it would've been disrespectful to your father to talk about the man who owned my heart before him."

She looks at me, but I stare straight ahead with my hands clasped in my lap. I need to hear this, but I don't need to make it easy on her.

"When I was growing up, I always imagined Neo would be my husband. We loved one another, and I never thought anything could come between us—until I met your father. I tried to resist Trey at first, but I couldn't because we formed an instant connection, and it was so intense it almost blinded me."

Knots twist in my gut as the picture of the boy's face briefly flashes in my mind's eye.

She settles back in the couch as she reminisces. "I was so confused," she whispers. "I loved Neo, but I fell so hard for your father, and it wasn't long before I knew I loved him too. Nothing had happened between us," she says, quick to reassure me. "But we had been spending time together as friends, and I already felt like I'd betrayed Neo." She looks up at the ceiling, and I don't need to see the tears to know they are there.

"Your father was offering me everything I had ever wanted, but I turned him down. My loyalty to Neo was too strong to walk away. Trey made it clear he loved me and wanted to marry me, but he respected my decision, and he left me alone."

The couch shifts, and she moves closer, tilting my face to hers. "I was utterly miserable. I missed him so much, and nothing with Neo felt right anymore. He felt the difference in me too. A distance that hadn't been there before. I eventually confessed. Told him I was in love with another man. He was devastated, and he told me to leave. I spent the next few months on my own, trying to work out what to do. I had moved to Lowell, needing to put some physical distance between me and Neo, not realizing your father was renting there too. We bumped into one another in a coffee shop one morning, and we were never apart from that moment on."

She holds my face in her hands. "I never want you to doubt the love I had for your father. The love we shared was very real, and I will miss him every single day for the rest of my life." Tears spill down her cheeks. "His death destroyed me, Harlow. You are the only thing that kept me alive in those early days when I wanted to follow him to the grave. But I could never do that to you. He lives on in you." She clasps my face more tightly. "I see him every time I look at you, and it comforts me. Which is why I hate that I've hurt you now when that's the last thing I wanted."

She lets my face go, and I let loose a breath I'd been holding.

"It's too soon, Mom. You're still grieving, and he's taken advantage of that."

"I know it might seem like that, honey, but Neo is bringing me back to life, and he can protect us and take care of us."

Please tell me my mother is not that fucking naïve!?

"*I* can protect us!" I protest. "We don't need a man to take care of us. This isn't the eighteenth fucking century, Mom!" Panic bubbles up my throat, as I grapple with my emotions.

She tucks her hair behind her ears. "I'm not built to live alone," she admits, and I shake my head in disbelief.

I'm so disappointed in her. *Where the hell has my mother disappeared to?* "Do you even hear yourself?"

"You're leaving for college next year. You've got your whole life ahead of you, and I don't want to hold you back. I know how much you worry about me. I know you protect and shelter me." She pins me with shrewd eyes, and maybe she knows more than she's letting on. "And I've got my own life to lead now. I've always loved Neo. Even when your father was my everything. Trey knew. I was always honest with him. If your father were alive, Neo would remain my past. But he's not. Trey's gone. And Neo is here. Still loving me. Asking for another chance."

What perfect timing.

"It's been over twenty years, Mom. How do you know he's the same man you knew?"

"I know his heart, honey. And while this might seem fast to you, it feels like it's been a long time coming for me."

"What exactly are you saying, Mom? What is happening here?"

She gulps, and her tongue darts out, wetting her lips. "Neo has asked me to marry him, and I've said yes."

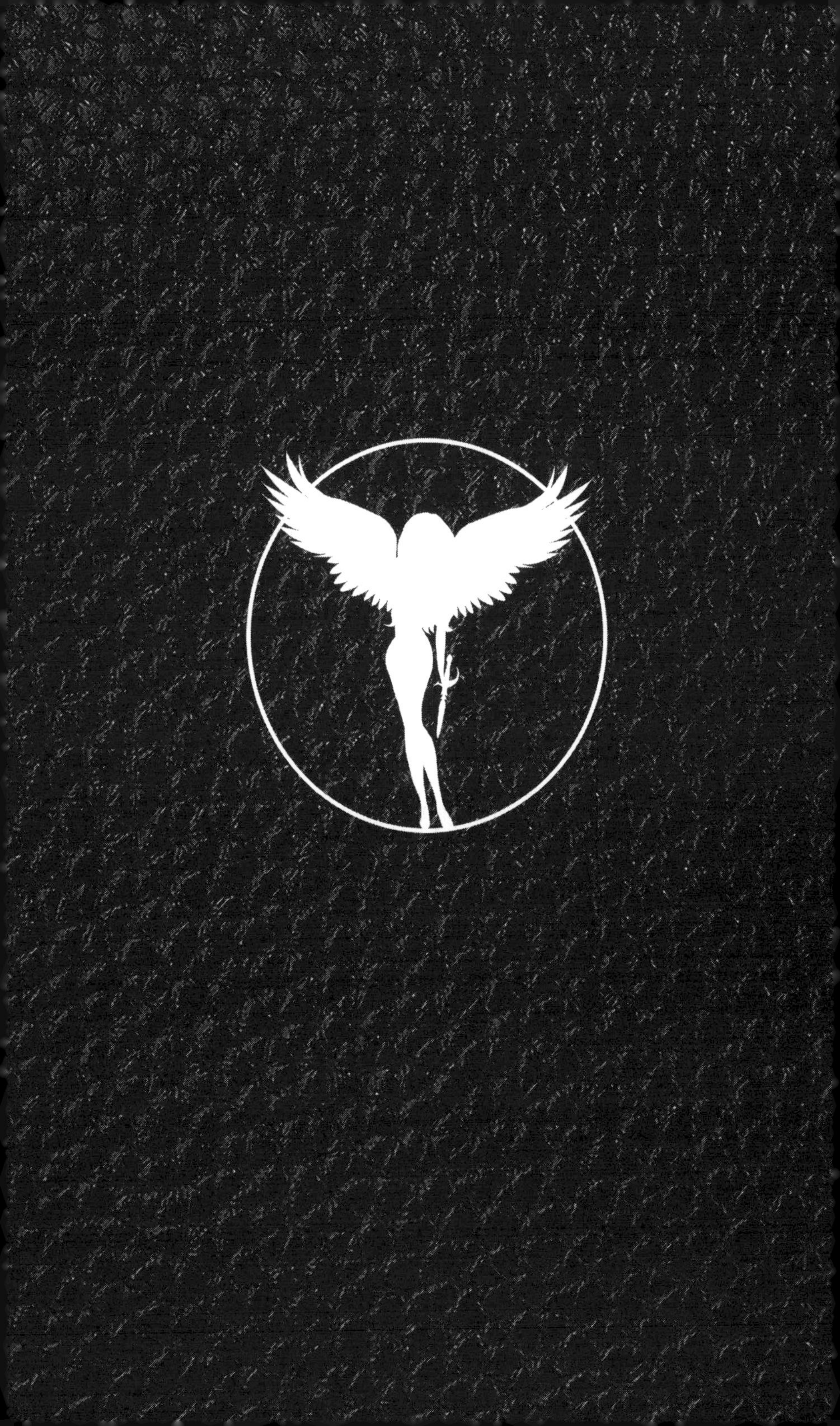

THE SAINTHOOD

CHAPTER 6

"Fuck my life," I mumble the following evening as I trail Sean and Sariah to the bleachers for the epic beatdown of the century. I've spent the day ignoring the envious looks and hostile glares from girls jealous I've been claimed as Sainthood property and hiding from said assholes, because in the mood I'm in, I can't guarantee I won't knife one of them to death.

I barely slept a wink last night. Troubled after my talk with Mom, I spent most of the night tossing and turning, trying to figure out how to get rid of Neo and then feeling guilty because I know this is partly my fault.

I doubt I'd ever be comfortable with Mom remarrying. No guy will ever replace my dad. Period. But, one way or another, I'll be leaving within the year, and Mom's still young. I can't dictate how she spends the rest of her life.

If it was genuine, and it was anyone other than Neo, I know I'd eventually come to terms with it.

But I will *never* be okay with this.

Especially when she's moving that asshole into our house this week.

I keep waiting for her to admit the rest, but she hasn't, and that doesn't give me a warm and cozy feeling. If I felt she was telling me the full truth, and that I could trust her one hundred percent, I might fess up.

But the awful truth is, I don't trust her not to run to him and tell him everything, and he can't know I know. Because then everything I've worked toward, everything I'm planning, will all be for nothing.

I'm in this alone.

Like I've always been.

Dad helped me a lot, but our motivations were different. We were both keeping secrets from one another, and I know he wouldn't want this for me, because it's risky and dangerous, but I have no choice. I won't run and hide for the rest of my life because that's not living.

I force my troubled thoughts from my mind as I settle on a bench between Sean, Sariah, and Emmett to watch the takedown on the field after classes have ended on Tuesday. Practically the whole school has turned out for this, and the stadium is almost full.

I've only just plonked my butt on the seat when a tall guy with a dull black hoodie pulled up over his head approaches. "Saint has a seat for you at the front," he says without extending a greeting.

I shove my middle finger up. "You can tell him that's my response."

He folds his arms, looking bored. "We can do this the easy way or the hard way."

My lips kick up as I stand. "What does the hard way look like?"

He moves to scoop me up, and I punch him in the face. Blood spurts from his nose as he winces. He glares at me, not so passive now. "I'm not opposed to hitting girls," he threatens, reaching for me again. "Don't tempt me."

I kick him swiftly in his left shin, and his leg buckles. He drops to his knees on the concrete step, cussing as he grabs the edge of the bench to steady himself.

I jerk my head up at the sound of running footsteps.

"Always so ladylike, princess," Caz Evans says, smirking. He extends a hand to the guy on the floor, yanking him to his feet. "Incapacitated by a female." Disgust washes over his handsome face as he shakes his head. "The shame." He shoves at him. "Get the fuck back down there, and try to at least pretend you've got a pair of balls between your legs."

I sit back down, feigning ardent interest in the two groups lining up across from one another on the field down below.

Caz sits on the end of the bench, half on top of me, forcing me to shunt over until my thigh is pressed right up against Sariah's. "I don't fold so easily," Caz says, cracking his knuckles as he shoots me a devilish grin. "And I thought you were smarter than this." He levels me with an all-seeing look.

"Go fuck yourself."

"I'd rather fuck you." His tongue darts out, playing with his lip ring in a way that's hugely distracting. His eyes are like furnaces as they skim me from head to toe, and I work hard not to squirm as my core throbs with need.

What is it with these guys? One heated look and they render me senseless. It's official—I've turned into one of those idiot girls in romance books who falls apart when faced with a hot guy.

It's embarrassing, and I'm glad no one has a hotline to my inner thoughts.

I press my mouth to his ear. "The only way your dick will ever enter my body again is if I'm laid out stone cold and bloodless on a morgue table."

"I've never given necrophilia much thought," he admits, running a hand through his jet-black hair, "but I'm game for trying anything once." He grins, his chocolate-colored eyes alight with mischief, and it pisses me off.

"Get lost, Evans. Haven't you got some buttheads to beat on the field?" I jerk my head to where things are heating up. Finn and Saint are locked in an intense conversation, with their supporters lined up behind them, flexing their arms, rolling their necks, and clenching their hands as they prepare to beat the shit out of one another.

Something cold slips over my skin, and I jerk my hands back, but I'm too late. Caz has already secured the handcuffs around both my wrists. Grabbing me by the shoulders, he yanks me to my feet. "Don't get involved," he warns Sean and Emmett as they stand along with Sariah. "Harlow is Sainthood property. She's ours to do with as we please." He steps out of the row, gesturing for me to follow.

"Eat shit." I kick the side of his leg with my booted foot. Caught off guard, he stumbles forward, grabbing the guy in front to stop himself from falling.

His nostrils flare as he straightens up, all humor gone, and he roughly grabs my hair, yanking my head back at an awkward angle. "I'm running out of patience, princess. Stop. Fucking. Fighting." He leans in to my ear. "Unless you want me to tell your bestie you're hiding shit from her."

He's bluffing. He doesn't know what I have and haven't told my best friend. And he doesn't know the extent of all I'm hiding. No one does.

However, the Saints trade in secrets. And they have the resources to dig deep. I can't take any chances. If Sariah finds out what I've done, she'll never look at me the same way again.

So, I shut my mouth and let Caz drag me down the steps, in front of the whole student body, thrusting me at some goon when we step foot onto the field. "Keep her there." He points at the bench by the sidelines. "Sit on her if you have to."

"Hey, asshole," I shout at his retreating back. "Forgetting something?" I raise my cuffed hands.

He turns around, walking backward as he faces me, showcasing a wide grin. "I happen to like that look on you. Suck it up, princess."

I hide my irritation, claiming a seat at the end of the bench, deciding I might as well settle in for the show.

I keep my eyes peeled, my gaze roaming the two gangs squaring off on the field, committing faces to memory. Both gangs have at least twenty supporters backing them up today, and I know, in the Saints' case, that's only the tip of the iceberg. The guys don't typically handle the grunt work themselves. They have access to a large gang they can call on when needed, and most of those guys stick to the shadows.

It doesn't take long for the violence to start, and I'm riveted as I watch the guys annihilate Finn's pathetic little school gang with minimal effort.

Saint, Galen, and Caz are lethal. Pounding the enemy into a bloody pulp while barely raising a sweat. Theo is no lightweight either, and what he lacks in body mass and strength he makes up for in pure rage. It's not difficult to see the broken, lost boy hiding beneath his bad boy façade.

Parker screams and shouts from the other sideline, but she's too far away for me to hear what she's saying. From the way she's throwing her hands around and stomping her feet, I know she realizes she's on the losing team. I wonder how long it'll take her to switch sides and how Saint will react to that.

It's all over in less than ten minutes, which has got to be some new kind of record.

Finn's crew lies broken and beaten on the field as the Saints stand victorious. They stride toward me, looking like their shit's the bomb, gloating as if it's all in a day's work.

And I suppose it is for them.

Saint lifts the hem of his shirt to wipe his brow, exposing the chiseled abs that are a regular feature in my dreams. His jeans hang low on his hips, and the V indents on either side of his body are clearly visible. My tongue longs to trace the curves and to dip lower, to wrap my lips around his cock and suck hard.

Saint grabs my chin painfully, lifting my head and stretching my neck as far as it will go. He swipes roughly at my mouth. "You had a little drool there."

I move to swat his hand away, remembering at the last

second that I'm still cuffed, and all I can manage is a feeble sideswipe that barely registers.

He smirks, whipping his head around to where Caz is propped against the entrance to the bleachers with his feet crossed at the ankles. "Nice touch."

"I thought so," he agrees, lighting up a cigarette. A smear of blood is spread across his brow, and the side of his shirt is ripped.

"Although I'd prefer if she was naked and cuffed to my bed," Saint adds.

"I thought you don't go back for seconds," I coolly reply.

"We don't," Galen retorts. "And who said anything about sex?"

"We could add a few more scars to your body," Saint suggests with a dark glint in his eye. A few guys chuckle as they walk by, heading up the steps.

"We're known for our creative torture techniques," Galen adds. "And I've already got a few new ideas in mind for you."

I shrug. "If you're trying to scare me, you'll have to try a lot harder than that." I stand, thrusting my shoulders out and refusing to be intimidated.

Most girls would probably be ashamed if they bore the scars I bear, but I'm not like most girls.

I wear my scars proudly.

It's why I've never shied away from wearing belly tops or sleeveless shirts or bikinis, and the shocked stares I picked up during swim class never fazed me, because these scars prove I'm a survivor, so why the fuck would I hide them?

"We'll see." Galen folds his arms, pinning me with the usual venom, and I decide to test the waters.

"You can't still be sore about what went down when we were kids? Or you always take rejection so personally?"

He shoves me back onto the bench, caging me in with his arms, pressing his body down on top of mine. One hand wraps around my throat, and he squeezes. I hold his gaze without flinching. "I will fucking end you, Westbrook. You can sit there acting all smug and innocent, but we know the truth." He squeezes my throat harder, and he's glaring at me with so much hatred in his eyes I wouldn't put it past him to strangle me in front of an audience.

Saint pulls him back. "Not here."

My breath oozes out in grateful relief, but I make no other sound, refusing to show emotion.

Saint glances up at the crowd who is loitering, watching us with bated breath. Over Galen's shoulder, I spot Parker watching the altercation with beady eyes, taking it all in and mentally parking it for dissection later, no doubt.

"Get the fuck home," Saint yells, his voice carrying across the bleachers. Kids instantly scramble until all that's left are the injured bodies on the field and a few stupidly brave stragglers.

The sky darkens, casting a gloomy blanket over the ground below as rain threatens.

Saint grabs my hands, releasing one of my wrists from the cuffs, and, for a second, I think he's going to let me go, but he locks the handcuff around the bench I'm sitting on, leaving me trapped.

"How original," I deadpan, rolling my eyes.

This time, it's Saint who invades my private space, leaning into my face. "We haven't even started." His eyes momentarily lower to my lips, and I smirk. A muscle pops in his jaw as he rips his face away from mine, casting a derogatory glance over my body. He straightens up, planting a shit-eating grin on his face. "You think you're invincible. We're about to show you you're not."

They walk off, and I sit there watching Parker scream in Finn's face as he struggles to climb to his feet. The guys on the field are limping away, using the entrance on the far side to flee the scene of their demise with their bloody heads hanging low in shame. Parker glances at me and grins at my predicament as she reluctantly helps her boyfriend hobble away.

I whistle under my breath, glancing up at the ever-darkening sky, wondering if it will actually rain.

Footsteps approach, and I don't need to look over my shoulder to confirm it's Sariah. I roll my jeans leg up and remove my blade with my free hand as my bestie, Sean, and Emmett appear in front of me.

"Fucking asshats," Sariah seethes, taking my blade and unfolding it for me.

"I can handle the Saints," I say, taking it from her and twiddling with the lock on the cuffs.

"Why are they interested in you?" Sean asks, and Emmett splutters, looking incredulous.

"Have you not seen the tape?" he asks, and I stop what I'm doing to lift a brow.

He has the decency to look sheepish. "Sorry." He shrugs, shoving his hands in the pockets of his jeans. "I watched it before I knew you were coming to Lowell High and before I knew you were friends with Sean and Sariah."

"Which is why *I* haven't watched it," Sean confirms.

"I watched it," Sariah says, and I grin. We watched some of it together when it was first leaked because I wanted to know exactly what was out in the public domain.

Dad always said knowledge is power, and I agree.

"Picked up a few new moves," she adds, winking at her boyfriend, and he throws his head back laughing.

"It was fucking hot," Emmett says, waggling his brows.

"Is that your way of saying you want to fuck me?" I inquire, as the lock pings open and I free myself.

"Every guy at this school wants to fuck you after that tape," he replies, while I rub my sore wrist.

"Or at least they did," Sean adds, as Sariah hands my backpack to me. "Until the assholes laid claim to you."

I throw the handcuffs inside, zip it up, and stand. "Well, at least, they've done me one favor," I quip.

"I've been checking up on them," Emmett says, as we climb the steps together, and my admiration elevates a few levels.

I knew he was smart.

When people threaten my family, I dig into their pasts to uncover every seedy little secret in the hope I can find something to use as leverage. Emmett clearly didn't take kindly to Theo threatening his sister, and I don't blame him.

Anyone who ignores a threat from The Sainthood is an idiot.

Those guys don't make idle threats.

"And they've never claimed any girl before," Emmett continues. "Hell, from what I've discovered, they basically shun girls after they've fucked them. So why have they claimed you?"

I have my suspicions, but it's nothing I can share. "I guess I'm just that good of a lay," I joke, grinning as I loop my arm through his and we hurry out of the stadium.

THE REST OF the week is an exercise in slow, silent torture as I wait for the shit show to unfold. Patience isn't my strong suit, and the hours tick by like minutes.

The Saints insist on sitting at my table at lunch, and if any of them are in my classes, they force kids aside so they can take the seat behind me, each one of them enjoying breathing down my neck in an attempt to make me uncomfortable.

They largely ignore me, with the exception of a few carefully chosen insults and threats, but I know we're all biding our time, and I just want all the cards laid out on the table.

Friday rolls around, and when I arrive home from school and see the red truck parked outside the front of the house, I know D-day has arrived.

I drive past Neo's truck, ignoring the asshole as he comes out of the house to unload more boxes, parking in the garage beside Mom's car. I climb out of my SUV and lock it with the key fob, pausing a moment to stare at Dad's collection of sports cars.

Besides Mom and me, they were his pride and joy, and

I always feel a pain in my chest whenever I look at them. A hideous thought infiltrates my mind, and I rush toward the lockbox mounted on the wall at the rear of the garage, removing the keys to all of Dad's cars and slipping them in my bag.

I'm damned if Neo is driving any of them, and I vow to find some safe place to move them to. The cabin is the ideal solution, and I make a mental note to ask Diesel if he can help me to transport them without anyone knowing.

If Neo gets his hands on any of these cars, I will pepper his body with so many bullets he won't resemble anything even remotely human when I'm done.

All week I've been dreading this moment until I concluded this is actually a good thing.

Keeping your enemies close is a well-known adage that most people dismiss without any thought.

But there is wisdom in the age-old saying.

Having Neo here means I can keep an eye on him in a way that won't raise suspicion. He might believe he has the upper hand, but I know more than he realizes, and if he knew what I knew, he might not be so confident about moving in here.

At the very least, if he's under my roof, I have access to kill him.

I don't want to go to jail for that bastard, but I will if there's no other option.

I might have to sleep with one eye on my door from now on, but so does he.

I try to keep that thought at the forefront of my mind when the doorbell chimes a couple hours later. I skip down the stairs, getting to the door before Mom or Neo, because I want to have some fun with this.

I open the door, shove my middle finger up at Saint and the guys, and slam the door in their faces before they can barge their way in.

One of them—my money's on Galen because he's the most hotheaded—presses his finger to the bell and doesn't let up. The shrill ringing is like music to my ears as I step away from the door, resting my back against the wall, grinning like a goober while I wait.

Mom and Neo appear a few minutes later. Mom frowns when she spots me, and Neo grins.

"Harlow. What is going on?" Mom asks as Neo flings the door open with more force than necessary.

"Man, am I glad to see you guys. Come in." Neo ushers the four guys into our hallway. He slaps Saint on the back, dragging him into a one-armed hug. "Welcome to your new home, son."

THE SAINTHOOD

CHAPTER 7

I CAN TELL from the shock splashed across Mom's face she had no idea they were moving in, and that goes some way toward reassuring me. "Neo?" Her face registers confusion as she faces her asshole fiancé.

"I'm sorry I didn't mention they were moving in with me, darling," Neo says, reeling Mom into his arms.

I dig my nails into the backs of my thighs and work hard not to project my disgust.

"I wasn't sure they were going to come with, and I didn't want to get your hopes up for nothing."

I smother my snort of hilarity. *And they say women are drama queens?* The bastard clearly planned it like this so he could intimidate me a little more. I'm glad he thinks I'm an imbecile, because that means he underestimates me, and I can use that to my advantage.

Truth is, the second I saw Neo Lennox sprawled all over my mother, I knew this was coming.

A light bulb goes off in Mom's eyes as she glances at the guys. "Oh my gosh. Saint." She reaches out, touching his arm.

"You're so grown up." Her face softens when she notices his cousin. "You too, Galen." She palms his face, and he smiles at her like he adores the ground she walks on. "You're both so handsome." The smile fades when she notices Theo, and she runs her fingers through her hair in a nervous tell. "Theo. It's nice of you to help the boys move in," she says after a few beats.

Neo clears his throat, shooting me a smug look over his shoulder. I like that he's not even pretending this isn't all about me. "Theo and Caz are moving in here too. The guys are undergoing initiation, and they need to stick together. I probably should've asked you, but it's not like you don't have the room. This place is massive."

Mom doesn't look surprised at the mention of initiation, but why would she? She grew up in Prestwick. Galen's mom, Alisha, was her best friend, and she was going out with Neo's brother, who was also a member of The Sainthood. Mom was Neo's childhood sweetheart, and she would have been with him when he was undergoing initiation from junior to senior level.

The truth is, Mom knows everything there is to know about The Sainthood.

Including the fact Neo is now the leader of the Prestwick branch and president of the entire national organization.

And she thinks it's a good idea to move him in here and make him my stepfather.

Way to pick 'em, Mom.

Neo smooths a hand up and down her spine, and I shiver at the thought of his touch. I don't know how Mom can bear him to touch her. I can't even look at him without wanting to flay my skin from my bones.

If his touch is like his son's, then you totally get it, my gnarly inner demon whispers in my ear, and I scowl.

Saint notices, misconstruing it as a smug grin crosses his mouth.

I flip him the bird, and his grin expands.

I'm going to enjoy wiping it off his face.

"I thought they'd be good company for Harlow." Neo continues lying. "She must get lonely in this big old house by herself when you're away or working late."

Mom turns to face me. "Honey, are you okay with this?" Her nerves betray her, and I know it's not just for me. This has her on edge too. I want to tell her I'm fine with this, because I'd rather they were here, letting this play out right under my nose, than sneaking around behind my back planning shit I can't predict or control.

But I can't admit any of that, so I stick to the role I've created for myself. "No, Mom. I'm not okay with this." I glare at the guys before forcing my lower lip to wobble. "I didn't know who they were," I lie, pushing off the wall and moving toward her with fake upset on my face.

Her brow creases as she eases out of Neo's embrace. "I don't understand. What—"

"They're the guys from the tape," I blurt, cutting her off. "I fucked all of them. Except Theo although he watched, and he did jerk off on my tits."

Saint trades looks with his father as Mom's face pales.

Inwardly, I'm clapping my hands with glee and wondering why I never tried out for drama class because I'm definitely getting a kick out of this.

I know my little charade won't change anything, but it will throw a wrench in the works, and I'm reacting predictably and naturally, which is most important. Neo doesn't look ruffled in the slightest, because he knows he'll talk her around, but I hope she gives him hell for at least a few days.

"You can't expect me to live with them." I pout, crossing my arms. "Not after they filmed me without my permission and shared the content online."

"Did you know about this?" Mom asks Neo, glaring at the boys she was so warmly welcoming a few minutes ago.

"They're teenage boys." Neo shrugs, yanking her into his side and flattening his palm against her ass.

My mouth curls up at the corner, and I want to rip him apart every time he touches her.

Living here with all of them will be a true test of self-control and patience. It's a test I intend to ace, so I relax my features and remind myself they are all getting what is coming to them in time. "I'm sure you remember what we got up to when we were their age?"

"So, you and my mom had group sex with other Sainthood members, and you recorded it without her permission and then shared it with the world?" I plant my hands on my hips as I challenge him.

"No, but we were like rabid bunnies, fucking any chance we got."

Ugh. That so backfired. "You're disgusting."

He smirks. "We're all adults here, and you seem sexually promiscuous, so I think we can all agree you are overreacting. My boys made you a star. You should be thanking them. I bet you have dudes lining up to pound your cunt since the footage aired."

My nostrils flare, and anger boils my blood at his disgusting slur.

Mom pushes Neo away, hurt flaring in her eyes. "Neo," she gasps. "That is completely inappropriate as well as being untrue. Your boys betrayed her trust, and you shouldn't condone that behavior." She glowers at all of them, and I silently champion her. "You owe my daughter an apology." She prods her finger in the air, moving it around them. "All of you."

"We've already explained ourselves to Harlow, Mrs. Westbrook," Saint says, looking like butter wouldn't melt in his mouth. "We weren't aware Galen's mom had cameras in that room, and we weren't the ones who shared it online. We were just as upset as she was when the tape aired."

"Bullshit."

"Are you accusing my son of lying, Harlow?" Neo asks, pinning me with a cautionary look.

I maintain eye contact with him, refusing to show fear.

"Because taking such a line would upset me greatly,"

he continues, "and I'm sure you don't want to do that." The underlying meaning is crystal clear, and fun time is over. "You're going to be my daughter. You and Saint will be stepsister and stepbrother, and I'm sure none of us want to get off on the wrong footing."

Mom glances between both of us, conflicting emotions raging in her eyes.

"I apologize if my comment offended you. I merely meant you seem sexually confident," he says, and he might be fooling Mom, but he's not fooling me.

"It's fine, and you're right," I lie, smiling sweetly. "What's in the past should remain in the past. This is a clean slate." I extend my hand to Saint, watching as he examines me closely, his gaze drilling holes in my brain as he attempts to extract the truth. "Welcome, *brother*. I hope you'll be very happy here."

"So that's why they claimed you," Sariah says the following night as we sit side by side in the old abandoned warehouse, drinking warm beer from bottles while we watch the largely inebriated crowd jump around the makeshift dance floor.

This party is in the rougher part of Lowell, a scene I usually avoid. It's especially risky attending, because The Arrows are known to frequent these parties, but I couldn't stomach bumping into the Saints at Beth McCoy's bash. Beth is Parker's bestie, and she's throwing a party in the woods behind Lowell High to try to salvage relations between Finn and The Sainthood. But she's an idiot because Finn made his bed, and now, he must lie in it. He should have taken Saint's offer and at least held on to his dignity.

Now Saint will go out of his way to humiliate and shun Finn.

At least, it might deflect some of the heat off me.

School next week should be fun.

"Yep," I lie, because I know Saint hasn't claimed me

because I'm to become his new stepsister. But it's handy to have a reason the public at large will accept.

"Has your mom lost her mind?" she asks, as I rip pieces of the label off my beer bottle.

"I never would've thought Mom would shack up with a degenerate like Neo Lennox, but I clearly don't know her as well as I think."

"I can't believe she's letting them live in the same house as you after they pulled that shit." She shakes her head, leaning back against Sean as he comes up behind her.

"I'm choosing to focus on the positives." I smile as Emmett climbs up on the old dresser beside me.

"Which is?" he inquires, clinking his bottle against mine.

"I can murder them all in their beds and claim it was a home invasion."

We all laugh, but I'm only half-joking. The thought *has* crossed my mind.

The other thought that's crossed my mind is that I need to come clean to Sariah. At least about some of it. Her association with me places her in danger, and I can't make that decision for her. She needs to know enough to make her own choice. But I'm terrified of that conversation because she might choose to walk away. And then, I'll truly be all alone.

The next hour passes pleasantly, and the more I drink, the more I relax. Emmett has only left my side to grab more beers and I'm enjoying talking with him. Sariah and Sean are dry humping one another on the dance floor, and I can't help smiling. If anyone deserves to be happy and in love, it's my bestie.

"You want that?" Emmett asks, tilting his bottle at the dance floor, in the direction of our friends.

"Someday, sure. Doesn't everyone?"

He nods. "I know I do."

"How is it Lowell High has two atypical jocks? You and Sean have got to be blowing some stats to smithereens somewhere."

He chuckles. "Not every guy on the team is a manwhore douche. There are plenty who are in it for the sport and the camaraderie. You must be reading a lot of the same books as my sister. The ones that paint jocks as man sluts. Don't believe everything you read."

"This is your sister who's ill?" I ask, remembering what Theo had said that day.

He nods, his expression turning serious. "She has leukemia, and she's been in this experimental trial the past four months, which is delivering results. We're hopeful she'll pull through."

I touch his arm. "I'm glad to hear that, and I hope she does."

He moves a little closer, staring at me, and we share a moment. "She's the only reason I'm not making a move on you right now." Apology shines in his eyes.

"You don't need to explain or apologize. I'm glad you're taking the threat seriously because those assholes don't mess around. I'd hate anything to happen to you or your sister because of me." I bring the bottle to my lips, taking a long swig. "Besides, I'm not in the market for a boyfriend, and I'm not planning on sticking around long after graduation. Your energy would be wasted on me."

"I disagree, but I'm not one to dwell on something for long. I hate those bastards, but I refuse to spend any time thinking about them. And they never said we couldn't be friends, right?"

I nudge his shoulder, smiling. "They didn't. And I don't have many friends. I'd be honored to call you that. You're a good guy, Emmett, but I should probably elaborate on a few things before you make a friendship commitment. I need to speak to Sean and Sariah too, so let's grab dinner at the diner next week, and I'll fill you in."

"It's a date."

I shoulder check him, rolling my eyes. "Between friends."

"Aw, look at you," a voice from my past says, dragging my gaze from Emmett's. "Always scouting new fuck buddies."

I fold my arms and level a dark glare at Darrow. "What do

you want, Dar?"

"I heard your mom is engaged to that fucktard Lennox. That true?"

I've nothing to gain by denying something that will be common knowledge once the official engagement party takes place tomorrow night. "Unfortunately, yes," I admit, sipping my beer as I eye my ex, wondering where he's going with this.

"And those assholes are living with you now?" His eyes burn with naked hatred, but I can't tell if it's directed at me or the Saints.

"Same response," I drawl, eyeballing him.

"You still fucking them?"

I snort. "You seriously have to ask that after what they did to me? What *you* did to me?"

"You disrespected me, Lo. What else did you expect me to do?"

I point my beer bottle at him. "You disrespected me first."

"Tempest's a slut. A nothing." He shrugs. "It doesn't even compare."

I shake my head. Man, he's a piece of work. "Wow. So, she's not your current girlfriend?"

"That doesn't change facts." He reaches out, toying with the ends of my hair. "You know I'd dump her for you in a heartbeat." His features soften, and it's the closest Darrow's ever come to showing me true emotion. "I was an idiot, Lo. I wasn't thinking straight, because I wouldn't have cheated on you with that slut if I had been. Don't confuse my mistake. I still love you."

Darrow doesn't know the fucking meaning of that word, and what we had most definitely wasn't love, but I'm not about to split hairs. He's approached me for a reason, and I'd like to know why.

Emmett is listening intently to our conversation, studying my face, and I can tell by the way he's holding himself rigidly still that he's waiting for my cue to lay one on him. He obviously doesn't know who Darrow is. Dar may not be in The

Sainthood's league, but you still don't want to mess with him. I've watched him gut guys for less.

"Is there a point to this nostalgia, or you're just hoping for a sly fuck? Because that's never happening."

He sighs, letting go of my hair. "I know. You've got more class than that." He scrubs a hand over his prickly jawline, and I spot Bryant staring at me from the corner of the room. Tempest is there with a face red enough to match her hair. "I have a proposition for you," he says, holding up a hand when I level him with another dark look. "Not a sexual one. I think you and I could help one another."

I jump down off the dresser, cautioning Emmett to stay put with my eyes. "I think I know where you're going with this," I say, looping my arm through Dar's and peering up at him with a dreamy look on my face.

He chuckles. "You still can't resist pushing buttons, huh, Lo?"

I beam up at him. "She fucking deserves a little payback." My gaze flits to where Bryant is now physically restraining Tempest from coming at me. I smirk before turning my back on her. I straighten up, all hint of playfulness gone from my tone and my expression. "Let's talk outside. See if we can't serve our mutual interests."

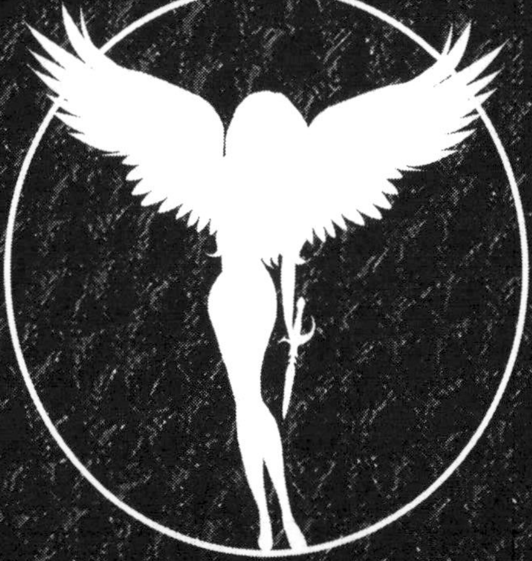

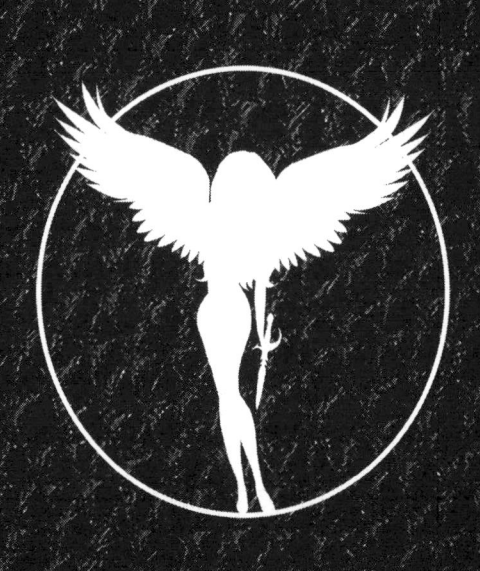

CHAPTER 8

I SCOWL AT the ceiling as the hot water beats down on my bare flesh, bracing myself for this nightmare of a party. Mom and Neo seem hellbent on a short engagement and a quick wedding, and I'm so torn over what to do.

How can I stand by and watch my mother marry that monster? Does she honestly love him? Does she truly understand what she's getting involved in? Or is she really that naïve? Or maybe, this is the byproduct of grief?

I lather shampoo in my hair as I ponder these questions. Steam envelops me in a cloudy haze as I drag my fingers through my hair, washing the product down the drain.

There is a way to stop this—I tell her the truth of what happened four and a half years ago.

But what if she already knows? What if she's always known? What if it doesn't make any difference?

I never would have considered these thoughts even a week ago, but learning my mom was previously engaged to Neo "Sinner" Lennox has diminished my confidence in her. I can't possibly know the real her if she could spend years with such a disgusting human. She must know the things he's done. The shit he's involved in.

So why would confirming it change anything except showing my hand?

I can't interfere.

I've got to let this play out.

At least, for now.

I rest my head against the tile wall, closing my eyes and wishing Dad was still here. Even if only as the voice of wisdom in my head, because I don't know what I'm supposed to do with this.

Hot water rolls down my spine as I contemplate my options, but I'm no closer to an answer as I switch off the shower and step out.

A muscular arm covered in tats darts out, offering me a towel, and I scream as adrenaline floods my system and my body reacts automatically to the perceived threat.

Saint chuckles, stepping forward, his hungry eyes drinking me in as he shamelessly ogles every inch of my bare skin. "Get the fuck away from me." I grab the towel and shove past him, charging into my bedroom with water dripping all over the floor.

I slam to a halt as three sets of male eyes flit to my naked form.

Whatever. It's not like they haven't seen me naked before.

Taking my time, I wrap the towel around myself, tucking it securely under my arms as I glare at Caz, Galen, and Theo. The latter is sitting on the edge of my bed, tapping away on a tablet while Caz is rooting through my bedside table, and Galen is—

"Give me that!" I march toward him, grabbing the new dress Mom bought for me to wear to her engagement party from his large hands. Water trickles from my sodden hair all over the hardwood floor, and my damp fingertips leave small wet patches on the black gown. I hold it up in front of me, grinding my teeth to the molars. "What the fuck did you do to my dress?" I give Galen the evil eye.

He lights up a cigarette. "Made some improvements. You like?"

I inspect the torn sleeves and the angular cut in the side of the dress extending across the midriff. "It's ruined." He smirks, and I snatch the cigarette from his lips, stubbing it out on a plate on my dresser. Caz chuckles, while Galen looks two seconds away from ending my life. "Your lungs will thank me some day." I push my face in his. "And after you destroyed my dress, you're lucky I didn't stub it out on your pretty face."

"No need to be so dramatic," Saint says, stepping up behind me and gripping my hips. "It's perfectly wearable."

"I doubt Mom wants me to look like a slut at her party." I scowl as I watch Galen light up another cigarette.

"Unless she plans on trading her daughter in for a new model, that's what she's stuck with," Galen replies, deliberately blowing smoke circles into my face. He leans in close, breathing icky smoke breath all over me, and I jerk back on instinct, pressing up against Saint's broad chest in the process. "What you wear won't change that fact."

"You're a bigger slut than me," I say, shoving his shoulders and trying to ignore the feel of Saint's hard-on pressing into me from behind.

He straightens up, his smirk deepening. "Jealous, *angel*?"

I snort. "Hardly." My lips twitch as I prod him in the stomach. "I was the one who rejected you, remember?"

He blows more smoke in my face, and it's irritating as fuck, but nothing can wipe the smug smile off my face. A muscle clenches in his jaw as he loses the smirk, narrowing his eyes at me. Thank fuck, my fourteen-year-old self pushed him away that day.

"We're wasting time," Saint says, trailing his fingers along the hem of my towel. "Dad wants us downstairs before the guests arrive." With the way he's toying with the towel, I know he plans on exposing me to the room again, and I refuse to give him that power.

This is my bedroom, and these dicks don't get to come in

here and act like they own the place and me.

Without stopping to overthink it, I let the towel drop to the floor, standing assertively in front of them. I'm proud of my body, scars and all, and I'm not going to bow down before these jerks.

Theo tilts his head up from his tablet, his eyes locking on the scars covering my stomach and upper arms before his gaze meets mine. I flip him the bird, because fuck him for his too late pity. He looks at me with the saddest expression before lowering his head to whatever he's doing.

"Get dressed." Saint rubs his erection against my ass, trailing his fingers up the side of my body, brushing against the swell of my breasts. Galen stares at Saint, and some unspoken communication filters through the air, bringing Saint to his senses. He slaps me on the ass and shoves me at his cousin. Galen instantly thrusts me at Caz, scowling and rubbing his hands down the front of his jeans as if I'm diseased. But his eyes roam my body, even as he sneers, and he can't disguise the reaction poking the crotch of his jeans.

"Get the fuck out of my room," I demand, my hostile gaze bouncing between them.

Caz holds on to me, running his hands all over my body, as his eyes flare with need. "Nah. The view's much better in here, and it's fun watching you squirm."

I dig my elbow into his ribs and wrench myself free. "Suit yourselves." I stroll into my walk-in closet, silently talking myself off the ledge. I'm three seconds away from grabbing my gun and riddling these assholes with bullets.

I yank my undies drawer open, removing a black lace bra and panties set. Nimble fingers pull them from my hands, tossing them aside. I spin around, glaring at Saint. "What the fuck is your problem?"

"Not slutty enough," he says, rubbing his chin as if my underwear choice is worthy of lengthy contemplation.

Pushing me aside, he rummages through my drawer, extracting a trashy red lace bra and matching crotchless panties

I bought to entertain Darrow last Valentine's Day. He thrusts them at me, his inked fingers brushing against the swell of my left breast. "Put those on."

"Fuck off." I throw them on the ground, unzip the altered dress, and step into it, holding it up with one hand as I use the wall to steady myself. Then, I slip my feet into the five-inch black and gold stilettos I'd laid out to wear.

Something akin to admiration flits across his face for a fleeting second, and then, the mask comes down again. His eyes trail the length of my body as I shimmy the tight-fitting dress on. Keeping his gaze pinned on me, he walks right up to me, spinning me around and pressing me into the wall. He moves my damp hair to one side, running the tip of his finger down my spine.

I could have him off me in seconds, but I'm interested to see where he's going with this, and how far he intends to push it, so I don't struggle or protest, holding my breath as his fingers latch around the zipper and he slowly pulls it up. My skin vibrates in all the places where his fingers touch my exposed flesh, and I bite down hard on my lip to stifle a moan.

He takes his time zipping me up, and it's a slow form of torture. Between the warm breath on the back of my neck, the touch of his fingers scorching my skin, and the heat rolling off his body as he presses up against me, I'm soaked and already regretting my reckless decision to forgo underwear. This dress is short, and I'll be lucky if I can sit down without flashing the goods.

As if he's a mind reader, his hand drops low, his fingers inching up under the hem of my dress.

"Get your hands off me." It comes out less of a threat as I'd intended.

He chuckles before placing his lips on the back of my neck while his fingers move higher and higher up my thigh. "Try to sound convincing next time," he rasps as his hand moves to cup my crotch from behind.

This time, I don't smother my moan in time, and he

chuckles again. "We own this," he purrs, rubbing his fingers up and down over my pussy. "No one touches this cunt but us," he adds, sliding one long digit inside me. "Understood?"

"I thought you weren't interested," I pant.

"We're not," he says, adding another finger and pumping them leisurely in and out of me. "But we're quickly learning what we need to do to keep you in line."

His words snap me out of the sexual bubble I'm trapped in, and I enjoy his howl of pain as I slam the heel of my shoe into his shin.

"Fuck!" He leans down, rolling up his jeans as he stabs me with a dark glare.

"The sooner you learn you won't keep me in line, the better this goes for both of us," I say, looming over him with my hands on my hips.

"That's not how this works," he hisses, unfurling to his full height. "The sooner you do what we say, the easier this is on you."

I snort. "I've never taken orders from guys, and I'm not about to start now."

I flounce out of the closet and over to my dressing table. Saint hobbles out behind me.

Caz chuckles. "I'm beginning to think we need to wear full body armor or our Kevlar vests when we're around the princess."

The nickname pisses me the hell off, but I'll never let them know that.

Ignoring them, I focus on blow-drying my hair, gloating as the noise drowns out their conversation. They refuse to leave, sprawling across my room, watching me studiously, as I style my hair and apply my makeup.

Instead of the signature tees they usually wear to school, they are all wearing fitted shirts with skinny jeans.

Saint's shirt is rolled up to his elbows, showcasing his muscled arms and the heavy ink on his skin.

Galen has the top few buttons of his shirt open, highlighting the colorful tats creeping up his chest and onto his neck.

Caz's shirt is stretched so tight across his back and shoulders it looks like it's two sizes too small.

Theo is wearing a gray shirt that hugs his lean abs, and he's made an effort with his hair. Instead of the usually messy blond waves, he has it slicked back and tucked behind his ears.

They scrub up well even when they're only making minimal effort, and I fucking hate how much my libido notices these guys.

I caution my hormones to calm the fuck down as I inspect my reflection in the mirror, deciding to roll with this.

I already look like trailer park trash with my ripped dress exposing the scars on my stomach and upper arms, so I might as well make the most of it.

Instead of the smooth, sleek hairstyle I was originally going for, I use a shit ton of volumizing product on my hair until I resemble something from the eighties with my puffed-out back-combed look. I apply thick eyeliner to my smoky eyes, finishing with a couple layers of heavy mascara. Full red lips complete the look, and I can't help grinning at my reflection.

"What's that smile for?" Saint asks, not even pretending he hasn't been watching me intently.

"Mom is going to flip out." I stand, smoothing a hand down the front of my dress, as I grab my purse.

Galen glowers, and it's getting old. "Continue scowling like that and it might stick," I taunt, sauntering toward him. I brush my fingers along his brow, smoothing the lines out, and he slaps my hand away. "It'd be a pity to ruin such a pretty face." He glowers harder, and I laugh.

Man, it's way too easy to wind Galen Lennox up.

And, so far, The Sainthood's intimidation tactics lack substance and sophistication.

I should have known that wouldn't last too long.

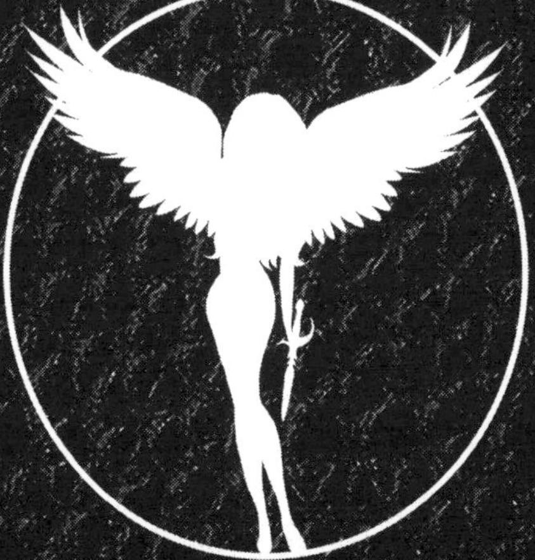

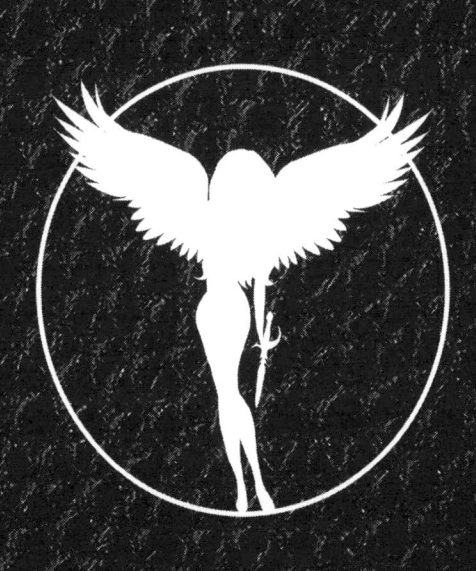

THE SAINTHOOD

CHAPTER 9

I WANDER AROUND the crowded downstairs of our house, counting down the minutes until I can slip away. Mom's face was a picture when she saw the state of me. The old me would've felt guilty, but I have zero guilt anymore and zero respect for my mom. She raged at Neo for his harsh treatment of me for all of five seconds before she forgave him. And she's let the assholes move in here and treat the place as if they already own it.

Dad must be turning in his grave.

Although I could kill for a proper drink, I pour myself a large soda, steering clear of the obvious gang members and the four jerks clinging to their coattails. There is no way even a drop of alcohol is passing these lips when there are so many dangerous men in my house. I need to keep my wits about me. While I recognize some of them, there are a lot of faces I haven't come across before, so I take a few photos on the sly when no one is watching.

Neo introduces me to a few scary-looking dudes, and I don't like the way their eyes roam my body or the curiosity that alights in their eyes when my identity is confirmed. But dudes are suckers for a pretty face and a show of skin, and I use it to my advantage—flirting and laughing with them, extracting some key details like their names and how long they've been members. All intel which I file away to decipher later.

The entire time I'm talking to the outlaw dicks, Saint's gaze drills holes in my back. I don't need to turn around to know all four initiates are watching me, but Saint's intensity is almost physical in the way I feel his eyes scorching a path over my body. I flirt outrageously, knowing it's most likely pushing Saint's buttons, and I'm only surprised he doesn't yank me away.

I'm guessing he's behaving tonight under Daddy's watchful eye, because Neo is also watching proceedings carefully, and his eyes work the room like a pro.

I can see where Saint gets it from. That cunning ability to observe all and know all. He's clearly learned it from Sinner.

Mom mustn't like the way they're looking at me either because she finds an excuse to extract me from the conversation, pulling me over to her work colleagues instead.

Mom's business associates are giving Neo's crew a wide berth, and the atmosphere is awkward in the extreme, the conversation stilted and tense. From the looks being shared around the room, I know I'm not the only one who thinks Mom's lost the plot.

It's like two opposing worlds colliding, and I've no idea how Mom plans to make this all work. When news gets out about her new gangland affiliations, I think she'll lose a lot of clients. Being connected to The Sainthood is bad for business no matter how you look at it.

My cell pings with a text from Sariah, wondering how much longer I'll be, and it's a welcome distraction. I tap out a quick reply as I slip out of the living room and walk the empty hallway toward the downstairs bathroom.

Leaving soon.

The cell is suddenly ripped from my hand, and I'm pulled

sideways into Dad's study. Neo shoves me into the chair in front of Dad's mahogany desk—the one passed down from his father in his will. Watching the asshole lean against the edge of the desk with my phone in his possession has my blood boiling for several reasons.

"Planning on ditching already?" he asks, reading the message from Sariah before scrolling through my phone like he has every right.

"Give that back." I thrust out my hand, pinning the full weight of my animosity on him.

"Shut up," he snaps without looking at me. He sifts through my messages, and all the tiny hairs lift on the back of my neck when he opens the photo files, deleting every single picture I took tonight. Lucky I already saved copies to the cloud and wiped the activity from my log. I move to stand, but he pushes me back into the chair, planting one firm hand on my thigh, keeping me in place. He puts my phone down on the desk and leans in close to me.

Bile swims up my throat at the malice burning in his eyes.

"I've been watching you for some time, Harlow." His words send shards of fear slicing through me. "And I've got to admit, I'm impressed."

I bottle my fear, schooling a neutral expression on my face. "Am I supposed to be grateful?"

He tightens his grip on my thigh, and his eyes drop to my bare skin for a brief moment.

A new layer of panic simmers underneath the surface.

"I'm not easily impressed, and it doesn't often hold, so you have a choice here." He leans down closer, putting his face all up in mine, and even though my natural instinct is to spit in his face, knee him in the balls, and get the fuck out of Dodge, I hold myself still, keeping a lid on my mounting fear. "Cooperate and live your best life," he says as he moves his hand up under the hem of my dress.

I grab hold of his wrist, stalling his upward trajectory, because that shit is *not* happening. "And if I don't?"

"Then mommy dearest pays the price."

My stomach plummets. I might be pissed at Mom now, but I don't want him hurting her because of me. I dig my nails into the underside of his wrist as he attempts to move his hand up to my bare pussy. I've never regretted my stupid decision to go sans underwear more than I do right now. "I knew this was bullshit. That you don't love her."

"Oh, but I do," he says, his jaw taut with tension as our hands battle for supremacy underneath my dress. "Your mother's the only woman I've ever loved. But she betrayed me, and she needs to be punished for that. The severity depends on you."

"Why?"

"Let's cut the bullshit, *Lo*. We both know why." He pulls back, removing his hand, and I fight hard to disguise my abject relief. "The mourning period is over. This is a new dawn. You will do what I say or you and the lovely Giana will suffer the consequences."

I don't hold back, leveling him with every ounce of hatred I feel in my heart. I don't know how, but someday, that man is going to die, and I'm going to be the one with my finger on the trigger.

He drops my cell in my lap before walking off, pausing at the door. He turns to watch me. "Your destiny was set in motion the second Giana left me for *him*. I don't give a fuck about fairness or what's right and what's wrong. If you want someone to hate, hate your parents, because it's always been their fault." His mouth pulls into a cocky grin, and he blows me a kiss before exiting the room, leaving me frozen in place.

All the panic I've kept at bay surges forward, and my pulse throbs wildly in my neck as potent fear sluices through my veins.

I haven't been fooling him at all! That he's been watching me is no surprise, but the fact he knows I know is. "Fuck it!" I throw my cell at the wall, watching it shatter, as my stomach twists and turns.

I need to implement my plan, and fast.

Movement out of the corner of my eye captures my attention, and I whip my head up. My eyes latch on familiar blue eyes as Saint steps out from behind the shelving unit. Anger rolls off him in waves as he strides toward me slowly.

I climb to my feet, quickly recovering my composure. "Does Sinner know you're spying on him?" *Did Sinner sanction it, or Saint has doubts about his father, especially around me?*

"What did he mean?" he growls, gripping my forearm and tugging me into him.

That same charge is in the air, and I sway in his arms as he lowers his fierce gaze to my lips. His erection prods against my stomach, and sheer liquid lust competes with raw rage on his face. He looks torn between wanting to strangle me and wanting to kiss me, and I can relate, because he invokes the same reactions in me. He reeks of unrestrained anger and danger, and I'm fucked in the head because I press in closer to him, turned on instead of being disgusted. His eyes darken, holding me a prisoner in place, and I couldn't move right now even if I wanted to. Which I don't, because my hormones have clearly eviscerated all sense of self-protection and logic.

"I asked you a question."

His words warn me not to fuck with him, and his eyes burn through me, searching, probing, and attempting to strip me bare, to see everything I can't let him see. But I'm powerless to break eye contact, drowning in those dangerous blue depths until I can't feel where he ends and I begin.

His penetrating stare takes me back to the moment we bonded, and I don't believe he's forgotten.

I know I'm imprinted on his soul the same way he is on mine.

"You already know the answer," I whisper.

"What the actual fuck?"

Galen's snippy tone breaks us apart, and I turn my head to the door where the other three guys are watching us with matching suspicious gazes.

I've dropped my barriers, and I'm feeling too much right now. It's a rare moment of vulnerability, and I'm wide-open in a room full of sharks.

I need to get out of here before I reveal something important.

I dash to the door, pushing my way through the testosterone barrier and fleeing to the safety of my bedroom.

No one stops me, but I know I'm on borrowed time.

THE SAINTHOOD

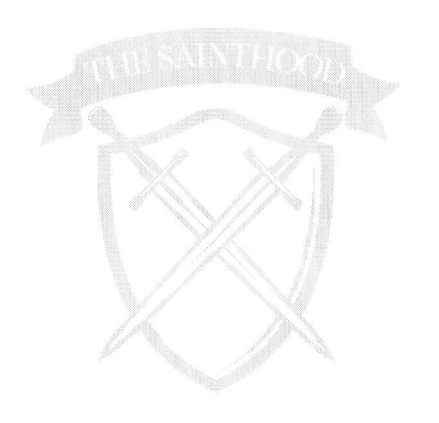

THE SAINTHOOD

CHAPTER 10

"HERE," EMMETT SAYS, handing me a beer the instant I plop my butt down on the threadbare couch in Sariah's living room. Her grandma is at bingo tonight, so we have the place to ourselves. "You look like you need it."

"Man, do I ever." I drain half the bottle in one go, sinking back into the couch as I finally relax. My muscles were wound tighter than Bradley Cooper on Oscar night.

"That bad, huh?" Sariah says coming into the room carrying a massive bowl of chips. Sean is behind her carrying a couple of dips.

"It was like outlaw central. Mom's definitely lost a few friends tonight."

Thank God, I eventually managed to convince my bestie to sit this one out. She wanted to come to support me. The three of them did. But I put my foot down. Bringing them tonight would have put them directly in The Sainthood's path, and I'm already risking their lives as it is. I won't deliberately put them at risk, which is why I've already told all of them they are banned from my house whenever Neo is there.

I know firsthand how gangs work. They target friends and family and use them to force cooperation. Over my dead fucking body will Neo use Sariah, Sean, or Emmett to make me toe the line. And that's the main reason why I'm here tonight. They need to know what's at stake, and it can't wait for our diner date. They need to hear this now.

I take another sip of my beer as I consider how best to start this conversation. But, honestly, there's no good or easy way to say this, so I just rip the Band-Aid off.

"I need to explain some stuff, because things are seriously fucked up. Anyone connected with me is in danger."

Emmett sits up straighter, angling his body so he's looking me more directly in the face. "What kind of danger?"

"The life-ending kind of danger."

His chest heaves, and he gulps. "What's going on?"

"Are you sure you want to know?" My eyes move around the room. "I won't fault anyone for walking away before it gets too deep."

"I'm all in." Sariah doesn't hesitate.

"Sure?"

"Hundo P. I've got your back. Always."

A layer of stress flitters away, and my heart swells at her instant loyalty.

I fucking love this girl so hard. "Right back at ya. I'm always here for you."

"I'm in too," Sean says. "You're as much my friend as Sariah's, and we don't abandon friends in times of need."

I nod, smiling despite the tension swirling in the air. "Truth, and I'd do the same for you."

I refocus on Emmett, and I won't hold it against him if he wants no part of this. He's not as invested as Sariah and Sean, and our friendship is still new. "You need to protect your sister. I totally get that. While I will do everything in my power to keep all of you out of the firing line, if you're privy to this, I can't promise they won't come after you."

He runs a hand through his messy hair, and strands of dark

brown hair tumble over his forehead. "I'm already involved. I'm already on their radar. And no one dictates who I can and can't hang out with. Provided we're smart, we can keep my sister out of this."

"I won't fault you for walking away, Emmett. You're the least invested here."

He shakes his head. "Nope. I'm in. Hit me with it."

Air whooshes out of my mouth in grateful relief, and I don't have the words to express how incredible it feels to not be alone. "I love you guys," I choke out in a momentary burst of emotion.

"We love you too, Harlow," Sean says. "And whatever it is, we'll deal with it together."

Tears sting the backs of my eyes, but I know they won't spill because it's been years since I've cried. I pull myself together, remembering the seriousness of the situation, locking all my emotions up tight again.

"Before I explain, I need your cellphones." I hold out my hand, and one by one, they deposit their phones in my palm. All three of them share similar confused but curious looks as I remove the detection device from the pocket of my jeans and scan their phones for tracking devices. I doubt anyone is keeping tabs on my friends, but you can never be too sure.

I hand them back their phones and repocket the detection device. "I was checking for bugs or tracking devices," I confirm before anyone asks. "You're all clean."

"Shit, girl. What the hell is going on?" Sariah inquires, tucking her blonde hair behind her ears. "And is this somehow connected with your past?"

Sariah knows what happened to me, because she saw a news report at the time, and we've talked about it, but I haven't given her the whole picture.

I give her a terse nod before taking another swill of my beer, eyeballing Emmett. "You only moved to Lowell a couple years ago, right?" I'm only asking to be polite because I already know everything there is to know about Emmett thanks to the background check I performed on him.

"Yeah. I'm not from around here." His foot taps on the floor.

"So, you don't know my background." I look to Sean for verification.

Sean shakes his head. "I know you don't like people gossiping about you. I've never said a word." His solemn gaze radiates with the truth, and I thank him with my eyes.

"What don't I know?" Emmett asks, his gaze bouncing around the room.

"You don't need to do this," Sariah blurts before I can open my mouth. "I know how much you hate reliving it."

"I need to start at the beginning because that's where it all began." Although, if Neo's words tonight are to be believed, it began the instant I was born.

"You have my full attention." Emmett's face is a mask of seriousness as he leans his arms on his thighs and focuses on me.

"I was kidnapped when I was thirteen and held hostage for five days. I was only released after my father paid a three-million-dollar ransom."

Emmett cusses.

"It was in all the papers and all over the news," Sariah confirms.

"And most everyone in town knows who Harlow is because of it," Sean adds.

I wet my dry lips. "It gave me a certain level of notoriety. One I still hate to this day." I push the sleeves of my sweater up, showing him the scar tissue on my upper arms. A look of horror is etched upon his face as he leans in closer to examine the faded lines. "My captors did that to me. Every day I was their prisoner, they inflicted some new form of torture on me. They recorded it and sent it to my parents. Dad was scrambling to get the money together to pay the ransom and arguing with Mom. She wanted to go to the cops, but Dad knew involving the authorities would sign my death warrant."

Of course, I only learned this much later. At the time, when every minute felt like eternity, I thought my parents didn't care enough because they hadn't come for me.

Emmett's brow puckers. "But I thought it made the news?"

"It did, but only after I was released. No one knew what was happening at the time it was happening, outside of my parents."

I rub my palms down the front of my tight jeans. "My captors kept me blindfolded the entire time, and they were careful not to use their names around me. They stripped me to my underwear, tied me to a bed, and kept me locked in a cold room with only a thin blanket for warmth. Someone stood over me anytime I needed to use the bathroom. Strong arms pinned me to the bed every day when they inflicted new torture on me."

I lift my sweater up to my ribs, showing him the six puckered circular-shaped scars scattered across my stomach. "Sinner did that to me on the last day. He laughed as I screamed every time he stubbed his cigarette out on my skin."

Sariah's eyes almost bug out of her head. "What?" she screeches, nearly dropping her beer on the floor. But Sean has spidey senses, and he snatches the bottle before beer ruins her grandma's new royal blue carpet. "I thought you didn't see any of their faces?"

"I didn't until the last day when Sinner did this. He was alone in the room when he pulled the blindfold off."

"He wanted you to know it was him," she surmises.

"Yes, but I didn't know who he was until I figured it out years later."

"You should've told me," she huffs.

"Don't be mad." I beseech her with my eyes. "I didn't tell you to protect you."

"I don't understand," Emmett says, frowning again. "Who's Sinner?"

"Sinner is Neo Lennox a.k.a. Mom's new fiancé. President of The Sainthood and my soon-to-be stepdad," I explain.

His mouth drops open.

"Holy shit." Sean shakes his head, his face displaying his shock. "David Jennings is innocent?"

I bob my head. "David Jennings was the scapegoat, because someone had to pay for the crime or the authorities would continue investigating."

"Who's David Jennings?" Emmett asks, scratching the back of his head.

"David Jennings was a business rival of Mom's. The Sainthood staged it so he looked like a vengeful competitor trying to bleed Mom's business dry and force her into bankruptcy. He protested his innocence the whole way through the trial, but he was convicted and sentenced to ten years in jail. He was also forced to hand over the ransom money along with compensation. His business and personal finances were drained overnight. His family was run out of town."

Sariah chews on the corner of her mouth. "How long have you known The Sainthood were responsible, and how did you find out?"

I hate fudging the details, but I've already decided there are certain things I can't tell them. I'm telling them as much as they need to know, because it's safest that way.

"I pieced things together over the years and properly figured it out a couple years ago. Dad changed after I was kidnapped and tortured. I know he blamed himself, and he went into full-blown Rambo mode to keep me safe. I attended self-defense classes, and once a month, when we told everyone we were going on camping trips, he actually took me to this cabin he owns where I was trained in hand-to-hand combat and a bunch of different weapons by a guy named Diesel. Diesel also taught me some computer and hacking skills and gave me access to a ton of high-tech tools and equipment." I tap the pocket of my jeans, pointing at the device I've just used on their phones that I have courtesy of Diesel.

"Is he a spy or?" Sariah leaves her question open ended on purpose.

RESURRECTION

I shrug. "I don't know. Dad told me never to ask. All I know is, Diesel must've been trained by the government at some point because the stuff he knows is serious shit. Either that or he's part of some badass mercenary organization."

"Doesn't sound like a bad guy to have in your corner," Emmett supplies.

"He's a great guy to have in my corner, but I still don't fully trust him because of that element that remains hidden."

I like to think I'm a good judge of character, and Diesel has been nothing but loyal and supportive, but Dad instilled a lot of advice, and the thing he drilled into me over and over again was not to trust anyone completely. That even allies can end up being foes.

"Did your dad know?" Sariah asks.

"We never talked about who took me. The only thing he asked me about my kidnapping was if they had raped me." Sean and Emmett turn pale. "They didn't touch me like that even though I was pretty well developed at that age and I'd already had my period." I grind my teeth to my molars. "They were more about inflicting pain. I didn't see their expressions, but I could feel their smiles as they burned me with cigarettes, cut me with knives, and took a blowtorch to my skin."

Sean gulps, and Emmett reaches out, taking my hand in his. "It's okay," I assure him. "I was broken for a long time after I was released, but Mom got me into therapy, and Dad helped me a lot. Knowing that I can defend myself fully gave me back a lot of my confidence and helped me overcome my trauma and my fears."

"If your dad went to all that trouble, he must've known it was The Sainthood," Sariah says, moving over to sit on my other side. "Because David Jennings was in prison, but it sounds like your dad believed the threat was still ever present."

I pull my hand from Emmett's tucking both my hands between my jean-clad thighs. "He knew. I'm sure of it. It's why he went to such extremes to protect me. But he never told me, and I never told him I'd figured it out."

"Why would The Sainthood kidnap you?" Sean asks, looking perplexed.

"Dad was a lawyer, and I think he was working for them." I hate admitting that, because I've had Dad on a pedestal for years, and acknowledging he was tied up in shady shit means he wasn't who I thought he was either. But it's the only truth that makes sense. "Something must've happened, and they kidnapped me to threaten him."

"Does your mom know?" Sariah asks, her mouth pulling into a tight line.

"We sheltered Mom from everything. That was the way Dad wanted it. She doesn't know about the cabin or my training. Dad said we had to protect her, but now, I'm rethinking my theories."

Sariah rubs at a spot between her brow. "If your mom was once engaged to Neo, and your dad knew that, then maybe he didn't tell her to protect her or—"

"Or he didn't trust her," I blurt, cutting Sariah off. "And I'm guessing Mom is the reason Dad was mixed up with them in the first place. Although that's only speculation because he's dead and I can't ask her because I don't trust her anymore."

"Fuck, Lo." Sariah yanks me into a hug. "This is a shitstorm."

"It's a lot worse than that," I say, easing out of her embrace. "It's not a coincidence that Neo has reappeared in our lives. It's all connected, and I think it's tied up with something my dad knew."

I pause for a second to gather my thoughts. I'm sure the answer is somewhere in the paperwork Dad left at the cabin, but most of the files are written in code, and in the four months since I discovered the documents, I haven't been able to crack it. I want to tell them about the secret files, but it places them in too much danger, and I'm already risking so much by telling them this.

"What do you think is going on?" Emmett asks, concern transparent on his face.

"Everyone knows The Sainthood controls the guns and drugs on the streets and that they are behind most of the violence and unsolved murders. I suspect they are involved in a ton of other shit too. The authorities know it, but they can never pin them down. It doesn't help that they have so many cops and judges in their pockets. I think my dad was collecting evidence to use against them."

Acid crawls up my throat, and pain stabs me through the heart. I look down at my hands, needing a moment. Sariah rubs my back.

I lift my chin up, trying to ignore the agonizing pain ripping me apart on the inside. "Dad was on edge in the months leading up to his death. He bought me my SUV as an early birthday present, and he was anal about it being the only car I drove. It's bulletproof, fireproof, bombproof, and about as indestructible as you can get. I thought he was overreacting, but now, I think he knew the danger had escalated."

I blow air out of my lungs, staring at my bestie, as I force the words out of my mouth. "I think The Sainthood found out what my dad was up to and they killed him for it."

CHAPTER 11

I'M DISTRACTED MONDAY at school because I'm itching to put my new plan in place. These past four months, my aim was to decode the paperwork, and once I understood what I was dealing with work out a way to take The Sainthood down.

But Neo making the moves on Mom has changed things. And after his guarded message last night, I know he's going to start making demands on me. I can't spend more time trying to decrypt the files.

I need ammunition, and I need it *now*.

I might have to move my timeline up and consider the very real possibility of fleeing before I graduate.

Unless I can prove Neo is behind my father's death.

So, I'm refocusing my energies on the car accident that claimed my father's life.

I tap out two messages on my new cell under the desk during math class before sliding my phone back into my pocket. Feeling eyes on me, I glance over my shoulder and stare blankly at Theo.

He stares back, giving nothing away, and I flip him the bird before turning back around and focusing on the class.

"Who were you texting during math class?" he asks when we are seated in the cafeteria at lunchtime. Being forced to sit with the four jerks every day is a pain in my ass, but I've tried ditching them, and they just follow me around.

Dicks.

Everyone knows Saint is set to become my stepbrother, and they've all jumped to the conclusion that's why they've claimed me. Now, girls are climbing over one another to hit on them, and I'm forced to watch as they lap up all the attention even if I know they are just humoring the girls in a bid to fuck with my head.

I hate to admit it's kinda working, and I'm trying really hard to retain my usual "don't give a fuck" attitude.

"None of your business, and get the fuck out of my space," I reply, elbowing Theo in the ribs because his chair is way too close to mine.

"There was a time you enjoyed Theo being all up in your space, wasn't there, princess?" Saint says, purposely moving his chair in closer to me on the other side so I'm trapped between both jerks.

I peer into Theo's face, but he's giving nothing away. "You told them."

He ignores me, shoveling a large forkful of pasta into his big mouth.

I press my lips to his ear. "But did you tell them the whole story?" I whisper loud enough for the others to hear.

He briefly squeezes my thigh in warning, his eyes challenging me with the promise of retaliation if I fuck things up for him.

I could blurt it all out now, but I'd rather hold it in reserve to use at an optimal time.

"We know he took your virginity when you were fifteen," Galen says, louder than necessary. "And that you've been whoring yourself out ever since."

A few catcalls and giggles ring out from the jocks and

cheerleaders table, but I ignore them. "Guilty as charged," I admit. "Although I call it taking control of my sexuality. It's the twenty-first century, Galen. Women have the same right to enjoy consensual sex as men. Your comment just confirms your ignorance and lack of intelligence."

I lean back in my chair, cocking my head to the side and smiling at him. Out of the corner of my eye, I spot Saint struggling to contain a grin. I think he secretly loves it when I challenge any of them—no matter how he tries to portray it. "Continue peddling your particular brand of bullshit, and see if I care," I tell Galen.

A throat clearing claims his attention before he can retaliate. I work hard to keep my emotions in check as I glance up at Parker. She's wearing a tight red top that's cut low at the front with her ample cleavage on full display. Her shapely hips are encased in a pair of skintight leather pants, and she's forced her ugly feet into a pair of sky-high stilettos. Her makeup is so thick it looks like it's been applied with a shovel, and her hair is so full of hairspray it doesn't move when she shakes her head.

"Galen." She purrs at him, sliding her tongue over her gloss-slicked lips. "Saint." She turns her head to their leader, her gaze raking up and down his body as she unashamedly eye-fucks him in front of everyone.

My hands clench into fists of their own volition, and a burning sensation spreads across my chest. I struggle to stifle my unfamiliar feelings when Sariah kicks me under the table, cautioning me with her eyes.

I compose myself, schooling my features into a neutral expression, before anyone else notices.

"What can I do for you, Parker?" Saint asks in a pleasant tone I've never heard him use. I almost gawk at him but recover in time.

"Could I talk to you in private?"

Saint smirks, and his chair screeches as he stands. Galen, Theo, and Caz stand too. "Stay with the princess," he commands Theo and Caz, taking Parker's arm and moving her over to the far wall where there are fewer ears. Galen shoots me a mocking smile as he follows them.

"Yo, Finn," Sariah hollers to the table behind us. "Your bitch is disrespecting you."

"Shut your trap, Roark," Finn shouts, digging his nails into the Formica tabletop so hard it's bound to crack.

"Talk to my girl like that again," Sean says, turning around in his seat to glare at Finn, "and I'll permanently wire your jaw shut."

"Bite me, asshole." Finn flips Sean the bird, clearly aggravated at the lack of public respect. Seems someone is having a hard time handling the loss of power.

I watch Parker preen and pout, flirting up a storm with both Galen and Saint as they listen attentively to whatever she has to say. I glance at Finn again, and he's seething, but he makes no move to retrieve his errant girlfriend, and that's how I know this is a strategic play, and he's definitely involved.

His face is a testament to the epic beatdown he secured last week, his skin every color under the rainbow. His left eye is still badly bruised, and his nose is swollen and covered in cuts, and he's never looked so weak in every sense of the word.

Galen barks out a laugh, and I swing my gaze back around. Saint is smirking, Galen is chuckling, and Parker looks like the cat that got the cream. Her hands roam Saint's chest, and his gaze flicks to mine for a nanosecond while she busies herself pressing her body up alongside Galen. She's draping herself all over them, and both those assholes are letting her.

Caz chuckles, slurping noisily on his straw as he drinks his soda. "Jealous, princess?"

I snort. "Of that dumb bitch? Hardly."

"Sure looks like it," Theo adds, not lifting his eyes from his phone.

"Don't pretend like you know me." My tone is snippy, and Sariah quirks a brow. I know I'm letting them get to me, and it's infuriating. But every time I'm in their company, they scramble my thoughts, crank my hormones to Richter-scale level, and seriously mess with my sanity. No one pushes my buttons more than The Sainthood, and it's getting harder to hold onto my cold, emotionless state.

"I do know you," he says, lifting his eyes to mine.

"No. You don't."

Parker's high-pitched giggle assaults my eardrums, and I turn my head just in time to watch Saint squeeze her ass before sending her back to Finn. I grind my teeth so hard to contain the vitriol that begs to be unleashed it feels like I've given myself lockjaw.

"The princess doesn't like Parker's hands on you," Caz tells Saint as he reclaims his seat beside me.

"Too bad she doesn't call the shots," Saint drawls, smirking as he clamps his hand down tight on my thigh.

"Listen up," Galen shouts, jumping up on his chair. "Party at our place Saturday night." A succession of pings rings out in the room, and everyone moves to check their cells. "Free booze and baggies. Invite only. Check your cellphones."

Sariah checks her cell, opening the invite she's received, cursing as she shoots daggers at Saint. "Momma Westbrook will never permit you to throw a party at her house."

Truth. It's Mom's pride and joy. She'll cut their balls off if they trash her house.

"What she doesn't know won't hurt her." Caz grins, winking at me.

"And she won't be a Westbrook for much longer," Saint adds with a sneer.

I wonder if she's ever truly been a Westbrook. *Has she been a Lennox all along?*

"How are you planning on getting her out of the house?" I ask, idly tapping my fingernails off the tabletop as if I'm bored.

"She didn't tell you?" Saint's lips curve up. "Dad is whisking her away for a romantic weekend. We'll have the whole place to ourselves Thursday to Sunday." He slides his hand higher up my thigh, but at least, I'm clothed this time *and*

I'm wearing underwear. He strokes his fingers at the apex of my thighs as he presses his hot mouth to my ear. "Think of all the fun we'll have."

Mom is up bright and early Thursday morning to cook breakfast for everyone before she and her obnoxious fiancé leave for their weekend of debauchery. Saint referred to it as a romantic weekend away, but I doubt Neo has a romantic bone in his body.

Tying women up and torturing them is more his style.

The eggs I'm chewing feel like sandpaper in my mouth as the thought lands in my mind, and I find myself fearing for Mom until I remember she's a lying cow who invited a monster into her bed while it was still warm from my dad.

She's on her own with this.

I shovel another forkful of eggs into my mouth to avoid engaging in the lively wedding conversation happening around the dining table.

Who knew teenage delinquents were so invested in wedding planning?

The four assholes are full of suggestions as they use fake charm to try to woo Mom to the dark side.

It's not taking much, which only confirms my suspicions.

"I was thinking you could wear a dark purple dress to match Saint's tie," Mom says, dragging me kicking and screaming into the conversation. "It would look great in all the photos."

I take my time chewing the food in my mouth, before dabbing the corners of my mouth with a napkin, and then I speak. "I thought one usually wore black to funerals."

"Harlow, please." Mom's eyes well up, but I'm not falling for it. Not now I know she's had a lifetime to practice her acting skills.

"If you're insisting on forcing me to participate in this

fucking charade, I'll only wear black." I throw my napkin down, pushing my chair back and rising to indicate I'm done with this convo.

Strong hands land on my shoulders, pressing me back into the chair. "You'll wear whatever the fuck your mother wants you to wear," Neo says, his voice sending chills down my spine, and they're definitely not the good kind. "And you'll act like you fucking love it. Something tells me you're experienced at faking it, so I'm sure you'll manage." He digs his hands into my shoulders, inflicting pain, but I don't even flinch.

The underlying threat is crystal clear, but I would've relented without it, because I'm playing a carefully constructed part. "Fine," I snap. "I'll cooperate." I push Neo's hands off my shoulders, unable to feel his touch on any part of me without my skin crawling like a thousand fire ants have burrowed their way under my flesh. I stand, leveling Mom with one of my special death glares. It's a look I've never had cause to send in her direction before. "I'll be the model daughter even if I'm hating every second of it. You faked being the model wife long enough; I'll just take my cue from you." She gasps, but I ignore her, grabbing my half-eaten plate and walking to the sink. I scrape the dried eggs and overdone bacon into the trash can underneath.

"Harlow, baby, please." Mom chokes on her words, her eyes sad as she reaches for me, but I sidestep her.

"Enjoy your weekend, *Giana*. Don't forget to pack your first aid kit. I have a feeling you'll need it."

THE SAINTHOOD

CHAPTER 12

"MOTHERFUCKING ASSHOLES," I yell, kicking my punctured tire. I glance at my watch, cursing under my breath. If they'd just deflated one of my tires, I could've changed it and still gotten to school in time, but the assholes have punctured all four tires on my SUV.

"New rules," Saint says, entering the garage from the house. "You ride to and from school with us from now on."

"Eat shit, asshole."

I brush past him, but he grabs hold of my elbow. "Your little temper tantrums are getting old. Just be a good whore, and do what you're told."

I smile sweetly in his face as I slam the heel of my boot down on his foot. Instead of loosening his hold on me, he tightens his grip on my arm, his fingers digging painfully into my skin. A muscle pulses in his jaw as his other arm rings my neck and he squeezes tight. "I'm all out of patience, princess. And I'm done asking nicely." I snort out a laugh, and his eyes narrow to slits. "I have no qualms about hurting women if they deserve it. Especially lying, thieving, manipulative whores," he threatens.

He lets me go, pushing me away, and I fall back into a hard, warm chest. "Like father, like son," I coolly reply, straightening up. Saint stands rooted in place, exuding rage that is both silent and lethal. He flexes his knuckles as he pins me with a look loaded with venom and the promise of retaliation, and a shudder works its way through me, but I quickly shake it off. "And the only manipulative whore around here is my mother."

I spin around, shoulder checking Galen as I brush past him. He grabs a fistful of my hair, yanking me back. "Where the fuck do you think you're going?"

In a move Diesel taught me, I twist around underneath Galen's arm and punch him in the nuts. He roars out in pain, instantly letting me go as he drops to his knees on the unforgiving concrete.

Saint grabs me by the shoulders, and he looks seconds away from going postal on my ass. But there's begrudging respect there too although he disguises it so fast I'm not sure I didn't imagine it. Saint hands me off to Theo. "Put her in the car."

"I need to go to my room."

Saint levels me with some serious evil eye.

"I'm on my period, and I forgot tampons," I lie, and my sugarcoated tone matches the fake sugary-sweet smile on my lips. "Unless you're happy for me to bleed out all over your shiny, new Land Rover." Not that it'd be anything new. I'm sure the guys are used to cleaning up blood.

The gangster business must pay well because all the guys have sweet rides, and I can admit to myself that I'm dying for a spin in Caz's Mitsubishi Eclipse.

"I'll take her," Theo says, clasping my arm.

I wrench out of his grip and pin him with a look Voldemort would be proud of.

"Hurry the fuck up," Saint snaps, extending an arm to haul Galen to his feet.

Galen grabs my neck before Theo can shepherd me away.

"Touch my dick again and I'll chop off your tits and shove them down your filthy mouth."

"Not before I castrate you and shove your dick up your ass!" I bite back.

"Get her out of here before she winds up dead," Saint says, and I grab my backpack, letting Theo usher me away.

He drops my arm when we reach the kitchen, and I stare straight ahead, pretending I don't see Neo's hand moving under Mom's skirt as she leans over the sink, rinsing dishes. I fold my arms around my body and ignore the rancid churning in my gut.

"He's not so bad once you get to know him," Theo murmurs as we climb the stairs.

I shake my head in disbelief. "I already know his soul is pitch-black."

"Things don't have to be so hostile, Lo. We don't have to be your enemy."

I twirl around at the top of the stairs and jab my finger in his chest. "Don't act so fucking naïve. We're on opposite sides, and everyone knows this is the way it has to be. Pretending otherwise fools no one." I head toward my bedroom with his footsteps heavy behind me.

He catches up to me just as I reach my room, spinning me around and slamming my back into the wall. My bag drops to the ground as he presses the length of his body against mine, holding me in place. The familiar feel of him against me raises a host of feelings I've worked hard to bury. "You're still so fucking stubborn and so fucking angry."

"I've good reason, Theo."

He sighs, cupping my face as he peers deep into my eyes. His hazel eyes are more green than brown today, and a pang of longing for the past jumps up and slaps me out of nowhere. "I know, babe." He looks at me the way he used to look at me. With comfort, familiarity, adoration, respect, and love, and it fucking slays me inside.

He doesn't know this, but at one time, Theo was my savior.

The reason I got up out of bed every day. The reason I chose to fight and not give up. Until he abandoned me and I lost the last parts of my soul. "Don't call me that." Hurt rushes to the surface, and I avert my eyes.

"If I said I'm sorry, and that I've regretted my actions every day since, would it help?" he pleads, caressing my cheek with his thumb.

"Not one bit. Your apology is too little and too late," I say, shoving him off me.

Being around these guys is dangerous for me on so many levels.

"I'm sorry I hurt you, Harlow. I—"

I slam my hand over his mouth. "I don't want to hear it, Theo." I harden my heart and plaster a matching emotion on my face. "I. Don't. Care. And I sure as fuck don't care about anyone or anything connected to The Sainthood either."

He shakes his head, pleading with his eyes and his tone. "All that kind of attitude will do is get you killed."

I shrug. "I'd rather die staying true to myself than live a life that's a lie."

"Why haven't you told them?" he asks quietly.

I shrug again, playing it casual. "That's not how I roll," I lie.

"It doesn't have to be this way. I can bring them around if you just give them what they want." He steps in closer, gripping both sides of my face in a tight hold. "I don't want anything bad to happen to you. Please, I'm begging. Just do what Saint says. He's a good guy, Lo. And if you get him on your side, he can keep you safe."

I contemplate his words for about point five of a second. "Fuck you, Theo. And take your hands off me unless you'd like to be nursing your balls like Galen."

He steps back, shaking his head, a muscle ticking in his jaw, as his expression morphs into something familiar. "You're smarter than this. Engage your fucking brain, Lo." He jerks his head at the door. "You have three minutes. Get your fucking shit, and let's go."

I grab my bag, slam the door shut, and lock it from behind, racing to my closet. I pull the carpet back and lift up the loose wooden panel in the floor, removing the box I keep hidden there. I grab the keys, before securing the box and rushing out to my window.

I climb out and shimmy down the side of the house in a well-practiced maneuver, slipping into the garage on the far side, ducking down low as I scan the layout. Saint's Land Rover is gone, so he must be waiting in front of the house for us.

Perfect.

I dash to the Gran Turismo, taking a quick moment to run my hand along the sleek, black bodywork before throwing my backpack inside and sliding into the driver's seat. I haven't driven this car in ages, and I'm glad Dad's cars haven't been transported to the cabin yet. I decide on the spur of the moment to keep this car here as a backup because I doubt this is the last time the assholes will tamper with my SUV. I make a mental note to ask Diesel if it's possible to get tamper-proof tires before I kickstart the engine, welcoming the familiar feel of the car as I floor it out of the garage.

This car can go from zero to sixty-two miles per hour in mere seconds, and I whizz by Saint's vehicle as Theo emerges from the front door with a scowl on his face.

I flip them the bird, throwing back my head and laughing as I fly past them, taking the small wins where I can.

"MAYBE THEO IS right," Sariah says, washing her hands in the sink as I touch up my makeup in the mirror. We're early, thanks to our speedier than usual journey, and the bathroom is empty. "Perhaps, you should play along and act more amicable."

I slick lip gloss on my lips and thread my fingers through my hair. "They'd smell a rat if I started cooperating all of a sudden."

Sariah dries her hands on a paper towel, her brow creased as her mind works overtime.

I'm so glad I told her and the guys and that they are solidly behind me. It helps to have someone to bounce stuff off.

"Maybe you could play a different angle," she muses, tossing the used towel in the trash.

"What do you suggest?" I ask, straightening the straps on my top.

"Maybe you should seduce them," she says. "Get them to lower their guard and let you in."

"I've considered that, but it won't work."

"Why not?"

I lean back against the wall with a sigh. "Because they're already fucking with my head, Sar. I'm struggling to keep my emotions on lockdown around them, and getting closer could majorly backfire on me."

"Please tell me you're not falling for them?" she groans.

"Things are complicated between us. You know the backgrounds. And if Mom goes through with this wedding, which I think she will, then I'm tied to them more permanently. I need to find a way of getting the intel I need without falling into their trap."

She taps a finger off her chin. "Focus on Caz. You don't have shared history with him."

I rub a hand across my chest. "Maybe, that'd work." I push off the wall, slinging my arm around her shoulders and tucking the little pint-sized beauty into my body. "It's worth considering at least."

"Whatever it is you're planning, it won't work," a whiny voice says, pushing into the bathroom, and I stifle a groan. It's too fucking early to deal with Parker's shit.

She's flanked by Beth McCoy and another girl I don't know.

"Whatever it is you've come to say, say it." I separate from Sariah, and we stand tall with our shoulders back, facing the three girls.

"Saint is mine."

I burst out laughing. "So fucking delusional."

Her mouth pulls into an unattractive sneer. "I have something he wants, and he's willing to trade."

"What does Finn think is happening?" I ask, crossing my arms over my chest.

"Finn is none of your concern!" she exclaims, and I'm tempted to tell her.

"And Saint is none of yours," Sariah says.

"If either of you stand in my way, you'll be sorry. This is a friendly warning. Next time, not so much."

Her threat holds about as much weight as Nicole Richie. "Gee. I'm quaking in my boots," I deadpan, snatching our backpacks up from the floor. I pass Sariah's to her, and she slides it over her shoulders.

"You should be, whore." She steps right up into my face.

I smile. "Your desperation makes you pathetic and careless." I let the smile slip off my face on purpose. I don't have time for petty distractions, and Parker is as inconsequential as the dirt under my boot. "Trust me, you don't want to make an enemy of me, and that's the only warning you're getting."

CHAPTER 13

"Wow." Emmett whistles under his breath as I guide my friends into the house Saturday night. "Your place is something else."

"I'm betting it'll be fucking trashed by morning," Sariah says, shedding her jacket and handing it to me.

"I'm betting it won't." I hang their jackets up in the closet and steer them toward the belly of the house where the party is in full swing. "This whole setup reeks of Neo's involvement, and he probably has a cleanup crew scheduled to clean the house before Mom returns."

"Fuck. You look hot," Emmett adds, casting appreciative eyes over my short black leather dress.

It's got a straight neckline and a myriad of straps that crisscross from my bust up over my shoulders, wrapping around the nape of my neck. It offers a glimpse of cleavage without being too slutty. The dress dips to midway down my back, showcasing some of my tattoo. "That's a work of art," he murmurs from behind as he inspects my ink.

"It's an avenging angel," I confirm.

"I fucking love it, and it's so you."

"Thanks." I offer him a genuine smile as I smooth a hand over my scalp. My hair is pulled back in a sharp ponytail, and I've gone all goth with my makeup with thick black liner and mascara and my signature red lips. The few vodka cranberries I've enjoyed before my friends arrived have taken the edge off, but I'm still in control, and that's important because I want to be firing on all cylinders tonight.

A topless waitress steps forward carrying a tray of drug baggies. My mouth turns dry as my eyes fixate on the branding etched on the front of the small plastic bags. It's The Sainthood's signature branding, the same drawing that members have inked on their skin—a dark circle with a burning cross in the center.

Senior members get the symbol inked on their chests once they attain full membership, while junior members are branded on their backs. A shiver works its way through me as I stare at the bag. On the bottom of the infamous symbol it reads Lowell Chapter in capital letters, and my skin crawls at the confirmation The Sainthood has moved into town and intends to stay.

"With the compliments of The Sainthood," the pretty girl says, blatantly eye-fucking Emmett from head to toe.

The Sainthood isn't pulling any punches tonight. They are making sure every person at school is locked down tight, and in a couple of strategic moves, they've wiped the board with Finn and his paltry opposition.

Controlling the drug trade at Lowell High is a smart move, but Lowell Academy is a loftier prize, and owning the streets is where the real money is made. I'm guessing they'll be making moves to go after that turf as well.

We might as well avail of the free weed, so I grab the entire contents from the tray, distributing the bags among us. I stuff a bunch right down the front of my dress, concealing them behind the tight leather.

"You can't—" the girl starts to say, shooting daggers at me.

"This is my house, so I think you'll find that I can, and I just have." My stare dares her to challenge me, and she instantly backs down.

Emmett chuckles as we walk past her toward the living room. "I think your sass turned her on. Her nipples went rock hard when you challenged her."

I roll my eyes, scoffing. "Don't play dumb, Emmett. We both know you're the one who creamed her panties and turned her nipples hard."

He laughs, sliding his arm around my shoulders, as we step into the den of iniquity, formerly known as our living room.

"Ho. Lee. Shit." Sean's eyes pop wide as we stop at the entrance to the room to take it all in.

"This is hardcore," Sariah admits, shaking her head in disbelief as she looks around.

"They had people here all day transforming the place." All the overhead chandeliers have been draped in red and black coverings, casting a garish glow over the proceedings below. The gray walls are concealed behind tall black and red freestanding panels that rim the room on all sides.

Mom's furniture has been moved out to make way for modern black and red leather couches grouped around low, glossy black coffee tables with ornate floral centerpieces and buckets of beer and vodka on each table. All the couches are positioned around the sides of the room, leaving the middle of the space free. Music thumps from mobile speakers in the four corners of the room, and a teeming crowd jumps around the makeshift dance floor.

The scent of weed is strong, and everyone in the room is high even if they're not smoking it.

More semi-naked girls man the temporary bar set up at the top of the room, and hordes of horny male seniors, with obvious hard-ons, crowd the space, ogling the girls. At a separate counter off to one side, our classmates line up to snort complimentary lines of coke.

I smoke weed on occasion, but I steer clear of other drugs

because that shit messes with your head, and my head's fucked up enough as it is.

Our fellow seniors are idiots. Falling into the trap like gullible fools.

After tonight, the guys have Lowell High sewn up tighter than a nun's panties.

After tonight, the guys will reign supreme.

And I fucking hate how easy everyone made it for them.

"Fuck me." Sariah stares at me like this is insane.

And it damn well is.

None of our usual parties come even close to matching up.

"Oh, you haven't seen the worst of it yet," I add, gesturing them forward. We move across the room, stepping over writhing couples and avoiding flailing limbs as we circle the outside of the dance floor. I grab us some vodka shots from the bar before we pass out into the back hallway, leading to the game room at the rear of the house.

My phone pings, and I jump on it, but it's only another text from Mom. She's called and texted daily since Thursday, but her faux concern doesn't fool me. I delete the text without reading it, biting on the inside of my cheek, and the pain helps ground me.

The door is closed but the sounds and smell of sex permeate the air as we approach. I turn with my back to the door, lifting my shot up. "Down the hatch!" I toss back my shot, and the others do the same. I grin at them. "Prepare yourself because I'm pretty confident when I say you've seen nothing like this before."

I move to open the door, and Emmett circles his arm around my shoulder again, but I brush it off this time. "The goon squad is through here, and you need to stay back."

Emmett chuckles as he slinks away, putting distance between us.

"It'd be good if you hooked up with someone," I suggest, and he shrugs noncommittally.

"I hope you're not queasy," I joke as I open the door and

lead the way.

The same décor has been used to transform this room, and the usual furniture has been removed and replaced with a bunch of mattresses strewn across the floor. Everyone in here is naked or semi-naked except for the assholes lording it over everyone else from the raised dais at the back of the room.

"Are they sitting on thrones?" Sean chokes out.

"Yeppers. They really are that obnoxious." I glare at the four dickheads as they smoke and drink from gold-plated thrones while they watch the orgy unfolding before them.

Everywhere I look, people are fucking, and there's zero discrimination and zero limits here. I ignore the grunting, groaning, and thrashing bodies as I pick my way toward the makeshift stage.

Saint hones in on me, his eyes practically burning my dress off my body as I slowly approach. His gaze treks down my long legs, and I know I made the right call ditching my thigh high boots in favor of the stilettos. My long, slim, shapely legs have always been one of my best features, and I'm not opposed to using my body for gain when there's a need. I draw the line at full-on prostitution, but most everything else is fair game.

Saint clicks his fingers, and one of the minions standing guard at the side of the stage moves forward to meet us. He stops directly in front of me. "Your friends are welcome to stay if they're participating." He looks over my shoulder. "Get naked or get out."

I glance behind me. "I'll meet you back out in the main room."

Sariah slants a look at me, and we silently communicate. I nod, and she takes her boyfriend's hand, drawing him away. I quirk a brow at Emmett. It's his call.

He casts a wary eye at the group of four guys and two girls on our left. It's a total free-for-all. Two of the guys are fucking the girls, and the other two guys are fucking one another. "I'll pass," Emmett says, adding, "You sure you want to do this alone?"

"I'll be fine." I subtly raise the hem of my dress on one side, showing the blade strapped to my upper outer thigh.

His eyes blaze with heat, and I caution him with a firm look. I've no doubt Saint is watching us, and that guy misses nothing.

"Okay. But if you're not back in fifteen minutes, I'm coming to get you."

"I think someone has a hero complex," I tease.

"I fucking mean it, Lo."

He levels a glare at the stage, and I tug on his arm to capture his attention.

What the fuck is he doing antagonizing them?

"Think of your sister," I whisper, and that snaps him into place. He turns and leaves, and I watch until he's closed the door behind him before turning back around and walking toward my soon-to-be stepbrother.

"Princess. How good of you to join us," Saint drawls, patting his lap like I'm a dog.

"Thrones?" I ignore him, quirking a brow and placing my hands on my hips. "Really? Aren't you guys supposed to be *saintly* and shit?"

He cocks his head to the side, that smug superior grin plastered on his mouth as he pats his lap again. I guess the guy is used to chicks obeying his every wish and command. He'll soon realize that's not me.

"You'll have to change your name to The Kinghood." My lips twitch. "Or maybe The Dickhood would be better," I add in a deliberately breathy tone as I lean down into his face. "Because you're all such dicks."

I straighten up, smirking as his nostrils flare. Saintly did *not* like that.

"Looking sexy, babe. C'mere," Caz calls outs from his slouched position on his throne. "That dress is straight fire." His leg is thrown over one arm of the chair, and he's doing nothing to hide the massive bulge in his dark jeans as he smokes a blunt and shamelessly ogles me. The guys are all bare chested, and I'm sure it's a calculated move to have every female in the vicinity panting after them.

I'm doing my best not to fall into that category, but damn, all four of them are sporting impressive chests and abs, and I know what they're packing behind their boxers too, which does nothing to dampen my ardor.

"You want to peel it off me?" I taunt, taking a step toward Caz.

"Fuck yeah." He thrusts his hips forward, unbuttoning his jeans. "Come ride me, princess."

"Caz," Saint commands in that deadly low tone of his as he grabs my wrist, tugging me down on his lap. "Pull your shit together." Saint whips his head to Galen while settling me on his lap. "Cut him off now."

Galen tugs the blunt from between Caz's lips and slaps him across the face. "Sober up, shithead."

Caz flips him the bird as Saint's arm wraps around my body, holding me in place. He blatantly stares down the front of my dress, and I glare at him.

"Seriously, asshole? Everyone here knows you're going to be my stepbrother. I'm off-limits, so that means keep your grabby hands to yourself." I attempt to pull his arm away, but it's like trying to move a ten-ton weight.

He looks at me with a familiar amused grin. "We're not blood related. I can fucking stare at you whenever I want and touch you however I like." He lowers his gaze to my chest again, and his arm moves higher, brushing the undersides of my breasts.

This guy is so confusing. He says he hates me, and he looks at me sometimes like he wants to rip my insides out and hang me from my entrails upside down. But I know he feels the intense chemistry between us too, because other times, he blatantly undresses me with his eyes and his dark, lust-fueled gaze speaks to all the naughty things he wants to do to my body.

I think it's fair to say Saint is as torn up about me as I am about him, and he doesn't know what the fuck to do about it either.

But I didn't stay home tonight to attend this party only to be distracted. I have two things to achieve, and I'm determined to handle both before the night is over.

THE SAINTHOOD

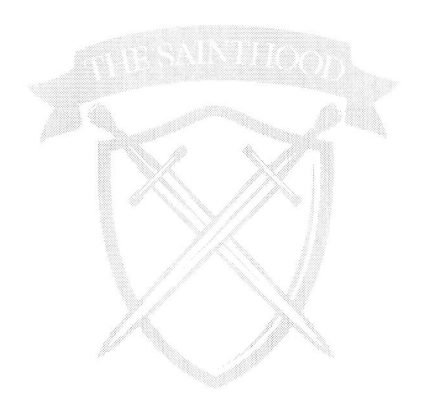

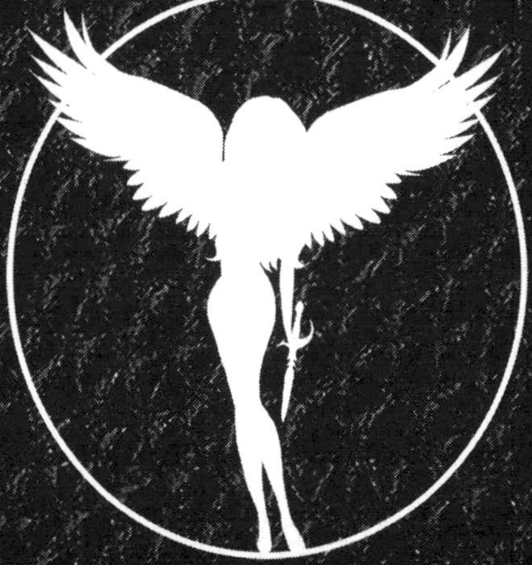

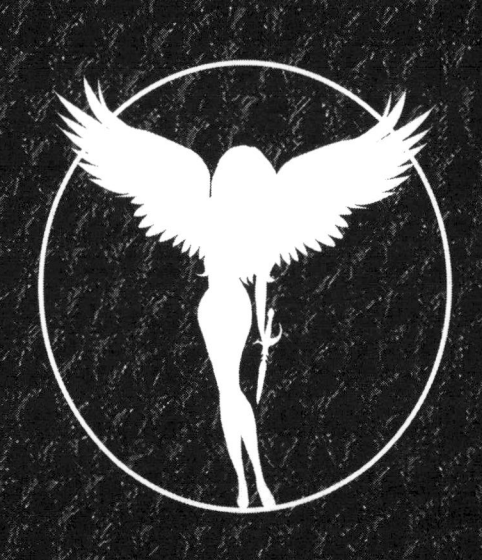

THE SAINTHOOD

CHAPTER 14

My gaze latches on to agenda item number one, and I stare at Parker and Finn as if I'm looking through them.

I spotted them entering the room a little while ago and that's when I snuck a quick look. The guys didn't notice me poking my head in here, or I'm sure they would've had one of their minions drag me in. I've spent the hours before Sariah and the guys arrived dodging the Saints' hired hands and watching my cell like a demented person, waiting for Darrow to call.

I don't have complete faith he can do this, and I hope I haven't made a worthless deal with the devil, but I haven't written him off just yet.

The Arrows despise The Sainthood, and I'm relying on that hatred to work to my advantage. But I'm under no illusion when it comes to Darrow's loyalty. He's loyal to himself first and foremost, and I'm only a means to an end, irrespective of his professions of love.

Darrow would throw his own mother under the bus if he thought there was something in it for him.

I swivel on Saint's lap, feeling his solid erection press against my ass, as I look down at him. His eyes darken, and the hold around my waist strengthens. "What?" he asks in a guarded tone and it's almost comical.

I sweep my fingers across his brow. "I think the drugs must have gone to your head. Why else would you invite Finn, Parker, Brooklyn, and Beth? Losing your touch, *Saintly*?"

He smirks, and his tongue darts out as he purposely trails his gaze to the mattress where Parker is blowing Finn while his bestie Brooklyn fucks her from behind.

Beth is lying flat on her back underneath them, sucking on Parker's tits as Brooklyn fingers her cunt. From the glazed looks in their eyes, I can tell they are all completely wasted.

Saint watches me watching with a calculated edge to his expression.

"Nothing I do is without reason, princess." He pauses for a second, his eyes meeting Parker's as she turns her head in his direction, eye-fucking Saint while she's sucking Finn's cock and taking Brooklyn's dick for a ride.

She really is a conniving, disloyal bitch.

"Parker has something I want," he admits.

"Well, it can't be her mouth because I've seen grannies suck popsicles with more skill than that."

Caz chuckles. Galen smirks. And Theo warns me with a sharp look. The latter's attempts to ingratiate himself to me are wearing thin.

Saint's eyes glint with wicked intent. "You could do better?"

"In my fucking sleep." I pin sultry eyes on Caz. "I don't remember Caz complaining." I deliberately omit mention of Galen even though I sucked his cock too, because neither of us need reminding of that.

"Our princess gives good head," he confirms, waggling his brows.

Galen snarls. "You can put that on your résumé. At least you'll have one skill set you can brag about."

"I have a 4.1 GPA and plenty of skills I could brag about." Sliding my blade out, I lean toward him, brandishing it in his face. "Care for a demonstration of my knife skills? I can carve your pretty face up quicker than you can draw a breath."

Saint takes my wrist, pulling me back from his cousin, his eyes roaming appreciatively over my Strider SMF. "Do you always bring blades to parties?"

"Does a bear shit in the woods?" I quip, sliding my blade back into the holder strapped to my thigh.

He grins, holding my gaze prisoner with that lethal lens of his, and I return his stare. "You made your point, princess."

"And you still haven't answered my question." I keep my eyes locked on his. "Why do you need Parker, and don't insinuate it's her cunt or her cocksucking skills because we both know that's bullshit."

He plants my feet on the ground and stands. Clasping my hand, he walks me down the stage toward Finn and his pathetic crew, while I try to ignore the tremors zipping up and down my arm from his touch.

He stops in front of them, keeping a tight hold of my hand.

Finn glances warily at Saint before sharing a look with Brooklyn. Brooklyn slows his thrusting pace while Parker's mouth makes a loud popping sound as she releases Finn's dick.

"Don't stop," Saint says. "The princess is going to give you a few tips." He shoots me a wicked grin.

Asshole.

"She deems your cocksucking skills lacking."

Her eyes narrow calculatingly. "I could always give you a personal demonstration, Saint," she purrs, ignoring the scowl her boyfriend sends her way. "And you can make your own assessment."

Saint scrubs a hand along his prickly jaw, looking like he might actually be considering it. "Tempting," he says, winking at her. Finn growls, and he truly is an idiot. Saint grins like all his birthdays have come at once. "But we have a rule about sharing."

Parker's eyes legit light up. "I can blow you all." Her eagerness is spew-worthy.

"Parker!" Finn snaps, glaring at his girlfriend as his erection noticeably wilts.

"You're used to being shared," Saint adds, licking his lips as if he's genuinely interested. "We'll put it to a vote."

"Like fucking hell you will," Finn spits, swaying a little as he attempts to face up to Saint. "She's mine."

"News flash." Saint grins viciously. "I don't think your slut got the memo." Saint reaches down, caressing her cheek, and she stares adoringly at him despite his slur.

Unbridled rage courses through me, and I'm done pussyfooting around. "It's her loss, Finn," I cut in, keeping my voice level and my face devoid of the red-hot jealousy slaying me on the inside. "And my gain."

I yank my hand out of Saint's, shoving him aside so I can press up against a very naked Finn. "You know I suck like a pro and can go all night. How long did we fuck at Robbin's party that time?" I pretend to count in my head. "I believe it was six hours straight." I smile seductively, piercing him with a lustful look. "I'm game for a repeat if you are."

Parker loses her shit, as I predicted. "You fucked that stupid slut?" she screeches at Finn, jumping up and lunging at me.

But she's high, drunk, and a fucking imbecile, and I'm way faster on my feet. I have her in a headlock with my knife pressed to her neck before she's even realized it. "Why am I the slut and your boyfriend isn't? Huh? Haven't you heard it takes two to tango?" I smile smugly at Saint as I spy Galen, Caz, and Theo approaching from behind. "To be clear, he wasn't your boyfriend at the time. We were both single and free to fuck our brains out all night long, which we sooooo did." I press the knife into her neck as she wriggles against me, and the blade cuts her skin.

She screams like I've just gutted her, and I remove my knife from her throat before I accidentally kill her.

If I end up in jail, I want it to be for something worthwhile.

Stepping back, I thrust her at Finn. "You deserve a fucking medal for putting up with that shit. I'm guessing her pussy is a better ride than her mouth because there sure as fuck isn't anything else going for her."

"Galen. Escort our guests to the front door. They've overstayed their welcome," Saint instructs in a clipped voice. The veins in his neck are bulging, and the venom oozing from his eyes says he wants to throttle me and Finn.

"What?" Parker shrieks, her heavy tits wobbling with the motion. "You can't throw me out! I came through for you."

"And you'll be rewarded in another lifetime for your cooperation," Caz says, smirking.

"I'll fucking warn them. I'll—" Caz slams his hand over her mouth, silencing her before she says too much.

Warn who and about what? My mind starts working overtime. *What does she have or who does she know that gives Parker leverage with the Saints?* I need to dig into her connections to see if I can find out.

Finn looks at her with disdain, grabbing his clothes and stalking toward the door without giving her another look. Beth slides her hand in Brooklyn's, and they walk off too.

Saint pins his full death glare on Parker as he pushes his face into hers, and she shrinks back from the potent evil radiating from his gaze. "You open that useless mouth of yours and it will be the last thing you ever do." His voice drips with menace and lethal promise.

She gulps, nodding, her eyes wide with fear.

"Get her the fuck out of my house," Saint says to Theo.

"*Your* house?" I plant my hands on my hips, giving him some serious stink eye.

Parker offers no protest as Theo takes her arm, scooping up her clothes and hauling her out of the room. I'm sure once she recovers she'll come after me like a rabid junkie seeking her next hit, and I curse my damn emotions for getting the better of me. Parker doesn't even rate on the scale of threats I'm dealing with, but she's an annoying gnat I could do without. I should've shut my mouth and ignored my jealousy.

Saint lifts his head, piercing me with a look so full of hatred it has to be seen to be believed. His eyes are like laser beams slicing me clear in half, and my heart picks up pace as my body floods with adrenaline at the impending threat. It takes iron-strong willpower to hold my ground when he pushes up into me, wrapping his hands around the nape of my neck and squeezing in a way he knows hurts.

"My house," he grits out. "My pussy." He grabs my crotch through my dress. "My rules." His face darkens and his chest vibrates with naked anger, and God help me, I'm seriously fucked in the head because it should completely terrify me, but instead, my panties are drenched and I ache for him as my body craves his in a way I don't fully understand.

Saint oozes power, authority, danger, and pure raw sex in equal measures, and I'm attracted to all parts of him. There's no point trying to deny it anymore, and maybe, Sariah is right, and I need to change the playbook.

"I will hurt you, Harlow." He digs his nails into my neck and squeezes my crotch. My body thrums in a mixture of agony and ecstasy. My heart pounds in my chest, and blood shoots through my veins, electrifying me. "I will make your life intolerable." He shoves me off him forcefully, and I lose my balance, falling back on the bed. He crawls over me, and I hold myself still as he hovers on top of me. "You will obey me, or the torture you suffered as a kid will pale in comparison to the suffering I'll inflict on your body."

THE SAINTHOOD

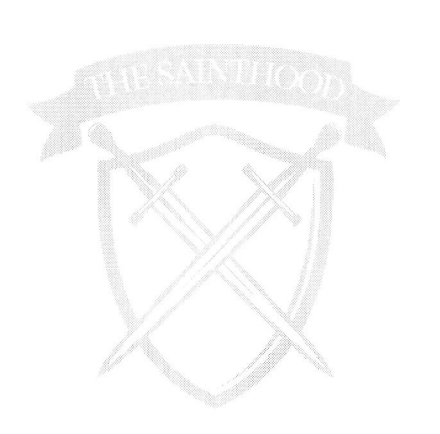

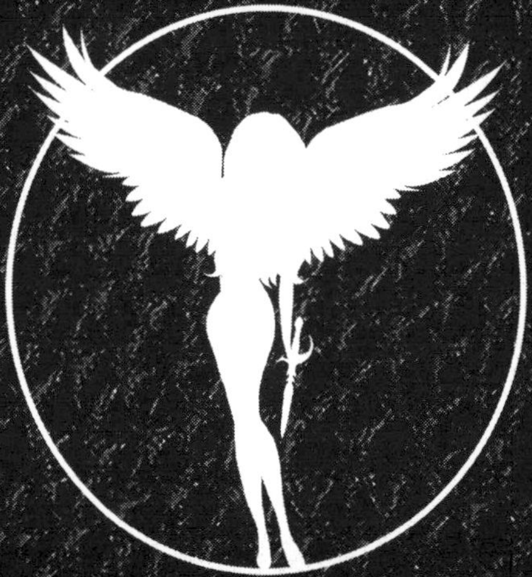

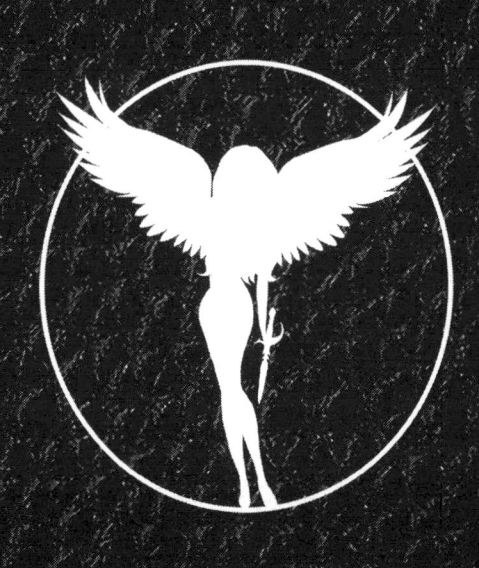

CHAPTER 15

*H*E REMEMBERS. *H*E *knows.* That's all I'm thinking after Saint tosses me out of the room and I make my way back to my friends.

I've never blamed that boy for anything, but now I know who the man is, I'm wondering if I've been wrong about it all these years. It only adds to the fucked-up-ness in my head, and I'm trying to figure out how this fits into the puzzle as I pick my way through the living room, searching for Sariah's blonde head.

An arm shoots up from a section in the top left corner of the room, and I spot Emmett waving at me.

"You're alive!" Sariah says, handing me a beer.

"And still in one piece," Sean adds, giving me a quick onceover to ensure I'm uninjured.

"We saw Parker, Finn, and company being kicked out," Sariah adds.

"Man, that chick has some set of lungs on her," Emmett supplies, sipping his beer. "She was screeching like a banshee."

"She is going to be gunning for my ass at school on

Monday," I say, quickly filling them in on what went down.

"She can try," Sariah says. "You were right to put her in her place. Bitch needs taking down a few notches."

"I'm more worried about you pushing Saint too far," Sean says, shifting on the couch and wearing a troubled expression. "There's been a lot of talk at school, and these fuckers don't mess around. You need to be careful, Lo."

"I know. He hasn't gained his reputation for no reason. Rumors say the woods behind Prestwick are full of his kills."

"Full of *all* their kills," Sean says, lowering his voice and scanning the room.

"Murder is only one of their skill sets," Sariah says, her voice laced with anger. "I've heard they're fond of torture, extortion, setting fire to shit, and all-round mayhem. We can never underestimate them."

"They should never underestimate me," I supply as my phone pings. I read the message from Darrow and stand. "I need to do something. I'll be back in a few. Keep an eye on the assholes, and message me if they move out of that room."

I grab my jacket from the hall closet and trade my stilettos for my boots before slipping out the back through the kitchen. The noise of the party fades as I cut across the grass, aiming for the pool house. I cast a glance behind me, ensuring I'm not being followed, before I step inside. A form moves in the pitch-black, and I draw the drapes before switching one of the lamps on.

"Do you have it?" I ask, moving toward him.

He holds out his hand, thrusting a piece of paper into my palm. "He's reliable, and his work is of a high standard."

I fold the paper carefully and tuck it down the front of my dress. "Thanks."

"You'll need serious cash."

"Not a problem." Dad left me a sizable inheritance, and the compensation I received from the kidnapping was invested wisely, so a large chunk of change landed in my bank account the instant I turned eighteen.

"When will it be set up?"

"I'm putting it in motion tonight."

"I want full access."

I snort. "Not happening. I'll pass the intel over as soon as I have it."

He steps up close. "I'm counting on you to come through, Lo. My rep is on the line if I don't deliver."

"I said I got this, and I do. I just don't know how long it'll take me."

"Don't make it too long," he warns before lowering his mouth to mine.

I push him off before his lips reach mine. "Don't mistake what this is, Dar. It's purely business. Go home to Tempest." I stand, stalking toward the double doors. "I'll be in touch."

I message the others as I'm walking back toward the house, asking them to meet me in my bedroom.

They are there first, and I close and lock the door behind me after checking the coast is clear. "I need your help," I say, propping my butt up against my dresser. "I'm planting cameras in the guys' rooms, and I need lookouts. Two downstairs, and one up here."

"Emmett and I will cover downstairs," Sean says. "It will seem more natural for Sariah to be upstairs, in case of discovery." He grins at his friend. "And it'll keep Emmett alive."

Thank fuck, the Saints implemented a strict "no upstairs" policy and ensured everyone was aware of that when they arrived. The orgy room helped eliminate any complaints—as long as people have somewhere to fuck, they don't care.

"Cool. Message me if you spot any of the goon squad coming upstairs." The guys leave while I move to the closet to retrieve my box of goodies. I extract the small bag Diesel procured for me and rejoin my bestie in my bedroom. "Can you keep watch out in the hallway and alert me if you hear anything suspicious?"

"Got it."

All the guys have locked their rooms, as expected, but I know how to pick a lock in less than sixty seconds. I'm guessing the guys do too, but I haven't installed the new padlock I bought for my room yet as I want to see what form of surveillance they have in store for me.

I'm scanning my room daily, but so far, there are no cameras and no monitoring devices on my cell phone or my tablet. I know it's only a matter of time before they try something, so I'm letting them plant what they want, and then, I'll figure out how best to use that to my advantage.

Sariah grins as I break into Saint's room first. Using the flashlight on my cell, I do a lightning-fast scan of his room.

It's unbelievably tidy for a dude.

The large king-sized bed is dressed in crumpled black silk sheets, and the previous gray walls have been painted black and red. Posters of naked chicks, heavy metal rockers, and MMA wrestlers cover the walls. Some schoolbooks litter the top of his desk, and he has a locked notepad and pen by his bed. Apart from some clothes on the floor and on the back of his chair, there is nothing else left in plain sight, and this room gives nothing away. I wish I had time to search his closet and the bedside tables, but today's mission is to install the cameras and get the hell out before I'm caught.

I unscrew the light socket by the door, drilling a pin-shaped hole in the plastic and inserting the tiny camera chip like Diesel has shown me.

He said this is the latest high-tech equipment, and it will give me image and audio access. After I secure the socket back in place, ensuring it's tight, I step back to inspect it. There's no way you'd spot it unless you were looking for it or examining it under a microscope. The guys might find them, especially if they scan the room for devices, but it's unlikely they know I have access to this type of equipment and the intel to install it. I doubt they're expecting it, and I'm banking on that.

I leave Saint's room, moving on to Galen's much messier room. This place is a pigsty. He has clothes and empty pizza boxes and bottles strewn around the place, and it reeks of cigarette smoke and stale beer. A guitar propped against the wall surprises me, and I wonder if he's any good or if it's more for show.

I install the camera and move into Theo's room next.

Predictably, his room is crammed full of technical equipment and books, and it's even neater than Saint's room. I'm just locking his door when my cell pings the same time Sariah's does.

"Shit. Galen is heading this way," she confirms as I read the same message.

"At least, I got three of them installed. I'll get into Caz's room another time." I loop my arm through hers, and we head downstairs, passing a grumpy-looking Galen on the stairs. He ignores us, and we ignore him, and that suits me just fine.

"Why is he always so crabby?" she asks when we hit the bottom of the stairs and he's disappeared upstairs.

"Who knows." I shrug.

"It must be in his DNA."

"He wasn't that ill-tempered as a kid," I say, remembering that time we met as clearly as if it was yesterday. "If I had to guess, I'd say it's to do with his home life. His mom turned into an out-and-out junkie after his sister died, and then, her husband overdosed a couple years later."

"That's no fucking excuse," she hisses, and I rub her arm in understanding. Sariah lost her entire family, and it hasn't turned her into a cruel, moody bitch. "Everyone has shit to deal with."

"I'm not making excuses for him, and you're right. There are plenty of people with troubled or dysfunctional backgrounds and they're not assholes like Galen Lennox."

My friends leave a short while later, and I wander into the kitchen to grab a snack to bring to my room. I avoid going through the living room where things are pretty out of control, and I go nowhere near the orgy room for fear of what I might find.

Remembering Saint pressed up against me, and the feel of

his hands on my body, has me horny and pissed, and it's not a good combination. Briefly, I consider joining the party and finding someone to fuck, but it'd be selfish to bring the wrath of The Sainthood down on some innocent just because I want to get laid.

I guess it will be my purple electric friend and porn for me tonight.

I make a sandwich, grab a bottle of beer and a bottle of water, and walk out to the hallway.

My eyes drink in the scene awaiting me with interest as I approach the stairs.

Caz is halfway up the steps, with his back stuck to the wall, as he fends off the advances of some young kid. She is wearing the skimpiest dress, and she's plastered in makeup, but it's obvious she's real young. She can't be any older than fifteen, max.

She's pawing at him like he's hers to do with as she pleases, and he's struggling to shake her off in his inebriated state. Which is pretty fucking hilarious if you think about it, because it's like the Hulk facing off against Thumbelina, and he could stomp on her without any effort. For a split second, I consider leaving him there. But I intervene for the girl's sake. She's way too young to get caught up in their shit.

"Hey, jailbait." I call out to her as I climb the stairs. "Get lost before I call your parents."

She glares at me. "Fuck off, ho, and mind your own business."

Wow.

I walk past them and up to the top of the stairs, setting my plate and the two bottles down. Then, I calmly retrace my steps, taking the girl by the arm and physically pulling her off Caz. She lets loose a string of colorful expletives. "I'm doing you a favor," I say, dragging her down the stairs screaming. "He's one of the Saints, and you can't manhandle him like that. Not unless you've got a fucking death wish."

"Get off me, you jealous bitch." She wriggles in my arms

as we reach the lobby.

"Think whatever you want," I say, opening the front door. "But this is my house, and you're no longer welcome." I shove her outside. "Say hi to the *Paw Patrol* for me." She flips me the bird as I slam the door in her face.

Caz chuckles. "*Paw Patrol*?"

"It's a popular kids' show," I confirm, walking up the stairs to meet him. "These kids I used to babysit were hooked on it. Mind you, they were only four and five, so I doubt she appreciates my comment." I shrug, uncaring if I offended the little minx. She'll thank me for it one day.

He strokes the hard-on in his pants. "I knew she was too fucking young, but try telling that to my cock."

I slap his chest, and I almost break a bone against the rock-hard wall of muscle I meet. "Jailbait wouldn't have sated your needs," I purr, pushing my chest against his. "But I sure as hell can."

The heated look he gives me confirms he's down with this plan, but the conflict in his eyes says I'll need to try harder. I palm his dick through his jeans. "Unless you don't want my lips wrapped around your cock while I play with your balls and finger your ass?" I tease.

"Jesus, fuck." He grabs my butt, pulling me in tight against his erection as his eyes drop to my mouth. "I'm horny as hell, and I never got to drill your cunt the last time. I'm game, babe, but Saint will rip me a new one if I touch you."

I scoff, outlining the shape of his dick through the denim with my finger. "One, he's constantly telling me I belong to the almighty Saints, and two, you always let that asshole cockblock you?" I unbutton his jeans and slip my hand inside, my brows climbing to my hairline as my fingers meet hot flesh. "Commando, huh?" I say, impressed, as I begin stroking him.

"Aw, fuck. Stop," he mumbles. It's a pathetic effort, and we both know it.

I snicker. "If you'd said that like you meant it, I might've taken pity on you."

I wouldn't.

He's horny, and he wants me, and I'm horny, and I want him too. It's been a while since I had a release, and I know he's a good lay. We can get off, and I can stick two fingers to Saint while I'm at it.

Win-win, if you ask me.

"We're not allowed to fuck girls without the others," he confirms, and I nearly fall down the stairs in shock.

I know they like to share, but I didn't think they had strict rules. That seems extreme and unfair; although maybe, it's a rule to stop anyone from catching feelings. To ensure no girls interfere with gang business. Sounds like something Neo might've introduced, considering how my mom fucked him over back in the day.

"And it's you," he cryptically adds. "He'll chop my cock off for sure if he finds out."

Now, I'm even more determined to screw him. I pump him harder, and he thrusts his hips into my hand, moaning as he rocks back and forth, and I know I have him by the balls.

Literally.

Keeping my hand wrapped around his cock, I stretch up and kiss the corner of his mouth. "It can be our little secret." I slide my hand down his dick and fondle his balls, silently high-fiving myself when his eyes roll back in his head. I kiss the other corner of his mouth. "Saint never has to know."

If Caz wasn't as stoned or as drunk as he is right now, I would never get away with this. But he's aching and desperate, and it's no secret guys are ruled by their dicks. I unbutton his jeans fully, free his cock, and dip my head down, laving my tongue against the precum beading at the tip of his crown.

"Sweet fucking Jesus. Do that again."

I give him a quick lick before straightening up. I'm not doing this on the stairs and risking Saint coming along and putting a stop to it.

My pussy is thoroughly invested now, and I need to fuck him. I tuck his cock back in his jeans, take his hand, and pull him up the stairs, passing by my sandwich and drinks. I'm a different kind of hungry now, so I leave my food behind without a second glance.

After he's opened his bedroom door, I forcefully push him inside. I close the door and shove him toward the bed, meeting his lusty grin with one of my own. He grabs hold of me, lifting me up by my ass, and I screech as he throws me down on the bed. "Prepare yourself, princess," he rasps, running his beefy hands up my bare calves. "Because I'm going to fuck you like you've never been fucked before."

THE SAINTHOOD

CHAPTER 16

WE'RE NAKED, LYING sideways, head to feet, on Caz's bed, pleasuring one another with our mouths and our fingers when he stops me. "I want to come in your pussy this time," he rasps before swiping his hot tongue along my slit. I grip his mammoth thighs, running my hands over the solid block of muscle, while I slowly trail my lips up and down his shaft. "Get up here and ride my face," he commands as his dick pops out of my mouth.

I crawl over his gorgeous ripped body, positioning myself over his face. Before I can lower myself down, he grips my hips, yanking my pussy to his mouth, and dives in.

Fucking hell.

I grab the headboard as he frantically works me over, his tongue lapping, his teeth nipping, and his mouth sucking, and it takes mere seconds before I'm shattering into pieces above him.

He's that good.

My legs quiver, my limbs wobbling like Jell-O as I rest my head against the headboard, trying to regulate my breathing.

"Ho. Lee. Shit," I pant, looking down at him. His tempting lips glisten from my juices, sending a new flood of heat gushing to my core. "You are so fucking good at that."

He smirks, reaching up to pull my body down flush against his. "I've had plenty of practice."

"Just what every woman wants to hear when she's in bed with a guy," I deadpan before planting my mouth on his.

We ravish one another, our tongues dueling for control, as our lips crash together, over and over again. The stubble on his cheeks chafes the skin around my mouth, but I welcome the pleasurable sting.

"I need your pussy, princess," he murmurs while sucking on my neck. I moan and writhe against him as delicious tremors of pleasure ripple along my skin. He kneads my tits, his fingers expertly rolling my nipples, and I'm so aroused again I'm close to climaxing already. "Fuck me, babe," he demands, clasping my face in his meaty hands. "Fuck me like your life depends on it."

"Your wish is my command," I quip, sliding down his hard body, stopping to lick his chiseled abs on the way.

He hands me a condom, and I roll it on before situating myself over his cock, watching his expression as I slowly lower onto him. His brown eyes smolder with lust as I take him all the way in, and we both groan in unison. "Feels so fucking good."

"Ride me, princess. Show me how much you want my cock."

His dirty talk is like a match to a flame, and I lift up and slam back down on him repeatedly, quickening my pace as I use my thighs and hips to control my movements.

"Fuck, yeah, princess. Hug my cock tight, just like that."

I squeeze my inner muscles as I bounce up and down on him and his hands glide up my body.

He roughly grabs my tits, tugging and flicking at my nipples, and the pleasure-pain sensation reverberates throughout my body.

I grind on top of him, slightly changing the angle so the tip of his cock is hitting the perfect spot, and the only sounds in the room are our joint grunts and the slapping of skin against skin.

Until the door crashes open and I whip my head around, inwardly smiling as Saint stalks across the room with a thunderous look on his face. I ignore him, turning back around and refocusing on Caz as I increase my speed and start super fucking him like he's the last man on the planet and I need to orgasm to survive.

I'm ripped off him without ceremony, and I thrash about as Saint lifts me up by the waist, pulling me away from the bed.

"Dude, seriously?" Caz glares at his leader. "You couldn't let me finish?"

"Shut your fucking mouth." Saint's entire body is shaking behind me, and he radiates anger. "Blue balls are the least of your worries." Saint spins me around in his arms, thrusting me at Galen. "Lock her in her room."

Galen clamps his arms around me, holding me in a vise grip. "Let me go, asshole. I'm perfectly capable of walking myself to my room." I wriggle in Galen's arms as he, predictably, glowers at me, throwing a look in Caz's direction. Caz is sitting up in the bed, his face flush with desire, his dick proudly jutting out, and my pussy pulses with need.

Fuck that fucking motherfucking cockblocking asshole Saint.

"Rain check, babe," I call out, blowing him a kiss, but Caz doesn't even look my way.

He's too highly strung, currently focusing his energies on a brutal face-off with Saint, and neither of them is paying me any attention.

"Highly fucking doubtful," Galen drawls before throwing me over his shoulder and slapping a firm hand on my ass as he obeys his boss and walks out of the room. I lift my head up and glare at Theo as he follows us.

Galen opens my door, kicking it wide with his booted foot,

as he storms into my room, tossing me down on the bed. I'm madder and hornier than earlier, and I'm not ready to let this go. Reaching over to my bedside table, I remove my purple electronic friend from the drawer and switch it on.

Galen stops retreating, watching me with hostile desire, his green eyes sparking with heat, his nostrils flaring, as I bring the vibrator to the apex of my thighs.

Theo is propped against the door, his eyes not fixated on his tablet for once, also watching intently.

I flop down flat on my back and spread my legs wide so they have a front row seat as I slide the device into my vagina, pushing it in as far as it will go. With my free hand, I fondle one breast, rubbing my nipple, as I pump the vibrator in and out of my pussy, moaning and writhing for added effect.

I maintain eye contact with Galen. He wears his usual hateful mask, but he can't disguise the desire in his eyes or the tent in his jeans. I continue moving the vibrator in and out of my pussy as I sit up and maneuver toward the edge of the bed. I look at him through hooded eyes, my gaze flitting from his lips to his cock. "Hate sex is my favorite," I purr, removing the device and placing it on the bed before standing. I close the gap between us, pushing my body into his as I stroke his hard-on through his jeans. "And I want a real cock to finish the job." I unbutton the top button of his jeans, sliding my hand inside his boxers to wrap around his erection. He jolts in my hand, his body moving in sync with my movements, even though conflict rages on his face.

He hates his attraction to me as much as I hate my attraction to him.

Theo is silent, but I daren't look at him because it won't take much to break Galen out of his lustful daze, and I intend to milk this as far as I can take it.

If Saint was mad about Caz and me fucking, he will lose his shit if I seduce his cousin too.

Taking a risk, I stretch up and kiss Galen hard on the mouth as I pump his shaft in his boxers.

He doesn't kiss me back at first, his hips thrusting as I stroke him harder, but then, something snaps inside him, and he starts moving his mouth against mine, biting on my lip and drawing blood as he devours my lips with savage brutality. I whimper into his mouth, and he lifts me up. My legs automatically encircle his waist, and we fall back on the bed, mouths suctioned together. I rip his T-shirt from his body, while he fumbles with his jeans. His jeans and boxers are halfway down his legs, and his big cock is heavy in my hand, when Saint cockblocks me for the second time tonight.

"Has everyone lost their motherfucking minds?!" he roars, stalking into the room and yanking Galen off me. Galen trips on his clothing, falling on his butt and scowling as Saint lifts me up off the bed.

Pulling back the covers, he roughly shoves me onto the mattress as my vibrator rolls onto the floor. He tugs the covers up to my chin before retrieving my electronic friend and tossing it at me. "Knock yourself out, princess, because that's the only cock you'll be riding the rest of tonight."

"You're an asshole," I calmly reply, sitting up and letting the covers pool at my waist. His eyes graze my tits, and the veins in his arms bulge as he flexes his fists. "What's the big deal? You've claimed me as Saint property and forbidden me from fucking anyone else. Unless you want my pussy to shrivel up and die, that means I only have three guys to fuck, because we all know you're off-limits, stepbrother dearest." I fling the covers off and stand. "Or is that the real issue, huh?" I plant my hands on his chest and look up at him. "You want to fuck me, Saint, but you can't, so no one else can have me either. Is that it?"

"Shut up, Lo."

He steps back, and I walk forward, eliminating the space between us. I palm the bulge in his jeans. "Your body doesn't lie."

"I'm a horny guy. You're a naked slut shoving it in my face. Of course, my body will react."

"I'm not a slut," I say, keeping my voice neutral, as I purposely step back. "And I'd rather fuck my vibrator than fuck you."

He closes the distance this time, grabbing me around the throat and forcing my head back. "Careful, princess. Don't poke the beast unless you're prepared to play."

He lets me go without another word, and they leave, slamming the door shut behind them.

I walk to my bathroom with a big-ass smile on my face and then finger myself to orgasm in the shower while I figuratively pat myself on the back for a successful first seductive mission.

The smirk is wiped off my face when I emerge from my bathroom to the sound of a drill at my door. I pull at the door handle, but it doesn't budge. I tug on it a few more times, but the result is the same. The bastards have installed a lock on the outside of my door, and I'm trapped.

My hands ball into fists and anger pummels my insides until I remember the cameras. I dash to my tablet, pulling up the app and quickly configuring the settings. I pull up the screens, zooming in on Galen's room because that's where it's all going down.

I plug in my headphones and settle back with a fresh smug grin on my face.

"Is it done?" Saint asks when Caz steps into the room.

"Yes," he snarls, leaning against the wall and glaring at his leader.

"You, I understand because you lose every brain cell when you're smashed," Saint says, poking his finger in Caz's direction. "But you," he adds, narrowing his eyes at Galen, "know better. Or is the venom all an act?"

Galen seethes. His arms are folded across his chest, and a vein throbs in his neck. "You know I hate the bitch, but she's hot. Sue me if my dick got hard."

His words penetrate deep, and pain slices across my chest. I can't believe this is all because I refused to make out with him that day. There's got to be more to his hatred than that. But our paths never crossed afterward. Not until now.

"What happened with you two?" Theo asks what I can't.

"Why should I spill my guts when you're still lying about what went down between you and her," Galen tosses back in his face.

Theo runs a hand along the back of his neck, and messy blond waves fall into his face, shielding his eyes.

"I don't give a fuck about what happened in the past," Saint barks. "What matters is right now. Sinner will be fucking pissed if we don't deliver results soon."

I sit up straighter in my chair, and blood rushes to my head.

I wasn't sure how much Neo had told them, but it seems they're fully up to speed.

Shit.

My mind whirls as I run ideas through my brain.

"I told you this wouldn't work," Theo says, swiveling in his chair. "She's not like most girls. She's smart as much as she's sexy, and she's not easily intimidated."

"She's a formidable enemy, and it's clear there's much we don't know." Saint's tone is borderline reverential, and warmth seeps into my tense bones.

Fuck. When did I get so needy that the words of an asshole have me practically blushing?

Saint runs his hands over his cropped dirty-blond head, looking deep in thought. "We need to revise our strategy," he says after a few beats. "And I think I know how." A malicious glint twinkles in his eye. "Party's over. Clear the house out."

The guys move without question, stopping at the door when their saintly leader speaks again. "What happened tonight won't happen again." His threat drips with hidden meaning. "No one fucks her without my consent."

They all nod, and I scowl at the screen, flipping the bird at the cockblocking jerk.

"It's clear we've underestimated the princess." He cracks his knuckles, smiling devilishly. "That's the last time she gains the upper hand."

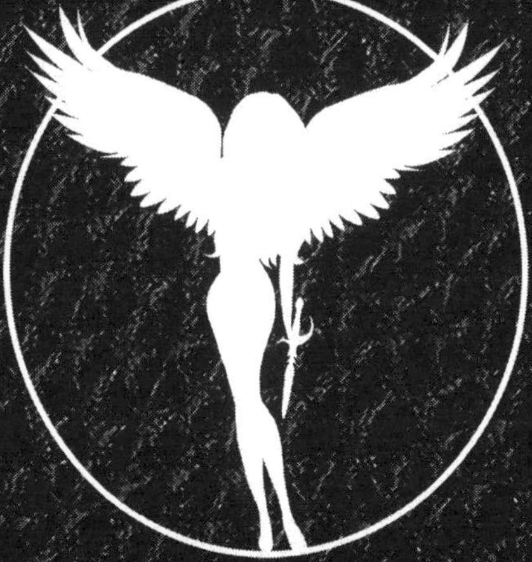

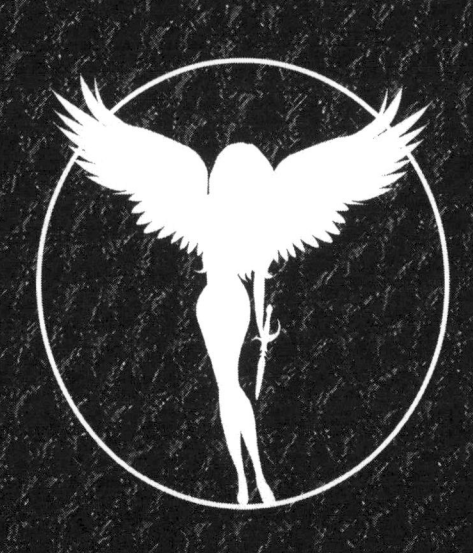

THE SAINTHOOD

CHAPTER 17

THE ASSHOLES CLEAR the house and head out, leaving me to my own devices. I dress in black yoga pants, a hoodie, and my Vans and climb out the window. I shimmy down the drainpipe and enter the house from the rear using my keys. Finding Dad's drill in the garage, I head up the stairs. Before I remove the giant padlock from the front of my door, I break into Caz's room and install the last camera.

I stash the padlock in a cupboard in my closet before crawling into bed in the early hours of the morning. The guys still aren't back, and I want to stay up to see their reaction to the missing lock, but my eyes have other ideas, and I pass out without conscious thought.

MOM AND NEO return from their mini vacay Sunday evening looking all loved up, and it turns my stomach. He misses no opportunity to grope her in my presence, and I know it's a blatant move to force my hand, but I've boxed my emotions up again, and I keep my distance from everyone.

They insist on taking us out to dinner that night, and I pick at the food on my plate, a silent bystander as they act like the fucking Brady bunch. Well, a tattooed, pierced, hotheaded, scary-looking version of the legendary family.

The guys purposely ignore me all week, and I wonder if this is their new tactic. Can't say I'm complaining. I still sit with them in the cafeteria at lunch, at our new table, at the head of the room, but I stick to chatting with my friends, while they entertain the never-ending line of gushing fans.

Their party was a huge success, and now, everyone toes the line. The Saints reign supreme over Lowell High, and it's embarrassing for Finn how easily they managed to take over his patch.

No wonder, he's keeping a low profile and hasn't shown his face in here all week.

The guys are barely at the house, sometimes only coming home just before we need to get up for school, and the camera footage, so far, is giving me jack shit. Dar has messaged me a couple times, and he's not pleased at the lack of progress, but I can hardly pull the intel out of my ass. I remind him that patience is a virtue and ignore his texts the rest of the time.

At some point, Theo installed a camera behind the TV in my room, but I don't remove it, enjoying tormenting them by prancing around my room naked at every opportune moment and indulging in a nightly live porn show involving various scraps of lingerie and an assortment of different dildos and vibrators.

But I do remove the tracking device on my cars and my cell, and my firewall blocks Theo's attempts to gain remote access to my tablet.

I'm not naïve. His skills vastly outweigh mine, so it's only a matter of time before he infiltrates my system.

Hence why I spent the earlier part of the week transferring all important documents to the cloud and wiping the tablet clean. I can access the cameras in their room via the cloud too, so I'm feeling pretty confident in my self-protection skills as I head into the city after school ends on Friday to execute the next part of my plan.

At least, their lack of interest affords me time to set some things in motion. Diesel already arranged for a guy to move Dad's cars to the cabin, and the text he sent to my burner cell earlier confirmed the op was a success.

Honestly, watching the expressions on the guys' faces when they entered the half-empty garage this morning was priceless and worth the pretty penny it cost me to get Dad's cars to safety.

I pull into the familiar law offices a half hour after leaving school with an ache in my heart. I cut the engine and sit in the SUV for a few minutes, looking up at the impressive glass building with a weight pressing down on my chest.

All of Dad's colleagues attended his funeral, but the only person who has reached out to me in the months since is Lincoln, Dad's assistant and righthand man.

They were close.

More akin to best friends than work colleagues, and I know Dad respected and trusted him. Which is why I've taken a risk, and I'm on my way up to meet him.

I get out of the car, grabbing my bag and heading toward the entrance. After I check in at the plush reception desk, I'm kept waiting for a few minutes, and then, Lincoln appears, enveloping me in a big hug before guiding me to one of the smaller meeting rooms on the ground floor.

"You look good, Harlow, but how are you really?" he asks when we are seated across a table from one another.

"I'm doing okay. I still can't believe he's gone, and I miss him so much, but I have to keep going. I know that's what he'd want for me." I shrug, downplaying it.

Truth is, I don't let myself think about Dad too much.

Because it has the potential to break me, and I can't let that happen.

"This place isn't the same without him," Lincoln says. "He

always had this all-consuming presence, and he commanded a room just by stepping into it. More than that, I respected and admired him, and he inspired me in a way no one else ever has."

"He was one in a million, and he'd be proud to know that."

He taps a finger off the top of the table. "I heard about your mom's engagement." He scrutinizes my face closely. "It seems a bit…sudden."

I snort. "That's one way of putting it." I sit up straighter, leaning my elbows on the table as I peer earnestly into his eyes. "You know who's she engaged to?" He slowly nods. "And you know who he is?" He nods again, but I'm not surprised. Dad and I may not have talked about it, but I know The Sainthood was pulling his strings. I guessed Lincoln would be clued in.

"I debated about whether to contact you when I heard the news," he volunteers. "But I didn't know if you knew."

"That The Sainthood were the ones behind my kidnapping and Dad was under their thumb?" I ask, because why beat around the bush.

His eyes pop wide. "Shit. You knew that?"

"Only relatively recently," I confirm. "And I never talked to Dad about it."

I regret that now.

I regret so much of what has transpired over the years.

But I can't turn back the clock. I can't undo my mistakes.

I can only try to make them right.

"He would hate that, you know." His expression turns sad. "He tried so hard to protect you."

"I know he did, Linc." I knot my hands on my lap, slouching a bit in my chair. "He worked overtime to protect me and to equip me with skills whereby I can defend and protect myself, but he should have confided in me, because this isn't over just because he's not here."

Linc's brow furrows, and he leans in closer, his chest pressing against the edge of the table. "What exactly do you mean?"

"Why do you think Neo 'Sinner' Lennox is now engaged to my mom?"

"Neo has always been hung up on your mom, Lo. It's how the whole sorry mess started."

Now, it's my turn to look shocked. "You know about that?"

He nods. "I know a little. Your dad was always very circumspect in what he told me. He never wanted to involve me, but I figured it out not long after I came to work for him. He was using his connections to obtain confidential information which enabled The Sainthood to avoid prosecution for crimes everyone knows they have committed."

It was a lot more than that, but I don't articulate that thought.

"Did my mom know?"

He shakes his head. "Your father protected her too. He didn't want her falling back into Neo's clutches for fear of what he would do in retaliation." A pained expression washes over his face. "He would be so disappointed in me," he adds, his voice barely louder than a whisper.

"Why? What have you done?"

"I should have warned her to stay away from him, but, quite frankly, he scares me."

"She's not your responsibility, and she knows what she's getting herself into. She spent years with that monster. She's not an innocent." My cutting tone is obvious in the extreme.

He reaches out, taking my hand in his. "She doesn't know they were the ones who kidnapped you. If she did, she'd never let that bastard anywhere near you."

I snort, and my tone turns bitter. "She doesn't care about my feelings, and I very much doubt she's as ignorant as you think."

He jerks back, extracting his hand from mine. "You think she knows?"

I nod. "Yeah, I do. I think she's a lot smarter than Dad gave her credit for."

A look of utter horror appears on his face. "You need to get out of that house, Harlow."

"I'm working on it," I mutter. I've already reached out to Darrow's contact. I'm just waiting for him to set a meet so I can get that ball rolling.

"Why did you ask to see me?" he inquires.

"I need copies of the police and medical examiner's report from Dad's accident. I know you can get them for me."

I'd thought of asking Diesel, but that's not the type of stuff he usually procures for me. I don't know his background, and I've no clue if he has those type of connections, so I thought it best to ask Lincoln first. If he can't deliver, I'll ask Diesel then.

He shakes his head. "You don't want to look at that, Lo."

I drill him with a deadly look. "I wouldn't ask unless I did."

"Why?"

"Because I don't believe it was an accident."

He jumps up, clawing his hands through his hair as he paces, and it's like watching a caged lion prowl an enclosure. He stops abruptly, crouching down in front of me. "I'm begging you, sweetheart. Please let it go."

"I can't, Linc."

"It's not safe, and you won't learn anything from those reports," he says, confirming he has copies. I know those reports are manufactured and riddled with lies. But I want to know who wrote them and who was involved, and then, I intend to dig up dirt on them I can use to blackmail them into telling me the truth. There has got to be someone, or something, I can locate to prove my dad was murdered.

"I still want a copy."

His face hardens, and he stands. "I can't help you. I'm sorry."

I grab my bag off the floor and rise, eyeballing him. "If you won't help me, I'll have to resort to other, less safe, measures."

"You're not a little girl anymore, Harlow. You're an intelligent young woman with a good head on her shoulders. I know you know a lot more than you've said here today. Please drop this. Your father would not approve. And his death will be in vain if you end up dead too." He clasps my shoulders, pleading with his eyes. "Let it go, Lo. Please, please, just drop this. You have the resources and the wherewithal to get the hell out of Lowell. If you want my help fleeing town, I'm all in, but I won't help you seek revenge."

He pauses for a beat before saying, "That's what got your dad killed in the first place, and I'll be damned if I help you do the same."

THE SAINTHOOD

CHAPTER 18

I RETURN HOME empty-handed, in a foul mood, further compounded when I hear sounds coming from Dad's study. I'm mad at Lincoln even though I know he's a good guy, and he believes he's protecting me. But he's clearly forgotten how stubborn I am, especially when I set my mind to something, and I'm not backing down.

I remove my boots and pad quietly toward the door to the office, peering through the gap, watching with mounting anger as the guys rifle through my dad's things.

Theo is sitting at the desk like he fucking has a God-given right to sit in my dad's chair, tapping away on Dad's laptop with a concentrated expression on his face. Saint is rummaging through Dad's filing cabinet, Caz is going through his desk drawers, and Galen is sifting through a few boxes of paperwork I've never seen before. They are resting on top of the mahogany table, just inside of the door, and each box is clearly labeled. It's definitely my dad's stuff, because I recognize his handwriting.

Where the fuck did they find those? And how the hell did I miss them because I went through this office with a fine-tooth comb after Dad died looking for evidence. I obviously missed something, and I mentally kick myself. I can't afford to make mistakes like this, and I'll have to redouble my efforts.

"What the actual fuck?" Galen roars, removing a bunch of photos from one of the boxes. The others drop what they are doing, walking over to the table. They stand behind him, trading worried looks as they stare at the pictures as Galen flips them over, one at a time. His hands are shaking, and the look on his face is downright furious. "I want to dig that motherfucking bastard up out of the ground and kill him all over again."

A red glaze coats my eyes and my blood is boiling as I instantly conjure up various ways to murder Galen Lennox.

Pulling out my knife, I charge into the room, launching myself at Galen without hesitation. Caz gets to me before I can reach him, snatching my wrist and digging his fingers into my flesh until I drop the knife. I knee him in the balls, ducking down as Saint reaches for me, grabbing the thick hardbound legal book on the desk, and swinging it in Galen's face. A loud whack rings out as it slams into his face, sending him sprawling backward.

He loses his balance, falling into the cabinet behind him, the glass panel on top shattering with the vibration of the heavy impact, raining shards of glass on top of us.

It doesn't stop me or the murderous intent flooding my veins. Galen slumps to the ground, cussing, and I jerk my head back, slamming it into Saint's head as he makes another grab for me.

Pain rattles through my skull, and my vision blurs in and out as I sway on my feet for a few seconds. Behind me, Saint is cursing profusely and wincing. Caz is still incapacitated, cupping his balls and groaning, while Theo has jumped back a few feet to avoid the glass.

I pounce on top of Galen on the floor, slamming my fist into his face, ignoring the splintering pain as glass embeds in my skin. "Fuck you, you fucking asshole!" I shout, punching him in the nose. Blood spurts, spraying over my shirt, but I barely notice it or the pain in my knuckles as I keep hitting him. "How dare you talk about my dad like that!" I thrust my sore fist into his jaw this time. "I will gut you to shreds and leave you to die a gruesome death," I threaten, snatching a jagged piece of glass from the floor and pressing it to his throat.

Cold metal presses against my temple as Galen stares at me with unforgiving eyes.

The clicking of the gun pulls me back to my senses. "Give me the glass, Harlow, or I'll blow your fucking brains out," Saint coolly warns.

I hold my hand firm, keeping the glass pinned to Galen's throat, despite the way my body trembles all over.

"Lo." Theo's voice is soft as he comes closer. "You don't want to do this. This isn't you."

I bark out a laugh, and it sounds crazy even to my own ears. "You don't know who I am anymore, Theo."

I don't know who I am anymore.

"I know how much you loved your dad and that he wouldn't want you to do this." He places his hand on my arm, and I let him pull it away from Galen's neck.

The glass has cut him, and a line of blood is visible along his throat. His face is covered in scratches, and drops of blood trickle down his chin. A bruise is already forming on his temple where the book slammed into him, and there is other discoloration on his jaw and his cheek.

I'm guessing I haven't fared much better. Feeling is returning to my numb body, and my face and my arms sting with a multitude of tiny cuts. I'm chilled to the bone as I climb awkwardly to my feet, brushing Theo's arm away when he attempts to help me.

Saint helps Galen to stand, and we stare at one another with mutual pain and hatred in our eyes. "Talk shit about my dad again and I will end you."

I turn to leave, and my eyes land on the photos scattered

across the hardwood floor. I crouch down, swallowing back bile as I inspect them.

The woman in the photos is reed thin and pale with gaunt cheekbones and sunken eyes. The telltale hazy look in her eyes confirms she's totally wasted as a variety of different guys fuck her every which way from Sunday. Acid swirls in my gut as I flick through them, growing more and more disgusted.

I drop to my butt, staring at them in horror, wondering what the hell they were doing in my father's things. I glance over at Galen as he crawls toward me, wincing in obvious pain.

Is this why he hates me?

He shoves me aside, grabbing the photos, his jaw taut, anger and pain oozing from him in spades.

I stare at him as my brain scrambles to make sense of this. "Is this—"

He clamps his hand over my mouth, muting me. "Don't say one more fucking word. You think you know it all," he says, releasing me as he staggers to his feet, clutching the photos protectively to his chest. "But you don't know shit." He stumbles out of the room as I sit on the floor, numb and in a daze.

"You need to go," Saint says, lifting me up by my upper arms. "We'll clean up before the oldies get home." He nudges me toward the door. "Theo." He looks over his shoulder. "Grab the first aid kit and tend to Harlow and Galen."

"I've got my own first aid kit. I can look after myself," I mumble, still staring at the empty doorway.

"Of course, you do," Saint says in an exasperated tone, grabbing my face and forcing my gaze to his. "If you breathe a word about this to your mom or my dad, they will be the last words you ever speak. Understood."

"They would be the last people I tell anything to," I blurt, too shellshocked to play the game.

He peers into my eyes, nodding as he sees the truth. "Go. And stay in your room."

I walk on wobbly limbs toward the door, clutching on to the

doorway as I cast a glance over my shoulder. "Why did my dad have those pictures of Galen's mom?" I ask.

He stares at me as Caz starts cleaning up the mess and Theo gathers his things.

The connection between us kicks in, shooting electrical currents across the room, and it's like being hit by a lightning bolt.

His brow creases, and for the first time, Saint Lennox looks less than assured. "I don't know, but I intend to find out."

THEIR RETALIATION IS swift and not entirely unexpected. However, I didn't anticipate being dragged out of my bed in the middle of the night and thrown into the back seat of their car. I'm in my pajamas with no shoes, a rag stuffed in my mouth, and a bag over my head wedged between two of the assholes as we drive along a bumpy road in the dead of the night. They don't talk, because the heavy metal blaring through the speakers is too loud to converse.

If they wanted to deliberately unhinge me, kidnapping me is their best chance of success. My nerves are frayed, and I sit stiffly in between them, wondering what fresh hell this is.

I don't know how long we drive for, but it's long enough to leave the town boundary. If I had to guess, we're going to Prestwick, because that's their main stomping ground.

The music cuts off when we come to an abrupt stop. I'm yanked out of the car unceremoniously, and I cry out against the gag in my mouth when my bare feet land on rough gravel. I stumble, almost tripping until someone grabs a fistful of my shirt, pulling me upright. A gun prods into my lower back as I'm marched forward, stumbling over the uneven path until my feet meet damp grass.

Without my vision, I put one foot in front of the other, walking blindly ahead, hoping I don't faceplant a tree or run into any wildlife with big teeth. My balance is wonky, and I'm wobbling and swaying like I'm drunk or high. I urge my errant pulse to calm down while I concentrate on my surroundings, remembering what Diesel has taught me. The chill night air coasts over my prickly skin as we walk. It's deathly quiet out here. The only sounds are the soft tread of our footsteps and the occasional hoot of an owl. I start counting my steps, trying to make sense of which direction we're going in, but it's challenging.

I have a pretty strong idea where I am. My money's on Prestwick Forest, their usual burial ground, which does little to help my unease.

If they decide to kill me, no one will ever find my body out here.

Bits of fluff adhere to the inside of my mouth, and I gag, almost choking. A cold pair of hands pulls me back against a solid chest, and someone rolls the covering up to my nose, removing the cloth from my mouth. I splutter, coughing out bits of fuzz, before swallowing lungsful of crisp, clean, pine-smelling air.

"Keep moving," Saint commands, his voice close to my ear, confirming it's him I've been leaning against. He lets me go, keeping the gun prodded into my back as we forge ahead. Giant goose bumps sprout on my frosty skin, and I wrap my arms around my shivering form to try and keep warm.

I jump when some animal lets loose a bloodcurdling howl, a whimper escaping my mouth before I can stop it, and they all laugh.

The bastards.

Eventually, we come to a stop after it feels like we've been walking for miles. Cuts and blisters cover the soles of my feet and they ache. The covering is removed from my head, and hands sweep my tangled hair back off my face.

"Screw off." I swat the hands away, smoothing my hair behind my ears and leveling a glare at Caz as he watches me with evident amusement. He's firmly back on the anti-Harlow team, and I doubt my next seduction attempt will be as successful.

I look around, taking in the environment. We're deep in a forest, and tall, ominous-looking trees hover over us as we trek across a grassy path. The moon is high in the sky, casting creepy shadows on the ground below.

"Tie her hands behind her back," Saint instructs.

Galen steps forward, circling me with an evil grin, like a serial killer hunting his next victim. His face is mottled with cuts and bruises, and I take some small satisfaction from that fact. He takes enormous pleasure in yanking my arms back so tight they almost wrench from the sockets. That's clearly a specialty of his, and he's waiting for me to cry out, but I don't make a sound. Not even when he ties the rope too tight and it feels like he's cut off my circulation.

"On your knees," Saint demands, and before I've had time to even consider complying, Galen thrusts his knee in my back, and I faceplant the ground. The muddy grass is cold and squishy under my cheek, but at least, I avoided eating a mouthful of it.

Saint yanks me up by my hair, fisting it around his hand and keeping me steady on my knees. He stands at my side, while the three stooges stand in front of me with their arms folded, wearing mutual inhumane expressions. They are all dressed warmly in hoodies, jeans, and boots, and a shudder works its way through me as I remember how fucking cold I am.

Saint removes a gun from the back waistband of his jeans. "Open your mouth." His blue eyes pierce mine as he attempts to look deep into my soul.

My instinct is to tell him to go to hell, but my sense of self-preservation is stronger, so I open my mouth wide, keeping very still as he slides the muzzle past my lips.

"Suck on it," he commands, and I'd arch a brow if I didn't have a fucking gun in my mouth and I wasn't concentrating so hard.

I do as he asks, licking all sides of the gun while keeping

my gaze trained on his.

"Fuck, that's—"

Saint whips his head around, and Caz breaks off midspeech. When Saint turns back around, his gaze is like a heat-seeking missile as he watches me with dark intent. A knowing, proud smile slightly curves the corners of his mouth, and I don't know if he realizes it, but he's let the mask slip, and he's broadcasting his feelings pretty loud.

I'm eye level with his crotch, and there's no hiding the monster bulge tenting his jeans.

Where Caz is turned on at the sight of me sucking a gun, Saint is aroused because I'm *obeying* him.

I have totally been going about this all wrong. And whatever tonight is about, it gives me an opportunity to change my playbook.

"Good girl, princess," he says, releasing the tight grip on my hair and caressing my face with his free hand. He pulls me to my feet, reeling me in flush with his body. He nudges my hip with his erection, and I suck in a gasp as heat floods my core. Movement in the background is only noise as I peer into Saint's eyes. "Do you know where we are, princess?" he asks, sliding his arms around my back.

"Prestwick Forest."

"Smart deduction, and you're correct." He pins me with a shit-eating grin. "And do you know what happens out here?"

"You kill people and bury them in the woods." They all chuckle at that, and I wonder what I said that's so funny.

"Do you know what else we do out here?" he inquires, poking further. I shake my head. He smiles wider, rubbing his thumb along my mouth, eliciting a wake of shivers in his trail. "Good." He glances over my head. "Ready?" he shouts. After a few beats, he looks down at me, grinding his cock against my pelvis and smushing his chest against my hard nipples. His eyes feast on my breasts, and I shiver all over. He smirks, letting me go, and I lament the loss of his body heat. "I really hope I'm not wrong about you, princess," he whispers in my ear before tugging me through the trees by the elbow.

The others are standing around an opening in the ground, looking down and sharing wicked grins.

"It's set," Galen says, his voice cold and unfeeling.

"Down you go, princess." Saint brings me to the edge of the pit, where a rope ladder has been slotted into the ground.

I lean over, peering into the pitch-black pit, shivering uncontrollably. "I'm not going down there."

Saint shakes his head, gripping my elbow tighter. "Already disappointing me."

"Let me clarify," Galen says, approaching me with lethal menace. "Climb down, or I'll gladly throw your ass in there." His eyes drop to my chest, and I hate that my nipples are rigid and poking through the front of my thin sleep shirt. He lifts his head, smirking, and his know-it-all demeanor grates on my last nerve.

"They're hard because I'm cold, asshole, not because I'm aroused."

"You can lie to yourself, angel, but we all know the truth." He leans in close to my face. "You're every bit as fucked up as we are. Maybe more so."

He's quite possibly right, but I'm not confirming that out loud.

"What's it to be, princess?" Saint says. "You going willingly, or not?"

My gaze meets Theo's, and his eyes urge me to climb down, his expression suggesting he's got my back. For a split second, we're co-conspirators again until I remember where I am, who I'm with, and how I got here.

"I need my hands," I say, averting my eyes from Theo and staring back at his annoyingly hot leader.

Saint's amused smile irks me. "So use them." The meaning is clear, and I think he knows, as well as I do, that I could've freed myself the minute Galen tied me up.

It takes me longer than usual, because that asshole tied them super tight, but I manage to get free a couple minutes later, and the rope falls to the ground at my feet. Galen and Saint share a look as I step up to the ladder and start climbing down.

The lower I go, the more my trepidation builds, but I refuse to let fear get the best of me, so I focus on my movements and my breathing, ignoring the way my heart is racing, my palms are suddenly sweaty, and blood is rushing to my ears.

I plant my feet on the muddy ground, shuddering as I look around. It's not actually that deep, and I can still see the guys standing around the edge, looking down. But it's deep enough that as soon as they whip the rope ladder away, and I realize I have no way out of here, panic starts to crawl up my throat.

"Let's see what you're made of now, princess," Saint says, shining a flashlight on my face. The light illuminates my surroundings, and my panic accelerates to coronary-inducing levels as the myriad of bones littering the muddy ground comes into clear view. Some still bear remnants of decaying flesh, confirming these are more recent kills.

I tremble all over, and this time, it's not from the cold.

Chuckles ring out from above, followed by a succession of wails as they howl like wild animals. They throw slabs of bloody meat into the pit, and I shriek as Galen throws his offering right at my face, darting to the side just in time. I scramble back as my foot hits the side of a skull, screaming before I can stop myself. They laugh again, and I bristle with rage, but I clamp my lips shut, because I won't plead or beg. They would love that, and I won't give them the satisfaction.

It turns dark again when Saint switches his flashlight off, but it brings zero comfort. Another shudder works its way through me, and I cross my arms over my chest as my teeth chatter.

"Wild wolves are known to roam these woods at night," Saint says, his voice tinged with glee. "I wouldn't stay down there too long, princess. Unless you want to become wolf nom, nom."

THE SAINTHOOD

THE SAINTHOOD

CHAPTER 19

I STAND IN the center of the muddy pit, in the pitch-dark, in my now filthy pajamas, shivering and shaking from the cold and uncontrollable rage. I listen to the guys laughing and joking as they saunter off, leaving me to my fate, and I want to tear those assholes limb from limb and feed them to the wolves when they come hunting. But my furious thoughts aren't going to help me escape, and I don't plan on spending long down here.

First, I hurl the lumps of bloody raw meat out of the pit, one at a time, offering silent thanks that Dad got me interested in kickboxing at sixteen. Between classes and regular bouts with the punching bag in our basement gym, I have decent strength in my arms. Enough that I can toss the stinking piles of wolf bait out of the pit and away from me. I don't think I've thrown them far though, and the scent will most likely carry on the breeze, so I need to get my ass out of here stat.

Ignoring the icky feel of slimy bones under my feet, I scale the perimeter of the small pit, using my hands to explore the muddy walls for anything to grip on to, but I can't find any markings I can use to climb out of here. The mud is quite soft to the touch, almost clay-like in substance, as if they built this pit on purpose solely to drive me demented.

I pace the small clear space in the middle of the pit, racking my brains for a solution.

When it comes to me, I almost throw up.

Adrenaline courses through my veins, and bile swims up my throat, but I can't identify any other plan, and even though I don't know if this will work, I've got to try.

I attack the wall I climbed down using my long nails to dig, pulling clumps of mud away. When I've gouged a deep enough hole, I swallow my distaste as I crouch down, tentatively reaching out and grabbing the first bone I feel. I don't think about the fact this belonged to a living, breathing being at one point in time, focusing on the fact I need to get out of here before *my* bones join this gruesome collection.

I wedge the bone into the hole I've dug, covering it with the clay-like mud, but leaving the end part jutting out just enough to climb on. I pack the mud around the edges, compacting it as tightly as I can, and then I repeat the process, lining bones up in a crisscross pattern, choosing bigger, wider bones for my feet and smaller ones for my hands to grip onto. I go as high as I can reach, hoping that I can close that final gap using my hands and pull myself the rest of the way up.

I'm covered in mud and sweat after my exertions, but at least, I'm no longer shivering.

Here goes nothing. I start to climb, and it's clear straightaway that the bones aren't going to hold long, so I scale the wall as fast as I can, almost slipping a couple times, until I've reached the last marker. I stretch my arms up, my breath oozing out in relief when my fingers grip the top of the pit. My footing gives out as I grab the top with my second hand, and I dangle from the edge, literally holding myself up by my arms and my fingers. I dig my hands into the earth above, grunting as I use my upper body strength to haul myself up and over the edge.

I roll onto my back, breathing heavily, my heart pounding furiously in my chest, arms throbbing like a bitch. But I'm silently triumphant because I'm out! I force my aching body to move, staggering to my feet and glancing all around.

Daylight is starting to creep into the dark sky, offering some small illumination, but I still have no clue what direction we came from. I remember the sound of their voices as they walked away, and I think they were heading in a westerly direction, so I take off that way, praying I'm not going deeper into the woods.

My desire to get the hell out of Dodge before any wolves make an appearance has me running even on blistered, cut feet.

The entire time, I'm conjuring up imaginative ways to dismember the guys.

I come to a small clearing, stopping for a minute to find my bearings and to draw a long breath. A gap in the woodland on my right grabs my attention, and I head toward it, smiling when I spot the fresh imprint of boots on the soft grass. I sprint through the gap, jogging along the narrow grassy path, my breath puffing out in cloudy circles, my limbs tired and protesting, but I keep going until I come to a much larger clearing and discover a defined path. I follow it for a mile or two until I reach the main entrance to the forest. I only know it is because I came up here one time with Darrow for a party.

I lean over the worn wooden railing to catch my breath while scanning my surroundings. The road outside is long and seemingly never ending, with thick forest running on either side, but I detect a small property about a quarter mile up ahead, and I take off in that direction.

I stick to the little grassy strip on the side of the road, forcing my tired legs to cooperate for another stretch.

When I reach the building I spotted, I see it's a small one-story log cabin. A trickle of smoke filters from the chimney as I stand at the front door and knock. No one answers. I figure they're most likely asleep, so I rap harder. When no one appears after I pound the door, scraping my knuckles in the process, I try the handle, but it's locked. I walk around to the rear of the house, trying the back door, but it's locked too.

Fuck.

I don't want to add B & E to my resume, but I'm low on options. I've no money, no cell, no shoes, and there isn't another house in sight. I need to get to a phone to call for help. I have no choice.

Wiping sweat off my brow with the back of my hand, I look all around for something I can use to break in.

What I wouldn't give for my lock-picking kit now.

I'm about to use my elbow to break the glass panel in the door when I spot a large plant pot at the corner of the cabin. Figuring I might as well check, I pull it up, and a laugh rips free from my mouth at the sight of the key.

Someone up there is looking out for me.

I open the door, calling out hello as I cautiously step inside. I check all the rooms, but no one is here. But they can't have gone far because there's a toasty fire going in the living room and something is cooking in the oven.

I move to the wall-mounted phone and place my call. It takes five attempts to rouse Sariah because that girl sleeps like the dead, but finally, she answers, promising she's coming as fast as she can.

Although it's tempting to conk out on the comfy couch in front of the fire, I don't want to overstay my welcome, so I exit the way I came in, cringing at the muddy footprints I leave behind. I replace the key under the pot and retrace my steps toward the entrance of the forest.

I'm slumped against the wooden railings, utterly exhausted, when Sariah shows up a few minutes later.

"Jesus Christ," she exclaims, climbing out of her grandma's battered red Volkswagen Golf. "What the hell did they do to you?"

I'd only given her the cliff notes version on the phone, so on the drive back, I fill her in on everything that happened last night.

"Those motherfucking bastards!" she seethes, gripping the steering wheel in a tight grip. "You could've been eaten by wolves! Or some psycho out burying bodies might've come across you. This means fucking war!"

"That's what they'll be expecting, but I'm altering my strategy."

After I go postal on Saint's ass, I decide, tiptoeing into my house fifteen minutes later. Sariah wanted me to come home with her, but I'm not hiding from them. They don't scare me, and they need to know they won't get the better of me.

I go straight to my bedroom, retrieve my knife and my kit, and step back out into the hallway, picking Saint's lock as quietly as I can.

When I'm inside his room, I stare at the asshole as he sleeps. He's flat on his back, sprawled across the king-sized mattress, the black silk sheets bunched at his waist, his chest inflating and deflating as he breathes deeply, as if he hadn't just left me alone in the freaking forest.

Slivers of buttery light slip through the blinds, bathing him in a dim glow. He looks magnificent with all that toned, tan skin on display, and the ink on his arms and one side of his chest only adds to the attraction. His face is all angular masculine lines, his jaw covered in a smattering of hair I find so sexy on guys.

I wish he was an ugly fucker because it might help to make it easier to hold on to my anger. But, somehow, I know that wouldn't make any difference. Saint exudes this aura, this magnetism, that sucks me in, and it's less to do with how he looks and more to do with his dominant personality, his cutting humor, the dark intensity he brings to everything, and the power of the connection between us.

A connection forged in a split second in a stolen moment when we were kids.

Right now, that connection means jack shit, and his gorgeous looks aren't distracting me from my anger either.

I move with purpose toward the bed, leaving a trail of

muddy, bloody footprints on the gray carpet.

I'm a dirty, sweaty mess, my hair is knotted and caked with mud, and I stink to high heaven. I'm covered in cuts, my feet are bleeding, and there isn't one part of my body that doesn't hurt as I climb up over him, straddling his thighs and pressing the sharp edge of my knife to his dick through the sheets.

His eyes blink open the second my body weight presses down on him, and he's instantly wide-awake, his gaze taking in the filthy state of me before lowering to the knife pointed at his family jewels. He turns his head to the bedside table, glancing at the time before facing me again with a cocky smile. "I'm impressed," he rasps, his voice dripping with raw sexuality, doing funny things to my insides.

Focus on your anger. I give myself a silent pep talk because the shithead is not getting away with what he's done to me. "I'm not," I snap, angling the knife over his crotch. "I'm livid and I have a tendency to act recklessly when I'm mad." I rip through his silk sheets until the tight black boxers he's wearing are revealed.

Bending his arms at the elbows, he tucks them under his head, grinning at me like I'm no threat.

It infuriates me, and I rip a hole in his boxers, exposing some skin and curls of wiry hair.

"If you want to see my cock, princess, you only have to ask."

"Mock me again and I'll slice your dick off."

I expect him to wince and attempt to protect his manhood, but he smiles instead. A smug smile that indicates he's not concerned, because he clearly underestimates how mad I am, he thinks I won't attack, or he's just not like normal guys who would cower in this scenario. "No, you won't. You love it too much."

I bark out a laugh, pressing myself down over him, loving that I'm soiling him with my dirty, mud-spattered skin, and holding my blade against his face. "Delusional much, Saintly?"

"You're not the only one who feels it, princess," he says,

running the tips of his fingers up my arm. "And I'm tired of fighting."

"Then maybe, you shouldn't have kidnapped me in the middle of the night and dumped me in an open grave in the fucking woods!"

He cups my face, uncaring I have a blade flattened against his cheek. "It was a test, princess, and you passed with flying colors." His blue eyes burn with the usual intensity, and when his tongue darts out, I catch a glimpse of metal in his mouth. The tongue piercing is new.

"Explain." I sit up, pulling my knife back, unable to think clearly when I'm that close to his face. Bile swims up my throat, and my stomach is tied into knots. It takes colossal willpower to ignore the feel of his growing erection under my ass, but I do because his words have thrown me.

"Theo has been championing your cause," he says, sitting up with me on his lap. He leans his back against the headboard, and I slide lower on his body.

"I never asked him to."

"Neither did we, but he's right." He grips my face. "We don't have to be enemies."

I smell a rat, and I'm not buying the bullshit he's peddling for a minute, but I'll play along. "What are we then?" I inquire, leaning into his face.

"We could be allies."

"Who says I need an ally?" I ask, working hard to keep my tone neutral as he moves his hand to the nape of my neck and his gaze drops to my lips.

"War is coming to Lowell, princess, and you don't want to find yourself on the wrong side."

I lean in closer until there's barely any gap between our mouths. Our noses brush, and he snakes his arms around my back, pulling me in close, uncaring that I'm dirty and messing up his bed. "What if I'm Switzerland," I whisper over his mouth. "And I don't want to choose a side."

He rubs the skin at the back of my neck, and all the tiny

hairs lift. "You don't get to sit this one out. You're going to be a Lennox, and Lennoxes always side with the winning team."

I break free of the bubble he's coaxed me into, tipping his beautiful face back and placing my knife against his Adam's apple. "Let's get one thing straight, Saintly. I'm a *Westbrook*, and I will *never* be a Lennox. Not while there's blood still flowing through my veins."

I'm glad for the reminder, and the anger he dialed down with his seductive charm flares to life again.

In a move he didn't predict, I lean back, cutting both sides of his boxers, tossing the torn strands away and leaving him fully exposed to me. I press the tip of my knife into his dark-blond pubes, enjoying the flash of fear glimmering in his eyes. "Your cock really is quite magnificent," I purr, using my free hand to stroke his shaft. Slowly, I move my knife down lower, and his Adam's apple bobs in his throat. "I'd hate for my hand to slip and cut it." I let the full extent of my venom show on my face as I press down on the knife, meeting flesh, and I'm sure I've drawn blood. I let go of his cock, eyeing it like I might just cut it off.

Saint holds himself deathly still. He's scared to death I'll lob off his precious dick. A fit of giggles bubbles inside me, but I smother my laughter, biting down hard on the inside of my cheek to maintain a cold exterior.

This is fucking priceless and the best payback.

"I researched eunuchs after watching *Game of Thrones*," I admit, swirling the tip of my knife through his pubes while I watch him try not to flinch. "Did you know there are many leaders throughout history who were eunuchs?" I quirk a brow.

"And your point is?" he says, trying to act blasé and failing miserably.

I move my knife even lower, placing the blade against one side of his cock. I swear he stops breathing. "Just that you'd be in good company if I did, you know, decide to castrate you for pulling that little stunt." The grin I give him is downright wicked, and the potent fear on his face is something he can no longer hide.

"You weren't in any real danger," he blurts. "I made that shit up about the wolves, all right? You've proven yourself resourceful, and we knew you'd make it out."

"And if I hadn't?" I ask, pulling a handful of his pubic hair and cutting it off in one swift move.

He lets out a roar, his hand automatically moving down his body to protect his cock. "What the fuck?"

I slap his hand away. "You really don't want to test me right now, Saintly." I smirk as the next words leave my mouth. "You deserve to be punished. We can do this the hard way, or you can make it easy on yourself."

"What are you going to do?" he croaks, his eyes wide with terror.

"Don't worry," I say, patting the crown of his cock. "I won't slice your dick off. This time," I add, grinning. "Provided you lie back and keep nice and still while I give you a little trim."

He blinks repeatedly, staring at me like I've gone mad. Perhaps, I have because I'm enjoying this far too much. I move the knife closer to his dick again. "So, what's it to be?"

"You know I'll make you fucking pay for this."

"Oh, I've no doubt you'd like to try, but you'll give me this." I drill him with a deadly look. "You *owe* me this." I hold his gaze without hesitation.

"You're actually fucking serious?"

I nod, already seeing the resignation on his face.

"You breathe a word to the others, and I'll make you suffer," he cautions, and I know I've got him right where I want him.

"It can be our little secret," I purr, and the smile that spreads across my mouth is so wide it threatens to split my face. "Now, keep still, and I'll try my best not to draw blood." I grab his pubes, lower my knife, and begin slicing.

THE SAINTHOOD

CHAPTER 20

After my little grooming session with Saint, I saunter back to my room, whistling under my breath, in a much better mood now. I shower and then toss some clothes over my TV, deliberately blocking the camera so they can't see what I'm doing. Using dad's drill, I fit one of the padlocks to the inside of my door and secure it before packing a bag for the weekend. I dress in workout gear and message Diesel on the burner cell before climbing out of my window. It's still early, and Mom usually doesn't surface before eleven a.m. on the weekends, so she won't know I'm gone for hours.

I take Dad's Gran Turismo because I need to blow off some steam even if I know it's risky because Dad wanted me to drive the Lexus to keep me safe. But I'm still on edge after everything that happened last night, and I need to let loose on the open road—and there's only one car for the job.

I turn my cell off, ignoring the latest string of messages from Darrow, in case the Saints try using satellite systems to track my whereabouts.

Keeping Dad's cabin off their radar is vital. It's my only

sanctuary from the shitshow that's my life, and it's also where Dad stored all his important paperwork, so I need to keep it hidden.

I'm still puzzled over the boxes Galen was rifling through in the study yesterday. *Where the hell did he find them? And are there any more?* I thought I'd uncovered everything I needed to know about Dad, but he's still surprising me even from the grave.

And why were the assholes going through Dad's stuff anyway? What is it they're looking for? I've guessed by now that Neo knows Dad was building evidence against him, so they must be looking for that. *Those photos of Galen's mom were some form of evidence, because why else would Dad have them?* It's not like either of my parents had any association with Alisha Lennox anymore.

All I remember from the party at Galen's grandma's house when I was fourteen is that his mom and mine seemed to be friends. Now I know Mom's history with Neo, it makes sense. Alisha was going out with Neo's brother the same time Mom was dating Neo.

But why were my parents at the party if they'd cut ties with that world before I was born? And how come Neo and Saint weren't there that day?

I blare the music and lower the window a little, letting the slight chill in the air blow the cobwebs from my mind. So many questions remain unanswered, and I know part of the key to all this lies in the past. But I'm going to give myself an aneurysm trying to work it all out.

I make good time, pulling up to the cabin ninety minutes later. I'm glad I came here—even if I was tempted to crawl into bed and rest my achy body. I need to put distance between me and the Saints before I end up arrested on a murder charge. And I need to regroup, to map out my new strategy.

I strip down to my undies and get into bed, instantly conking out. The shrill ring of my burner cell wakes me sometime later, and I feel around the top of the bedside table for it. "Hey," I mumble in a sleep-drenched voice, pulling myself upright in the bed and yawning.

"Did I wake you?" Diesel's amused tone filters down the line.

"Yep. I didn't get much sleep last night."

Initial silence greets me. "ETA in a half hour, but I can't stay off the grid for long."

"It won't take long. Thanks for meeting me on such short notice."

"I told you I'm here for you, and I meant it."

His words send a flood of warmth coursing through my chest. "Thank you, Diesel. That means a lot."

"I'll see you soon," he says before hanging up.

I pull on a pair of gray sweats and a white tank top, knotting my hair into a messy bun on top of my head, and pad down to the kitchen in my bare feet. I switched the heating on when I arrived, and the warm floorboards are a salve to my injured feet.

I make a pot of coffee, grab some fruit and a bagel, and patter into dad's office to switch on the computer.

When Diesel arrives, I press the button to open the electronic gates, watching him speed up the long driveway in a blacked-out Land Rover that instantly has me thinking of Saint.

I prop one hip against the front doorway, sipping my coffee as I wait for Diesel to arrive.

He climbs out of his vehicle, wearing aviators even though it's not sunny, and he reminds me of a much taller, more dangerous version of Tom Cruise in *Top Gun* with his dark hair, masculine jawline, and confident, cocky stride. "Hey, sweetheart," he says, bending down to kiss me.

I act instinctively, moving my head to the side so his lips hit the corner of my mouth instead of the intended target. Awkwardness seeps into the air as he straightens up, pulling his shoulders back, and I drag my lower lip between my teeth, concerned I've upset him.

I need Diesel, and I can't afford to mess this up. And, more than that, I care about him and don't want to see him hurt.

"Hey." I soften my expression and my tone. "I thought we'd agreed this would be strictly professional from now on." We hadn't spoken the words, but we both communicated with actions the last time we slept together.

"What if I said I'd changed my mind?" he inquires, tenderly cupping my face.

"You know we can't do this. The timing's all wrong." I shuck out of his embrace, walking into the cabin with a heavy heart, knowing he'll follow me.

"It's because of them, isn't it?" His voice is clipped, but there's a hint of sadness and concern at the back of it.

I lean back against the kitchen counter, wrapping my hands around my mug as I examine his face. "Who?"

"Don't play games, Lo. That's not who we are. You know who I'm talking about."

I set my mug down and shove off the counter, walking toward him. "I try not to need people in my life, Diesel, because it's hard to find people I trust and because association with me is risky." I place a soft hand on his arm. "But I need you." My eyes scan his. "I need you to be on my side. To continue training me. To continue helping me. I won't survive this otherwise."

His hard features soften, and he sighs, bundling me into a friendly hug. "You know you have me. Whatever you need, I'm always on your side."

Thank fuck. I ease out of his embrace. "Then, you know why we need to keep this platonic. We had fun, but if we kept going, someone was bound to get hurt. I can't risk that, and you are more to me than a hot body to fuck."

He loosely holds my waist. "The guy you end up falling for is going to be a lucky son of a bitch, because you truly are one of a kind, Harlow Westbrook."

"Careful," I tease, needing to defuse the atmosphere. "You don't want to give me too many compliments. It might go to my head."

"I very much doubt that, but I hear you loud and proud, little squirt."

I grin at his familiar endearment although it's been a few years since I heard it, but I know we're going to be okay. A layer of stress lifts off my shoulders. "Coffee?" I ask as I grab my cup and move toward the pot.

"Please," he says, pulling himself up onto a stool at the counter. "You weren't the only one who didn't get much shuteye last night." I grab another mug from the overheard cupboard and pour him a cup while I refill mine. "Speaking of, do you want to tell me what's going on? Why are you covered in scratches and cuts and walking like you've got a limp?"

I hand him his mug and claim the stool beside him. "Saint and the other assholes decided to test me." I shrug, wanting to downplay it. "It's nothing I couldn't handle, and I think they're finally realizing I'm not easily intimidated."

"Be careful, Lo. They may be only junior chapter, but they have rap sheets as long as my arm. At least Saint, Galen, and Caz do. Theo is the invisible ghost orchestrating stuff from the shadows."

I level him with a stern look. "You don't have to warn me about The Sainthood. I know what I'm dealing with, and I'm taking the necessary precautions."

"And are you protecting your heart?" he blurts.

My mouth hangs open. "Seriously?"

"C'mon, Lo. You're gorgeous, intelligent, feisty, and you can hold your own. You think I don't know they're hitting on you? You think I don't know about the tape?"

Well, shit. I've never discussed that with him.

"I didn't watch all of it," he adds before I can ask. He removes his aviators, locking his gaze on mine. "But I saw enough. There's chemistry there, and that's worrisome. If they can't get to you through intimidation, they will revert to more seductive measures."

Based on the convo I had with Saint before I left, I've already deduced that. But I made the decision to seduce them first, and if they want to play this game, I'm more than ready to play ball.

They might think they can win me over, but I'm not like other girls.

I never give my heart away, and I sure as fuck won't start now.

"I'm already two steps ahead of them."

He scowls, and his eyes burn with envy. "That's what I was afraid of."

"Please tell me you're not jealous and this is just concern."

He has the decency to look ashamed. "It's mostly concern, and I'm working on the jealousy part."

I'm so glad I ended things with him last time because it's obvious now that he was already invested. My heart aches a little, because, in a different time and different place, I could see us making a go of things.

But we are where we are, and there's no point dwelling on what-ifs.

"Work harder," I suggest, my tone brooking no argument.

"What is it you wanted to ask me?" he says, and I'm grateful for the subject change.

"I need you to get me the accident paperwork."

"What are you planning, Lo?"

"I know Neo had my dad murdered, Diesel, and there's got to be some evidence I can use to put him away."

"You think Neo hasn't dotted all his I's and crossed his T's?" He shakes his head. "I know you want to see justice served, but you can't expect to go up against an organization like The Sainthood and win?"

It hasn't escaped my notice that he didn't balk at my claim or dispute it. Diesel believes they killed Dad too, and not for the first time, I wonder exactly who he is.

"I won't know unless I try." I fold my arms over my chest. "Can you get me the paperwork or not?"

"You won't let this drop, will you?"

I smirk. "You know me well."

He sighs heavily. "I don't like this, Lo. I don't like this one bit. I don't want you getting yourself killed, so I'll agree to get it for you—on one condition. You promise you won't go snooping by yourself. We do it together."

"Why are you so invested?"

He threads his fingers through mine. "You may have forgotten the scared little girl you used to be, but I haven't. I made a vow to myself when your dad brought you to me. That I'd keep you safe and never let anything or anyone harm you again. I intend on keeping that vow." He stands, pressing a kiss to the top of my head. "I need you to promise, Lo."

I look up at him, seeing nothing but concern and compassion. "I promise," I say, hoping I can keep it.

AFTER DIESEL LEAVES, I spend some time going through Dad's files, the uncoded ones, looking for something of interest I can give to Darrow. My ex is really starting to get on my nerves, and his harassment is pressing my buttons. Fact is, the guys are home so infrequently I'm getting fucking nothing from the cameras. They don't even sleep in the house some nights. I'm beginning to lose confidence in my ability to identify the location of the warehouse for Dar. The meet is set up with his contact for tomorrow, and I really don't give much of a fuck after that. But Dar has already proven how nasty he can be when he feels betrayed, so I want to give him something to ease the sting. I have enough shit on my plate without adding more petty squabbles to the list.

And speaking of petty squabbles, I dig through Parker's background, in the hope of finding some dirt, but I come up empty-handed. Guess I'll need to dig deeper. Everyone has something they want to hide, and a girl like Parker must have a treasure chest full of secrets. I'll discover where she's hiding the truth and crack that beast wide open.

I spend the rest of the night scanning the coded files to

an encrypted cloud folder, feeling more assured now I have a backup, in case anything should happen to the originals. On instinct, I copy a few confidential files from dad's other folders onto a USB stick, disguised as a tube of lipstick, and slip it into my purse. No harm in having some insurance in case I should need it.

The next morning, before I head to the meet, I message Sariah to get together at the gym downtown. Although my body still throbs like a bitch, I seriously need to vent some pent-up anger, and going a few rounds in the ring with my bestie is the perfect cure.

I PULL UP to the biker bar on the outskirts of Prestwick and park out front. Wiping my sweaty hands down the side of my jeans, I double-check the coordinates Darrow's guy sent to me. I'm in the right place, and it doesn't surprise me that this shady fucker conducts business here.

I walk from my car with purpose, stepping into the dimly lit bar, aware of several sets of eyes looking in my direction. My knife is strapped to the outside of my thigh on purpose, and my gun is tucked into the waistband of my jeans. I'm glad I dressed down for this meeting because I fit right in with my dirty jeans, scuffed boots, rocker tee, and black leather jacket. I approach the bar. "I'm looking for Johnny. Darrow Knight hooked me up."

"Wait here," the bleached blonde says in an unfriendly tone, throwing me a look before ducking behind the bar.

I stare straight ahead, ignoring the eyeballs glued to my back and the inquisitive stares from the two older dudes sitting at the counter.

Blondie returns with an even bigger scowl on her face. "Back there," she huffs, jabbing her thumb behind her.

I walk through the swinging double doors into a small private room. The three guys inside stop talking, watching me as I step forward. "Which one of you is Johnny?" I ask, grateful my voice holds steady.

"That'd be me, darlin'," the guy slouched on the couch, rolling a joint, says, giving me a blatant onceover. "Come join me." His hair is dark with strips of gray. It's unkempt, falling into his big brown eyes and matching the straggly beard that runs from his chin to his chest. Laughter lines crease the corners of his eyes and his mouth, and his weather-beaten tan skin attests to countless hours outside. His belly tumbles over his belt, and his arms and legs are chunky.

I sit down on the couch and face him, waiting for his next move.

"Why's a pretty girl like you in need of the services of an old coot like me?" he asks, lighting his joint.

"It's better that you don't know," I say, removing the envelope from my back pocket. "That's the down payment you requested."

"Chewie!" He jerks his head at the guy with the waist-length hair and long thick beard. "Do the honors."

Chewie takes the envelope and counts the cash. "It's all there, boss."

Johnny nods, and Chewie backs away, sliding the envelope into the inside pocket of his plaid shirt.

"My guy'll need to take photos," he says, blowing smoke circles in my face. "I'll send you the details of the location once I set it up. Then, it'll take two weeks to get all the IDs together."

"That's fine."

He jerks forward suddenly, slamming his lips down on mine. Before I can protest or push him away, he reels back, grinning madly. "Nice doing business with you, girlie." I stand, and he swats my ass. "Now scoot before Chewie starts getting ideas. He likes 'em young."

I've never run out of a place faster, scrubbing at my lips, and I don't release the breath I'm holding until the bar is a blip in the distance.

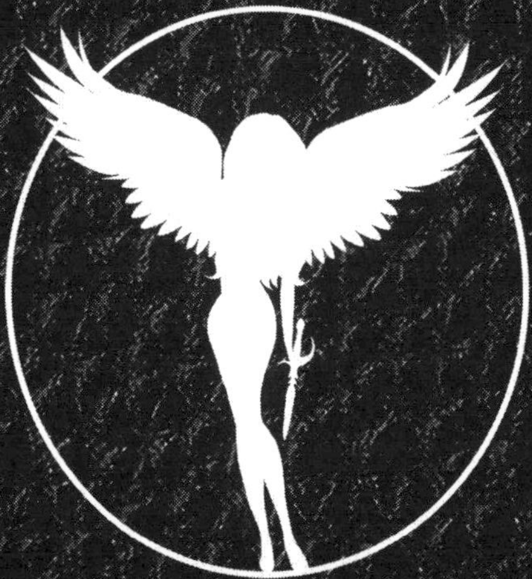

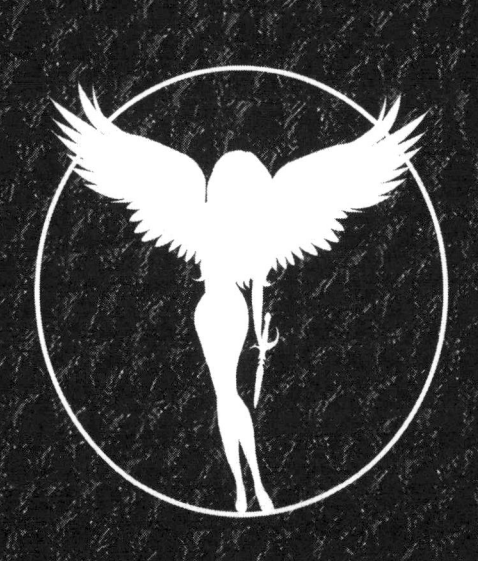

THE SAINTHOOD

CHAPTER 21

I MEET SARIAH downtown and work out some aggression in the ring. Then, I shower and change, and we meet Sean and Emmett at the diner for something to eat. The guys are all worked up over what the Saints did to me and my new plan to stop fighting them, but I talk them around, assuring all three of my friends that I know what I'm doing.

"How's your sister doing?" I ask Emmett after the waitress has refilled our sodas.

"She's good, thanks. You'll have to drop by the house sometime. I know she'd love to meet you."

My eyes climb to my hairline. "You told your sister about me?"

"Course I did." He shoots me a cocky grin. "I tell her about all my crushes."

I throw a few fries at him across the table, and he laughs. "Relax. I told her we were friends, and I might've mentioned you take kickboxing classes. She'd love to join, but it's out of the question while she's so ill. I think she wants to live vicariously through you."

"I can drop by sometime and talk to her about it."

"Cool."

The bell over the door chimes, and a deathly hush settles over the room as footsteps enter the diner. I don't need to look around to know who it is because my body is already so attuned to Saint Lennox I can detect whenever he's close. That crazy connection between us sparks to life when he's near, lifting all the tiny hairs on my arms, making my heart beat faster, my skin heat, and my body ache with need.

It freaks me the fuck out.

Because I always thought it was a myth authors created to make readers believe in soul-mate love.

I have zero desire to live in my own twisted romance novel.

The Sainthood lit a flame to my childhood and murdered my father, and they've stolen my mother from me. Saint, Galen, Caz, and Theo may not have been directly involved, but they're part of the same organization. They own the same crimes.

I do *not* want this connection with him.

I don't want to feel the way I feel when I'm around *any* of them.

I've spent years successfully caging my emotions, and they are breaching barriers left and right. They are breathing new passion into me, bringing me back to life, and I hate them for it.

If my friends knew I felt like this, they would nuke this new plan of mine without hesitation, because it's hella risky.

Yet I don't feel like I've much choice. Saint has already decided, and it'll work better for me if I appear to be going along with it.

Footsteps approach, and even if I didn't already know who it was, the dark glare from Emmett would confirm it. I kick him under the table, cautioning him to get with the program.

"Get that to go, princess," Saint says, looming over our table. "We need to leave."

"For where?" I ask, pretending I don't notice how hot

he looks in his creased, worn black leather jacket and ripped skinny jeans. My stomach flips when I spot The Sainthood logo on his jacket, and I know all the guys have the same logo inked on their skin.

"Get. Up." He challenges me with his eyes. "Unless you want me to make a scene." He cracks his knuckles, drawing my gaze to the intricate ink on his hands, as he grins wickedly. "You know how much I love that."

"No need to get your panties in a bunch. I'll go with you. I was just wondering where." I grab my bag, plate, and my drink. "Catch you guys at school," I say to my friends. They mumble their goodbyes as I wait for the waitress to bag my food. Then, Saint grabs my elbow and steers me out of the diner, surrounded by the other three goons.

"Where the fuck were you all weekend?" Saint asks as we walk toward his Land Rover.

My eyes lower to his crotch. "How's the aftermath of the manscaping?" I inquire, lowering my voice but not whispering. "Bet you're itchy as fuck, right?" I can't help smirking.

If looks could kill, I'd be ten feet under with the way he glares at me. "Keep your voice down," he murmurs. "You're lucky you're still breathing."

"Now, now." I pat his arm. "Don't be like that. We had a deal. I was pissed at you. You were pissed at me. Now, we're even."

He audibly grinds his teeth, and I feel like bursting into song. Every time I thought of his trimmed pubes over the weekend, I doubled over laughing. I'm going to milk this for as long as I can.

"Where did you go?" he asks again.

"I'll trade ya. An answer for an answer." I stuff a few fries in my mouth, making a big deal out of licking the salt off my lips and my fingers.

Caz chuckles, and Galen scowls, shoving his hands deep in his pockets. Theo is mute as he dutifully follows at the rear.

Saint's jaw tenses, and he opens his mouth to say

something but stops himself in time. He opens the passenger side door, and Galen shoves past me, but Saint stretches his arm across, blocking him. "Princess is sitting with me today."

Galen's back turns rigid, and the glower he gives me as he turns around would annihilate weaker mortals. But I'm made of strong stuff, so I ignore him, not even gloating, because I'm pretending to be nice.

That seems to rile him up even more, and he yanks the door open to the back seat, almost pulling it off its hinges.

"Calm the fuck down," Saint warns, drilling him with a look before he gestures for me to climb up. He shamelessly ogles my ass as I get in, and I'm grateful my tee hangs below my jacket. He swats my butt, grinning before closing the door.

What is it with douchey guys thinking they can slap my ass today?

The three guys are squished in the back, and Galen sends daggers at me through the mirror as I bite into my burger. I chew my food, and he glares at me the whole time. When I've swallowed, I swivel in my seat, the leather squelching with the motion. "What the fuck is your problem with me?"

He sits up straighter, leaning forward so he can pin me with the full extent of his hatred. "Your very existence annoys the fuck out of me. That good enough for you, angel?"

Saint rolls his eyes as he starts the car and glides out onto the road.

"You just need to skullfuck the shit out of someone," Caz says, and every pair of eyes lands on him.

Saint smirks, Galen snarls, and Theo is passive. As usual.

Caz beams like he just won a fucking award.

"You are so freaking weird," I admit, taking another bite of my burger.

Saint watches me eat with a wolfish grin on his face.

"It's his word of the day," Theo says, and I arch a brow.

Caz elbows Galen in the gut as he leans toward me, his warm brown eyes lit with excitement. "You know what the Urban Dictionary is, princess?"

Now, it's my turn to roll my eyes. "Well, duh," I mumble over a mouthful of burger.

"Caz is addicted to it," Theo continues explaining.

"And he drives us fucking insane," Saint cuts in. "He picked skullfuck from the list of trending words this morning, and he's been trying to fit it into the conversation all day."

I finish my burger, crumple up the empty paper bag, and throw it on the floor of Saint's pristine new ride. The wolfish grin vanishes from his face, and I silently fist pump the air as I turn to face Caz. "I think that's pretty cool. And I'm game to play."

The goofy smile on his face matches the smug glint in his eyes as he flips Saint off. "The princess loves my geekiness. I've just died and gone to heaven."

I snicker as I extract my cell and power it on. I can practically feel the hostility radiating from Saint. I've noticed he doesn't like it when I give the others attention, and I've added that to my arsenal of dirty tricks.

Ignoring the multitude of fake worried texts from Mom, I log on to Google and type in the name of the site. I can hardly contain my laughter as I read the definition. "Skullfuck. The action of inserting one's erect penis into the eye socket of another person and proceeding to thrust your hips back and forth, thereby fucking their skull." I knew what the word meant, but I still make a face. "Ew. Gross. What kind of sick fuck would do that?"

"Rumor has it the SoCal Sainthood chapter did that a couple years back to a bunch of their rivals," Theo says in a deadpan voice like he's reading an encyclopedia.

"After they'd gouged out their eyes and before they pumped them full of bullets," Saint clarifies.

"They sent a video of it to the dead dudes' girlfriends and wives," Caz says, waggling his brows like it's the best thing he's ever heard.

"Never invite me to any parties in the SoCal chapter," I deadpan, shivering at the thought.

"I don't know why you're looking so pleased with yourself," Galen says, goading Caz with a look. "That was lame-ass."

"You're just pissy 'cause the princess beat your time," Caz retorts.

"What the what?" My confused gaze bounces between them.

"The pit was one of our initiation trials," Saint confirms, and I try to look like all the blood hasn't drained from my face. "And you beat Galen's time by ten minutes."

I frown. "How can you tell?"

Did the assholes have eyes on me in the woods?

"We based it off the time it took for you to return to the house," Saint replies.

I slant my best puppy-dog eyes at Galen. "Aw, beaten by a girl. How tragic."

"Consider it a freebie," he snarks. "It won't be happening again."

I chew on the inside of my cheek, my mouth tasting like sandpaper. "Whose idea was it for me to replicate one of your trials anyway?"

Saint picks up on something in my tone, and he scrutinizes my face closely before he's forced to return his attention to the road. "Mine. Why?"

"I doubt your dad'd be pleased. Girls have a clear role in the organization, right? I thought they were either wives, girlfriends, or hoodrats?"

"Correct, but why would us dropping your sexy ass in the same pit ruffle Sinner's feathers?"

I shrug. "Just an observation."

"Neo wouldn't give a fuck," Galen says. "You crawled your way out of a pit. Big fucking deal."

"One of these days, I'm gonna carve that grumpy look off your face and give you a new smile, à la Joker style," Caz replies, attempting to lighten the tension in the air.

"One of these days, I'm gonna hack the Urban Dictionary

site and wipe it off the face of the planet," Galen retaliates.

"Shut the fuck up. I'm sick of this shit talk." Saint grips the wheel tight. "We've got business to attend to, and I need everyone's head in the game."

"Then, you should've left the slut at home," Galen supplies. "Because all she does is stir shit."

"I haven't done a fucking thing," I protest, flinging my hands in the air. "Not my fault you've got a giant stick up your ass."

The car screeches to a halt in the middle of the road, and cars swerve to avoid crashing into us, honking their horns, the drivers waving angry fists as they pass by.

Holy fucking shit.

Saint is a law unto himself.

"You're acting like spoiled children, and I won't tolerate insubordination," Saint roars, glaring at his friends. He pokes his finger at his cousin. "You're giving me a fucking headache. Knock it off."

Galen folds his arms, challenging Saint with a look that suggests he won't back down.

"I'm in fucking charge," Saint continues, "and you'll do as I say. If you don't like it, I can always have a word with Sinner. See how well that goes down."

"Drive the car, asshole," Galen hisses, gripping the back of Saint's chair. "And fuck off with the lecture. We don't need a reminder of who's in charge." A snide smile graces his lips. "But not for much longer." He prods Saint in the back in a deliberate move. "Just remember, once we complete initiation and graduate school, we'll be members of the senior chapter. You'll only be a small fish in a big pond then."

"I'm the prez's son. My word will still be king." Saint's bloodcurdling tone sprouts goose bumps all over my body. "And like my father, I'll move through the ranks quickly." He sends a bone-chilling look in Galen's direction. "You'd do well to remember that, *cousin*."

Galen bleeds frustration as he stares out the window,

seething. He's a melting pot of restrained aggression that's going to erupt and destroy everything around him someday.

Saint starts up the car, and we move forward again. "I know shit is eating you up," he says after a while, glancing at Galen through the mirror. "We'll get to the bottom of it. I promise."

Hmm. That's interesting. *Is he referencing the pics of Galen's mom?* Everyone knows she's a junkie, and I doubt anyone is shocked she's hooking. I'm only surprised because my dad had them. *Am I missing something here?*

"You seriously need to get laid," Caz adds. "Blue balls make you cranky as hell."

Galen grunts, and I feel the daggers digging into my back. "Not like that's happening anytime soon."

I twist around, smiling sweetly. "I'll crawl in there and fuck you right now if it means you stop being an almighty pain in my ass."

"You hate him," Theo reminds me, looking up from his tablet to join the land of the living for a change.

I shrug. "I don't have to like him to have sex with him."

Saint whips his head to mine. "If you didn't have a great rack and a sweet ass, I'd almost mistake you for a dude."

I scoff. "Don't be sexist. If I was a guy and I made that statement, you'd all be whooping and hollering and patting me on the back. Why can't I enjoy sex and speak my mind, no matter how salacious my thoughts might be?"

"Because it's not very ladylike," Theo replies, becoming more invested in this conversation.

"I've zero interest in being a lady."

"I don't think your mom would be pleased," he adds, inciting my rage.

"Like I give a fuck what that backstabbing bitch says." I spin around in my seat, folding my arms across my chest, annoyed at Theo's comments and the fact I've just shared a part of myself with the dickheads.

"Lo—"

"I'm done talking about her, Theo," I say, interrupting him

before he can probe any further. I stare at the side of Saint's head as he drives us toward the rougher part of Lowell. "Where are we going, and what are we doing?"

"An answer for an answer," he says, eyeballing me.

I sigh, pursing my lips for show. "Fine. I was at a hotel in Channing. The Regent."

Disbelief is etched across his face as he shoots me some serious side-eye.

I pull the papers Sariah gave me from my jeans pocket. "Here. Check the receipts if you don't believe me." Thank God, I made a reservation for Sariah and Sean at the hotel last night. I had a feeling I might need proof.

He glances at them briefly. "A suite? You better have been alone." He narrows his eyes, and a chill tiptoes up my spine.

I was savvy enough to book it in my name alone, and Sariah snuck Sean in for some sexy time. I glare back at him. "I was alone. Plotting ways to murder you all in your sleep."

His lips tug up. "Come up with anything creative?"

"I'm all about the art, baby," I purr, licking my lips.

"You can get creative while I sleep anytime, princess." Caz holds the back of my chair as he leans forward. "*My* blue balls would thank you."

I might be imagining it, but I swear I see Saint shivering.

I reach around and pat Caz's hand. "I'd take care of that for you if it wasn't for the moody cockblocker in the driver's seat."

"You'll take care of it when I tell you you can take care of it," Saint says. "Right now, we need to focus because we're only five minutes away."

I sit up straighter. "I answered your question, so now it's your turn. Where are we going?"

He turns to me, grinning. "To blow some shit up."

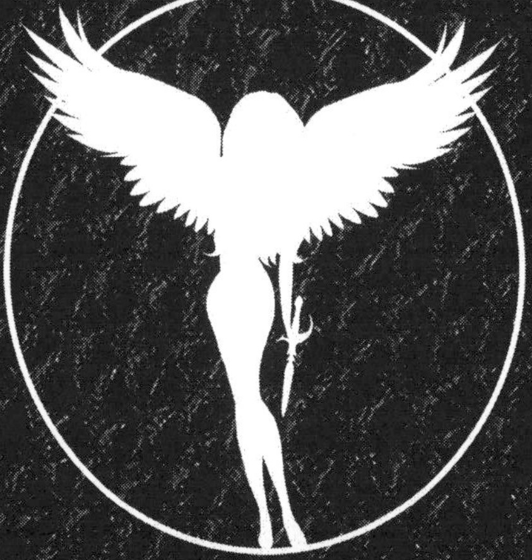

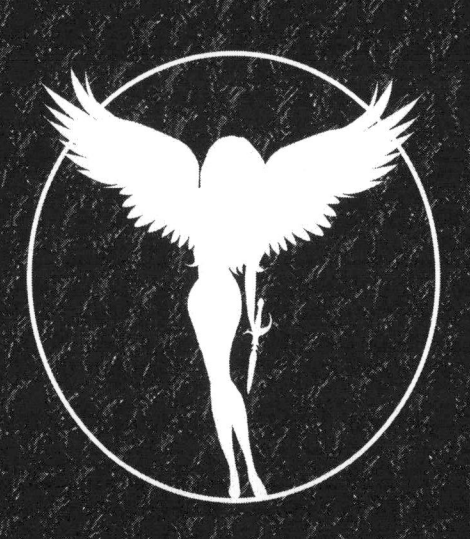

THE SAINTHOOD

CHAPTER 22

"WHAT ARE YOU blowing up?" I ask as we slow down across from a row of houses. A couple of them are boarded up, a few are in obvious need of a paint job, and others have neglected gardens, giving the entire area a run-down feel.

"That place," Saint says, stopping across from the house at the very end of the street.

The exterior is painted in a duck-egg blue, the paint flaking away, revealing rotten panels of wood underneath. Several tiles are missing from the roof, and the garden at the front is so overgrown it could pass for a jungle. The forest runs along the far side of the property, stretching across the other side of the street and beyond, farther than the eye can see. The blinds are down on all the windows, and if it wasn't for the trickle of smoke fleeing the chimney, I'd put money on the house being abandoned.

"And it's *we*," Saint adds. "You're a part of this too."

"I'll sit this one out. Thanks." I offer him a tight smile.

"Who said you had a choice?" We face off for a few minutes, and I give up first on purpose.

"Fine."

"You're so much prettier when you agree."

I flip him the bird, grabbing my gun from my purse and stuffing it in the back waistband of my jeans. I feel heated eyes on me, and I look up. All four guys are watching me intently—even grumpy-ass Galen. "What?"

"You sucking that gun is permanently etched into our retinas," Caz says, earning a sharp look from his leader. "That was so fucking hot." He adjusts himself in his jeans. "And now, I'm hard as a rock. Great."

"Maybe Saintly will be nice and let me blow you later."

"Be a good girl and do what you're told, and I just might," Saint says.

"Are we getting out or what?" I ask after a couple minutes of silence.

"Not yet. We're scoping out the place." Saint looks over his shoulder. "Well?" he asks Theo.

"Four heat signatures. One of them is McKenzie."

Saint rubs his hands together. "This night just got even better."

"Who's McKenzie?" I inquire.

"A lowlife scumbag who deserves to die a slow and bloody death."

"I'm sorry I asked," I murmur, wondering what the fuck I've gotten myself involved in.

We sit in the car for another half hour, all quietly observing the house, and not talking per the domineering asshole's instruction. Just when I've decided I'll probably die from boredom, Theo speaks up. "They're in the back room now. I say we make our move."

"Agreed." Saint gets out of the car and opens the trunk.

I climb out at the same time as the others, watching them distribute some serious hardcore weapons. Caz hands me a rifle, but I back away. "Yeah, no." I pat my waistband. "I'm good."

Like hell I will carry one of their weapons. I've no gloves

with me, and I'm not giving them my fingerprints on one of those things.

Caz shrugs, swinging a duffel bag over his shoulders and sauntering across the road with Galen, both of them making zero effort to conceal their movements. It's dark out now, but it's still brazen as fuck. I watch with reluctant admiration as they stick blocks of explosive to the exterior walls of the house.

Saint closes the trunk. "Let's move out." He grabs my hand. "You stay with me, princess."

Adrenaline flows through my veins as we creep around the side of the house and around to the back. The guys line up at the rear right-hand-side window, standing a good distance back. The wooden blinds are closed, obscuring our view of the room inside, but Theo confirmed there were four people inside, and things are about to get real.

An ominous sense of foreboding washes over me, and I've a real bad feeling about this.

"Get ready for mayhem, baby." Saint winks, releasing my hand and steadying his finger on the trigger of his rifle before nodding at the others.

The four of them open fire in sync, sending a barrage of bullets flying through the window. The glass shatters explosively, scattering broken shards all over the patio. The noise is deafening until Saint raises his hand and the shooting stops. Shouts emerge from inside, followed by the sound of running footsteps and the slamming of the front door. The guys grin at one another, looking pumped up and ready to shoot more rounds, while Theo pulls his cell out of his jeans. "It's clear." I guess he has the same tech on his phone as his tablet.

Saint lowers his weapon and grabs my hand, and we stride with urgency around to the front of the house. "We're good here?" he asks, and Galen and Caz nod.

"It's all set."

"Perfect." Saint tows me back toward the Land Rover, pointing his gun at a few brave neighbors who risk popping their heads out to see what all the commotion is about. As soon as they take one look at his face and The Sainthood emblem on his leather jacket, they hightail it back into their houses.

"What if they call the cops?" I ask while Theo removes his tablet from the back seat and starts tapping away on it.

"They won't," Galen says, taking the rifles from the others, placing them carefully in the duffel bag, and putting it back in the trunk. "They're too afraid of retaliation."

"What's in that house?" I ask though I've already guessed.

"It's a meth lab. The main one supplying Lowell High," Saint clarifies.

I nod. "The competition. Right."

"They had a choice," Saint adds, nodding at Theo when he looks to him for direction. "And like Finn, they chose poorly."

Theo presses a button on his tablet, and the house detonates as each block of explosive blows a hole through the dilapidated property. Plumes of smoke billow into the dark night sky, contrasting with the bright red flames licking a line around what's left of the place.

A shot pings over our heads from behind, and the sound of approaching footsteps has me reacting on autopilot. I whip the gun from my jeans, turn around, and fire off a couple rounds without stopping to think. It's an instinctive reaction to a threat;—one I've been trained for.

A body slumps to the ground, and my stomach drops to my toes. "Shit." I step forward to investigate, but an arm wraps around my waist before I can round the front of the car, stopping me.

"Careful, princess," Saint whispers in my ear, dragging me back. "Let Caz and Galen check first. He might only be injured."

Please just be injured, I repeat over and over in my head like a mantra, as Caz and Galen approach the prone body from either side of the car with guns elevated and pointed at the shooter. They disappear for a few seconds, and my heart rate accelerates.

"Clear," Galen shouts, and Saint lets me go, clasping my

hand in his again as we round the car and move to where the guy is bleeding out on the ground.

"Fuck," I exclaim, watching the pool of blood under his head grow bigger. His eyes are open, staring vacantly up into the sky.

He's dead. I just killed a man.

"Nice shooting, princess," Caz says, admiration lacing his tone. He leans in closer to examine the shot in his skull and the second one embedded in his chest. Switching the flashlight on his phone on, he starts pointing it around, narrowing his eyes as he scans the area surrounding the body.

"Hand me some gloves," Galen says over his shoulder to Theo, and Theo pulls out a pair of clear plastic gloves from his pocket.

Mental note to self—start doing that.

I watch as Galen digs his fingers into the bullet wound in the guy's chest, rooting around in his damaged tissue, until he retrieves the bullet. He holds it upright in the air, his hand and the bullet soaked in the dead guy's blood.

"I've located the second one," Caz says, pointing at a spot just off to the left of the body. Galen stands, grabbing the second bullet and dropping both of them into a clear plastic bag Theo holds out.

Saint is talking on his phone, putting in a request for a cleanup crew, and awareness dawns on me. I grab Theo's arm. "I'll take those."

"Afraid not, angel," Galen says, smirking. "We'll be holding on to the evidence."

Saint ends his call, snatching the gun from my hand before I've had time to process the movement. He hands it to Theo. "Put that and the bullets into lockup. You know the drill."

"You fucking assholes set me up." I can't believe they outmaneuvered me.

Saint holds up his palms. "I'll admit I brought you along so you were an accessory, but I'd no way of knowing one of the guys would hang around."

"And no one forced you to shoot him," Galen adds.

"One of us might be nursing a bullet wound if she hadn't," Theo says, locking the evidence into a secure briefcase.

I'm not buying Saint's explanation, because it's too convenient. I wouldn't put it past him to have paid the guy to shoot at us, not expecting me to be such a good marksman.

"Who was he?" I ask.

Saint prods his foot in the dead man's side. "Luke McKenzie. A drug dealer and a pimp. Lately, he'd turned his hand to human trafficking." Saint spits on him. "Fucking degenerate. He was snatching girls as young as five to order."

I mash my boot into the dead guy's crotch, kicking him a few times, hoping he feels it in hell. "I don't feel so bad now," I admit even though it's still a fucked-up situation because the assholes are keeping the proof I committed murder, and no doubt, they intend to dangle it over my head to ensure I do their bidding.

"Asshole deserved it," Caz says, unbuttoning his jeans.

Saint grins as he drops my hand and joins his buddies. I'm not sure what it says about me, but I watch with begrudging amusement as the four guys piss all over McKenzie's dead body.

THE HOUSE IS empty when we return, but that's not a huge surprise. Mom is rarely at home anymore. "Everyone, shower and meet in the basement," Saint commands, and I salute him.

He pulls me into his body, squeezing my ass. "I'm going to enjoy this so much, baby." I drill him with a "fuck you" look. "We've got leverage now, princess." He squeezes my butt harder. "We completely fucking own your ass."

"Like hell you do." I plant my hands on my hips and tip my chin up. I've given this a lot of thought on the journey home. "So what if you have a gun with my fingerprints? It's unregistered and can't be traced back to me. And if the cops were to ever question me, I'd feed them some bull about how you tricked me into holding your gun. We do live together, remember?"

"That gun committed murder, baby." Saint's smug confidence grates on my very last nerve.

"If you turned it over, it'd implicate The Sainthood." I return his smug look with one of my own. "You think anyone in this entire town would believe your word over mine?" Although some might question my morals and my judgment over the tape, I've never been in trouble with the law, and what happened to me as a kid garnered plenty of good will. "I'm a model student, a model citizen, and a bereaved daughter who was once kidnapped by the very same organization accusing me of murder. Get fucking real. That evidence is worth jack shit, and you know it."

"What the hell did you just say?" Theo asks from behind, and I turn around.

"You heard me."

Galen, Caz, and Theo share puzzled expressions before looking to their leader. "What's she talking about, Saint?"

He steps forward, closing his eyes briefly and rubbing at his temples. "Shit."

That's all I need to know to confirm the others aren't clued in. He never said anything, and it's obvious that bastard Sinner didn't either. I'm not sure what to make of that or how it changes things, if at all, but I park those thoughts for now.

Saint opens his eyes, watching me with that intrusive lens of his.

I cock my head to the side. "Do you want to tell them or shall I?"

THE SAINTHOOD

CHAPTER 23

Saint insists we shower before talking as we're all covered in blood and reeking of smoke. He also insists on watching me scale the drainpipe and climb through my bedroom window, telling me if I end up falling to my death he'll have to explain it to my mom.

He's an idiot if he thinks I believe that.

Douche just wants to ogle my ass some more.

As I'm leaving my room after freshening up, I make a mental note to install the other padlock I bought to the front of the door because climbing in and out of my window is getting old real fast.

I saunter into the basement in a cloud of perfume, the musky, sensual tones of jasmine, vanilla, and sandalwood mixing with spicy dark fruits, swirling around me in an alluring haze. My freshly blow-dried hair is tumbling down my back in soft waves, and I love how each of the guy's gazes roams my tiny denim shorts and the off-the-shoulder short-sleeved black and silver top I'm wearing.

I'm slowly reeling them in whether they realize it or not.

I'm in my bare feet, and I know my legs look super long and slim and that the edge of my sheer, lacy purple bra is evident on the side where my shirt hangs low. Even dickhead Galen can't tear his eyes away. I swipe a beer from the bucket on the table and sit on the couch beside Saint, trying not to gloat. I purposely sit close enough that our thighs brush together. The other guys are on the leather couch across from us, their eyes glued to my body, as I get settled.

I bring the beer to my lips, tipping my head back in slow motion and savoring the glide of the cold liquid down my dry throat. I feel the guys' heated attention, and blood rushes south, making my core pulse with need.

Sexual tension is thick in the air, and my nipples pucker, poking through my flimsy bra and the thin material of my top. My eyes meet Caz's penetrating gaze, and he looks seconds away from pouncing on me. I lick my lips, tracing the tip of my finger along the rim of the bottle, and his Adam's apple bobs in his throat while he stretches his thighs out to accommodate the growing bulge in his jeans.

Saint clears his throat, eyeballing Caz. "I thought you wanted the truth."

"We do," Theo says, cutting through the heated atmosphere and refocusing our collective energies. His eyes dart to mine. "You told me you didn't know who kidnapped you. That they kept you blindfolded and they used initials for names."

"That was all I knew back then. It was only much later I discovered the truth," I admit.

"And how is it *you* know?" Galen asks, jerking his head at Saint. "I thought there were no secrets between us."

Saint scoffs. "Don't talk out your ass. Every person in this room is hiding something."

"It's not as if it matters much," I say, crossing one leg over the other. Four pairs of eyes greedily follow my movement. "It's in the past."

"Of course, it matters!" Galen yells. "It fucking matters a lot."

Why? He fucking hates me. I frown, wondering what else I don't know.

Galen scratches the back of his head as he shares a pointed look with his cousin. "How long have you known?"

Saint flexes his arms, glancing at me as he says, "I've always known."

"Explain that," Theo grits out, and I've never heard him use that tone with Saint before.

Saint ignores Theo, holding me prisoner with his intense gaze. "Am I the reason you figured it out?"

I stare into his hypnotic blue eyes. "It wasn't really one thing. It was a bunch of pieces slotting into the puzzle all at once."

"When?" he asks.

"About two years ago." After me and Theo were over.

"Can you stop talking in code and fucking tell us what the hell is going on?" Caz asks with a pout.

"I was kidnapped on my way home from school," I say, beginning to explain. "I was only three blocks from my house when a van drove up onto the sidewalk and a strange woman yanked me inside. She put tape over my mouth and a cloth bag over my head."

I take a sip of my beer as I relive one of the worst days of my life. "We drove for what seemed like ages. I couldn't breathe properly, and I was gagging, almost choking, before she removed the bag and the tape. She threatened if I made a sound she'd cut my tongue out. I was too frightened to disobey. When I was taken out, we were at an abandoned warehouse in the middle of nowhere. A few cars and trucks were parked out front. The woman walked me up to the entrance and forced me to face the other way while she argued with some man."

"Dad didn't know I'd snuck into the back of his truck," Saint interjects, picking up the story from his side.

I've always wondered how he came to be there.

"I was thirteen, and we'd just started getting more involved with the business, but this night, he said I couldn't come with. I was pissed and stubborn, and I went along for the ride anyway."

Caz rolls his eyes. "Not one bit surprised."

Saint flips him off. "Sinner had only been inside the warehouse a few minutes, and I was about to get out and spy through the window when a van pulled up. I watched Dad's latest piece of ass drag a girl out of the van."

He peers deep into my eyes as he speaks. "I could tell she was scared. She was trembling all over, but she never said a word. Didn't scream or protest. Just looked around, taking in her surroundings, knowing it would be futile to call out for help."

He brushes a stray strand of hair off my face, and his touch ignites a host of fiery shivers across my skin. "I wanted to rescue you," he says, lowering his voice. "I didn't know you or why you were there, but I just knew I needed to get you away. I was trying to work it out in my head when you spotted me."

"I never forgot your face," I whisper, my mind lost in the moment, trapped in the past, reliving those few seconds that bonded us instantly. "I saw the fear and determination in your eyes, and I silently begged you to help me."

"I know." He cups one side of my face, lost to the past in the same way I am. "And I wanted to, but he saw me. Just before the door closed after you went inside."

"What did he do?" Galen asks, his tone somber.

"He beat me bloody. Told me to forget I'd seen her. Said she would be released once her dad paid the ransom. He threatened if I told a soul, he'd kill her and then me."

"I fucking knew there was more to it!" Galen jumps up. "I remember that time. You could barely fucking walk for days. When I asked you why he'd been so savage, you told me you'd thrown shade at him while he was drunk." He looks at me, and for a brief second, there's no anger or hostility in his gaze. "I remember him throwing up when the news reports came out after the fact. He was distant and troubled for months."

"Galen." Saint silences him on the spot.

Galen swings his gaze to his cousin. "You should've told us."

"I wouldn't risk her life like that," Saint says, and my stupid heart swoons at his words.

For so long, I've been confused over that moment. Wondering if it was all in my head. If it was one-sided. If I'd imagined the troubled boy with the piercing blue eyes and messy blond hair. And when I figured it out, and I realized who he was, I wondered if he'd been a part of it.

Hearing his confession soothes me.

I know we're enemies. That this changes nothing. But, in this moment, there are no walls between us. There is only truth. And he's just proven, at one time, he cared for me.

Enough to suffer a beating.

To keep this a secret from his best friends.

"You should've told us that night during spring break," Theo says, his words carrying accusation.

"Why? Because it would've changed anything?" Saint radiates frustration and anger.

"Because it might've helped put things in perspective," Caz states, sighing and sinking back into the couch.

Galen sits back down, burying his head in his hands. He's always known I'm the girl who was kidnapped, so I'm not exactly sure why he's reacting so emotionally. Who kidnapped and tortured me didn't change the outcome, and he hasn't shown me much sympathy until now.

That guy is such a fucking mystery. One I hope to figure out sometime if only to gain some type of understanding or closure.

"The Sainthood has always been about protecting kids," Galen says, spearing Saint with a tormented look. "Or at least, that's what I've always thought."

A muscle pops in Saint's jaw, and he looks off into space.

"Why would they do this to...Harlow?" He almost whispers my name. "This was before Sinner was prez, so the order must not have come from him."

I snort, lifting my shirt up at the hem, pointing at the circular-shaped puckered marks on my stomach. "Your precious Sinner did that to me. He removed the blindfold and made me watch his face. He laughed while he stubbed his cigarette out on my flesh. His eyes were manic. His pleasure obvious. Trust me, he was definitely the one in control."

For years, I refused to think back to those last few hours because the pain was so unbearable. I did such a good job of blanking it out that I'd forgotten I'd seen his face. When I figured things out, and I pulled up photos of The Sainthood members, I picked him out almost instantly.

Galen's nostrils flare, Theo clenches his fists, and Caz gulps.

Theo jumps up. "This is such fucking crap!" He throws his hands in the air. "All of it!" He puts his face right up in Saint's. "We had a right to know. This is not unconnected. It can't be."

"None of us know that," Saint says, maintaining a cool tone. "And I said nothing because Sinner reminded me it was to remain a secret." He looks mildly apologetic as he meets my eyes.

"That is fucking bullshit, and you know it!" Theo screams in Saint's face, grabbing a fistful of his shirt. You could hear a pin drop in the room. "It's all a fucking lie, isn't it? I knew Lo wouldn't do that."

Saint shoves Theo away, jumping up and squaring up to him. "It's possible we don't know everything, and you need to watch your mouth."

I stand. "What's a lie? What do you think I've done?"

"Stay out of this," Saint barks, and it's clear our little trip down memory lane is over.

"Like hell I will! This is everything to do with me!" I scream.

"It's Sainthood business that doesn't concern you."

"Then, I'm done talking." Tonight's been a lot to process, and I need to retreat and assess everything. I swipe another beer and head toward the stairs.

Saint calls out to me as I walk away. "Neo can't know."

I spin around. "Why? He'll kidnap and torture me again?"

He walks calmly toward me. "That was child's play, princess." He tips my chin up with one long finger. "And trust me, you don't want to know what it's like to be on the receiving end of Dad's punishment as an adult."

CHAPTER 24

I AVOID THE kitchen the following morning, forgoing breakfast, and drive to pick up Sariah on an empty stomach. We stop off at our favorite diner, ordering coffee and doughnuts to go.

I park outside the front of the school building, cranking up the heater in the Lexus as we eat while I bring my bestie up to speed.

"What do you think is going on?" She props her feet up on the dash, blowing on her coffee.

"I'm not sure, but it's obviously something to do with the way they've been treating me. Sinner has asked something of them."

"And the revelation that The Sainthood were the ones who kidnapped you has them questioning shit?"

I shrug, stuffing the last bit of glazed chocolate doughnut in my mouth. I chew quickly, pondering it all again. "It seems that way. Even Galen looked thrown although I'm sure that won't last." I sip my coffee. "Theo was the biggest surprise. He blew up at Saint."

"He still cares about you."

"If that's true, why did he cut me off like I meant nothing to him? His reaction could be all part of the play."

"Maybe you should've let him in last night." I explained how Theo spent a half hour outside my bedroom door after the confrontation in the basement, begging me to let him in so we could talk.

"I'm feeling a little out of my depth," I truthfully admit, eyeballing my bestie and putting words to the emotion festering inside me.

"How so?"

I lean my head back, sighing, wondering how to articulate this. I sigh again, turning my head to the side so I'm facing her. "They're making me feel things, Sar. Things that scare me."

She analyzes my face, not saying anything for a few seconds. She clears her throat before speaking. "You know how much I hate The Sainthood for what they did to my family. I know your guys weren't directly involved in that, but the organization they're members of was responsible. I don't need proof to confirm what I know in here." She thumps her chest, right over the place where her heart is. "I also know how dangerous they are, and I've seen the shit they've pulled on you."

"But?" I ask, sensing there's one coming.

"But I see it too. They're coaxing you back to life." She takes my hands in hers. "I know why you work so hard to keep your emotions on lockdown. Why you protect your heart. Why you're so guarded about who you let into your life. I understand it all. And maybe, if I hadn't met Sean and I didn't know what it's like to be in love, I would feel differently about this. Truth is, I want you to open your heart, Lo. I want you to allow yourself to feel because you're only living half a life if you shut emotions and people out."

"I can't trust them, Sar. They have an agenda, and this is all part of it."

"Probably, but you're smart as fuck, Lo. And you're

playing them at their own game and winning. Feeling something isn't bad as long as you are in control of it."

I twist around. "That's the thing, babe. I'm afraid if I get sucked in deeper I won't be able to control it. And I'm afraid of—" I bite down on my lip.

"Admit it," she whispers.

"I'm afraid of getting hurt. I don't let guys in for a reason and these guys have the potential to cut me wide-open and make me bleed. Especially Saint because he has the ability to get inside me in a way no one ever has."

"You're afraid he'll use it against you? Or you think he'll see all that guilt and shame you're carrying?"

Fuck. Maybe I haven't been so successful at hiding my emotions. "You see that?"

She nods slowly. "I see it, but I don't understand it, because you're one of the best people I know."

"If you knew the absolute truth, you wouldn't say that."

She squeezes my hands tight. "There is nothing you could tell me that would alter anything between us." She smiles, but I can't return it because I don't share her confidence. "I'm always here for you, Lo. If you ever want to tell me, I will always listen."

MORNING CLASSES PASS me in a blur. It's hard to concentrate when my mind is so distracted. I'm quiet at lunch, sitting beside the assholes to keep up appearances, but I'm not in the mood to chitchat.

Saint picks up the untouched wrap from my tray, holding it out to me. "You skipped breakfast. Eat."

"I'm not hungry, and I had coffee and a doughnut."

"Leave her alone," Sariah says, spearing Saint with a look from across the table.

"Butt out. This doesn't concern you," Saint replies, twirling a bottlecap between his fingers.

"Listen here, asshole." Sariah leans across the table, aggression contorting her face. "Anything to do with my bestie concerns me, and I'm not scared of you."

"Sariah." Sean tugs on her elbow, pulling her back and wrapping a protective arm around her shoulders.

"You should be," Saint says. He eyeballs Sean. "Keep her in line." The "or else" doesn't need to be said.

"Knock it off, Saintly. Even look funny at Sar and I'll be happy to demonstrate more of my knife skills," I threaten.

Galen's head whips to Saint's. "What's she talking about?"

"Fuck if I know." He attempts to shrug it off. Under the table he pinches my thigh in warning.

"I'm done with this shit." I stand, my chair screeching in protest.

"I need to speak with you," Theo says, grabbing his bag and rising.

"Well, I don't want to speak with you." I storm off, and he chases after me, catching up to me out in the hallway. A few students loiter in the corridor watching as Theo grabs my arm and forces my back to the wall.

"Stop running away. It's infuriating." He cages me in, putting his face up close to mine.

"You'd know all about that," I huff.

"I messed up, Lo." His voice softens. "I messed up so bad with you, and it's one of my biggest regrets."

I plant a bored look on my face. "So you've said. We done here?" Out of the corner of my eye, I spot Parker and Finn lounging against a locker, pretending like they're not listening.

"We all need to sit down and lay our cards out on the table. It's the only way we're gonna get to the truth."

"What makes you think I'd trust any of you with the truth?"

His eyes scrutinize mine. "That's fair, but you know I'd never let anything happen to you."

"I know nothing of the sort, Theo. You dumped me without a second thought. Cut me out of your life like I never even existed."

He sighs as he takes my hand, threading his fingers in mine. "We both know it didn't go down like that."

I shake my head, removing my fingers from his and pushing him back a few steps. "Rewriting history now, Theo?"

A look of fierce determination crosses his face. Then he grabs my cheeks, pulls my head to his, and kisses me hard and fast. He presses my body into the wall, his arms curling around me, his fingers digging into my ass.

I push him away again, staring at him incredulously. "Seriously?"

Un-fucking-believable. Like, "beam me up, Scotty" level of unbelievable.

"Fuck off, Theo."

I move to walk away, but he holds on to my arm. "I'm not your enemy, Lo. And whether you like it or not, I'm going to prove I'm a true friend this time."

I don't dignify that with a response, walking to the bathroom to check my burner cell, shaking my irritation off with every step I take.

I lock myself in a stall and check my messages to see if Darrow replied. He has, and he wants to meet after school, so I tap out a response, power off the phone, and stow it in the hidden secret pocket of my backpack.

Parker is waiting for me when I step out. "Oh, joy," I deadpan, brushing past her and moving to the sink. "To what do I owe the honor?"

She props her hip against the sink beside me. "Trouble in paradise?" She smirks, twirling a lock of her hair like she's six.

"As if I'd tell you." I wash my hands.

"You're obsolete," she adds, grinning. "And I'll be taking that princess crown real soon."

"Wow, been studying the dictionary lately? Didn't think you had it in you." I dry my hands on a sheet of paper towel.

"I can't wait to knock that smug smile off your face."

"I hope you're the patient type, because that won't be happening any time soon." I put my face in hers. "Like ever." I push her back. "And I'm no fucking princess. I'm the goddamn queen."

She barks out a laugh. "I'll enjoy taking you down."

"Bitch, you come near me and the only one getting taken down is you."

"They won't protect you forever."

I fling my bag over my shoulder. "Who said anything about their protection?" I arch a brow. "I don't need any guy to protect me. I'm more than capable of defending myself. Come at me, and you'll find out the hard way."

I ditch school ten minutes before the bell rings so that I can get away without any of the assholes following me.

Pulling into the gas station on the outskirts of Prestwick fifteen minutes later, I park around the back.

Dar is already there, leaning against the side of his truck with his hands in his pockets. I secure the large brown envelope in my backpack and climb out, following Dar around to the shaded side of the building. This is quite a popular meeting spot in Prestwick whenever anyone is up to anything shady because there are no cameras, it's surrounded by wide open fields, and the owner turns a blind eye to the illegal comings and goings.

"Here." I hand him the envelope.

He frowns. "What's this?"

"Information which will get one of your guys out of jail."

He stares at me for a second before opening the envelope and pulling the papers out. He skims them quickly, before resealing them, folding the envelope in half, and tucking it into the back pocket of his jeans. "This is helpful."

I scoff. "It's more than helpful, and you know it."

"Diego will be pleased. He's been trying to extract Alfred for the past year, but it's not what I asked for."

"I can't pull the location of the warehouse out of thin air!" I hiss. "They're giving me nothing on the cameras, and they have some blocking software installed on their cars, which means the trackers I planted aren't working." I pull my jacket around my body as a gust of wind batters us from behind. "I'm getting closer to them, and I'm confident I'll get the intel. I just need more time."

"I don't *have* more time." He weaves his hands through his hair. "My graduation to the senior chapter depends on me finding that warehouse and destroying their supplies. It's the only way The Arrows will gain control of Prestwick Academy and start winning the lion's share of the business on the street."

"It's not their most closely guarded secret for nothing," I supply. "If it was easy to figure out where they're storing their supplies, then someone would have hit it before. I will get the information. It'll just take a little longer."

He grabs my ponytail. "How do I know you're not lying to me?"

I punch him in the stomach, and he lets me go. "You don't. You've just got to trust I hate them as much as you do."

"But do you?" he asks, rubbing his stomach and glaring at me. "Rumors are circulating, baby. Saint's put the word out you're under his protection. The Sainthood only does that for wives or girlfriends."

I didn't know he did that. I roll my eyes. "We're going to be family. I'm sure the protection extends to stepsisters too."

He straightens up, scrubbing a hand along his stubbly jawline. "Johnny was in touch. Checking I vouched for you. I told him to hold off setting up that new meet until he gets my approval."

Anger blooms in my gut. "You have no fucking right to do that!"

He steps into my face, sneering. "I have every right to do that. You'll get your meeting when I get the location of the warehouse. And you'll get your new IDs once I've blown their supplies to kingdom come." He grabs hold of my ass, reeling me in close to his body. "A deal's a deal, sweetheart."

I knee him in the balls. "Fuck you. I gave that motherfucker a five grand down payment. If you screw this up for me, you'll be sorry."

"Ditto, sweetheart. Fuck with The Arrows and see if you live to tell the tale."

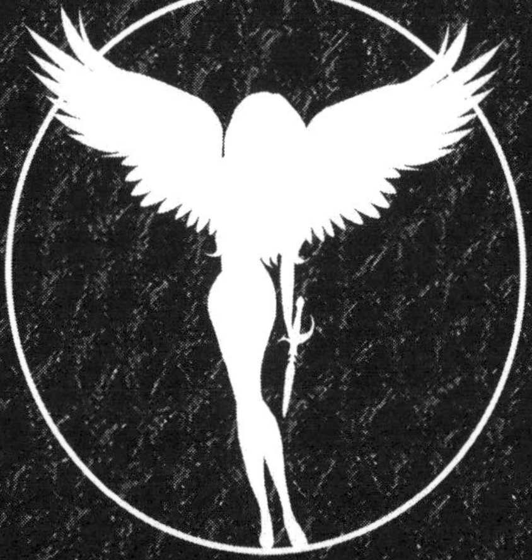

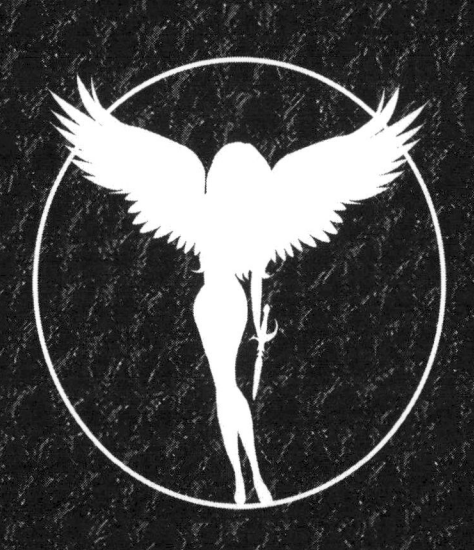

THE SAINTHOOD

CHAPTER 25

"Do you have plans this weekend?" Mom asks me Thursday night when we're all around the dinner table.

"I do now," I reply, shoveling a forkful of mashed potato in my mouth.

Sinner drops his silverware, and it clangs off the table. "Show your mother some respect."

"I'll show her respect when she's earned it."

Mom smiles, ignoring my comment and pretending the tension isn't so thick you'd need a snowplow to cut through it. "Neo and I are looking at wedding venues out of town this weekend. We thought you and Saint might like to come with us?"

What freaking planet does my mother live on that she thought I'd ever be down for that?

"That sounds fun, but, unfortunately, Harlow and I will be indisposed this weekend," Saint says. "She's helping us with some stuff."

I am? That's news to me. All week, we've been keeping our distance. Even Theo hasn't tried to come near me since he kissed me.

Mom's brow creases, and she glances at Neo briefly before asking Saint, "What stuff?"

I jump in with a reply before he can answer. "Our fans are begging us for 'Harlow fucks the Saints part two.'" I shrug, enjoying making Mom squirm. "We thought we'd get started on that." I smile sweetly at her, and I hope guilt is eating her up on the inside.

"Harlow." Saint's voice is low and deep, and how he manages to instill such warning with one word is true talent. "She's joking," Saint assures a pale-faced Giana. "We're working on school stuff," he lies, slanting her his best "butter doesn't melt" expression.

And, of course, Mom falls for it, because it seems she's just that gullible.

The guys are always on their best behavior around her. Smiling. Complimenting her. Never cussing and always mannerly.

And she falls for it every time.

It's like she's erased that part of her brain that knows they were the guys I had a foursome with. The ones who recorded it and helped broadcast it around the web. Even when I taunt her with that, she immediately dismisses it.

Honestly, it has to be seen to be believed.

"That's too bad," she says. "But I'm so happy Harlow is helping you out. She's always been a steady A student." She beams proudly at me, and I genuinely wonder if she's been lobotomized. "And it's great she's willing to help her new stepbrother." She pats me on the shoulder, and I almost choke on the chicken in my mouth. "I'm glad everyone's getting along."

Man. I've definitely wandered into some alternate realm.

THE GUYS ENJOY belittling Mom behind her back when I join

them in the basement later on. Mom and Neo have gone out, and Saint demanded my presence. I wanted to stay in my room and go through the files Diesel sent me earlier, but I need to get my head back in the game. Especially now that jerk Dar has thrown a new wrench in my plans.

Perhaps I should've gone to Diesel for the IDs, but for some inexplicable reason, my gut tells me I'm right to keep my escape plans hidden from him.

The guys are all freshly showered, so I guess they were working out in the gym. Dad built a pretty decent one down here in the enclosed space behind us. I usually work out every couple of days, but not so much since the guys moved in and invaded the territory. Now I'm no longer purposely avoiding them, I can start using it again.

"You obviously got your smarts from your dad," Caz says, patting my thigh as we sit side by side on one of the couches.

"Giana is smart too," Theo replies. "Dad hired her to run this big advertising campaign one time, and he was delighted with the response."

Mom's professional alliance with Mr. Smith's multimillion-dollar medical supplies company ended the same time my fake relationship with Theo did.

"She seems to have nuked all brain cells since my dad died."

Caz passes me the blunt, and I take it, inhaling deeply, before passing it to Galen on my other side. He's been sullen and quiet all night, and I still can't figure him out.

"She loves my dad," Saint says, swigging from a bottle of JD. "Why would you begrudge your mother happiness?"

"Because my father is barely cold in his grave and she's already planning her new wedding," I snap. "I wouldn't expect you to understand. You don't even know who your mother is!" It's a low blow, and I know it, but I'm sick of him pushing my buttons.

"Get over here now." He uses that low, gruff emotionless tone, the one that sends equal tremors of fear and lust shooting up my spine, and drenches my panties, every time.

"Fuck off." I cross my arms over my chest.

Saint angles his head at Caz, silently communicating with one look. Caz sweeps me up, depositing me on Saint's lap before I've had the time to protest.

Saint clamps his arms around my back, holding me firmly in place. My legs slide on either side of his thighs, and my chest is all up in his face. I'm only wearing a thin tank, so he has a bird's eye view of my cleavage. "Speak of my mother again and I'll strip you naked while we all take turns spanking your naughty ass."

Doesn't sound like much of a punishment to me.

My lips curl up, and I push further. "She abandoned you the minute you were born, right? She evaded Sinner and snuck out of the hospital. How does it feel to know she never wanted you?"

"Lo." Theo's voice holds clear warning.

Saint grabs the cheeks of my ass through my jean shorts in a way I know will leave bruises. "You truly have a death wish, don't you, princess?"

"Or she just likes spanking," Caz says, attempting to lighten the mood.

I glance over my shoulder, offering him my best seductive smirk, because you betcha, I do.

"I volunteer as tribute," he adds, and I laugh, turning around.

Saint tilts his head to the side, and a sly grin creeps over his mouth. "The princess would like that too much. I need a more appropriate punishment." He grabs hold of my waist, yanking me toward him, burying his face in my breasts. He tugs my top down, biting and sucking on exposed flesh, and I wriggle against his growing erection as my desire spikes. His hand moves to my crotch, and he rubs his palm back and forth along my pussy through my jeans. The friction of the zipper pressing against my sensitive core has me drowning in sensation.

It's been too long since I was thoroughly fucked, and if this is his idea of punishment, he can punish me any time.

He stands and I wrap my legs around his waist, clinging to him. Without warning, he dumps me on Galen's lap. "Blow my cousin, princess. He needs to de-stress."

"You've got to be kidding me." Galen snorts.

"You know you need this," Saint says, adjusting himself through his jeans. "And she'll hate every second."

"I'll hate every second," he says, contradicting himself as he clamps his arm around my waist, holding me on his lap when I attempt to climb off him.

They're both fucking insane. Or delusional. Because the only one who will hate it is Saint when he sees how much Galen and I enjoy it.

Saint's lips twitch. "Close your eyes and imagine she's Sariah Roark. You still dream of fucking her, right?"

I glare at Saint, and he laughs. I know all the innuendo about my bestie is another way of getting a rise out of me. But they're not the only ones who like to press buttons. "I'm not doing it," I lie. "You can't make me."

Caz chuckles. "You really don't want to go there, princess. He can and will make this happen." He turns his gaze on his leader. "I want one too." He cups the tent in his jeans. "I'm about to explode I'm that frustrated."

"I'll happily blow you," I offer, smiling as I apply some reverse psychology.

"And I'll happily permit it," Saint says, calling my bluff.

"I'll suck Caz's cock, but I'm not sucking the devil's cock." I fold my arms as I eyeball Saint.

"You'll do as I say." Saint crouches over me, yanking my head back by my hair. "There's no point in fighting."

"And if I refuse, how will you make me?"

"We'll give all the recordings of your nightly shows to Sinner. I'm sure he won't hesitate to share them with the guys. Let them get their rocks off to fresh, young pussy."

I stare at him in horror, unable to hide my natural reaction. I feel like slamming my head into the wall. Not that they've realized I know about the cameras, because I figured they knew that straightaway. I disabled all their other tech, so the fact the camera was still operational would've alerted their suspicions.

I knew they were keeping the charade alive because they were enjoying my little nighttime striptease and vibrator act. And I kept it alive because it played into my seduction plans. I knew there was a risk they could expose it, but the thought of the men who kidnapped me watching it makes me ill.

"I hate you," I say, tapping Galen's arm so he'll release me. He loosens his hold, and I slide to my knees on the floor in front of him.

"You love me." Saint's eyes flash darkly as he bends over me, cupping my chin. "And you love how much we want you, and you want us too. You don't need to say it. We all see it in your eyes."

So, he knows this isn't a punishment. *Unless he's punishing himself?*

I wrench out of his hold, turning around on my knees and reaching for the buttons on Galen's jeans. Our eyes meet, and I hold nothing back, letting my desire shine through. This isn't a punishment. I hate him, but taking control of his pleasure, watching him fight me on it and fail—because he will fucking love every single thing I do to him—is the ultimate power play. I will rule supreme over Galen Lennox in the next few minutes, and he's going to love and hate me in equal measure.

All protest has disappeared as he lifts his hips, letting me pull his jeans and boxers down his legs. He knows the state of play as well as I do, and he wants this too much to fight the inevitable any longer. He leans back in the chair, closing his eyes as he spreads his thighs wide. He's completely relaxed, not fearful I'll bite his cock off, because he knows Saint is right. My body is on fire right now, my core pulsing, and my mouth salivating at the prospect of sucking his giant cock.

If I close my eyes, I can remember the feel of him moving inside me, pounding my pussy so hard I saw stars.

Fuck Saint. Fuck him. Fuck him. Fuck him.

I hate he knows me this well.

I don't want him seeing too much.

And this is exactly what I meant when I spoke to Sariah. Because I'm me, I can't help one last retaliation before I get to the task at hand. I glance over my shoulder at Saint. He's back on the couch beside Theo, watching me with fire in his eyes. I pat the knife in my back pocket. "Maybe, I'll give him a little trim too."

Theo glances between me and Saint with an inquisitive look, but he doesn't ask the question. Galen is too in the zone to hear, and Caz is already stroking his bare cock, eyeing me with a predatory stare, flippantly dismissing my intentional dig.

"You're skating on thin ice, princess," Saint warns, and I smile demurely at him before dropping my eyes to the erection pressing against the front of his jeans. He clearly gets off on this too.

I turn my head again, ignoring the guys behind me as I lower my mouth to Galen's impressive cock. I lick the bead of precum at the tip, and his primal moan drenches my pussy in pure need.

I dive in, running my lips up and down his hot shaft while pulling the skin down and pumping the base of his cock. Then I wrap my lips around his crown, lowering slowly and taking him into my mouth. I suck hard, gliding my lips up and down his throbbing length while I also pump his cock with my hand. He thrusts into my mouth, his hips working overtime, and the sounds emanating from his throat are so hot I nearly cream my panties.

His eyes open, and he locks his gaze on mine, watching me suck him as he rocks into my mouth with urgent need. I sit up on my knees so I can position my head better and take a little more of him in, never losing eye contact.

I stroke him faster, aware of Caz cussing and moaning as he tries to slowly stroke his own cock, and it doesn't take long for Galen to detonate in my mouth. Warm, salty cum slides down my throat as Galen roars out his release, continuing to thrust his hips until I've milked every last drop.

He was desperately in need of that.

A popping sound echoes in the air when he pulls out of my mouth. In a surprising move, he yanks me up into his lap and slams his lips down on mine. His tongue forces its way into my mouth, and he devours me with a slew of drugging kisses.

I lose myself in the sensations he's evoking in me and the passionate way he's kissing me.

If I didn't know better, I'd almost believe he has more than hate in his heart for me.

I grab his shoulders, angling my head and deepening the kiss. When he moans into my mouth, every nerve ending on my body is on high alert, and I'm writhing against him like a woman possessed.

Angry sex is a favorite of mine, and I'd love to impale myself on Galen's cock now, but I've another man to take care of, and from the sounds nearby, Caz is on the verge of losing his load.

I pull back, staring at Galen as both our chests inflate in sync. His lips are shiny and swollen from kissing me, and I've no doubt mine are the same. He surprises me again, leaning forward to press a softer kiss to my lips, and I wonder if this is his way of declaring a truce. But his face gives nothing away as he lifts me up, handing me over to his buddy.

Caz holds my face painfully as he meshes our lips in a frantic, hard, brutal kiss. His tongue swirls around the inside of my mouth, licking and laving, and the thoughts he might be tasting his buddy's leftover cum gets me so worked up I grind down on his cock, rocking back and forth, needing the friction to set flame to the fire.

I tumble off the ledge, screaming into his mouth as I come, pressing my chest into his while I ride each turbulent wave. I'm panting after I come down from my high, momentarily resting my head on Caz's shoulder while I snatch a minute to recover.

"You are sexy as fuck, Lo." Caz breathes against my ear as his fingers weave through my hair. "That was one of the hottest things I've ever seen." He takes my hand, pulling it down between the gap in our bodies and pressing it to his cock. "And I need you to suck my dick now before I come without you even touching me."

I slide down between his legs, kneeling on the floor and leaning forward to take him into my mouth. He grabs the back of my head, shoving me down more forcefully on his cock, and he proceeds to fuck my face without abandon.

I stretch my mouth wider, taking him all the way in, licking and sucking as he grunts, jamming his cock in and out of my mouth, his powerful thighs rippling with the motion as he thrusts. I play with his balls, and the minute I prod the entrance to his ass, he comes apart, cussing and shouting my name as he also shoots cum down my throat. Caz is fond of a little ass play, and I wonder if he's ever experimented with other guys.

I fall back on my butt when Caz pulls his dick from my mouth. "Fucking hell, babe. You're like the queen of blowjobs."

I press a kiss to his muscular, hairy leg. "Why, thank you, kind sir. That's just what every little girl aspires to." I send him a saucy smile.

He chuckles, reaching out to tousle my hair in a surprisingly affectionate gesture.

"You're quite impressive yourself," I add, knowing this will piss Saint off. "You made me come without even touching me."

"Yep. I'm just that good, princess," he says, puffing out his chest, happy to take all the credit, and I laugh.

A growl rips through the air, and I swivel around on my butt, looking up at a furious Saint. He glares at Caz. He glares at Galen, and it's completely obvious now that he was punishing himself and he can't handle it.

I crawl toward him, kneeling up and reaching for the button on his jeans. His cock is straining against the denim, and he clearly needs this.

I'm dying to fuck him again, but he slaps my hand away, sneering. "Don't fucking touch me."

He shoots Galen and Caz one last hateful look before storming out of the room and stomping up the stairs, putting hotheaded teenage girls the world over to shame.

I swear, these guys give me a permanent headache.

"What crawled up his butt?" Caz asks.

"You really need to ask?" Theo says, rising. He's the only one who didn't take advantage of the situation though he has an obvious erection too. He extends his hand, and I let him pull me to my feet. "He's not as immune as he lets on." He eyeballs me. "Would it kill you to call a truce?"

I plant my hands on my hips. "I'm not the one who drew battle lines. And it's not my fault if he's his own worst enemy at times."

THE SAINTHOOD

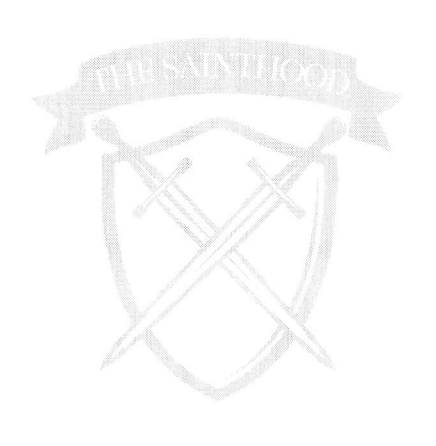

CHAPTER 26

A LOUD NOISE startles me from slumber in the middle of the night, and I bolt upright in bed, grabbing my knife from under my pillow and unsheathing it.

"Fuck." The shadow climbing through my window hits his head off the top of the window frame, cursing in a familiar timbre. Air whooshes out of my mouth in mild relief. I set my knife down on the bedside table and swing my legs out of bed as Saint staggers toward me.

"What the—"

"Shush." The asshole clamps his hand over my mouth, backing me up into the wall. "Don't wake the others." His rich, earthy breath sweeps over my face, and he ignites an inferno inside me when he lifts my left leg, pulling it firmly around his waist, his hands roaming the bare skin of my thigh. He rocks his hips into mine, and there's no mistaking the obvious hard-on.

My libido is now fully awake, and I press against him, clutching him tighter. "How drunk are you?" I murmur, trying not to be affected by the startlingly honest lust mingled with adoration on his face.

"Too drunk to talk," he says in a steady tone without even a trace of slurring. But the rich scent of his breath betrays his alcohol consumption. "But not too drunk to fuck."

"Saint, I—" I don't get any more words out before he slams his mouth down on mine.

I briefly debate pushing him away just to piss him off, because he was an asshole to me earlier and he doesn't deserve to fuck me.

But I'm high on the taste of his lips, the feel of his hot body pressing against me, and his hard dick thrusting into my groin, virtually obliterating his jeans and my thin lace panties, and I fucking want him too bad to reject him. The fact he climbed up to my room in the middle of the night is a major turn on too. It's like some fucked-up version of *Romeo and Juliet*.

I'm taking what I want, and it'll be on my terms.

"Don't think, baby," he murmurs, sliding his hot mouth down my neck. He sucks on the sensitive spot right at the point where my neck meets my collarbone, and I tremble underneath his skillful lips. "Just feel." He rocks his erection against my pussy, and a whimper escapes my mouth. "You feel me, babe? You feel what you do to me?"

I grab handfuls of his ass. "I thought you said no talking?"

His eyes glint with wicked intent as he rips my sleep top in two with his bare hands, exposing my upper body to his hungry gaze. The torn material slinks down my arms, falling to the ground, as he lowers his head and sucks my breast into his mouth.

My nipples are so hard they could cut glass, and I groan, tracing my fingers along his shorn blond locks while he feasts on my breasts. He alternates his attention between them, sucking and kneading, flicking and tormenting, and his callused fingers are not gentle. He tweaks my nipples roughly, plucking them like guitar strings until they're raw and achy.

The whole time I'm flexing my hips against his as we dry hump against my wall. He rips his mouth from my tits long enough to shred my panties and remove his jeans and boxers. We're frantic as we reach for one another again, and when he lifts me up, my legs automatically encircle his shapely waist. I barely contain my scream as he slams inside me in one swift move.

His mouth devours mine as he pounds into me, and I hardly feel my back scraping against the wall, because I'm too consumed with the way his cock is worshiping my pussy. Reality hits in a lucid moment, and I shove at his chest. "What?" he grunts, shifting me higher on his body and thrusting his cock in deeper.

"Condom," I rasp.

"I'm clean, you're clean, and you have the implant. We're not using condoms anymore."

I shove his shoulders harder, stifling a moan as his cock presses against my G-spot and I see stars. "How the fuck do you know that?"

"Theo pulled your medical records." He pins me with a devilish grin. "Don't get mad, baby. Just accept we know everything about you and relinquish control to me."

I bite down hard on his shoulder, and the moan that leaves his lips sends heat gushing through my core. I glare at him before his mouth descends on mine again, and then, I take it out on his tongue, biting and swatting it, and brutalize his lips with punishing kisses.

He yanks me away from the wall, planting my feet on the ground in front of my dresser and draping me over the back of the chair. "Need to go deeper. Spread your legs, princess."

Panic builds inside me as his hands trace up my spine. I slip out from under him before he can plunge back in. "I want to ride you." I grab his hand and tug him toward the bed, pushing him down. I move fast so he doesn't have time to argue, straddling him quickly and lowering myself over his warm, hard length.

"You're so fucking bossy." He grips my hips, digging his fingers into bone.

I grind down on top of him, using my thighs to slide up and down his dick, gripping him hard with my inner muscles. "You fucking love it," I pant.

"Only with you," he grunts, grabbing my arms and pulling me down toward him. "And one day, you'll submit."

"You mean when hell freezes over?" I slam down hard on top of him, and he grunts.

He flips me over superfast, pinning my arms above my head and thrusting deep inside me. "You'll do it and you'll love it."

"Keep dreaming, Saintly."

He smiles, and it's the first genuine smile he's ever given me. I doubt he even realizes he's doing it. I gulp over the sudden lump of emotion wedged in my throat, feeling his every thrust and stroke straight through to my soul.

No! This won't happen. I can't let it.

I channel the unmentionable emotion, molding it into anger, and I arch my back, lifting up, biting and sucking his abs and his chest. He lets go of my wrists so I can sit up straighter, and I claw my nails up and down his back, feeling the prick of blood under the tips of my fingers as I go to town on him. He thrusts into me harder, cussing under his breath when I dig my nails into his sweet ass cheeks, lashing out at his body while inwardly screaming at myself.

He takes it all, giving it back in spades, grazing his teeth over my nipples, leaving bite marks on my breasts and my collarbone, and sucking so hard on my neck I know I'm going to wake up covered in hickeys.

We fuck one another hard, pounding and thrusting, scraping and clawing, our tongues and our lips fighting for supremacy as we battle our natural instincts. He's got his tongue piercing in, and every time I feel the metal ball moving against my tongue or he licks the inside of my mouth, I let loose a primal moan drenched with sheer liquid lust. I drag my nails through his scalp, bite his earlobes, and scratch his face.

He yanks my head back by my hair, pulling it so tight it

makes my scalp sting, and then, he nips and bites along the edge of my jaw, the pleasure-pain sensation electrifying every cell and nerve ending in my body.

It's wild and out of control, and I'm loving every fucking second of it.

He is too.

We toss and tumble on the bed as we challenge each other for control, flipping one another over every few minutes. I slam up and down on his cock, and he pounds into my pussy, prodding my puckered hole with two fingers as his cock demolishes my cunt.

When he pinches my clit, I explode underneath him, and a rainbow of vibrant colors and emotions bursts behind my retinas. I cling to him, feeling his hot cum spill inside me, and I grip his cock tighter, keeping him close to me, both hating and loving how intimate this moment feels.

We hold on to one another as we ride the high and slowly come back down to earth. Our skin is sweaty, our breathing ragged, our heartbeats pounding, and the magnitude of the moment slams into me.

Powerful emotion batters me on all sides, and I'm drowning.

Tears prick my eyes, and for the first time since I was thirteen, I think I might cry on the outside.

Oh fuck. He can't bear witness to this.

I push him off me and hop up, unlocking the door and yanking it open. "Get out." My voice wobbles and my arm trembles as I point at the open door. "Get out and stay out."

He stands, watching me with that fucking, intrusive lens of his as he scoops up his clothes. He stops in the doorway and turns to face me, gripping my chin painfully. "Thanks for the fuck, princess." He tweaks my nose. "Guess it sucks to realize you're female after all."

I shove him out, slamming and locking the door behind him, grab a pillow, and scream into it in pure rage. Then, I lose it, tossing shit around my room, dragging the covers off my bed, pummeling my fists into the wall until the skin tears, and doing everything I can to purge the emotion lashing me on all sides.

It's preferable than giving in to the tears waiting in the wings, because I'll be damned if I give Saint Lennox my first tears in five years.

He can go fuck himself with an inflatable cock extender until his ass bleeds.

I slump to the floor, burying my head in my hands, fighting the storm raging inside me.

When I eventually calm down, I survey the chaos in my room with a sinking feeling, shaking my head as I internally berate myself for losing control.

I'm glad I removed the camera earlier so the guys weren't witness to my shame.

I climb awkwardly to my feet, my body drained from the rough sex and the emotional aftermath, cleaning the mess up in between yawns. As soon as I put my bed back together, I flop onto the mattress, drag the comforter up over my head, and attempt to erase the last couple hours from my mind.

"WHAT THE FUCK happened to you?" Caz asks the following morning when he enters the kitchen, gawking at the multitude of hickeys covering my neck and my collarbone. He moves in closer, his brows knitting together as he inspects the faint bite marks dotting my jawline. I've tried my best to disguise the marks on my face with makeup, but the ones on my neck are harder to hide. Even if I wear a scarf, something that would draw attention itself, it won't cover all of them because they go right up both sides of my neck.

"The same affliction that did a number on our fearless leader," Galen drawls, entering the kitchen with Saint in tow.

Caz inspects Saint's injuries with his jaw trailing the ground. Saint has hickeys all over his neck too and obvious scratches to his face that can't be hidden.

Guess we gave one another a real workout last night.

Caz crosses his arm, narrowing his eyes at Saint, because it's obvious as fuck what went down last night. "Is the rulebook thrown out, or are you making your own rules now?"

"You didn't go unsatisfied from what I remember," Saint coldly replies, brushing past me without acknowledgment and reaching for the coffeepot.

I'm already nursing my third cup of coffee, debating whether I should play hooky today. Yet hiding from the world feels like I'd be handing Saint a victory on a silver platter, and I'm in no mood to do that either.

"Still would've appreciated an invite to the party," Caz grumbles, popping some bread in the toaster.

"And end up looking like Chris Brown and Rhianna after date night?" Galen says. "No thanks. You can keep that shit."

I gasp. "Take that back! That was domestic abuse, and he was arrested for assaulting her. It's not something you should joke about."

"As opposed to you two angry fucking and slapping the shit out of one another?" Theo questions from his position by the doorway. He looks shocked and miserable, and he won't meet my eyes.

"It was consensual," Saint says. "And it's nothing the fuck to do with any of you."

"The hell it isn't," Caz shouts. "We're not allowed to touch her! You went apeshit on my ass when you found us fucking in my room. Now, what, that's suddenly okay?"

Saint pushes Caz out of his face. "Let me make it clear for you." He grinds his teeth, and anger rolls off him in waves. "The princess is mine to do with as I please. If you ask nicely, I might let you fuck her on occasion."

"Excuse me?" I bore a hole in the side of his skull. "I'll fuck whomever I want whenever I want, and right now, you're the last fucking cock I want to ride."

He smirks. "Try telling that to someone who believes it."

"This is fucking bullshit!" Galen roars, pushing his way in between them. "Can't you see what she's doing to us? She is going to rip us apart and then stand back and laugh."

"You have a mighty high opinion of me all of a sudden," I retort.

"I'm just calling it like I see it," he says, shoving past all of us. "None of this shit is going to end well."

"YOU AND SAINT are all anyone's talking about today," Sariah tells me at lunch. We're at a table at the back of the library pretending to study while we eat. I couldn't stomach the cafeteria today. Not because of the nosy looks—my fellow classmates can take their judgmental opinions and shove them up their ass—because I need distance from the Saints.

Things are becoming…intense.

In a way I can't explain.

One part of me loves how much I feel like I belong with them.

Another part of me hates how it feels like I'm losing my identity. Because I'm struggling to process my feelings when it comes to those guys, especially Saint.

"Hey, baby." Sean circles his arms around Sariah from behind as Emmett drops into a seat beside me.

"Jesus fucking Christ." Emmett's eyes pop wide as he scans my marked jawline and neck. His fists clench into balls as he jumps back up. "I don't give a shit who that bastard is, he's going down for this."

I tug on his arm, glaring at the few heads that lift and stare in our direction. "Sit back down." When he doesn't move, I peer up at him with pleading eyes. "Please, Emmett." He reclaims his seat, and I thread my fingers through his. "Saint didn't hurt me. It was consensual rough sex. Okay?"

He stares at me like I'm a stranger. "You get off on that shit?"

I sigh, rubbing a tense spot between my brows. "Things are complicated between us."

"I'll say," Sean supplies, slinging his arm around his girlfriend's shoulders. "And the step-sibling thing seems like the least of it."

"I should've just stayed in bed," I deadpan, biting into an apple. "Because this day honestly couldn't get any worse."

Famous last words.

I'm in world history class, at the end of the day, when the door bursts open and Emmett pops his head in. Ignoring the teach—because it's Shaking Sheila, thus known for her habit of shaking like a leaf whenever anyone raises their voice to her—he motions me forward with his fingers. "You need to come with me. Right now."

I don't need to be told twice, shoving my books in my backpack and striding through the door, out into the empty hallway, conscious of footsteps following me.

"Get lost!" Emmett snarls over my shoulder. "This doesn't concern you."

"Lose the attitude, or I'll gut you and spread your insides over the school walls," Galen threatens, pulling a knife on my friend.

I glare at Galen for a few beats until he relents, putting the knife away. I tug on Emmett's arm. "What's wrong?"

"It's Sariah," he says, striking fear into my heart.

"What happened?"

He takes my hand, pulling me along the hallway, and the tormented, troubled look on his face elevates my heart rate to coronary-inducing level. "She was found in the girls' bathroom over by the science lab, lying on the floor, unconscious, and beaten to a pulp."

THE SAINTHOOD

CHAPTER 27

I WRESTLE MY hand from Emmett's and take off running in the direction of the bathroom. Two pairs of footsteps run after me. Blood thrums in my ears and pounds in my skull as potent fear whizzes through my veins. Rounding the corner, I slam to a halt at the scene that awaits me.

Sariah is being carried out of the bathroom on a stretcher, surrounded by EMTs.

Sean's pale face is testament to his concern for his girlfriend.

Vice Principal Pierson has her arms locked around her body, and she's shaking her head in disbelief, her lips pinched tight, her expression a mix of sorrow and fear.

"Sean!" I jog to his side. "Is Sariah okay?"

He gulps, and his voice sounds scraped raw as he speaks. "I don't know, Lo. Nobody knows exactly how long she's been in there. Someone wedged a chair underneath the door before climbing out the window, so no one's been in there for hours. Cleaning staff was concerned when they couldn't get in, and they called Mrs. Pierson. Then, she came to get me, and

Emmett came with." He massages his temples. "I was sitting in fucking class while my girlfriend was bleeding out on the floor."

"You didn't know, dude." Emmett attempts to reassure him.

"Step aside, please," Mrs. Pierson says, gesturing us to one side. "We need to let the medical personnel do their jobs."

I clutch Emmett's arm as the EMTs carry an unconscious Sariah away. She's covered in blood, and there are bruises already appearing on her arms and her face. Her top is torn, and I glimpse more bruises on her torso.

The vice principal clasps a hand over her mouth, shaking her head, her eyes brimming with unshed tears.

Sean is distraught and struggling to hold it together. "He shouldn't drive," I tell Emmett, nudging him toward his friend and teammate. "You drive, and I'll follow you to the hospital."

"You sure you don't want to come with us?" he asks, casting a wary glance at Galen. He's thankfully kept his mouth shut, observing from the side as he fiddled with his phone.

"It's fine, Emmett. I'll meet you there in a while." I need to know who's responsible for this, and that's not something that can wait.

He nods, walking to Sean and squeezing his shoulders. I watch them walk off, vowing to rip through whoever did this to my bestie.

There are two prime suspects at the top of my list—it was either the bitchy cheerleaders who targeted her last year or this is Parker Brooks' doing. My money is on Parker, because the cheerleaders haven't caused any trouble for Sariah so far this semester. Parker's words from the other day resurface in my mind. She knows she can't touch me, so she went after my best friend instead.

Stupid fucking bitch will pay for this.

Gnawing guilt claws at my insides at the thought of my friend suffering for my sins.

I will fucking kill Parker Brooks and throw her into the pit in Prestwick Forest until her bones rot alongside the others already lining the muddy floor.

"Who did this?" I ask the vice principal, because I need confirmation before starting a new war.

"We don't know, but there will be a full investigation," she says. Her eyes narrow as she looks behind me at the sound of approaching footfall.

The fine hairs on my arms prickle, and I know Galen called in the cavalry.

"We've got it from here, Mrs. P," Saint says, snaking his arm around my shoulders and pulling me into his body. "You can go now."

She opens her mouth to reprimand him but obviously thinks better of it. Tossing a poisonous glare in Saint's direction, she walks off without a word.

"This was Parker and Finn's doing," Saint says.

"You know for sure?"

He nods. "There was a witness. She contacted us, and we left class immediately. We've just come from talking with her. She told us everything," Theo replies.

"Which is?" I ask, anger mushrooming inside me.

"Parker paid this freshman to keep watch in the hallway while her, Beth McCoy, and a few others cornered Sariah," Caz confirms.

"She fought back," Saint says. "But those aren't good odds."

"How long was she lying unconscious for?"

Saint squeezes my shoulder. "It happened at the end of lunch, just before the next period."

"Where the fuck is that freshman?" I seethe, my hands balling into fists. "That little bitch knew my best friend was lying beaten and bloody on the floor, and she waited hours to contact you? I'm going to make her wish she'd never been born."

"As much as that turns me the fuck on, we'll handle her punishment," Saint says.

"It's delicate," Theo explains. "Our rule is still fresh.

People need to feel comfortable coming to us with stuff, so we have to tread carefully."

"Beating her bloody would not send the right message," Caz agrees.

"And we need to keep her away from the authorities until we've handled it," Saint says.

"Fine. Forget the fucking twat. Just point me in Parker's direction, and I'll vent all my rage at her. She'll be in a wheelchair for life by the time I'm through with her." That goes for Beth and the other bitches too.

"All in good time, princess."

"Do not fucking patronize me, Saint." I shuck out of his hold. "If this was one of your guys, you'd have already smashed through the classroom door and gunned the bitch down."

"Actually, that's the last thing he would do," Galen cuts in. "Our violent rep may proceed us, but most of our attacks are skillfully planned in advance."

"And we know just how to take Parker down," Saint adds, grabbing my hand and lacing his fingers through mine. He starts towing me away.

"How?" I struggle against his hold, not willing to go anywhere until I know revenge will be mine.

"Parker was the one who gave up the meth house," Saint confirms, gesturing for me to keep walking.

"Go on."

"Her and that idiot Finn thought it would buy their way into our good graces if they betrayed their source, enabling us to eliminate the competition." Saint smirks.

"They were given a choice at the beginning, and they chose poorly. Sainthood only offers second chances where it's warranted," Theo says as we head toward the main entrance.

"And it would never be warranted in their case," Galen says.

"Finn didn't have the balls to negotiate himself," Saint adds. "Fucking pussy. And he made another mistake trusting his girl because she's had her own agenda all along."

"Let me guess," I say, pursing my lips. "She offered up the meth house and herself?"

Galen smirks, confirming it. "They both reek of desperation."

"And The Sainthood doesn't do desperation," Saint adds.

"So, you used them, they've just found out, and now, they're pissed," I surmise. Saint nods.

"I don't get why they came after Sariah though," Galen muses.

"Maybe, they found out about your little crush on her," Caz jokes, but it falls on deaf ears.

I send him a withering look. "My bestie just paid the price for your actions, and you think it's okay to joke about it?"

He has the decency to look sheepish as he tugs on his lip ring. "I was trying to lighten the tension. I meant no disrespect, Lo. Sariah's cool."

"I have an idea," Saint says, opening the double doors and pulling me outside onto the top step. "We'll set it up after we drop you off at the hospital."

"I want in," I say, walking down the steps. "This is my revenge as much as it's yours."

Saint stares at me. "We wouldn't dream of cutting you out."

"I want to end her," I caution as we approach his Land Rover.

"Agreed." He pulls me over to the passenger side of the car, opening the door for me. "Now, get your sexy ass in the car, and let us put things in motion."

I SPEND THE rest of the evening and most of the night at the hospital, waiting to talk to Sariah. But she's in a coma, and no one can tell if or when she'll come out of it. I share a taxi with Emmett when visiting hours end and we're forced to leave. Sean and Lorna, Sar's grandma, are with her, and I take some comfort from the fact she's not alone. Emmett wraps his arms around me in the back seat of the car, and I lean my head on his shoulder, consumed with worry for my best friend.

It's quiet when I return to the house, and I wonder if Mom and Neo have left for their weekend yet. They weren't around this morning, but sometimes, Mom leaves for work early, and that lazy butthead she's marrying is known for sleeping in late.

I'm yawning as I walk down the hallway, hunger gnawing at my insides, demanding to be fed. The lights are on in the kitchen, and the four guys are seated around the long dining table, devouring pizza.

All four of them look up at me as I step inside. "You look exhausted," Theo says, standing and pulling out a chair for me. Caz squeezes my shoulder as he brushes past me.

"How is Sariah?" Saint asks.

I drop down onto the chair. "She's in a coma."

The guys emit a litany of cusses. Saint pulls me over onto his lap, circling his arms around me. I'm too tired, and too scared to fight it, so I curl into him, letting him comfort me.

"You should eat." Galen slides a plate in front of me with two slices of pepperoni pizza on it.

Caz hands me a bottle of water before distributing beers to his friends.

"Did you make any plans?" I ask, uncapping the water and sipping it.

"We have everything set up," Saint confirms, running his hand up and down my side. "We're going to a club down by the docks in Fenton tomorrow night."

"Why? And don't attempt to hold back. I need to know everything."

Caz's lips kick up at the corners. Galen eyes me curiously while drinking his beer. Theo is watching my every move, his eyes radiating concern.

This interaction is new and completely unsettling.

I bite off a massive chunk of pizza, swallowing slowly, as I wait for Saint to explain.

"It appears Luke McKenzie was tied up with The Bulls, a gang operating out of Fenton," he says. "They're out for blood, and we're going to give them Parker and Finn on a platter."

I almost choke on a mouthful of pizza. I chew fast and swallow. "They didn't murder that douche."

"No one knows that but us," Theo says. The pizza sits in my stomach like a lead balloon. I've been cocky thinking the guys couldn't use that evidence against me, but this changes things.

"We're not going to use it against you," Saint adds, as if he's read my mind.

I peer into his eyes. "Why not?"

"That's something we can get into later. Right now, we focus on pinning the murder on Finn and Parker, and we let The Bulls deal with them." He nods over my shoulder. "Wipe it clean."

I turn around in time to watch Theo rub a cloth over my gun, removing my fingerprints. He cleans the bullets too, leaning down as he inspects the casings with a sharp eye. He lifts his head slowly. "Where'd you get these bullets from?"

"I found them in my dad's office after he died. The gun too," I lie. "Why?"

He scratches the back of his head. "Just curious." His false smile tells me everything he hasn't said. Something on the bullets has caught his attention.

Fuck. I need to ask Diesel where he got them and give him a heads-up.

Saint stares at Theo, and they have one of their silent conversations as he pulls me in closer to his body, kissing the side of my head. I don't think he realizes he's done it. Galen's mouth drops open, and Caz smothers a smile.

"So, The Bulls will be at the club tomorrow, I guess?" I ask, redirecting the conversation as I pick a piece of pepperoni off the pizza and pop it in my mouth, while snuggling in closer to Saint.

God, he smells divine. Like vanilla mixed with spice and

orange blossom in a thoroughly masculine way. It's both sweet and sour, just like him.

"We've already arranged a meet," Saint confirms. "We'll give them an altered version of the truth and hand over the evidence. They'll do the rest."

"What about Beth and the other bitches? They're not getting out of this unscathed."

"We thought we'd let you and Theo work on that," Saint adds. "Dig through their backgrounds, and find something we can use to bury them."

"I'd rather just bury a machete in their faces," I say.

Caz chuckles. "I'd pay good money to see that bitch fight."

"They'll be expecting retaliation," Saint says. "Let's make them sweat a bit. And if we need to extract a blood debt, we can make that happen in a way that won't get you arrested or expelled from school."

I lift my head up, staring directly into his blue eyes. "Why are you helping me? What's in it for you?"

"Your friend got caught up in our shit. She's lying in a hospital bed because of it. We always exact payback," Saint confirms.

"And we always clean up our own mess," Galen adds.

THE SAINTHOOD

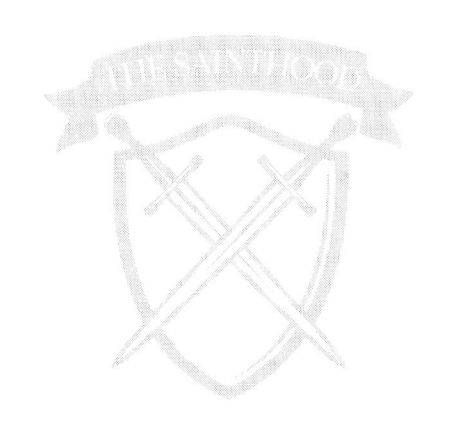

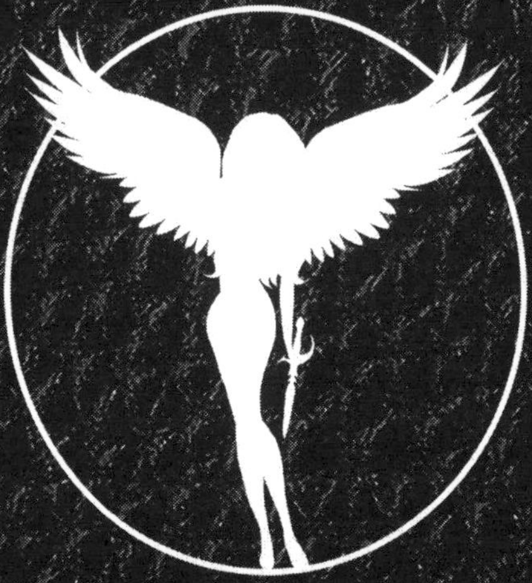

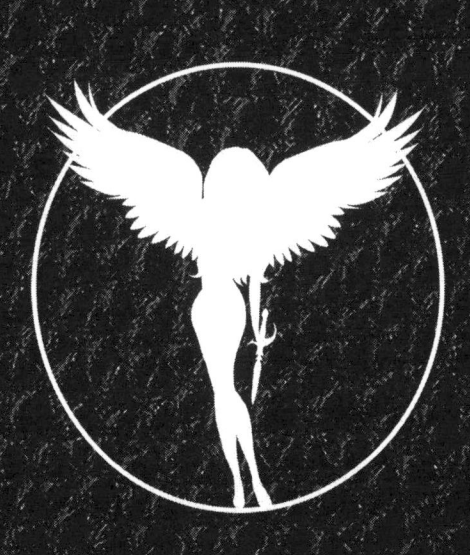

THE SAINTHOOD

CHAPTER 28

I STARE AT my reflection in the mirror, knowing I'll get a reaction from the guys in this dress. It's a tight black mini with embellished sequins overlaid on velvet fabric that hugs my curves in all the right places. The spaghetti straps are different lengths because the top of the dress is higher on one side. The material is ruched around my middle, and I've pulled the adjustable string tight over my left thigh, raising the hem higher on that side so I'm flashing a considerable amount of skin. High-heeled black ankle boots complete the look, elongating my long legs.

My hair falls in straight lines over my shoulders, and I've gone heavy with the eyeliner and mascara, sporting my usual smoky eye and red lips look.

With the hickeys coloring my skin, the scars on the tops of my arms, and half my back tattoo, on full display, I look pretty in a badass kinda way.

Should be perfect to fit into the crowd at the club tonight.

Grabbing my purse and my leather jacket, I leave my room, bolting the door behind me.

Mom had shown a glimpse of fear when she'd walked past my room as I'd been fitting the new padlock to the front of my door, but she didn't pass comment. I guess she truly doesn't give a fuck anymore.

"I think we should stay home," Caz splutters the second I come into view in the doorway of the kitchen. All eyes turn in my direction, and I hold my head up high as I walk toward them. Theo runs his hands through his hair, Galen tries and fails to look immune, and Saint devours me with a look that should melt my clothes from my body.

I haven't seen Saint since he crawled out of my bed sometime this morning. All I know is when I woke, he was gone, and I almost thought I conjured last night up. But I didn't imagine him holding me in his strong arms all night, offering silent comfort as I worried about my friend.

I spent all day at the hospital, where there's no change, and my bestie is still in a coma. I briefly considered ignoring the guys' plans. Visualizing storming into Parker's house and planting a bullet between her eyes. But I know that's only emotion talking. The smart plan is the one we're setting in motion tonight. I just need to be patient, and everyone will get what they deserve.

"Holy fuck, princess." Caz walks around me, inspecting every inch of my body. "You are the definition of sex on legs."

"Thanks, I think," I joke.

"You look stunning, Lo," Theo says, and I tip my head politely at him. We need to present a united front tonight, and I don't want to start the night off wrong, so I'm determined to be pleasant and amicable.

Saint pours a line of shots, and everyone takes one, knocking them back fast.

I surreptitiously check the guys out, and they all look hot as fuck in dark jeans, boots, and body-hugging T-shirts. They are wearing their gang-issued black leather jackets with The Sainthood emblem on the front. Combined with their tats, piercings, and ripped bodies, they exude "don't mess with me" vibes by the bucket load.

"Hey, you ever watch that movie *Girls Trip*?" Caz asks me out of the blue.

"Can't say that I have," I admit, accepting another vodka shot from Saint.

"Want to watch it with me tomorrow?"

Why does this feel like some kind of trap?

Still, I'm curious as fuck, so I'll play ball. "Isn't it a chick flick? Why'd you want to watch that?"

"It's got a scene with the grapefruit technique in it," he says, grinning widely.

Saint rolls his eyes, Theo smiles, and Galen groans as he hits his head repeatedly off the counter.

A light bulb goes off in my head and I make the connection. "That's your word of the day?"

"He shoots. He scores!" Caz fist pumps the air, and I laugh.

"You are such a dork." I shake my head, still grinning as I knock back my shot. "But it's weirdly endearing. And I actually know what that one means." I waggle my brows suggestively.

"You ever tried it?" His eyes light up.

"Have you?"

He shakes his head, and my grin expands. "Neither have I, but I'm down for trying anything in the bedroom at least once."

Galen splutters, and a wicked grin slips over Saint's mouth. "You would seriously wear a grapefruit ring around your dick while she sucked you off?" Galen asks Caz.

"Damn straight I would." Caz adjusts himself in his jeans, and I can see the idea alone is enough to make him hard.

"It'd be hot," Theo agrees, looking like he might like to give it a try too.

Although, I doubt he'd try it with me.

"It'd be sticky and messy," Galen protests, shuddering, and I crack up laughing.

"How else is sex supposed to be?" I ask.

"It sounds unhygienic," he adds, because the guy just can't

let anyone win an argument.

Caz and Saint snort with laughter. "You sound like a pussy," Saint admits, screwing the cap back on the bottle of vodka.

"And the secret is to warm the grapefruit up first and to wear a condom. Then, you avoid any potential infections or allergic reactions," I clarify.

"For someone so knowledgeable, I'm surprised you haven't done it before," Caz says.

I snatch my purse up, fighting a fit of giggles. "I might've asked Darrow to try it one time." Saint's good humor evaporates, and he purses his lips. "But he's as big a pussy as Galen," I admit.

Galen flips me the bird, and I lose my shit, laughing uncontrollably, bending over and clutching my stomach because I'm laughing so hard it physically hurts. I'm flashing a lot of cleavage bent over like this, and Saint and Caz notice, eyes fixed on my tits like they've never seen boobs before.

The energy in the room shifts.

My laughter dies, and I straighten up, my heated gaze bouncing between the two guys eye-fucking me like they wish they could strip me bare and sample *my* grapefruit.

Galen snatches the keys from Saint's hand, rolling his eyes. Saint hasn't taken his eyes off me for a second, and he looks ready to jump my bones.

I honestly wouldn't complain.

"I'll drive and Theo can take shotgun so you two can drool all over the back seat." Galen points between Saint and Caz, shaking his head as if he can't understand it when we all know that's bullshit.

He avoids making eye contact as he walks past me out into the hallway, and that's how I know he's definitely affected.

I drill a look at Saint as the others trail Galen out the door, waiting for him to say something. But he's quiet as he slides his arm around my shoulders, ushering me out of the kitchen, down the hallway, and out through the front door. "Don't leave my fucking side all night," he eventually says. "This place will be crawling with shady fucks, and the second they lay eyes on you, they'll descend like greedy vultures."

I think that's as close to a compliment as I'll get.

"I can hold my own," I say, raising the longer side of my dress to show the small knife strapped high on my thigh. "But I'll stay close. I promise."

He helps me up into the car, his fingers brushing over the backs of my bare legs as I climb inside.

I'm the meat in a Saint and Caz sandwich in the back seat, and I'm not, in any way, unhappy about it. Both of them ravish me with their eyes, and sexual tension sends sparks of electricity charging through the air. Saint places his hand on my thigh in a possessive gesture, but he doesn't protest when Caz starts running his hand up and down my arm, across the swell of my breasts, and generally touching any exposed skin he can reach.

I purposely spread my legs a little wide, knowing my lace panties are visible because my dress is just that short.

Galen almost crashes at least three times as he struggles to keep his eyes on the road, while I struggle to keep the smug grin off my face.

Saint pushes my thighs together, keeping my knees pinned shut as he levels me with a knowing look. "I'd rather get there alive," he drawls, and I can't contain my grin any longer.

By the time we reach the docks, I'm hot and horny, and I'm betting the guys are too.

"Remember what I said," Saint reminds me, gripping my hand tight as we approach the entrance to the large warehouse the club is at. "Stay glued to my side. If we get separated, for any reason, stick with one of the other guys." His beautiful blue eyes pierce me with a cautionary look. "Do not wander anywhere by yourself."

"Sheesh." I swat his arm. "I'm not an idiot. I got it. Relax."

He palms my cheek. "I know you're not an idiot. Just being here with us is risky enough without you looking like that."

He waves his hand in my general vicinity, and warmth spreads through my bones, heating every part of me.

I stretch up and kiss him.

Just because I feel like it, pulling back before it can develop into something we don't have time to indulge. "I won't wander off."

He nods, squeezing my hand, before focusing his attention on the two guys manning the entrance.

"All right, man." One of the burly bouncers raises his fist to Saint, and they do some elaborate knuckle-touch maneuver, before slapping each other on the backs. Then, Saint repeats the process with bouncer number two. The other guys move forward, and more knuckle touches and back slaps occur.

Dudes are such idiots, but I manage to control the urge to roll my eyes.

"Who's this pretty lady?" The second bouncer asks, moving forward a couple steps, his eyes roaming my body like he's mentally undressing me.

I'm already regretting leaving my jacket in the car. I'm not shy about my body, far from it, but I hate assholes who believe they have a God-given right to objectify a woman just because she's wearing a sexy dress. I should be able to wear whatever the hell I want without being perved on.

His blatant drooling earns him a death stare from Saint, and he gulps, instantly stepping back and averting his gaze.

"Harlow is with us. Spread the word. I'll gut anyone who even looks at her," Saint coolly replies, his words dripping with intent.

"Ruben's in the VIP area waiting for you," the first bouncer says, his anxious gaze jumping between Saint and his colleague, trying to break the sudden tense atmosphere.

Saint nods. "Thanks, bro." He eyeballs the other jerk. "You're lucky Ruben vouched for you."

"I'm sorry, man. It won't happen again."

He looks half scared out of his wits, and it's a timely reminder of how much power The Sainthood have around these parts. If this burly bouncer is terrified, and all he did was ogle my tits, what the fuck would they do to me if they knew everything I've done?

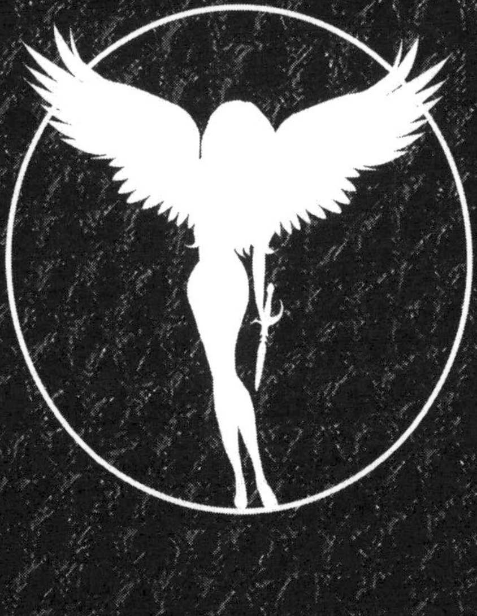

CHAPTER 29

THE BOUNCERS OPEN the doors and we step inside the industrial-sized warehouse. Sultry beats reverberate around the space as multicolored lights stream over our heads. The large open-plan room is packed. A big crowd dances in the middle of the floor watched by groups centered around booths on either side. At the top of the room is a large bar, thronged with people. Overhead, on a circular balcony, a DJ spins the latest tunes.

Saint leads us through the room toward the bar. People jump out of our way, while others nod respectfully at the guys. A few fools eye me up and down, and Caz sucker punches each one of them until everyone understands I'm off-limits. It's ridiculously alpha, and totally unnecessary, but I'm enjoying it.

Not sure what that says about me.

The sea of people at the bar part to let Caz through. He orders another round of shots for everyone but Galen. No money passes hands, and I wonder if that's always the case.

We down our tequila shots, and then, we're on the move again, rounding the bar. I take in our surroundings as we walk, observing everything and everyone. A bouncer guards an elevator at the back of the bar, but he moves aside to let us enter.

We pile in with Saint and me at the rear and the other three in front of us.

"These guys are dangerous assholes," Saint explains. "Be careful."

"That means keep your mouth shut and let us do the talking," Galen clarifies, and I shove my middle finger up at his back. "I know you're flipping me off," he adds.

"Only because it's most people's reaction to you," I retort.

He glances over his shoulder, grinning. "You say that like it's a bad thing."

"Only you'd think it wasn't," I whisper, just as the door opens on the upper level.

Saint holds my hand firmly in his as we walk along the narrow hallway and enter the VIP area. It's a decent-sized room with about twenty booths and its own private dance floor and bar. A glass window wraps around the front of the space, highlighting the main area below. It's virtually empty except for the five guys in black and red leather cuts occupying one of the larger booths.

A tall guy with muscles to rival Caz's ripped body stands and steps out of the booth to greet us. "Saint." Cue more stupid manly—I say that with a healthy dose of sarcasm—greetings.

"Ruben. Thanks for meeting on short notice."

Caz and Theo step up alongside me, while Galen flanks Saint on the other side. Ruben nods, his eyes flaring with interest when they land on me. He takes my free hand in his, and though I want his callused palm nowhere near my body, I don't object, because I don't want to ruffle any feathers.

All five Bulls are wearing pieces, and they're doing nothing to disguise it either. "I don't believe we've met. I'd never forget such a hot body," Ruben says, raising my hand to his lips and planting a wet kiss on my knuckles.

What a sexist pig.

I bite back my distaste, offering him a tight smile. "Harlow Westbrook. Good to meet you." I figure it's fine to confirm my identity because A, Saint introduced me as Harlow downstairs and B, if what Dar said is true, and the Saints have put the word out that I'm under their protection, then everyone already knows who I am.

"Pleasure's all mine." Ruben roams his gaze up and down my body, his eyes lingering on the hickeys on my neck before lowering to my breasts. I meet his gaze full on, not backing down, shooting venom from my eyes while keeping a fake smile plastered on my face.

Saint subtly grips my hand tighter, but outwardly, he's composed.

"Thought you guys didn't do girlfriends," a guy with a shaved head and bushy beard asks. He's slouched against the back of the booth with one knee bent, his thighs spread in a vulgar manner.

"Thought we were here to discuss business not pussy," Saint says, and I dig my nails into the underside of his palm.

Ruben chuckles, slapping Saint on the shoulder. "Let's grab some shots and talk by the bar. I'm sure my guys can keep your woman entertained."

Someone, pass me the puke bucket.

Saint pulls me into his arms, moving his mouth to my ear. "Stay close to Galen." He swats me on the ass before letting me go, and it takes colossal willpower not to slap him back.

Galen instantly moves to my side, threading his fingers in mine and guiding me to the booth.

Theo takes Ruben's vacated space on one side, at the end, beside three unfriendly assholes, and Caz slides in beside the bald bearded dude on the other side. A guy with long, greasy strawberry-blond hair sits on Baldy's other side, ogling me shamelessly as Galen takes the last seat at the end, pulling me down on his lap.

"That sharing rumor is true, huh?" Baldy says, grinning as he passes the guys a beer. He's got two gold crowns in place of his front teeth, and I briefly wonder if that's by choice or someone knocked them the fuck out of his ugly head.

He doesn't offer me a drink.

Chauvinistic asshole.

But Galen gives me his, and I'm pleasantly surprised he's taking his designated driver duties seriously. I don't think most gang members give a shit about driving drunk.

"We're not in the habit of discussing our private lives," Galen says, circling his arms around my waist.

"You're that bitch from the video," a guy with dark skin and dark hair says, smirking as if he's recalling it scene by scene in his head.

"Watch your fucking mouth, and show some respect," Theo says.

"Hoodrats don't earn respect around here," he replies, making a point of settling his gun down on top of the table.

"Harlow isn't a fucking hoodrat. She's our girl," Caz barks. Galen stiffens behind me, and Theo shows no emotion.

"Isn't she Lennox's stepsister?" Baldy asks, glugging his beer.

"You guys gossip worse than girls," I say, done with playing the silent, obedient type. "And I'm sitting right here. You don't need to talk about me as if I'm invisible."

"So, is it true, sweetheart?" Baldy asks. "You banging your stepbrother?"

"Every fucking chance I get." I smirk, bringing the bottle to my lips as laughter erupts around the table.

Saint and Ruben interrupt their conversation at the bar to look in our direction, and I blow them a cheeky kiss.

"What about the rest of these assholes?" the dark-haired guy asks. "You banging them too?"

"A girl has to keep some of the mystery alive," I tease, winking as I deflect answering his question.

The tension lifts a little after that, and the guys shoot the shit while things look intense over at the bar.

After a few minutes, I watch as Saint hands over the brown

paper envelope with the gun and the bullets, and they get up, slapping each other on the back. I drain my beer, watching Saint stalk toward me. He grips my hips and lifts me off Galen's lap, tucking me in under his arm.

"The Bulls won't forget this, brother." Ruben nods at Saint, and he returns the gesture. "Later, friends."

We go back the way we came, and when we step into the elevator, I turn to face Saint. "What happened?"

"It's handled. They will deal with Finn and Parker."

I stretch up and put my mouth to his ear, unsure if there is a camera in here. "Do they know we blew up the meth house?"

He nods, tugging at his ear. "They don't give a shit about that. Their involvement with McKenzie was on the sex trafficking side. His death has fucked stuff up with their contacts and jeopardized their supply."

I'm even more grateful the douche is dead now.

We emerge on the dance floor, and one of my favorite songs is blaring from the speakers. "I want to dance," I shout in Saint's ear.

"This is enemy territory," he shouts back. "We're not staying." He tugs on my hand, leading me away from the dance floor, but I grab the front of his jacket, pinning him with my best doe-eyed pleading look.

"One dance. Just this song." I bat my eyelashes. "Pretty please."

He lets loose a string of colorful expletives before gesturing to the guys and leading me out onto the dance floor. I immediately let loose, swaying my hips in time to the beat of the music and throwing my head back as my hands roam my body. Heat surrounds me from behind when Saint presses up against me. His hands take over from mine, sweeping all over my body as the other guys surround us, keeping prying eyes away. Caz pushes up against my front, his body moving in sync with mine as I find myself locked in another Caz-Saint sandwich.

Behind me, Saint brushes my hair to one side, gliding his

lips up and down the side of my exposed neck, and I just know he's appreciating his artwork. He rocks his hard-on against my ass, and I whimper. Caz grips my hips, grinding against me, and then, his lips descend in a punishing kiss I feel all the way to the tips of my toes.

The second the song is over, it's like the spell has been broken, and both guys step away with smug smirks. My hands clench into fists, and I'm tempted to punch the bastards. Saint leads me off the dance floor and out through the door with the others trailing us.

I take turns making out with Caz and Saint in the back seat on the way home, and I feel Galen's envious eyes burning holes in my back, so I'm confident a little repeat of our foursome is on the cards when we get home.

But Saint makes it abundantly clear that's not going to happen, locking my bedroom door behind us before any of his friends get ideas.

We need to talk about his possessiveness sometime soon, because he can't monopolize me. I like the group dynamic, and I want to explore it more.

I'm into the other guys too.

Well, maybe not Theo, because there are extenuating circumstances, but definitely Caz, and the love-hate chemistry Galen and I have going on is every bit as hot as it is annoying.

We strip our clothes off without speaking a word, falling into bed in a tangle of lips, tongues, arms, and legs, and when he enters me, something alters between us.

He fucks me hard and relentlessly, with the same savage ruthlessness I'm used to, but his eyes never stray from my face, and he showers me with kisses, unable to hold back, clearly feeling the connection burning between us the way I do.

When we come together, staring into each other's eyes, our hearts beating in sync, our souls fusing, I realize I'm fucked in more ways than one.

THE SAINTHOOD

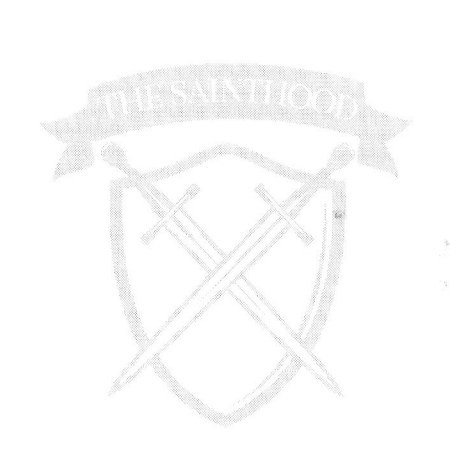

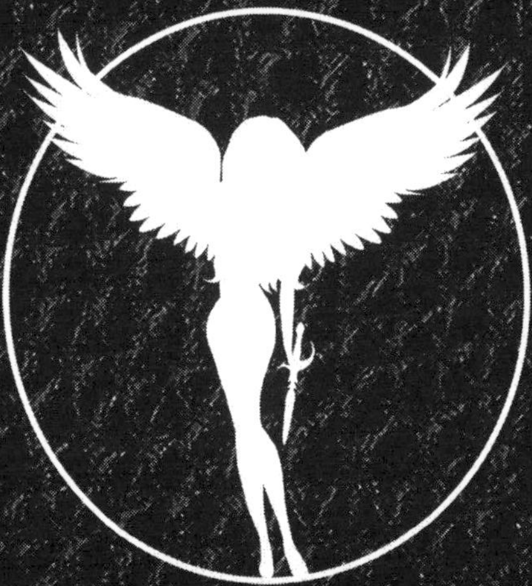

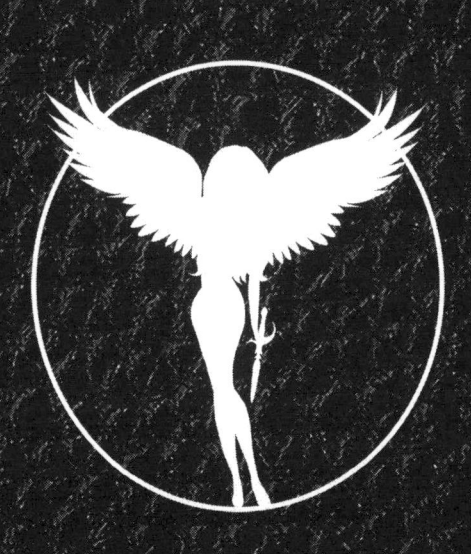

THE SAINTHOOD

CHAPTER 30

I HIBERNATE IN my room on Sunday morning, surviving on a stale protein bar and a warm bottle of water I found in the drawer of my bedside table, because I'm too chicken to risk going downstairs.

I'm freaking the fuck out after what went down last night.

And I'm not talking about sharing airspace with The Bulls knowing I'm the one who killed their guy.

That danger pales into insignificance in comparison to the danger of losing my heart.

Saint doesn't come near me, and he was gone again this morning when I woke, so either he's busy with crew shit or he's freaking out too.

After a shower, I change into skinny jeans and my old Paramore T-shirt and sit down in front of my iPad.

I spend a couple hours reviewing the files Diesel sent me on Dad's car accident, conducting some initial investigation. The police report was written by a cop who was conveniently gunned down on the street a month later, in an unsolved case, and the CSI tech report on the car was written by a new recruit who has since quit and moved overseas. I can't find anything in his background I could use for blackmail purposes. The guy seems squeaky clean, and I'm guessing he must have been intimidated into falsifying the report.

It looks like Lincoln was right, and this is a dead end. I'm not sure where I go from here. A heavy weight presses down on my chest, but I refuse to adopt a defeatist attitude. The Sainthood is smart, but everyone slips up. I will find evidence they murdered my dad. I won't give up trying.

I log on to the cloud surveillance app next, scanning through the most recent camera footage from the guys' bedrooms, out of habit more than anything else. I'm not expecting to find anything, so I bolt upright in the chair when I stumble across a conversation from earlier today that took place in Galen's room.

"We need to head out," Saint says. "Sinner's getting nervous. The Arrows have increased their efforts, and he wants to move the supplies from Landing's Lane until the risk has passed. He's secured a new temporary warehouse by the docks in Prestwick. It'll be handy for the shipments coming in this weekend."

"That shit'll take forever to load." Caz groans.

"Not with every member helping out," Saint adds, slapping him on the back. "C'mon. The sooner we get there the quicker we get the job done."

The conversation ends, and they leave. I shut off the footage and sit back to think, tapping a finger off my chin.

I've already come to the conclusion the guys have some other place they go to, to manage business, because they never discuss shit in their bedrooms. It's got to be the same place they crash sometimes. I wasn't expecting to get anything from the cameras, and, honestly, I've only kept them live because I enjoy watching Caz jerk himself off every night.

So, why are they, all of a sudden, talking business here? Could this be a setup?

It's not unfathomable to think they're on to me, no matter

how careful I've been.

I mull it over for ages, debating the pros and cons, before I decide to Google Landing's Lane. It's an old abandoned army base straddling the borders between Prestwick and Fenton. I attempt to locate visuals on Google maps, but there are none, which is hugely interesting. If that is where The Sainthood stows their supplies, it makes sense it can't be found. I'd expect them to protect it from prying eyes.

I think the intel must be real, so I reach for my burner cell, pulling my knees into my chest as I tap out a message to Darrow. My finger hovers over the send button as I contemplate the enormity of this decision.

There is a lot resting on this, and it's not black or white. It's littered with gray areas.

Darrow can't be trusted to keep our deal a secret. I've known that all along. He'll love nothing more than letting the Saints know I was the one who betrayed them. It's the ultimate payback.

When I entered into the agreement with him, I didn't care because I didn't give a shit about what the guys thought of me. If this goes down, it'll mean war between the rival gangs. I want that to happen, need it to happen, because it'll distract The Sainthood long enough to enable me to dig deeper. To locate the evidence I need to get justice. For Dad, and for me.

I've no doubt they'll want revenge, but with a gang war to preoccupy them, along with the impending wedding, I figure it buys me some time. I wasn't planning on being here when their time came to seek vengeance, because I'd have my new identity and I'd disappear. But now, that's in limbo too.

I stare at the message, conflicted over what to do.

My gut urges caution.

If I go ahead with it, I know The Arrows will wage a full-blown war against The Sainthood. Blood will be spilled, and an increase in gang violence will be the new norm. And when Sinner finds out how it went down, he won't just be gunning for my ass; he'll be after the guys too for letting a woman gain the upper hand.

So fucking what? I don't owe any of them anything. Especially not Saint. Just 'cause he's given me a few mind-bending orgasms doesn't mean he gets a free pass.

Stop lying to yourself.

I put the cell down on the dresser, resting my head on top of my knees, biting down hard on my lip and drawing blood.

If I do this, and the guys find out, they'll hate me forever. Especially Saint.

Why does that statement almost induce a panic attack?

I shouldn't care.

I don't care.

They deserve everything coming to them.

I pick up the cell again, moving my finger to the send button, hovering over it as I continue my internal debate, but I can't do it. I can't push the button.

Because I do care.

Fuck.

They have come to mean something to me.

See? This is why I don't do feelings. All they do is fuck with your head and your heart and turn you into an overanalytical obsessive fool. And that's when I'm most likely to make a mistake, because I don't have a clear head.

But it's more than that.

It's about self-preservation too, and I can't be hasty.

I need to put more thought into this, so I switch off the cell and replace it in the hidden panel of my Prada backpack. Then, I slip my feet into my Vans, grab my black hoodie, and head out to the hospital.

MONDAY ROLLS AROUND, and it's super weird driving to school without my bestie in the passenger seat beside me.

It seems the school board is taking the situation seriously, and they've been busy over the weekend. Security cameras are now mounted in the hallways, and they've added some new staff to the security team. A couple of mean-looking dudes patrol the halls, their eyes taking everything in.

The rumor mill is in overdrive, especially when Finn and Parker are no-shows, and gossip is rife about The Bulls gunning for their asses.

Couldn't happen to two more deserving people, and I have zero remorse for the fact they'll pay for my crime. I couldn't give two fucks whether they live or die.

Beth is in my English lit class, and I wait until the teach has arrived before entering the room. I purposely head toward Beth's seat, glaring at the girl sitting behind her until she gets up and moves. Then I spend the full forty minutes sending daggers at Beth's back, breathing down her neck, kicking the back of her chair, and poking her with my pen.

She's stiff as a board, and quiet as a mouse, enduring my torment, because I'm sure she's freaking the hell out.

Finn and Parker are MIA, the school is scheduling interviews with students to try to uncover the truth, and, although there's no proof, because the guys have sent the freshman into hiding—preferring to seek justice the vigilante way—if it comes out, she is most likely facing an aggravated assault charge. She'll do time.

She knows all this, and she won't want to do anything to draw attention to herself, so she stays quiet, and I get to torment her in peace.

It's juvenile and petty, and completely beneath me, but I'll take the enjoyment where I can.

By the way she hightails it out of class, I know she's pissing her pants, and I fully intend to torture her any chance I get over the next couple weeks. By then, we should have a plan to ruin her.

"You enjoyed that," Caz says, coming up to my desk as I stash my books.

"Not as much as I'd enjoy breaking her nose and shoving her teeth down her throat," I honestly reply.

He slings his arm around my waist, steering me out of the room. "I'm starting to forget what it was like before you barged your way into our lives."

"Dull and boring as fuck," I quip, leaning my head on his shoulder in a rare show of vulnerability.

"Hey." He stops in the middle of the hallway, tipping my chin up. "She's going to be okay."

"You don't know that, Caz." I shake my head, worrying my lip between my teeth. "What if she's not? She's my best friend. The only person I truly know to have my back no matter what."

He brushes hair off my face. "We've got your back, princess." He rubs his thumb along my cheek, peering deep into my eyes. "The question is, do you have ours?"

THURSDAY IS ONE strange as fuck day. I wake up to Mom perched on the edge of my bed with her finger pressed to her lips. "There's no cameras in here, right?" she whispers, anxiously looking around.

I rub sleep from my eyes as I straighten up in the bed. "No," I confirm over a yawn. "I removed them. Why?"

She glances at the fading hickeys on my neck, frowning. "I need to ask you something." She moves her gaze to my face, straightening up. "Did you take anything from the study after Dad died?"

If Mom's asking questions, I guess something must've gone down or Sinner is resorting to her doing his dirty work.

Sneaky prick.

And he obviously thinks I'm a complete idiot.

"No, of course not," I say, deliberately appearing confused. "What would I have taken? I did find Saint and the guys in there recently going through Dad's stuff, so maybe, you should ask them."

"I will," she says, but she can't look me in the eye, so I know she's lying.

"What's going on, Mom?" I'm not expecting her to tell me, but there's still some teeny, tiny part of me that's hopeful.

She stares at me for ages without speaking, and I can almost see the wheels turning in her head. It's the first time we've been this close for weeks, and I'm only now noticing the purple shadows under her eyes and the newly formed worry lines at the corners of her mouth. Her voice cracks a little when she eventually speaks. "I know our relationship is a little tenuous right now, but I need to ask you for something."

Is this woman for real? A little tenuous? Try it's fractured and splintered with little chance of salvation. *And she's the nerve to ask something of me?* Not fucking likely. Still, curious minds want to know. "What is it?"

"Stay out of the house as much as you can over the next few days."

"Why?"

She knots her hands in her lap. "Just stay out of Neo's way, sweetheart."

He definitely suspects something.

"Why?" I repeat even though I know she won't tell me anything.

"Just do it, honey. Please. Do it for Daddy."

And that was totally the wrong thing to say. My jaw hardens, and I glare at her. "If that's everything, you can leave."

Her mouth opens and closes like a fish out of water, and she runs her hands through her unbrushed hair. Tears well in her eyes, but I'm immune.

She's reached a new low now.

Putting that bastard's needs before mine.

Coming here to try to extract information from me to pass on to him.

I am so done with her.

She swipes at the moisture spilling down her cheeks, standing and walking toward the door. She falters, turning to face me one final time. "And you should stay the hell away from those boys too," she adds, as if she cares. "I don't want to see you throwing your life away."

So, my day is off to a great start with that awesome conversation, and it only goes downhill from there.

At school, I come close to stabbing Beth purely because I need to vent my rage in someone's direction and she's the most likely victim. I sit with the guys in the cafeteria at lunch, toying with the knife in my hand as I glare at her across the tables.

"Put that away," Saint says, staring straight ahead as if he's not speaking to me. Things are even weirder than normal between us. He's building walls around himself, and with every passing day he appears to grow more and more frustrated with me.

Is it because he resents what's happening between us too or there's more to it?

"Eat shit and die," I retort, stabbing my knife into my apple and slicing it into wedges.

Galen slouches in his chair, folding his arms and crossing his ankles as he shoots Saint a knowing look. Saint ignores him, and Theo watches the interactions with the cunningness of an expert spy. Caz looks troubled, shoveling pasta into his mouth, looking like he's not even enjoying it.

"Hey, you want to get out of here?" Emmett asks, no doubt feeling the horrid tension too, and I'm grabbing my bag before he's even finished asking the question.

"We're ditching to hang out at the hospital," Sean adds, crumpling his uneaten sandwich up as he stands.

"I'm there." I clean my knife on the back of a paper towel and sheath it. "Let's go," I say, walking away from the table without looking back.

GRANDMA LORNA ENVELOPS me in a giant hug the minute I step foot in Sariah's hospital room. Sean immediately goes to Sariah's bedside, taking her hand, while Emmett walks to the window, looking out over the bleak landscape outside. "You look like someone who needs a hug," she says, squeezing me tight.

She's not wrong. It's been a shitty week and a particularly shitty day. But compared to my bestie, things are all rainbows and unicorns for me, so I tell myself to snap out of it and quit feeling sorry for myself. "Is there any change? Has the doctor been around to see her yet today?"

"No change," she replies, letting me go. "And he was here an hour ago. Her vitals are the same." She slumps down in the chair, looking sad and tired. Lorna is Sariah's mom's mom. She had kids early, as did her daughter, so she's young for a grandma and still in her fifties. Yet looking at her now, she looks like she's aged twenty years overnight.

I sit down beside her, patting her hand. "Why don't you take a break? Get something to eat in the cafeteria and maybe take a walk. I'll stay with her."

Sean takes a long hard look at Sariah's only remaining family and obviously agrees. "That's a great idea. I haven't eaten either. I'll come with you."

Sean takes Lorna's arm and escorts her out of the room.

"This must be so hard for her," Emmett says.

"I know. It must've almost killed her losing her daughter, her son-in-law, and her other grandkids in such a gruesome way. Seeing Sariah like this must be breaking her heart."

"How are you holding up?" he asks, moving to sit beside me.

"I'm fine. Worried, obviously, but I've had lots of practice at blocking shit out. I'm not thinking about the what-ifs. I'm just focusing on being here." I lean forward and take Sariah's hand, comforted at the warmth radiating from her skin. "Time to wake up, babe. I know you're going to because you didn't survive all those years ago to give up now." I kiss her brow. "C'mon, Sar. Wake up."

I need you. You're the only one who can help me sort through this mess.

I send those thoughts out to the universe, hoping someone up there hears me and takes pity.

I IGNORE MOM'S warning, returning to the house shortly after nine p.m. The downstairs is empty, so Mom and Neo must be out again. The sound of the TV wafts from the basement, and I'm guessing the guys are in their den, as usual. I've no desire to see any of them, so I trudge up the stairs to my room. Raised voices in the upstairs hallway root my feet at the top of the stairs, and I press my body into the small alcove, peering around the curve of the wall.

Sinner is jabbing his finger in Saint's chest, his mouth twisted into a cold sneer, as he threatens him.

"I told you I have it covered," Saint says, standing his ground and refusing to be intimidated. It helps that he's a couple inches taller than his dad. "You are freaking out over nothing."

Sinner stares at his son as he scrubs a hand over his jaw. "I hope you're right. For all your sakes."

"I've got this, Dad."

Neo's sinister smile slips off his face, and he nods. "You have the instincts of a natural born leader." He slaps his son on the back. "That's why I don't want you to get distracted by pussy even if she is one hot piece of ass."

"I'm playing Harlow perfectly." Saint's smug grin rubs me the wrong way, and pain rips across my chest.

Sinner squeezes Saint's shoulder, digging his fingers into his flesh in a way I know hurts. "I wonder if the daughter is as good a fuck as the mom." A sly sneer spreads over his mouth. "I might have to test that theory." He waggles his brows, and I puke a little in my mouth.

"Maybe, we can swap some time," Saint suggests with an equally matching sneer. "And compare notes after."

Neo roars out laughing, grabbing his son into a headlock.

"That's my boy!" He lets him go before thumping him in the arm. "Come with me." He lifts one shoulder. "I've something in my room I want to give you."

I watch them walk off as the tornado brews to epic proportions inside me. I slip into my room, lock the door, and dump my backpack on the bed, kicking off my boots and throwing my jacket on the floor.

I don't hesitate. I don't stop to second-guess myself or give it any more thought.

Fuck this shit. And fuck that asshole. Fuck all the Saints.

I take out my burner cell and send Darrow the message I should have sent him last Sunday.

"Take that for perfect play, asshole," I say out loud, grinning as I lock my bedroom window and head for the shower.

THE SAINTHOOD

CHAPTER 31

I SPEND A sleepless night, tossing and turning in bed, after the initial euphoria faded, wondering if I've made a colossal mistake. But it's too late to take it back now.

After I'm showered and dressed, I throw the burner cell on the ground and smash it to smithereens with the heel of my boot. It's like kryptonite now, and I need to dispose of it. I have a stash of burner cells, thanks to Diesel, so I can afford to toss this one. Wrapping the broken pieces in an old cloth, I place it in my bag. I'll get rid of it later, dumping it someplace it can't be traced back to me.

The guys are a no-show in the kitchen, and they don't turn up at school either, which does little to calm my nerves. I'm on edge all day, snapping and barking at people left and right. An ominous sense of dread builds momentum inside me, and I just know things are going to go belly up.

I stop by the hospital, but I don't stay long, because I want to get home and talk to Saint. I might be making an even bigger mistake, but I think I need to tell him what I've done. The more I reflect on the conversation I overheard last night, the more I believe he was lying to his dad.

It's what I've been doing to my mom.

And I know I'm not the only one who feels the connection between us. I know he has feelings for me despite what he told Sinner.

Caz's question has been niggling at me all week too. He asked if I had their backs, and it sounded like a test.

I think my initial gut instinct was correct.

I think the guys purposely had that conversation in Galen's bedroom to trap me.

I could be wrong. Maybe I'm grasping at straws because I want to know they care, but, even if I am, this is still the best course of action. The best way of conducting damage control.

The house is in darkness when I return, and all the guys' cellphones are switched off. I wear a line in my bedroom floor as I wait for them to come back.

It's after two a.m. when I eventually hear cars driving up the driveway. They are quiet as they trek up the stairs, disappearing into their bedrooms without talking.

I wait a couple minutes, fighting a sudden bout of nerves before I kick them aside.

I'm a goddamn queen, and if I fucked up, I will own that shit.

Pulling a light sweater on over my tank top and sleep shorts, I open and close the door softly, locking it behind me. I walk to Saint's door, pick the lock, and enter his bedroom without invitation. This conversation needs to happen one on one, and I don't want the others interfering so I can't risk knocking and them hearing. Galen will lose his shit if he finds out what I've done, Theo will be disappointed, but I think Caz will be pleased I'm fessing up.

As for Saint, I'm not entirely sure how he's going to react.

I close the door, scanning the empty room. The bathroom door is ajar, steam wafting out, the noise of water hitting off the tiles confirming he's in the shower. For a brief second, I consider joining him. Sex might butter him up. But I dismiss it almost as quickly. I'm not going to manipulate his reaction. I will handle whatever crap he throws at me with my head held high.

I sit on the edge of his bed, stretching my bare legs out in front of me, while I wait for him to emerge.

He walks out of the bathroom five minutes later, materializing in a cloud of steam, water dripping down his chiseled abs, disappearing into the towel slung low around his hips. He sees me and stops, staring at me in that alluring way of his, as if he's staring straight through to my soul. It takes huge amounts of willpower to avoid drooling over his gorgeous body, especially when he's only wearing a teeny towel. I find myself jealous of the beads of water clinging to his tan skin, and that's just pathetic.

I clear my throat and shake the haze from my brain, lifting my eyes to his stunning face. His jaw is clamped tight, a muscle flexing as tension swirls around us. "We need to talk," I say, standing.

He walks right up to me, leaving only a miniscule gap between our bodies. "Yeah. We do."

"I fucked up," I blurt. "But I want to make it right."

He walks to his dresser, with his back to me, and drops the towel. "I'm listening." His voice is gruff, his naked ass delectable, and I'm having a hard time concentrating.

Get a fucking grip, Harlow! You're acting like some hormone-crazed teenager. Note to snarky voice in my head—I *am* a hormone-crazed teenager.

Saint stares at me over his shoulder, his lips pulling into a knowing smirk. Asshole knows what he does to me. But at least, he's not wound up too tight. Maybe this might be all right.

"Put some damn pants on and stop distracting me," I hiss, finally dragging my eyes from his ass. I drop back down on the edge of the bed, focusing on the floor.

"Start talking, princess." His tone brooks no argument.

So, I do, telling him everything about my deal with Darrow,

how I planted the cameras in their rooms, and sent Dar a message with the coordinates of The Sainthood's warehouse.

The mattress dips as he sits down beside me. Thankfully, he has sweats on, but those lick-worthy abs are all up in my face, newly testing my self-control. "Why are you telling me this?" he asks.

This is the real hard part. I look him straight in the eye. "Because it didn't feel right to betray you." I pause for a beat. "I don't want to betray any of you."

It's the truth, but how do I separate them out from the larger organization who still must answer for their crimes?

And how much have the guys been privy to?

How involved are they?

These were some of the questions keeping me awake last night.

"So why did you?"

"I overheard you and Sinner talking last night." This is embarrassing to admit, but I can't hold back. "I was enraged when I heard you both joking about swapping me and my mom. I flipped and let my emotions get to me. Instead of stopping to cool down, I just went into my bedroom and messaged Dar. I've spent all day regretting it."

He smooths a hand over the top of his head, dragging his fingers across the shorn blond locks, frowning. "Are you saying you only told Darrow last night? Not on Sunday when you heard our conversation?"

"Yeah, it was last night. Why?"

He pinches his lips, looking deep in thought, and I wait him out. "Because The Arrows started making plans on Monday. We caught a couple of their guys scoping out the location in the dead of night."

"They already knew?" My brow creases. "How?"

He stands and paces. "I don't know. We thought you'd told him. That you'd fallen for our trap."

I rise. "So, you were trying to trick me? You've known about the cameras all along?"

Saint rolls his eyes. "C'mon, Lo. You're way smarter than this."

"You've been deliberately messing with my head."

He walks right up to me, grabbing the back of my neck. "At the start, yes. But not recently. We've begun to realize you're not our enemy. We set this as a test, to see if we could trust you."

"I guess I failed, huh?"

"You've just proven yourself now."

I focus on the other part of his statement. "Why did you think I'm your enemy? And why didn't you just come out and ask me about it?"

"Why didn't you?" he asks in a softer tone.

I sigh, wondering how best to answer that. We both know this is more than just their trap. "Because I wasn't going to do it."

He nods, and I see the acceptance in his eyes. "I pushed you to it last night." He grips the nape of my neck harder. "It was bullshit, babe. I told him what he needed to hear."

"If you thought I'd betrayed you, why wouldn't you have meant it?"

"You already know the answer to that."

Prickles of awareness dance around the room, and he's saying so much by not saying anything.

My tongue darts out, wetting my lips, and his eyes follow the movement greedily. "I've been so pissed all week that you did it. We didn't think you would."

I narrow my eyes to slits, because really? He smirks, instantly understanding my implication.

"Okay, Galen thought you would, but the rest of us bet on you remaining true to us."

"Figures Galen would be the doubting Thomas."

"Galen's got…issues," he says.

That's putting it mildly.

"Discovering The Sainthood was responsible for your abduction softened him a bit, but he still doubted your loyalties because it takes a lot for Galen to trust people."

"I can't dispute that, because I did do it in the end."

"You're making it right now." He pulls me into his chest, and I wrap my arms around his waist.

I look up at him, as his hands rest on my hips. "I'm sorry, and I regretted it the moment I did it."

"It's okay. There's no harm done, and maybe, it was a good thing." He takes my hand, bringing me back to the bed. He pulls back the covers, and I climb in.

"Why?" I ask when we're sitting up, side by side, with the covers pulled up to our waists, our backs leaning against the headrest. "What don't I know?"

"The Arrows have been making aggressive moves to take over our patch since we relocated to Lowell. They have gradually been getting braver. Sinner's going nuts, and he's not the type to sit around and wait to be attacked. He likes to bring the fight to his enemies."

This is something I already know.

"One of our initiation tasks was to come up with a plan to draw them out. To force them into making a move so we can begin to take back control. Everyone wants to know where our warehouse is. It's our most closely guarded secret." He threads his fingers absently through mine. "So, we came up with a strategy. We'd give them a false location. False details of a new shipment. And then lie in wait for them to attack. Neutralize the threat."

"The warehouse isn't in Landing's Lane?"

He shakes his head, grinning. "We use that premises for interrogation purposes, but we never store our supplies there. What most people don't know is, we have a number of hidden locations. That's just one of them."

"If I didn't fall for the trap, how were you going to lure them out?"

"We have a large crew who stays in the shadows. They have their finger on the pulse of the streets. They would've slipped the intel and ensured it got into the right hands."

I twist around on my side so I'm facing him. "I didn't give them the intel, so who did?"

"I have no idea, and that changes things."

"What does Sinner think happened? Did you tell him it was me?"

"Hell no!" He stares at me incredulously. "He thinks we planted the intel."

"And if I hadn't fessed up, would you have told him the truth?"

He shakes his head. "No way. I'm trying to keep you out of that asshole's net." My eyes pop wide. He cups one side of my face. "I meant what I said before. If he got a hold of you this time, he would fucking break you apart, Harlow. I couldn't save you last time, but I'm sure as fuck going to try to now."

I want to believe him, yet it doesn't explain their treatment of me at the start. "You obviously didn't care about that when you first came here, so what's changed?"

He caresses my cheek with his thumb. "A fuck ton of stuff. But mostly, we know Sinner and the controlling board of The Sainthood have been lying to us. They told us you had evidence that could put half the organization in jail. We were told to intimidate you. To scare you into telling us where you were hiding it. But you fought us every step of the way, gaining our respect and admiration. And everything that's happened since has us questioning the whole fucking thing. It reeks of something darker at play." He holds both my cheeks in his hands. "We know you're planning something, and I think it's time we joined forces." He rubs his thumb along my lower lip. "War is imminent, and you need to be on the right side."

The implication is clear, and if it was just standing by their side, I could handle it. But there is a lot more to it than that.

Can I stand beside The Sainthood in this battle, even if it's a lie? If it brings me closer to the truth, then yes, I can and I will do it. But I risk losing them if I hide my true agenda.

I stare into his eyes, pondering what to say.

I want to trust him so badly.

But I just can't.

"He killed my dad, Saint. And even while he was alive, he made his life hell. Of course, I want Sinner to pay and I'm doing everything I can to make sure that happens."

"Unfortunately, your father sealed his fate the instant he laid eyes on Giana," Saint admits. "It's unfair as fuck what's happened to him and to you, but you've got to understand Sinner is a fucking psychopath. I'm scared for you. I know he's got plans. If you have what he's looking for, we need to consider giving it to him. We might be able to use it to negotiate a way out."

"What is it he thinks I have?"

"Video footage showing members of The Sainthood raping, torturing, and killing Commissioner Leydon's wife."

THE SAINTHOOD

THE SAINTHOOD

CHAPTER 32

"THE SAINTHOOD DID that?" I remember it well because when Daphne Leydon went missing, after failing to return home from work one evening, a manhunt was immediately launched. The case went global because she's not just the police commissioner's wife, she's the niece of the US president.

"You really didn't know?" he asks.

"Look at my face." I point at myself. "I'm telling the truth. I don't have any video."

"The murder weapon is missing too."

I shake my head. "I don't have either of those things. I swear." I'm so confused. So much of this doesn't add up.

"I believe you." He rests his forehead against mine for a moment. "But Sinner thinks you have it because your dad had it and now it's nowhere to be found."

"That's why he killed him?" I ask, joining the dots, and Saint nods. Silence engulfs us for a few minutes, and I use the time to think.

"Dad was trying to build a case, so if he'd had that

evidence, he would've used it. I don't know how or why Sinner thinks we have it, but he's wrong."

Saint drops his hands from my face, turning on his side so we're looking at one another. "What kind of evidence do you have?"

"A few case files that would challenge convictions. Prove The Sainthood tampered or planted evidence, but it's mostly low-hanging fruit that wouldn't stick." That's not a lie, but it's only half the truth.

"Something isn't right with all this." He rests his hand on my hip, fighting a yawn.

"I know."

"But we're not going to figure it out at three a.m. when we're both beat."

"When's it all going down?"

"Tomorrow at five."

"I want to be there."

"Absolutely not. It will be fucking mayhem."

"I'm good with a gun, and I know how to protect myself." I've no plans on killing anyone, but I want to be there for a number of reasons. Maybe, I can get some stuff on camera I can use for leverage. I might glean some intel that could help me take them down. And I want to be standing with The Sainthood when Darrow and The Arrows show up. It will be immediately obvious I've double-crossed him, and he'll want my blood. Standing shoulder to shoulder with the most powerful criminal gang in the state will buy me some protection and some time.

"You're not getting anywhere near that shitshow tomorrow. It's not safe." His expression tells me not to bother arguing, but he doesn't know me very well if he thinks I'll let it drop this easily.

"It's not safe to leave me unprotected. Especially when Darrow finds out I've betrayed him for you guys again."

He sighs, pulling me into his arms. "Can we have this fight tomorrow because I need to fucking sleep." He says this even though I see the agreement in his eyes. He knows I've made a valid point.

I snuggle into him. "Okay, but I'm not backing down."

"So fucking stubborn," he mumbles, his voice already laced with sleep.

"I've three words for you," I say. "Pot. Kettle. Black."

He laughs, hugging me tighter, and I fall asleep feeling more content and less alone than I have in ages.

THE DOOR SLAMS against the wall, and we jolt upright in the bed, instantly awake and on guard.

"Well, isn't this cozy?" Sinner drawls, leaning casually against the doorway as he stares at both of us.

"What is so urgent you had to barge into my bedroom at"—Saint glances at his cell phone through sleepy eyes "—seven a.m. on a weekend."

His dad pushes off the wall. "You need to come with me."

"Why?"

"Don't fucking talk back, boy. If I say I need you, I need you. Now get up."

Saint sits upright in the bed, gritting his teeth. "I'll meet you downstairs. I need to grab a quick shower," he lies.

The look Sinner gives his son is one I've rarely seen him direct at Saint, and it starts alarm bells ringing in my ears.

"Sorry, sweetheart," Sinner says, cocking his head and smirking at me as his eyes drop to my chest. At some point during the night, I removed my sweater, so I'm only in a thin tank top that leaves little to the imagination. "A quickie is out this morning."

Saint yanks the covers up over my chest, and Sinner narrows his eyes at his son as he walks toward me. My instinct is to run and hide, but I'm not going to cower from this bastard. He needs to realize I'm not a frightened thirteen-year-old any longer. I tip my chin up and meet him with a fierce gaze, remaining stoic as he traces his fingers along my collarbone. "But I'll be in the mood to celebrate tonight." He edges his fingers lower. "You should test drive a real man for a change."

Saint grabs his wrist before his fingers dip under the edge of my top. "Take your hands off her."

"Or what?" Sinner grins at his son, and it's downright evil.

"Or you can find some other goons to put their lives on the line today." He shoves Sinner's hand away, pulling me in under his arm.

"Careful, son. Don't play with fire unless you're prepared to get burned." He walks to the door. "Get your ass out of bed. You really don't want to keep me waiting." He leaves the door open on purpose, and Saint jumps up, slamming it shut after him.

"Fucking psycho," he seethes.

I get up. "I want to help."

"Not now, princess," he snaps, and I grab my sweater off the floor.

"Don't take that tone with me, and don't even think about stopping me from coming today," I add, sliding the sweater down over my head. "I'll expect a call later."

I curl my hand around the door handle when he sidles up behind me, pulling me back into his warm body. "I'm leaving Galen here with you today. He'll keep you safe."

I twist around in his arms, scowling. "I don't need a babysitter."

"I showed my cards, babe. And I don't trust him not to try and take you, purely to spite me. I'm not leaving you unprotected. I don't have time to argue about this."

"Can't you leave Caz? Galen will just piss me off and get on my nerves all day."

The asshole grins. "Don't pretend that you don't love that shit, and you can't have Caz. I need him."

"Fine. I'll agree to it on one condition—you let me come today."

He closes his eyes for a second, exhaling heavy. "Do you

ever give in?"

"Nope." I smile sweetly at him. "And you can lie all you want, but I know you like me like this."

"Must enjoy torturing myself," he murmurs, and I swat at his chest before pushing him away. "Go get dressed before that bastard comes back."

He grabs my head, pulling my face to his and slamming his lips down on mine, morning breath be damned. The kiss is brief, but it still leaves me swaying on my feet. "Go. I'll see you later."

I fling myself at him, hugging him quickly. "Be safe." He shoots me one of his irritating amused looks, and I'm back to wanting to slap the shit out of him again, so I leave before I punch the cocky jerk.

I don't know what type of instructions Saint gave Galen, but the annoying douche drags me to the basement and forces me to sit through *The Fast and the Furious* franchise. It's not much of a punishment, because, come on, the eye candy is to die for, but I don't admit that because I enjoy winding Galen up too much.

Especially since he appears to have regressed, and he's back to hating me with his usual intensity.

But I get it now.

He thinks I've betrayed them. I consider telling him the truth, to clear the air, but it'll only make things worse because he'll be even more pissed with me then. Somehow, I don't think Galen will be as forgiving as Saint. So, I say nothing, content to let Saint fill him in later.

He watches his cell as often as I watch mine, and we share matching scowls. "What did Saint tell you before he left?" I ask for the umpteenth time.

He tweaks the peaks of his faux hawk, looking like he's ready to throttle me. "I already told you."

"He must've said more than that."

He grits his teeth, glaring at me. "I spoke to him for thirty seconds. Guard the princess with your life is all he said. Now, quit whining because that shit's never attractive."

"So, he didn't say you were to bring me when you were leaving?" I thought it was agreed, and if he reneges, I'll swing for him.

"Ugh." He buries his head in his hands. "Someone, please save me."

A deep chuckle breaks out behind us, and we both whip our heads around. "Sir Caz to the rescue." Caz bows, sweeping his arm out in a flourish as he smirks.

I jump over the back of the couch, catapulting into his arms. "Thank fuck, you're here. Galen wouldn't shut up. My ears are hurting."

Galen gives me the evil eye before turning it on his buddy. "A call would've been nice." He slaps Caz on the back.

"We were fucking busy."

"I'm a part of this too. Not some fucking glorified pussysitter."

"And you were just accusing the princess of whining?" Caz says, his brows climbing to his hairline.

"Are we trading off?" Galen asks.

Caz shakes his head. "Boss wants everyone at the warehouse." I open my mouth to protest, and he slams his palm over my lips. "You too, so no need to rip me a new one."

"You've got to be kidding me?" Galen throws his arms around, aggression and frustration leeching into the air.

"Saint says it's too risky to leave her here unprotected."

Before they can change their minds, I run up to my room while Caz heads to the bathroom. Grabbing my spare gun, I check the safety is on before sliding it into the holster and securing the belt around my waist. I sheathe my knives on my other hip and shove a spare clip in the pocket of my hoodie, pulling it down low so it conceals the belt. Then, I braid my hair, lace my sneakers tight, pull on black gloves, grab my cell, and skip downstairs to meet the guys.

"Oh joy. It's Sports Barbie," Galen deadpans, as Caz approaches behind him.

"Barbie was blonde," I point out, letting Caz open the front door for me. His car is parked right outside.

"I bet you dye your hair," Galen retorts, pulling the door shut behind him.

"I bet you kill puppies for shits and giggles."

"Enough bickering, children," Caz says, holding me at the waist as he steers me around to the passenger side of his sports car. "Daddy needs to concentrate on driving." He tugs up the back of my hoodie unexpectedly, raising it and my tank well above my butt, and I instantly tug it back down, turning around and scowling. He holds up his hands. "Whoa! Calm down there, princess. I felt the gun belt. No need to look at me like I ruined your favorite sweater in the wash."

"You don't get to put your hands on me whenever you feel like it."

Galen snorts. "Could've fooled me." He opens the passenger door, shoves the seat forward, and gestures for me to get in the back.

"Princess is riding up front with me," Caz says. "I want to feel her up in those tight yoga pants."

Galen growls. "Who the fuck wears yoga pants to a fight?"

I prod him in the chest. "Someone who knows how important it is to remain flexible and alert, but I don't expect you to understand that. Not with that giant stick shoved up your ass. Can you even walk with that thing?"

"Okay, amusing and all as this is, we've got some heavy shit going down today, and you two need to zip it; otherwise, someone might get hurt." Caz is dead serious as he warns us with his eyes.

Galen climbs in the back without further protest, and I get in the front, and neither of us utters a word to one another the entire journey. Caz strokes my thigh while he drives, eliciting a rake of delicious shivers, and it distracts me from the upcoming fight.

We pull up to the abandoned military base thirty minutes later. It's bigger than I expected with a bunch of dilapidated buildings scattered around the vast area. Dirt kicks up behind us as Caz drives on bumpy, cracked roads toward a larger building on the western side of the plot. As we approach, I notice the peeling brown paint, broken roof, and cracked panes of glass on the high row of windows at the top of the structure. The warehouse is bordered by woodland at the side, a large overgrown field out to the front, and rusted iron gates at the rear that appear to be only loosely secured

Two lookout towers stand idle on either side of the building, and I guess that's on purpose. Ambushes generally only work if you have the element of surprise. From the outside, it looks like the place is derelict, but once Caz maneuvers his car inside the space, it's like Armageddon on steroids.

There must be close to one hundred men here, all lined up in rows, wearing matching black combat pants, boots, and black leather jackets. Every man is clasping a gun, mostly machine guns, from what I can see, and sporting killer expressions. The amount of testosterone in the air is enough to light a bonfire.

Behind them is a myriad of bikes, cars, and trucks, and Caz parks his car at the end beside an armored truck. It's open at the rear and weighted down with boxes of weapons and bullets. There's a small door at the far righthand side of the structure, but other than that, the entire space is open plan.

"Grab me that vest," Caz says to Galen.

Galen hands him a Kevlar, which he promptly thrusts at me. "Saint says you're to wear this."

Galen mutters under his breath, shaking his head and rolling his eyes.

I put up no argument because only a dummy protests when someone is trying to keep them alive. Saint's thoughtfulness stabs at the walls around my heart, threatening to pull them all down. I waste no time putting the vest on, securing my belt over it. I was cursing my lack of forethought earlier when it occurred to me that I needed my bulletproof vest. I keep it up at the cabin, because I've never actually needed it before, and I was always afraid Mom would find it and it'd invite questions.

I make a mental note to bring it home with me the next time I'm up there.

"Keep your hood up," Caz says, when I'm ready to go, "and your head down. Don't draw attention to yourself, and keep behind us where you're hidden. Saint doesn't want Sinner to know you're here."

"Doubt the yoga pants will help," the jerk in the back seat says because he just can't stop being a pain in my ass. He's been pricklier than a hedgehog in heat this week and back to hating me with his usual vigor.

"Galen," Caz snaps. "Zip it."

We get out, and I do as Caz says, keeping my hood up, my head down, and staying behind them. It helps that I'm tall for a girl, but I hate to admit that Galen is right. Everyone else is wearing the same battle attire, so I stick out in my yoga pants and hoodie combo, and the lack of leather jacket pins me as an automatic outsider, but there's nothing I can do about that now.

We stop at the armored van, and the guy in charge hands Caz some rifles, doing a double take when he spots me. "She's with Saint," Caz confirms in a low voice. "And we want to keep it on the down low."

"Sinner know?"

"Yes," Caz lies. "He's the one that requested the low profile."

The guy nods. "You know how to shoot, sweetheart?"

I bob my head in confirmation, and he offers me a standard rifle. I notice some AK47s and M14s in the back, and I jerk my head toward them. "I'd prefer one of those. I've used both in training."

Galen and Caz turn and stare at me with shock, a little disbelief, and slight awe although the awe is mostly on Caz's side. If anything, Galen looks even more suspicious of me now. The man looks amused. "How about you start with this," he says, shoving the standard machine gun at me.

I shrug, not willing to start World War Three, slinging the gun over my shoulder and motioning to the guys to move.

Caz keeps sneaking glances at me as we walk until Galen nudges him in the ribs. He's probably wondering who exactly I am, and if I had to guess, I'd say Caz is hard as a rock in his pants.

Facing forward, he walks us behind the last row of armed men. It seems the men are lined up in order of seniority with the senior crew members at the front and the junior members at the rear. Caz guides us to the end and up a few rows, stopping when we reach Theo and Saint. Both are wearing the same attire as everyone else, staring straight ahead with determination on their faces. They move sideways, and Caz nudges me in beside Saint. Neither of them looks at me, and I don't look at them either, looking dead ahead, showing no emotion on my face as I ready my weapon and prepare for battle. Caz stands beside me with Galen at the end. Galen leans forward, staring down the line, drilling a hole in the side of Saint's head, waiting for him to acknowledge him. Saint warns him to back down with one scathing look which reminds him who's in control.

"Heads-up!" Sinner shouts, entering the space from the rear door. "ETA in four minutes." He rubs his hands in glee as he stalks across the space with a swagger only genuine assholes inherit from birth. "Let's show these bastards that The Sainthood rules the world!" he shouts, and a chorus of lusty whoops and hollers echoes around the cavernous space.

Saint brushes his fingers against my hand, and I subtly turn to look at him. "You got this?"

"I got this."

He nods before whispering, "Now, the real battle commences."

THE SAINTHOOD

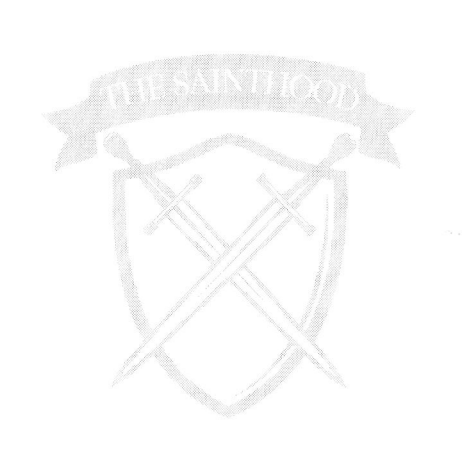

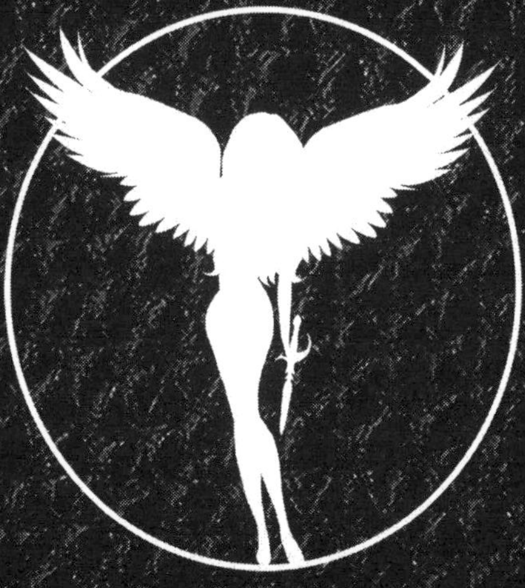

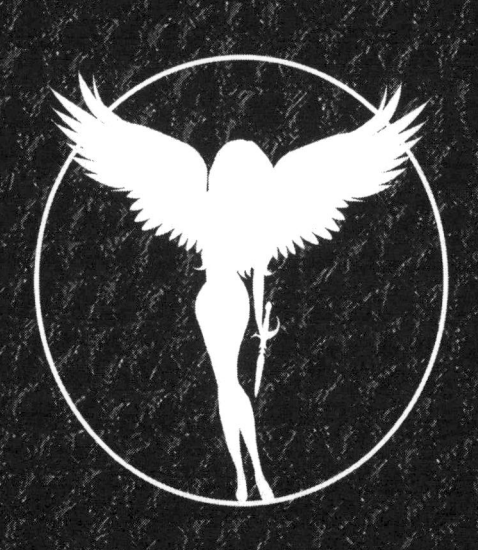

THE SAINTHOOD

CHAPTER 33

THE RUMBLE OF approaching vehicles signals the arrival of The Arrows. Anticipation is pungent in the air as we wait to strike. Nobody moves inside the warehouse, and I'm afraid to even breathe. When The Arrows push up the shutters at the front of the building, they get the surprise of their lives. The Sainthood opens fire instantly, and it quickly becomes a bloodbath.

The men surge forward, pushing their enemy back out into the field, and the battle turns vicious as most of them lower their weapons and start fighting with their fists. Saint cautions me with his eyes as we step outside, but I don't need the warning.

I stay back, flattening my spine against the wall, as they throw themselves into the melee. Discreetly, I pull my cell out of the pocket of my hoodie, turn it on, and start recording. I get a couple minutes of footage, enough to confirm what's going down and implicate the main players, and then, I switch it off and put it away. I can't risk filming for long because someone might see, and it could get me in a lot of trouble.

My eyes scan the field from left to right, lingering on the guys as they beat the enemy to a bloody pulp. They plow through their opponents, slamming their fists into faces, kicking and punching body parts, until bodies are lining the ground at their feet.

There's a violent elegance to the way they take their enemies down.

Galen slams the butt of his gun into some guy's face, barely breaking a sweat or blinking an eye as blood sprays everywhere. Caz flattens guys with a single powerful punch. I watch Saint snap some guy's neck like it's an everyday occurrence, and maybe it is, while Theo surprises me the most, fighting with skill and precision, using his full body to attack the guys lunging at him. He's a target because he's not quite as ripped as the others, but he is clearly no stranger to fighting.

I find it weird they've all put down their weapons to fight with their bare hands, but I've long since given up trying to understand the male brain.

A bunch of dead bodies litters the space directly in front of the warehouse, initial casualties of the ambush, and the ground is awash with blood. I remind myself all these guys have done tons of illegal shit and their deaths are no loss to the world.

The Sainthood is decimating The Arrows, and with their superior numbers, it seems likely they'll be the obvious victors.

Until more assholes arrive a few minutes later.

I push off the wall, cursing as I watch another forty or fifty people approaching. They rush forward, shouting and roaring as they immediately join forces with The Arrows.

Sinner barks out orders as he whips out a handgun and starts popping off shots left and right.

"What the hell?" I mumble to myself when I spot The Bulls in the midst of the enemy crew, flanked by Finn, Parker, and a couple of other idiots from school.

What the fuck is going on?

The Bulls don't hold back, clearly favoring firepower over fists as they shoot at members of The Sainthood, firing a stream of bullets, one after the other—*bang, bang, bang, pop, pop, pop*—like they're playing *Call of Duty*.

Shit.

Things are seriously fucked up, and now, the odds have switched, and it looks like I might be on the losing team.

At that moment, my eyes lock on Darrow. He has one of the senior members of the Saints in a headlock and I watch as he slits his throat from ear to ear in one slow motion, his gaze burning with hatred as he glares at me.

Fuck!

My mind whirls as I envision how things are going to go down, and I know I need to do something.

I race into the warehouse, grab an AK47 and dash toward the side door, running as fast as my legs will carry me. I yank the door open, glancing at the stairs leading to the basement, as I jog across the small landing, pushing through the exit door, and go outside. The lookout tower is about one hundred feet in front of me, and I sprint toward it without hesitation.

Just as my foot reaches the bottom of the ladder, I'm yanked back by my hair and spun around.

Caught off guard, the AK47 flies off my shoulder, and I faceplant the ground. Rough gravel grazes my cheek, and I wince as pain rattles my bones. But my survival instincts are strong, and I jump to my feet, whirling around and instantly ducking down to avoid Parker's clenched fist.

"You're going to die, bitch, and that crown will be mine." She points a Glock at my face, her finger curling around the trigger.

"Not fucking likely." I kick her shin and crouch down, sideswiping her legs with a low-flying sweep. She goes down hard, arms and legs flailing about, as she loses her balance. The gun flies out of her hand when she falls forward. I jump aside as she crashes to the ground, snatching the Glock up. I fist my free hand in her shirt, lifting her up and turning her around. She moans and whimpers as she falls flat on her back this time, and I jump on top of her, straddling her waist as I press the Glock into her forehead. "Now, let's see who's going to die."

"Don't do it," a voice calls out behind me, and I turn my head slowly around.

Sweat mixes with blood on Theo's face as he approaches. "You kill her and you're never coming back from that."

"Why do you care about this bitch?"

"I don't. I care about *you*." He stops beside me, towering over both of us, pleading with his eyes.

"He's right," Parker sobs. "Let me go, and we'll call it even."

I press the muzzle harder to her brow, and she starts full-on crying. "My friend is lying in a hospital bed in a coma because of you! We're not close to even!" I roar.

Sounds of battle continue in the background, and Theo keeps his eyes peeled, his gun raised and moving left to right as he scopes the area, ready to nuke any threat. I've never seen this side to him before, and it's hot as fuck even if my thought is inappropriate considering the situation.

"I can give you more intel!" Parker cries, desperation oozing from her pores.

I dig the muzzle into her forehead as I move forward, sitting down on her chest and compressing her air supply. "Talk!" I hiss.

Theo moves back a few steps, retrieving the AK47 and slinging it over his shoulder.

"Finn made a deal with Darrow," she pants, "and they approached The Bulls together with satellite footage confirming it was you who killed McKenzie. They won't stop until you're dead."

"Impossible," Theo says, shaking his head. "I took care of that evidence."

"Well, they got their hands on it," she rasps. Her wide, terrorized eyes pierce mine. "Can I go now?"

Theo and I exchange a look and share a silent agreement.

I get up off her, brushing dirt from my pants, while I keep the gun trained on her. She scrambles to her feet, and when she's fully upright, staring me straight in the eye, I shoot her in the head at close range.

The light goes out in her eyes instantly, and she falls to the ground on her back with a thud.

"I was going to do that," Theo quietly says, his voice radiating sadness.

"We both know that justice was mine. On behalf of Sariah."

His Adam's apple bobs as he holds the AK47 in his hands. "You know how to use this?" I nod. "Okay, let's go. I don't know how much longer we can hold out. The guys can't even get back to the warehouse to grab more guns."

"I'm going up," I say, pointing at the lookout tower. "Better vantage point from up there."

"You always were smart under pressure." He smiles. "C'mon."

I climb the ladder as fast as I can with Theo keeping pace behind me. When we reach the top, I settle into position on my knees with the gun on my shoulder. Using the scope, I home in on the guys and get ready. With a steady hand, I take out their opponents, one at a time.

They startle, looking around, no doubt wondering what the fuck is going on, and I see the moment Saint notices me, his eyes squinting in this direction.

Theo whistles. "Where the hell did you learn to shoot like that?"

"There's a lot you don't know about me."

"Obviously." He clears his throat, and I resume scanning the field, looking for more targets.

I locate Sinner, slashing at a guy with a machete, and I'm sorely tempted to kill him. He wouldn't even see it coming.

"You can't go there," Theo softly says. "I understand the temptation, but it'll only bring a world of hurt down on you and your mom. He's not just the president of the Prestwick and Lowell chapters. He's president of the entire organization. You kill him and you sign your own death warrant. Don't give him that."

I hate that he's right. I'm no martyr. Acting in a reckless manner would go against everything Dad tried to achieve. He wanted me to know how to protect myself, and he fought to try to give me back my life. Killing Sinner, and thereby sentencing me and Mom to death, will mean he died in vain. I won't dishonor his memory in that way, so, while it's hard to train the gun in another direction, I do.

Theo sighs in relief, squeezing my free shoulder in a show of support. "Don't go for the obvious targets," he suggests, keeping watch behind me. "No gang leaders because you're already in enough shit. Just take out a few more randoms. They'll run off scared."

I do as he says, and it's not long before the enemy disperses, afraid of being taken out by sniper fire.

When we're sure it's safe, when all the enemy vehicles are gone, we climb down and head around the front of the building to rendezvous with the others.

Saint runs toward us the instant he sees me with Caz following at his heels. I scan them from head to toe, checking for injuries, but apart from a gash on Caz's arm and a few bruises and cuts on both their faces, they are fine. Caz's injury, although bloody, seems shallow and not life threatening although he'll probably need a few stitches.

"Where's Galen?" Theo asks.

Saint shrugs, gripping my arm. "Get her out of here now," he barks. "Quick, before—"

"There you are, Harlow," Sinner says, materializing behind Saint like a creepy monster crawling out of the shadows. He walks around his son to me, sliding his arm around my shoulders. The vein in Saint's neck visibly pulses, but otherwise, he looks perfectly composed. "We need to have a little chat." Sinner squeezes my shoulder in a bone-crushing embrace. "Follow me."

We walk silently behind Sinner as he enters the warehouse and stalks across the room, barely pausing to survey the devastation around him. The surviving men are cleaning up the mess. Piling dead bodies in a truck and storing blood-soaked weapons in boxes. A makeshift first aid area has been set up at the back of the space, and a few women tend to men with injuries. I've no idea where they came from or who they are, but I'm assuming they are girlfriends or wives or trusted associates.

Theo's fingers fly across the keypad of his cell as he messages someone. Caz cracks his knuckles, a scowl marring his handsome face. Saint places his hand on my lower back as we walk toward the door that leads to the basement. "I won't let him hurt you," he whispers, stepping back as Sinner glances over his shoulder, stabbing Saint with a poisonous look.

I'm remarkably calm as I'm led downstairs to what I'm guessing is their main interrogation room. The floor is gross with evidence of dried blood and other DNA staining the concrete despite the drains on either side which I presume are used to wash away confirmation of their crimes. It seems they've used this room recently and haven't had the time to properly clean up yet.

I gag over the noxious smell, almost puking. It's a mix of stale piss, coppery blood, vomit, sweat, tobacco smoke, fear, and regret. I don't make a sound as I'm shoved into the only chair in the middle of the space. Not even when my sneakers land in a puddle at my feet. I'm guessing it's either piss or blood, and I'm doubting anything good happened to the previous person in this chair.

A silver table, the type you see in a hospital or a morgue, rests off to one side. Saint, Caz, and Theo stand just off to the left, working hard to mask their concern, while Sinner and three men I've never met before stand directly in front of me. One of them, a scary dude with a shaved head and tattoos halfway up his face, secures my arms and legs to the chair.

"That was a very impressive display out there," Sinner says, a brief flash of admiration appearing on his face. "I underestimated how well that bastard Trey prepared you."

I hold my chin up, grinding my teeth to the molars, saying

nothing even though I want to rage at him for speaking about my father like that. But I won't give him the satisfaction, and it's a known fact Neo Lennox will never say a good word about Trey Westbrook.

A fourth unfamiliar man enters the room, carrying another chair. He sets it down, and Sinner straddles it so he's facing me, grinning maliciously like the crazy, evil fucker he is.

"Tell me, *princess*." He smirks, knowing he's riling up the guys. "When did you figure it out?"

"Figure what out?"

He slaps me across the face, and my head whips back, my cheek stinging from the impact. Saint takes a step forward, and I shoot him a warning with my eyes. Caz tugs him back as Sinner looks at his son with obvious displeasure.

Neo refocuses on me. "Let's try this again." He cracks his knuckles. "If you lie to me, I will hurt you. Answer me truthfully, and I'll let you go."

Yeah, right. As if I believe that.

"When did you figure out we were the ones who kidnapped you?"

There's no point hiding it anymore or playing this sick song and dance we've been playing since he showed up at my house. "When I was sixteen." I eyeball him, and it's like staring the devil in the face. "Why did you kidnap me?" I have my theories and I'd like to see if I'm right.

"Your father was struggling to understand the implications of our...business relationship. He needed a reminder that he was tied to us for life."

"You used me to keep him in line. To ensure he continued doing dirty work for you." It's what I've always suspected, because the only way Dad would ever get into bed with those assholes is if they were holding me or Mom over his head.

He nods. "Did your father know you worked it out?"

"I never told him."

"But is that the truth?" he asks, arching a brow.

The guy with the missing tooth and an abundance of nose

hair on his right tilts his head to the side, his gaze roaming me from head to toe, and I've never been more grateful to be wearing an oversized hoodie. I wonder if these guys were part of the crew who kidnapped me.

"It's the truth. He died not realizing I knew."

Sinner grins, flashing me perfectly straight, perfectly white teeth that look so out of place in his sneering mouth. "That's where you're wrong. I think Pops did know. That's why he started feeding you false intel to pass to us."

My heart rate kicks up. "What false intel?"

"What do you mean?" Saint adds, his voice laced with confusion. "Why would Harlow be passing you intel?"

Sinner jumps up, grabbing Saint around the throat. Tension bleeds in the air. "Interrupt me again and you'll spend a week in the pit." Sinner shoves him away. "Shut up or I'll have you removed."

Sinner sits back down on the seat. "This is the part the board has trouble with." He looks up at the guys flanking him on both sides, confirming their status. "There are some of us who believe you weren't aware that the information you passed to us the last twelve months was bogus."

"It was fake?" I blurt, my brow puckering. "Why? I don't understand?" My gaze bounces between the men.

"It was orchestrated to trap us, and it almost worked." His jaw flexes, and murderous rage flits across his face. "Your father paid the price for that treachery, but do you need to pay the price too?"

"I didn't know," I protest, my mind whirling at this latest revelation.

It's true that when I'd figured out it was The Sainthood who had kidnapped me, and they were the ones I was spying on Dad for, I became more careful about the information I included in the monthly drop-offs. Before I knew the truth, I just copied the files from Dad's office intact and handed them over because I was a scared kid who believed them when they told me they would kill both my parents if I didn't cooperate.

They threatened me just before I was released, and, even as a young kid, I knew then I would never be free. They told me if I didn't do what they said they'd kill my parents and take me again, and this time it would be forever. They said, "It's simple. Just copy the files, bring them to the drop-off point, and no one gets hurt."

But there is nothing simple about betrayal.

The weight of that responsibility, and the pressure of the guilt, is something I've carried with me every day since.

The drop-offs were always in the same place, and I never saw anyone. I used to leave the envelope in the mailbox at the assigned time and go home. I remember being tempted to hang around to see if I could catch a glimpse of my kidnappers, but I never did it because I was terrified they'd follow through on their threat and kill my family.

After I discovered their identity, and I was old enough to understand the information in Dad's work files, I left stuff out on purpose, only handing over minor shit but enough to avoid arousing suspicion. However, if what Sinner is saying is true, and the information was fake, it means Dad knew I was stealing his paperwork and handing it to the enemy.

I can't keep the torment off my face as pain, loathing, and guilt battle for supremacy inside me. I hope he understood that I didn't have any choice. I hang my head in shame, feeling the weight of the guy's shock boring imaginary holes in my back.

I don't know if the fact Dad knew makes it better or worse. I've carried the guilt for his death these past few months. Knowing he was deliberately feeding them fake intelligence should ease the burden, but I know it won't. Even if it's shared, I will forever live with the knowledge that I helped get my dad killed.

I didn't complete any more drop-offs after Dad died, because there was no fresh information, and, at first I'd thought they didn't know he had more evidence. Until they showed up at the house, Neo got engaged to Mom, and the guys started harassing me. Then, I knew the stakes had been raised and the strategy had changed.

Right now, I've no idea where Sinner is going with this except he's hoping to cause a divide in the bond I have with his son and the other Saints. The unpredictability of his actions has me on edge, and I'm working hard to hold on to my composure.

Sinner shifts closer to me on the chair, gripping my chin and forcing my head up. "I came to a realization recently. We've been going about this all wrong. I sent my son and the other initiates into Lowell High to intimidate you"—he sneers at Saint—"and I was so disappointed in their failure, but I'll admit I might've been wrong. I didn't realize Trey had taken his protection to such extremes." He holds my chin painfully. "He's prepared you well. I see now that intimidation and manipulation won't work, so it's time to flip it on its head."

"Stop speaking in riddles," I say, earning another slap.

"I know you know a lot more than you're admitting. I know you know where your dad kept the evidence. You won't tell us shit while you're on the outside, so it's time to bring you in."

"What?" Saint croaks, looking thoroughly confused when our eyes meet.

Sinner stands, grinning. "Give a warm welcome to our newest initiate, boys, because Harlow is joining the ranks."

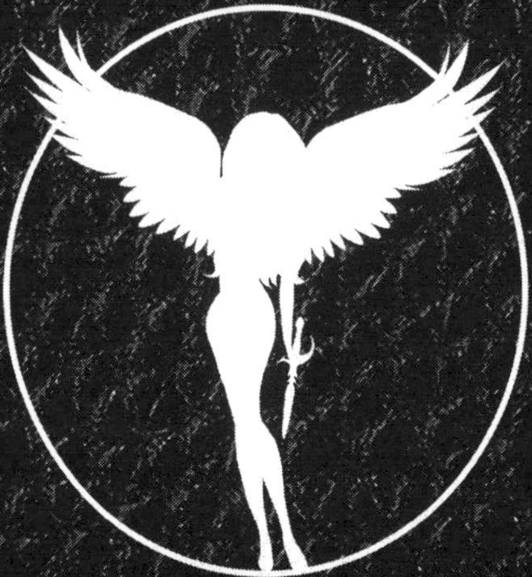

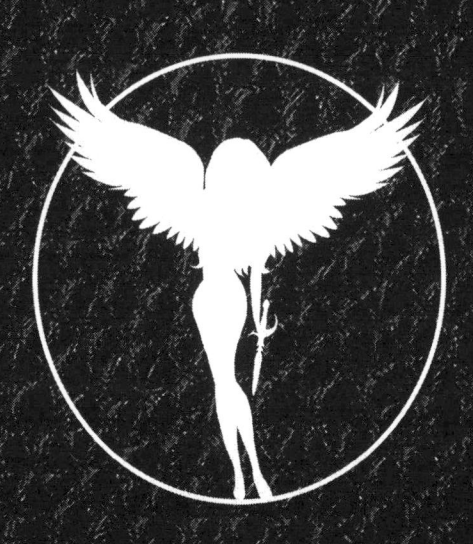

THE SAINTHOOD

CHAPTER 34

"What?" I stutter. "Women can't be members." I cast a glance at the guys, and shock is evident on all three of their faces.

"They can now." Sinner starts removing the bindings from my arms. "We took a vote recently, and we've decided, in certain circumstances, to allow some women to join The Sainthood."

"Why would you agree to that?" Theo asks, risking his ire by speaking up.

"Because we're coming under a lot of heat from the authorities. Our contacts on the inside can only help so much. Initiating women into the membership means we will have a new layer of members to support us. Cops won't suspect the women."

"You want women to do your dirty work for you," I say, as he frees my arms.

Bending down, he unties the rope at my feet. "Exactly." He yanks me up off the chair. "And in your case, your obvious skill set could be an asset."

"I won't do it." I cross my arms.

"You will."

"No, I fucking won't." I stand my ground.

He grabs my face, digging his nails into my cheek. "I will beat that stubborn streak out of you."

"You can try," I retort.

His eyes darken as his lips curve up at the corners.

"You won't kill my mother," I blurt, knowing this will be his new threat. No one fights this hard to win back their childhood sweetheart to turn around and shoot her dead.

I wrestle against his hold as he drags me toward the table.

He cranks out a laugh. "I would put a bullet in Giana's skull in a flash," he admits, proving there is a fine line between love and hate. "But that won't keep you in line." He lifts me up, throwing me over his shoulder and slapping my ass. Out of the corner of my eye, I watch Saint seething. "So, I'll keep her alive," Sinner continues, as I wriggle and pummel my fists on his back. He slaps my ass even harder, and I bite down on my lip.

"For every act of disobedience, I will take it out on your mother." He slams my butt down on the table, and his fingers move to the zipper on my hoodie. I try to swat his hands away, and he lashes out, slapping me in the face again. "I will beat her. Cut her. Drug her. Fuck her till she bleeds from every orifice. Pimp her out."

It's not the first time he's threatened to use Mom to keep me in line.

He strips my hoodie off me, eyeing the Kevlar vest and my weapons belt with an amused smile. It's one I've seen on Saint countless times, and I hate they have that in common, because every time Saint looks at me like that, all I see is his murdering bastard of a father.

"So what?" I say. "It's no secret I hate her now."

He grabs my neck in his meaty palm, yanking my head back. "So callous. So ungrateful." He sneers, and it's not hard to see how much he loves gaining the upper hand.

Not for long asshole.

I don't know how, but I'm going to make him pay.

I regret not taking him out on the field. I should've riddled the monster with bullets and taken my chances.

"The only reason she's with me is a feeble attempt to protect you."

"What?" I splutter. "You're lying."

"Am I?" He smirks, removing the Kevlar vest and the gun belt and forcing me to lie down on my stomach.

My brain churns a hundred miles an hour as I try to make sense of this.

Does Mom have her own plan? Is marrying the enemy, and keeping him close, the best way to protect me? Or is Sinner just fucking with my head?

I don't know who to trust anymore. I can't figure out who is a friend and who is a foe.

Sinner uses my own knife to rip my tank top up the middle, leaving me in my bra.

I know what's coming, and I squeeze my eyes shut, hating that everything Dad fought to stop happening is going to happen anyway.

Sinner pulls my yoga pants down a little, exposing the top of my black thong and the full extent of my back tattoo.

"Your father really thought of everything, didn't he?" Sinner says, running his fingers up and down my spine. I shudder as strong repulsion washes over me. "If I didn't hate everything about him, I might feel some grudging respect."

"Dad, what's going on?" Saint asks.

"Come here, son."

I close my eyes as Sinner runs his hand along my lower back, his fingers brushing the curve of my ass. "If you'd stopped to examine her ink when you were fucking her, you might've noticed," he says.

"What the…" Saint's voice trails off as I feel his fingers probe the place where the fiery logo is inked on my skin.

"What is it?" Caz inquires.

"The initiation tattoo," Saint says in a clipped tone. "Harlow has the same tattoo we have."

Every time I've seen it on their lower backs, it served as a reminder, and I've wanted to throw up. I successfully blocked it out, but now, there's no avoiding it.

"What the fuck?" Theo says, and I know he's cursing himself for not seeing this when we were together. To be fair, the tattoo artist Dad hired to cover my entire back did a fantastic job and you would only notice it if you were looking for it, because the flames surrounding my avenging angel disguise it well. Still, anytime the Saints came close to my back, I freaked out at the thought they might see it.

I've always known it means I belong to them.

But I never understood why Sinner did it. Despite his explanation, I still don't. He was the one who insisted on it. He was the one who held me down while the man etched it on my skin.

I knew this day would come, and I'd hoped to be long gone by then, but I've run out of time. And I'm all out of options.

Sinner lifts me up, planting my feet on the ground. The other board members ogle my chest in my sports bra, but that's the least of my concerns. Saint stares at me as if he hardly knows me. And I suppose, in a lot of ways, he doesn't.

Sinner shoves my hoodie and belt at me, groping my breasts in the process, before thrusting me at Saint. "Harlow is to be one of you. She will receive full training and undergo initiation. You will bring her to the training facility immediately."

"What will you tell her mom?" Saint asks in a voice devoid of emotion.

"I'll handle Giana. Just do it."

Saint nods as Caz helps me into the hoodie, avoiding eye contact. I strap the gun belt around my waist, showing no emotion on my face.

Sinner would love me to break down.

To scream and protest.

To grant him an excuse to hurt me.

But I won't give him the satisfaction.

Saint grabs my wrist, preparing to walk off, when Sinner clamps a hand down on his arm. "Don't even think about crossing me."

Saint snarls. "You honestly think I want anything to do with the lying bitch now?" He glares at me in the way he used to at the start. "She's dead to me."

Sinner scrutinizes his son's face. "Go. I'll meet you back at the house later."

No one speaks as we exit the basement, walk across the warehouse floor, and climb into Saint's Land Rover. Caz's Mitsubishi is missing, and I figure Galen must have taken off in it. Saint taps out a message on his cell before fitting it into the holder on the dash. Music blares from the car speakers, making talking impossible, but I'm not even sure what I'd say.

The tension is terrible in the car, and I know we all feel it. This whole scenario seems inevitable and a little anticlimactic, and that makes me nervous.

We drive for ten minutes, and I sit up straighter in the passenger seat as Saint pulls into the entrance of Prestwick Forest. *Is the training facility in here?*

Saint parks in the gravelly parking lot, cutting the engine. No one speaks, and I grow tired of the awkward atmosphere. "Someone, say something." My gaze jumps between them. "Anything. Even if it's you hate me."

"Lo." Saint leans across the console, taking my face in his and smashing his lips down on mine in a surprising move. He ravishes my mouth, kissing me like he's afraid he might never get to do it again.

I barely hear the other vehicle pulling up alongside us because I'm so consumed in his kiss. He pours it all out, letting his lips do the talking.

"What was that?" I ask when we break apart.

"This is fucked up, babe." A muscle pops in his jaw. "He can't get his hands on you."

Things slot into place. They're not taking me to the training facility. They're taking me someplace else. "Where are you taking me?"

"Someplace safe," he replies.

I grab onto his arm. "You heard him. He will kill you if you cross him."

"We'll figure it out," Caz says, poking his head through the gap between the front two seats.

"We're not letting him do this to you," Theo adds, determination transparent in his tone and his face.

"You're one of us," Saint says, grabbing the back of my neck and planting a hard kiss on my mouth. "And we protect our own," he confirms when he rips his lips from mine. He climbs out of the car, rounds the front, and opens my door.

"Stay safe, princess," Caz says, tilting my face and leaning forward to press a forceful kiss to my lips. His tongue swirls around my mouth, and I sigh against his lips. When we break apart, he rests his forehead against mine before sitting back in his seat.

"We'll see you soon," Theo says, planting a tender kiss on my cheek. It's a genuine, concerned gesture that gives me so many feels. As he conveys silent promises with his eyes, I swallow over the messy lump in my throat, not properly understanding why they would go against their president for me but grateful they are.

Galen gets out of the Mitsubishi, eyeing me with suspicion. "What's going on?"

I slide out of Saint's car.

"I need you to take Harlow to the safehouse out by Grenlow."

"Why the fuck are we taking her anywhere?" he demands.

"There isn't time to explain," Saint says, opening the passenger door of Caz's ride and ushering me inside. "Just protect her until we get there. I'm counting on you."

Galen stares at his cousin as if he's insane. Then, he slowly shakes his head, walking back around to the driver side and getting in.

Saint crouches down before me, taking my hands. "We're going to grab some shit from the house. I'll get some of your things, and then, we'll follow you up there. Galen will keep you safe."

I wish it was anyone but Galen I was going with, but Saint calls the shots, and he knows what he's doing. I need to place my trust in him because I don't have many options right now. "Okay."

"Give me your cell," Saint commands, and I hand it over. He smashes it with his foot until it resembles nothing more than scraps of metal and glass. There wasn't time to save the footage from the field to the cloud, so the recording is lost to me now. "I'll bring you a burner," he adds before nodding at Galen and walking off.

Galen starts up the car, backing out as we watch Saint get into his Land Rover.

We don't speak, but that suits me fine, because the waves of hostility rolling off Galen aren't comforting. I lean my head against the window, closing my eyes but not falling asleep, because I need to keep my wits about me.

When we pull into the gas station on the outskirts of Prestwick a short while later, I sit up straighter, my head whipping to Galen as prickles of apprehension skate across my skin. I reach for my gun, but cold metal presses into my temple.

"I'll blow your brains out without hesitation," he threatens, pushing the muzzle in harder as he drives around the rear of the building one-handed. "Take the belt off and toss it in the back seat."

I do as he asks, glaring at him the whole time. "Whatever you've done, you should reconsider."

He snorts. "Shut your mouth. There's nothing you can say that'll get you out of this. I'm not like the others. I'm not so easily manipulated."

He parks the car, keeping the gun pressed to my skull as he switches off the engine. He hauls me over the console, dragging me out the driver side on my hands and knees, keeping the gun pointed at my head.

A pair of blood-spattered boots lands in front of me, and my apprehension increases tenfold.

Galen reels me to my feet, grabbing my arm painfully and pressing the weapon into my lower back.

"Lennox," a familiar voice says.

"Knight." Galen nods at my ex. "We still have a deal?"

"Hell yeah," Darrow says, glaring at me. "I want the traitorous bitch dead as much as you do."

"Kill her someplace remote." Galen passes me to Darrow.

Darrow immediately spins me around and pulls a knife out. He presses it against my throat, holding me against his body with my back to his chest.

"You're making a mistake. You don't understand. I'm—"

Galen stuffs a rag in my mouth, cutting me off. "I'm done listening to your bullshit. You're a lying whore. The others are too blinded by your pussy to see what's right in front of them. You think you could rat us out to the enemy and get away with it?" He sneers. "I don't care how justified you feel. No one betrays The Sainthood and survives."

"When will we get our cut?" Darrow asks, nicking my skin and drawing blood as he presses the knife against my throat.

"When I have proof that she's dead."

TO BE CONTINUED

To read the bonus scenes from the guys' POVs, type this link into your browser: https://smarturl.it/ResurrectionBonus Rebellion, book two, is available now in ebook, paperback, and audiobook format.

ABOUT THE AUTHOR

USA Today bestselling author **Siobhan Davis** writes emotionally intense young adult and new adult fiction with swoon-worthy romance, complex characters, and tons of unexpected plot twists and turns that will have you flipping the pages beyond bedtime!

Siobhan's family will tell you she's a little bit obsessive when it comes to reading and writing, and they aren't wrong. She can rarely be found without her trusty Kindle, a paperback book, or her laptop somewhere close at hand.

Prior to becoming a full-time writer, Siobhan forged a successful corporate career in human resource management.

She resides in the Garden County of Ireland with her husband and two sons.

You can connect with Siobhan in the following ways:

Website: www.siobhandavis.com
Blog: myyanabookobsession.com
Facebook: AuthorSiobhanDavis
Twitter: @siobhandavis
Instagram: @siobhandavisauthor
Email: siobhan@siobhandavis.com

BOOKS BY SIOBHAN DAVIS

KENNEDY BOYS SERIES
Upper Young Adult/New Adult Contemporary Romance

Finding Kyler
Losing Kyler
Keeping Kyler
The Irish Getaway
Loving Kalvin
Saving Brad
Seducing Kaden
Forgiving Keven
Summer in Nantucket
Releasing Keanu
Adoring Keaton
Reforming Kent

STANDALONES
New Adult Contemporary Romance

Inseparable
Incognito
When Forever Changes
Only Ever You
No Feelings Involved
Second Chances Box Set

Reverse Harem Contemporary Romance

Surviving Amber Springs

RYDEVILLE ELITE SERIES
Dark High School Romance

Cruel Intentions
Twisted Betrayal
Sweet Retribution
Charlie
Jackson
*Sawyer^*
*Drew^*

THE SAINTHOOD (BOYS OF LOWELL HIGH)
Dark HS Reverse Harem Romance

Resurrection
Rebellion
Reign
The Sainthood: The Complete Series

ALL OF ME DUET
Angsty New Adult Romance

Say I'm The One ^
*Let Me Love You^*

ALINTHIA SERIES
Upper YA/NA Paranormal Romance/Reverse Harem

The Lost Savior
The Secret Heir
The Warrior Princess
The Chosen One

The Rightful Queen

TRUE CALLING SERIES
Young Adult Science Fiction/Dystopian Romance

True Calling
Lovestruck
Beyond Reach
Light of a Thousand Stars
Destiny Rising

Short Story Collection
True Calling Series Collection

SAVEN SERIES
Young Adult Science Fiction/Paranormal Romance

Saven Deception
Logan
Saven Disclosure
Saven Denial
Saven Defiance
Axton
Saven Deliverance
Saven: The Complete Series

^Release date to be confirmed

Printed in Great Britain
by Amazon